***

The Not So Ancient Mariner

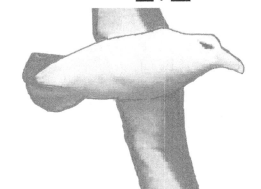

M·G·Lewis

Copyright © 2021 Michael Gene Lewis
All rights reserved.

ISBN-13: 9798542622804

Cover photo by author

This book is a work of fiction. Names, characters, places, and incidents are the product of the author's imagination or are used fictitiously. Any resemblance to actual events, locales, or persons, living or dead, is entirely coincidental.

Also by M.G. Lewis

Gabe Bergeron Mysteries
Death on Daugherty Creek
Foreseeable Harm
Beauty in Ashes
Deep is the Chesapeake
Mr. Boghossian Loses a Tenant
The Nuptials of Ezmeralda Gutierrez
Keypunchers & Other Villains
Bornheimer's Demise
On Farm Deadly
Waters Ebb, Rocks Emerge
Really Not His Fault
The Not So Ancient Mariner

Other
Rune's Riddle

Nesrady Clone Series
The Clone Who Loved to Bake Bread
The Clone Who Loved to Fight
The Clone Who Loved to Swim
The Clone Who Loved Voltaire

Monday
8:00 am

He had parked in the garage on South 16th Street and was making his way to work. It was a lovely day in April, and there was a bounce in his step; not quite a skip but skip-adjacent.

He might have burst into song except that a dark van pulled up in front of the Mahr Building, the home of the moderately-reputable, accounting firm of Garst, Bauer & Hartmann, his employer.

His first guess was the FBI.

Not that he had done anything or possessed any information which might draw them hither. Well, that he knew of.

He was about to resume skipping when Andy "Bolty" Boltukaev popped out of the black van and helped Jennifer, his lady wife, make the journey from van to door.

This was not from an excess of chivalry on Andy's part; not that he wasn't a nice guy. This was due to the fact that Jennifer was great with child; her third. And presumably Andy's third also.

The said father-to-be spotted him and waved. Andy was about his height but twice as wide, being banded with slabs of muscle about his body, arms, and legs. He had blond hair, blue eyes, and steel cheekbones.

Andy said, "Gabe's here."

Jennifer swiveled her enormous torso. "He is?" She glared at him for no good reason. "Okay. You get going. Gabe will help me inside."

Andy smiled the smile that had led to Jennifer being in her

current condition, kissed her, and flew to his van and away; probably to an exciting day of locksmithing.

He smiled at Jennifer. She was tall with long brown hair and not unattractive. She was also his boss and granddaughter of the Garst in Garst, Bauer & Hartmann. "How are you doing?"

She renewed the glare and upped the intensity to the hyper-lethal range that would kill even tardigrades. "How does it look like I'm doing, Bergeron?"

He had fallen into this trap before. Her face was drawn and sallow and telegraphed her discomfort if not outright agony, but it was unwise to tell her that she looked like she was about to knock on Death's Door; equally unwise were the words "glowing" or "blooming."

"It won't be long now?"

She snarled and rolled her eyes, but she didn't have the strength to do either properly. She looked ill. If he didn't know she was eight months pregnant, he would be profoundly worried about her. He was still a little worried but he tried not to think about it.

He picked up the bags and her briefcase which Andy had dumped on the sidewalk and opened the door for her.

She tottered inside. Once in, he said, "Do you want to take my arm?"

She snorted but she locked onto him. He wanted to offer to put an arm around her, but he wasn't sure where to grab?

They were progressing slowly toward the elevator when a scarlet Lexus pulled to a halt out front.

Both doors flew open like a cardinal spreading its wings. Harry Baldacci, his friend and coworker, leaped out of the driver's side as Carla Wong-Baldacci, also his coworker and Harry's wife, struggled to get out on the passenger-side.

The struggle part was due to Harry's low-slung Lexus and to Carla's rotundity.

He was reliably informed that she was six months pregnant, and he saw no reason to doubt it.

He waved at Baldacci. Harry was also his height and also wider, but his width was not due to muscle. Harry was not fat; maybe stocky was *le mot juste*?

Of course, he had been putting on the stocky for some time now. He had receding, black hair and scampish, brown eyes.

Carla slapped Harry's hand away when he tried to pull her from the car, but she couldn't extract herself on her own.

Once on her feet, she pushed Harry away again. Harry followed, head bowed, two steps behind her into the lobby.

She was wearing one of her signature charcoal suits, but this one was cut on a grander scale than her previous suits. She looked like an oddly shaped filing cabinet. The ruby cravat could only do so much to enliven the ensemble.

She patted her very black, very frizzy hair.

He smiled at her and Harry. "Hi Carla. Hi Harry."

Carla glared at him, but she looked at Harry. "Go park the car. I'll ride up with Bergeron and Jennifer."

Harry said, "You're sure?"

She pulled a machete from her briefcase to decapitate and emasculate Harry with two savage blows.

Well, she didn't but only because she had forgotten to pack her machete.

"Yes, I'm sure! I'm not helpless, Harry."

Harry smiled and ran. They had been married a little over a year, and this was their first child. Harry roared off; it was unclear if he would ever return.

He pushed the button for the elevator just as Jennifer groaned and dug her nails into his arm.

Carla said, "Are you okay?"

More inarticulate groans and moans as she leaned against the wall. "Jennifer!"

But Jennifer took a deep breath. "It's okay. Just Braxton Hicks."

Carla nodded. "Is it gone?"

Jennifer nodded.

He knew that Braxton Hicks referred to false contractions; sort of a warm-up for the awful pain to come. Still he would rather not get into the elevator with Jennifer, but he couldn't see any options.

Jennifer and Carla were looking at him. "What?"

Carla said, "She isn't having the baby now, Bergeron."

"Are you absolutely sure?"

Jennifer smiled at him. "Yes, Gabe."

Which was good to hear. But Carla looked like she hadn't slept in days, and she was scratching her hands. Was this pregnancy related or some fell contagion?

He had to be brave. He hit the button to send them skyward.

A long pale limb halted the doors, and Dana got on board. Dana was the receptionist at Garst, Bauer & Hartmann. Well, she sat at the receptionist's desk and presumably was paid a salary, but her work ethic was as pale and anemic as her complexion.

She smoothed lank, brown locks. Her thin lips were fire engine red; her eyes circled with charcoal. Her skirt and blouse were skimpy and lime green; her legs and arms were long and spindly.

The general nakedness caught his attention, but the dangly, gold earrings clinched it.

She had last worn those when she had been "dating" Nemec, the late, unlamented, former partner of GBH.

He looked from Jennifer to Carla. They smirked at him. So everybody knew that Dana had a new boyfriend?

Nobody told him anything.

And then his keen powers of observation noted that Dana's columnar form was not quite so columnar as in earlier days.

Shit!

It couldn't be.

Well, it could. Easily. He looked at Dana's tummy and then at Jennifer and then back to the offending tummy. Jennifer might have smiled.

He was in an elevator with three pregnant women. He looked at the floor. If anybody's water broke, he was crawling out of the hatch at the top of the car and shinning up the steel cables.

He was spared behaving inappropriately by the ding of the elevator door as it opened on the eleventh floor.

He did not trample anyone getting out of the elevator.

He conveyed Jennifer to her office, got her seated in her

chair, inquired if she required anything further, and then ran to his cubicle. He may have shuddered for a bit.

Monday Noon

Harry looked like crap too. Not nearly as bad as Jennifer or Carla but not good.

They were alone in the breakroom. "What happened to you, Baldacci?"

Harry closed his eyes. "You don't want to know, Bergeron. Carla can't sleep. And she's going to the bathroom a dozen times a night."

"Frequent urination."

Harry looked at him. "That's not even half of it. She also...."

He held up a hand. "I don't want to know. No, Baldacci. You try to tell me anything, and I'll punch you in the face."

Harry smiled at him. "Wuss."

"Right. Absolutely. One hundred percent, Grade A Wuss."

Harry was staring at his cup of coffee. "And when she's not in the freaking bathroom, she's scratching. Or she's going on about her body...about the stretch marks and...."

He clamped a hand over Harry's mouth. "Last warning, Baldacci. If I wanted to know this stuff, I would date women."

Harry said, "You're so lucky...but don't tell Carla I said that, Bergeron! Don't even hint it!"

"I promise. Not a word." He smiled at Harry. "So only three more months?"

It was only because Harry was in the last stages of sleep deprivation that he made it back to his cubicle unscathed.

He was about to ask if Harry and Carla wanted to go to CoffeeXtra for lunch when Andy Boltukaev got off the elevator. He strode purposefully to Jennifer's office and started packing up her stuff.

Jennifer was pointing at him through the glass half of the wall. He could pretend he didn't see her, but she was too pitiful to mess with.

He leaped to obey her summons. "Yes, Jennifer."

"Sit down and close the door."

Jennifer and Andy had fixed him with their gimlet eyes. He wasn't sure why? He hadn't done anything.

"Gabe, I'm going home. I might come in tomorrow...."

Andy was shaking his head.

Jennifer said, "Or maybe not. I may work from home."

Andy nodded.

"Only sensible, Jennifer."

She smiled at him. "And I want you on your best behavior."

"Of course! As I always am, Jennifer."

She smiled some more; Andy did not. He wasn't scared of Andy. Well, he was, and Andy knew it.

"And I want you to help Carla. She's not feeling well."

He shook his head. Andy initiated a threat display that involved flexing his whole body from his tiny seashell ears to the toes inside his boots. Well, he couldn't see the toes but everything else was battle hard, battle ready. "I mean I would be glad to help her but she would never let me touch her clients, Jennifer. You know that."

Jennifer smiled benignly like Mary from the manger. "Then you help Harry with his clients and let Harry help her."

"Right. Okay. I can do that. So is she not doing so well? Over and above the regular...problems?"

He had been going to say "horrors" but he thought they might not like that.

Jennifer nodded. "So you will help Harry to help Carla."

"Of course. I will do whatever I can. No worries. Go home and put your feet up. Take a nap. Everything here will be ship-shape."

She smiled at him. "Thanks, Gabe, I knew I could count on you." She smiled at Andy. "I have to go to the Ladies' Room, and then we can go home."

Andy smiled at her as Dana helped her to the Ladies' Room.

When the door closed, Andy put a hand on his chest and pushed him against the wall. It was difficult to read Andy's chiseled features but he was pretty sure Andy was not happy with Gabe Bergeron.

"Help Baldacci. Do not leave early. Don't get involved in any murders."

He smiled his very best smile. "I will, and I won't, and I absolutely won't."

Andy's smile wasn't reassuring as he moved closer. "She needs to rest, and she can't be worried about this place."

"I understand. I like Jennifer. I want to help her. Honest, Andy."

Andy nodded. He smelled of acetone, lemons, and Andy. The lemon thing was new, but it didn't detract from the enticing eau de Andy. The electric blue eyes were a little scary, but all in all, it wasn't bad being sandwiched between a plaster wall and a muscle wall.

He may have been enjoying the experience a bit too much when he said, "But what if something happens...."

Andy patted his face with a grubby, powerful hand and got closer still until they were rubbing noses. "Make sure nothing happens."

"Right. Understood." He was having a little difficulty in breathing. "Jennifer is going to be coming back soon."

Andy said, "Jennifer and Aunt Xava would be pissed if I broke your neck."

"I'm sure they would! Devastated! So how are Xava and cousin Vinnie doing?"

"But I think they'd be okay with an arm."

Which might be true. He tried to be stoic, but he didn't want a broken arm. Would Andy let him choose which arm? Still.

Andy gripped both of his arms fiercely and shook him just

a little. "You can be normal for a month, Bergeron."

"Of course, I can. Wait. I'm always normal."

Andy shook his head. "Dana's watching."

"And what? Reporting back to you? That really isn't necessary, Andy. Really."

"One freaking month, Bergeron." And Andy turned and marched out of Jennifer's office.

Monday
5:00 pm

He tried not to get pissed over Andy and Dana machinating against him. He was walking along Arch Street to his apartment. The birds were singing; the April air was semi-balmy. He was going to forget that he had been wronged.

He jogged up the stairs to his fourth floor apartment, but at the landing of the last flight he heard a familiar clanking.

He double-timed it and threw open the door. Cory was on the weight bench, pressing an impressive amount of iron.

He dropped his briefcase and threw his jacket on the sofa. He took up position to give Cory a spot for the last reps.

Cory smiled at him, and he smiled back. "What a very nice surprise, Special Agent."

Cory had shown up on Friday, and they had spent a most excellent weekend together but he hadn't expected him to still be around.

Cory was Corentin Georges Poirier, Special Agent of the FBI's Art Theft Team, and all around good egg. He was brave, true, stalwart, and only his mother called him Corentin.

And also handsome. His brick red hair had flopped over his face; his big blue eyes shone like Alpine lakes. Or whatever was very blue and nifty.

He was on lying on his back and naked to the waist, glistening with sweat; the ebb and flow of his pecs and abs and obliques and possibly other muscles that ordinary men did not possess was mesmerizing.

Cory grunted, "Gabe!"

He tore his eyes away from the panoply of muscles beneath him and realized that Cory needed assistance with this rep.

"Sorry!" Cory frowned at him. "I was distracted. It won't happen again."

Cory went for one more rep; he provided just the correct amount of assistance.

Cory relaxed and let his breathing slow before getting up. Cory smiled and squeezed his biceps like melons in the market. "You should do some reps, Gabe."

Cory glanced at the bench, and he grabbed the Special Agent round the waist and lifted him in the air. Cory might have three inches and forty pounds on him, but he was strong too.

He may have paraded Cory around the sofa.

Cory smiled some more and kissed his forehead. "Okay. So you're not the weakling you appear."

"No, I am not, Sir." He wasn't sure how much longer he could hold Cory.

But Cory smiled. "Down, Bergeron. Now. Before you hurt yourself."

"Nonsense, Sir. You are but a feather."

And then he dropped Cory, and they fell onto the sofa.

Cory rolled on top of him. "You have too many clothes on, Bergeron."

Cory had correctly analyzed the problem, but he was sure he could work out a solution.

Tuesday
6:30 am

He hadn't told Cory that Andy had threatened his radius, ulna, and humerus; Cory might take umbrage. And while he had no doubt that Cory would win any battle of the titans, he didn't want either of them to get hurt.

He had slipped out of bed leaving Cory to slumber and had made it into work by 6:00 am. He had looked at the empty office and been appalled to be there in the middle of the night.

He had sighed and set to work. He did want to help Carla by helping Harry, and he wanted Jennifer to be able to relax and not fuss over Garst, Bauer & Hartmann.

He was at his desk in his little cubicle all alone and working like a magical, accounting jinni when the elevator dinged.

He was hoping that it was Harry, but no.

Bradley, the FBI tech, stepped out, scanning the empty office. It had been five months since he'd seen Bradley...beside Sieta Dijkstra's corpse. How had he gained access to the building?

He may have ducked down. He needed to have a talk with the new security guard. The turnover rate was high among security personnel. At least, this one, though scruffy and scrawny and beady-eyed, had never seemed drunk or high.

He was considering crawling under his desk when Bradley spotted him.

"Bergeron?" He remained mute. "Bergeron, I know it's you."

"Do not."

Bradley was closing the gap between them. He pretended to pick up a pen from the floor and righted himself in his chair.

Bradley was in jeans and a sweatshirt. He was still smallish. His pale face was oval and equipped with large black eyes, fierce eyebrows, and an unremarkable nose and mouth. The mounds of luxuriant black hair and the noble forehead made his head seem just a tad too big for his body.

The unremarkable mouth was set in a grimace.

"Hi, Bradley. What can I do for you?"

Bradley shook his hand and then grabbed Harry's chair and pulled it close. "I'm not sure how to say this."

"Start at the beginning and proceed to the end." He held up a hand. "I can't take you on as a client right now. I'm swamped, inundated, drowning in clients. I have...."

It was Bradley's turn to hold up a hand. He had long delicate fingers that looked like they could dash off a respectable performance of a Chopin Polonaise.

"Why would I need an accountant? No. It's something else."

Shit. He had a sudden pain in his left arm. He had decided that should arm breaking become necessary, the left would have to take one for the team.

He shook his head *con brio*.

Bradley's eyebrows flexed into a predatory arc. "Just listen to me, Bergeron! Do you think I want to be here?"

"Then why are you?"

"My mom."

He looked around for a woman of middle years approaching ninja-style and failed to detect one. "I don't know your mother, Bradley, and I don't have time for you to explain why you're here or what it has to do with her...."

"Duke is missing!"

This was stated in a ringing tone.

He paused and looked Bradley over. "I didn't look for Chatterjee's cat...actually it was his grandmother's cat...and I don't find lost dogs either."

"Duke isn't a dog! Duke is just his nickname; he's Lars

Thorvaldsen, and he's been missing for a week, and he's my friend, and I'm worried about him. I tell Mom that he can take care of himself, but something is wrong, and the police won't do anything."

This was said in one breath. "Bradley? You work for the FBI." Bradley looked ever so slightly uncomfortable. "What? They won't do anything either? Wait. How old is this Duke?"

Bradley was staring at the worn, gray carpeting. "He's forty-six."

He knew he should just march Bradley to the elevator and get back to work. "So he's taking a vacation? Where does he work? Have you talked to them?"

"He's a licensed mariner."

"A what?" He had read the "Rime of the Ancient Mariner" a long time ago. He couldn't remember if he'd enjoyed it?

Bradley swept his black hair out of his eyes but it rippled forward rebelliously. "He works as an officer on merchant ships...hauling cargo. He was second mate on the SS Kerkyra sailing from Hamburg to Nigeria and just got home three weeks ago. And now he's gone."

He shook his head. "Wait. What is his connection to you and your mother?"

"Duke lives across the street from us...in his grandmother's old place. When he's in the country."

"And?"

A pinkish hue was blossoming on Bradley's pale cheeks. "He's my mom's boyfriend."

"I see."

"My dad died when I was ten, and Duke has been like a father to me, but now that I'm a man we're buddies. We went to a bar."

How old was Bradley? Early twenties. "And how old is your mother?"

"Forties. Why?"

"No reason. So what did your father do? For a living?"

"He worked for the Social Security Administration." Bradley was frowning at him again.

"Right." So Bradley's mother had once had a choice between an office drone and a lusty sailor who had heaved to across the street and thrown out his big anchor. He thought Bradley might want to avoid DNA test kits.

Bradley was staring at him. "I knew this was stupid."

He nodded. "I'm sorry but I can't help you, Bradley."

Bradley jumped to his feet and almost ran to the elevator, but it dinged before he could smack the button.

And a tallish woman debouched. He really needed to talk to this security guy about letting just anybody into the building.

She smiled at Bradley and ruffled his ebony locks.

She might be in her forties but time had not dimmed her charms. Well, barely. At least from across the office anyway. She had black hair and black eyes like Bradley. She was curvaceous enough to tempt lusty sailors. Or so he would assume.

She said, "What's wrong, Stevie?"

Stevie snarled at her. Well, he grunted. "He won't help."

She smiled at Bradley and stepped past him. She extended her hand. "Mr. Bergeron? I'm Susan Bradley, Stevie's mother. It's wonderful to meet you after the stories that Stevie has told me."

Every time she called him "Stevie" young Bradley flinched like he'd been lashed across the back with a cat-o'-nine-tails.

She was wearing little silver earrings, pale pink lipstick, and a pale gray suit. Her slippers were silver with sensible heels.

"I'm not sure what Stevie...Bradley has told you, but I'm just a bookkeeper who is currently overworked and underappreciated. I'm very sorry about Duke. Well, that you're worried about him. Couldn't he be fine? Just off on some adventure? Or on another ship second mating away?"

Her smile dimmed as she shook her head. "No, Mr. Bergeron. I would like to believe that he's fine, but I don't. I tried calling him but I got a message that his phone was unreachable. And we had plans for Saturday..."

So Duke had only been missing a few days?

She ruffled Bradley's locks again. "We were going away for the weekend. Duke had made reservations; he was going to rent a car. His old truck is a clunker." She glanced at Bradley. "We hadn't seen each other in months, you see."

So it was to have been forty-eight hours of passion. "Right. He would have called if he'd had a sudden work thing?"

She nodded. "He would. He's been working for a Greek shipping company lately. I called them, and they had no idea. I tried calling the captain of the SS Kerkyra and the first mate, but their phones were unreachable just like Duke's."

Bradley was staring at the carpet again. Once could be nothing, but twice was interesting. "They could still be in Nigeria, Mom."

She nodded.

"I really can't help you. I'm sorry about Duke but I have no idea what to do."

Bradley said, "Come to the house. Mom has the key to Duke's place. Just look around and do your thing."

She said, "Please, Mr. Bergeron?"

She had tears in her eyes, but it was well known that he was immune to tears. Shit. Bradley had tears too. It was unfair to double tear him.

Time was flying, and Dana might pop in at any time. Or Carla. He didn't want either of them to see Bradley and Susan.

"I can't help."

But they didn't appear ready to leave. Bradley looked at his mother but didn't say anything. She started telling him how dependable and kind and considerate and sweet Duke was, and how he would never, ever hurt her or worry her like this.

He sighed. "I suppose I could stop by and just look around the house. Not that it will do any good." They smiled. "But if you see a tall, garishly dressed, stork-like woman as you leave, tell her that you're accounting clients and keep moving."

He didn't actually drag them to the elevator. He sighed again when the door closed on them.

He meandered back to his cubicle. He was going to have a private chat with young Bradley about what he wasn't telling his mother.

No. He didn't want to know.

He would look around the house and leave, and that would

be that. Well, he could call Vonda and ask her to look into this Duke?

No. Even if his good buddy, Detective Golczewski, would make some discreet inquiries into Duke, it was none of his business. And the second mate might have a girl in every port. He hoped that wasn't so for Susan's sake but it could be. He might have to suggest that to Susan. Or Bradley.

The elevator dinged, and Harry and Carla walked out. Carla looked too ill to be working, but he wasn't brave enough to tell her that. And Harry wasn't either.

And then it hit him; he had managed to "be normal" for two days.

Well, that wasn't fair. He hadn't done anything except come in two hours early to work on some of Harry's clients. But he didn't have time to wail or moan; he got back to work.

Tuesday
7:00 pm

Harry had manned up enough to talk Carla into going home after lunch. Which was good. He had worked on Harry's clients the rest of the afternoon. His own clients were not so high maintenance. He had trained them well.

He just had to disabuse Bradley and Bradley's mother that he could help them, and he was golden. Well, semi-golden. There was still the matter of all the extra work he had taken on.

He was in his yellow Jeep crossing the Schuylkill River on the Walnut Street Bridge bound for West Philly and Bradley's home.

He knew he should have called and canceled. He still could, but he didn't like Andy setting Dana to spy on him like he was a child, a willful child. Or not normal.

And in his heart of hearts, he knew he was just a tad curious about merchant seaman Duke. But no one need ever know that; not Andy, Dana, or Jennifer.

His phone played the guitar riff from "Secret Agent Man." And especially not Cory.

"Hi Cory. Where are you?"

"In your apartment. What are you up to?"

"What did you hear? It isn't true, Cory. Honest."

Cory's silence was of an ominous nature. "What are you doing right now, Bergeron?"

"I'm driving in my Jeep."

"Gabe."

"I'm in West Philly...heading for the home of Susan Bradley."

"And why the Hell are you doing that? And who is Susan Bradley?"

"She's the mother of Steven Bradley."

"Gabe. I will track you down."

"While I'm always delighted to see you, that is totally unnecessary, Special Agent. Just stay at my apartment, and I will join you soon. As for Susan, she has lost a boyfriend named Duke."

"And?"

"And Steven Bradley is one of the FBI crime scene techs who worked on the Frisian art thieves case. Don't you remember him? Small, lots of black hair? Anyway, we got to know one another though he was rather mean to me and maneuvered me into looking at Sieta's corpse...."

"And he asked you to find Duke?"

"He did. He and Susan. They came to the office where I was working most diligently and implored me to lend a hand."

"They implored you?"

"They did. Tears were involved."

"Gabe."

"I know, Cory, but I had to get them out of the office before Dana arrived and telling them I'd come was the quickest option."

Cory sighed. "Tell me everything."

He did. Except for Andy threatening his limbs. And that it was possible that Bradley didn't want the FBI to know something about Duke. "So that's it."

"Gabe."

"No, it is, Cory. Look I'm already here."

"Give me the address, Bergeron."

"It's 9847 Williams Street. Well, that's Susan Bradley's row house. The boyfriend's house is across the street. I'll call you back after I peruse Duke's home. I promise."

"Be sure you do, Bergeron."

And Cory was gone.

He parked in front of what he thought was Susan's house. It

was the end home of a dozen, narrow, two-story, brick row houses jammed into the block. Each one had a bow window with a cornice projecting from the second story; there were window air conditioners and satellite dishes peppering the facades.

Each home also had a porch; the porch roofs were of different styles, materials, colors, depths, and intersected at non-Euclidean angles. Half of the homes had green, aluminum awnings projecting out from the porches.

They were well kept. Susan's had a bit of hedge in the front and big ceramic urns with plants. He jogged up the stone steps to the porch as Bradley came out the front door with keys in hand. Susan followed him but she stopped on the porch.

She waved. "Thank you for coming, Mr. Bergeron. You don't know how much I appreciate it."

He smiled. "I'll do what I can, Mrs. Bradley." Which was zero since his crystal ball was in the shop.

Bradley looked worn out, but he locked onto his hand and gave him a manly shake. "Thanks, Gabe."

"Sure." He may have smiled at Bradley. "You live with your mother?"

Bradley glared at him like an angry hamster. "No! I live next door." He pointed at the next row house. "That's mine."

He nodded and followed Bradley across the street. Duke's house, or his grandmother's house, was a long, narrow brick Victorian, half the size of Aunt Flo's house, but enormous for one old lady or one possibly lusty grandson.

It was a two story home with a turret rising from the ground floor to well above the main roof; somebody had covered the turret with white vinyl siding. The front porch frothed with the original, white gingerbread trim.

Bradley went up the stairs and through the door. He flipped a switch in the front parlor to dispel the dusky gloom. There were arched, double doors leading into what might be a dining room. Dark walnut wainscoting circled both rooms. Modest antique chandeliers hung from the ceilings. With a little loving attention, the rooms could be charming.

Bradley didn't appear all that eager to explore the house. He stopped in the parlor and fidgeted. "Duke lives in the back section."

They were standing beneath the parlor chandelier. The room was bare. A trail led through the thick dust on the floor. "Bradley?"

"Yeah?"

"What aren't you telling me? Or your mother?"

Bradley looked at him clearly torn between what might happen to this Duke if he told or if he didn't. "Nothing, Gabe."

"Right. Tell me or I'm walking out the door."

"It's nothing really."

He thought Bradley was shaking. It was so not nothing. "Spill, Stevie."

"Don't call me that!" He shook his head. "I just checked for any news about the SS Kerkyra."

"And discovered what?"

Bradley dug out his phone and was staring at it. "The ship was attacked by pirates in the Gulf of Guinea."

He may have snickered. "Pirates? I didn't see that one coming."

Bradley was pissed and mulling over the idea of punching him in the face. He may have ditched the smile and taken a tiny step back.

"It's true! It happens all the time in the gulf! And off the coast of Somalia and the strait of Malacca too."

He'd heard about Somali pirates; sort of. But Bradley proceeded to show him reports from news media in Lagos and Abuja centered on some place called Port Harcourt. They detailed the trials and tribulations of the SS Kerkyra and its crew.

"The pirates came on board and took the captain and first mate off the ship and held them hostage awaiting ransom from the ship owners."

He read the rest which managed to use lots of words to say nothing, but the upshot was that the captain had been killed in some kind of firefight with another group who might or might not have been pirates or brigands of some sort. The Nigerian government deplored the whole situation.

It appeared that Port Harcourt was located in Rivers State on the coast of Nigeria, and the state government was also in a deploring mood.

"Shit. So your mother doesn't know about this?"

"No."

"Right. And Duke was onboard when this went down?"

Bradley said, "He had to be."

"And you suspect him of what?"

Bradley shook his head and glared at him, bushy eyebrows scrunched into a defiant mask. "I don't suspect him of anything!"

He stood there staring at Bradley.

"I don't, Gabe, but he flew home as soon as the ship docked. I guess he docked it, being the second mate. He would have been in charge after the captain and first mate were taken."

"And he should have stayed with the ship?"

Bradley shrugged. "I think so? And he never mentioned it. Not a word."

"And you think he was involved somehow?"

Bradley got really close. "No!"

Bradley was two inches shorter and pounds lighter but vexed. "Take it easy. Look, what do you really know about this guy? Maybe he helped the pirates for a cut of the ransom?"

Bradley threw a punch. It was a punch as sad as one he might have thrown before Cory's training.

He blocked it and pushed Bradley across the room until he resisted, and then he grabbed his arm and basically fell down dragging Bradley with him and hurling him over his body.

Bradley landed flat on his back, and he was on top of him before the young tech knew what was happening.

"Do that again, and I will kick your ass."

Bradley gathered his wits. "Bastard! Get off me, and don't talk shit about Duke! I knew what you'd say if I told you! I knew it!"

Bradley stopped talking and lay there looking very upset.

"Are you going to behave yourself?"

Bradley glared at him, black eyes glistening with proto-tears. He tried to extricate himself for a bit before he gave up. "All right. But Duke is a good guy. He didn't have anything to do with any Nigerian kidnappers!"

"Right." He got to his feet and offered Bradley a hand which he took after some more glaring. He hoped Bradley understood that he wouldn't hesitate to *yoko wakare* his ass again.

They stood there staring at each other. He started to turn. He was going to exit Duke's house and the lives of Steven and Susan Bradley never to return; especially since he could be home with Cory.

Why was Cory in his apartment again on a weekday? It was great, but it was unexpected. He grabbed the door knob as he pondered what was up with Special Agent Poirier.

Bradley said, "Don't go."

He glanced back. "Give me one good reason?"

"Something happened last night."

"What?"

Bradley raked his long, black hair out of his eyes and straightened his back. "I haven't been sleeping too well, and just as I was drifting off after midnight, there were these noises...."

"Okay. So tell me about the noises."

He shook his head. "I don't know. A couple of crashes? Or thumps maybe. And a vehicle took off fast. I got a flashlight and searched all around Duke's house. The doors were locked. The windows hadn't been tampered with as far as I could tell. Duke's truck wasn't in the driveway or on the street."

"And you're sure the noises came from Duke's house?"

He shrugged. "Last night, I was sure."

"But you didn't go inside?"

"No. Mom's got the key, and I would have had to wake her up, and I didn't want to do that."

"Okay. So let's look around and see what we can see."

Bradley smiled at him or tried to. He looked exhausted and upset and had dark smudges under his eyes that no twenty year old should have.

He thought that Bradley was sure that something bad had happened to Duke, but he was fighting hard against believing it. He wanted to know the truth but not really.

"You'll still help?"

"Maybe. If I can. Which isn't too likely now that I know that Nigerian pirates are involved." He didn't mention the FBI.

Bradley moved out of the parlor and down a hall to an antique kitchen at the back of the house. It had been the cat's meow when Clara Bow had graced the silent screen.

There was a smell that should never be in a kitchen. It was faint but not nice.

The kitchen had enormous, single pane windows that surely let in more of winter's cold than they kept out. The yard behind the house was so overgrown with shrubs and trees and vines that he could barely see the back end of a row house on the next street over.

A pile of mail was on the kitchen table.

Bradley said, "That's Duke's mail from when he was away; Mom gave it to him when he got back."

"Right."

He sat down and went through it. He didn't see any bills or bank statements, just the usual junk mail.

"Duke does all his banking online. I showed him how to do it." A little smile that died quickly.

"Does he have any family?"

"No. None that we know of."

"Okay. Does he own any property other than this place?"

Bradley shrugged. "He's never mentioned any place. We can ask Mom but she would have said."

"Right."

He opened the refrigerator which was even emptier than his. Duke didn't even have ice cube trays. Just to be thorough he inspected every cabinet. He found a mummified mouse in the one over the refrigerator. Maybe that was the smell?

The kitchen faucet was leaking: drip, drip, drip. Rust from the water had stained the porcelain.

He tried smiling at Bradley. "Okay. Lead on."

They went down a hall to Duke's bedroom. It had originally been something else. Maybe servant's quarters?

In any case, the furniture had been acquired in the last

quarter of the twentieth century. The linens were of recent vintage and fresh. A chest of drawers held a dozen pairs of boxer-briefs in packs of three; red, black, green, and blue. Only one pack had been opened and was lacking two of the red boxer-briefs.

If he had to guess, he would surmise that Susan had purchased them along with the bed spread and the sheets. And probably the rug which was nice.

There was a metal rack that held a few pairs of pants and some shirts on hangers.

There wasn't a scrap of paper anywhere in the room. And it didn't smell very good either.

He looked at Bradley.

"I know. There's nothing here to tell us a damn thing."

"No, there is not. Wait. Does he have a safe deposit box?"

"Maybe?"

"We'll ask your mother. Where does he bank?"

"DW Bank."

But the bank wasn't going to tell a non-relative about any safe deposit box.

"So where's the bathroom? And any other rooms that Duke used?"

"The only bathroom in the house is upstairs."

He followed Bradley up the backstairs. The fifteen watt bulb in the overhead fixture hardly dispelled the gloom.

He wasn't sure why he was suddenly uneasy. He drew in a breath. There was an odor hanging in the air, like the smell in the kitchen and bedroom only stronger.

As they climbed the steps, the smell transitioned into a stench. He felt the hairs on the back of his neck rouse themselves in an atavistic response.

He grabbed Bradley's arm. "Hold up." He stepped around. The door ahead was closed. "Is that the bathroom?"

Bradley nodded; black eyes enormous.

He didn't know why he had to go first. He might be ten years older than Bradley. Or a bit more. But he was just as squeamish as the next guy. There were those who would say more squeamish; Bradley was one of them.

But he hadn't loved Duke.

He pulled out a handkerchief and covered his mouth and nose.

He turned the knob and peered around the door when the gap was six inches. The bathroom was dark; a glimmer of light was coming through one tiny, stain-glass window.

A thick, gag-inducing stench of corruption and bodily effluents was oozing out and coiling around them. This never boded well.

Bradley had shut his eyes. "The switch is on the right."

"This may be a case where more light is not a plus."

But he flicked the switch anyway.

Tuesday
8:00 pm

It wasn't as bad as it could have been. Well, not for him, but then he had no connection to Duke.

Bradley said, "What is it, Gabe?"

It was a large gentleman in an antique claw-foot bathtub.

He was not naked nor was he bathing since the bathtub held no water, but he was just as dead as the stench had indicated.

The blood that had congealed on his head and white t-shirt and the white-filmed, staring eyes clinched it.

"Bradley, take a deep breath and then stick your head in."

"What the Hell is it?"

Bradley had to know? He'd been to enough crime scenes.

And Bradley pushed into the room enough to see the tub and its occupant. He stood there staring.

And then he smiled. Which was not the reaction of a normal, non-serial killer type person.

Bradley noted his expression. "It's not him, Gabe!"

"Not Duke?"

"No!" He laughed. "This guy is older. And Duke has long blond hair."

What hair the dead gentleman had left had been graying and buzz cut. The guy barely fit into the tub. He had been six foot five or six and had big arms with tattoos. A capital "A" covered the left biceps, and a Greek letter was on the right. He consulted the old memory banks: "Ω" or omega.

It took him a second. Not the Latin "A" but the Greek "A"

for alpha. He looked at the massive fists; even from across the bathroom, he could see the scars on the knuckles.

Bathtub Man had gotten into fights often enough to christen his left arm as the Alpha and his right as the Omega; the beginning and end of anyone who crossed him.

"Okay. So who is he?"

Bradley shook his head. "I've never seen him."

He took some photos with his phone and backed out of the bathroom taking Bradley with him.

He dialed 911 and set in motion the mechanisms drawn up to handle violent death. Well, non-government sanctioned, violent death.

And then he made a more difficult call. "Hi, Cory."

"Gabe?"

"I might have a situation."

"Shit! Tell me, Bergeron...in ten words or less."

"Body in a bathtub; probably not natural causes."

Cory said a collection of Anglo-Saxon monosyllables in novel combinations. "Are you okay? Have you called the police?"

"Yes and yes."

"I'm on my way."

Which was good. Cory could help deal with the police, and he could get his scolding out of the way. He deserved it. He should have just canceled this visit.

He was standing beside his Jeep when the first squad car arrived. The officer was understandably wary so he put his hands up and smiled which led to the officer drawing his weapon.

"The body is in the bathroom on the second floor." He pointed helpfully at Duke's house.

"Put your hands on the Jeep and spread your legs. Now!"

His name tag read "Fuchs." Officer Fuchs patted him down.

He wasn't sure that Fuchs would appreciate any of the salient facts so he kept his mouth shut as more officers arrived.

In due time, Bradley and Susan came out of her house and talked to Fuchs.

Fuchs was tall and broad and so overcome with Weltschmerz that he could barely put pen to paper to record their names and addresses.

His light brown hair was trimmed short. He had a medium-sized nose, tiny ears, and eyes set too close together. They were of an indeterminate color; a pale shade of despair.

But in due course, a detective arrived. He had hoped that he might know the detective. Of course, it wasn't Oscuro so that was a plus.

Detective Fowler was about forty. He was as tall and world weary as Fuchs, but if Fuchs was slipping into terminal ennui, Fowler appeared more embittered.

He had a cigarette dangling out of his mouth. His tie was stuffed into a suit pocket, but the suit itself was pristine.

Fuchs had kept him isolated from Bradley and Susan. Fowler had talked to them, and now he was ready for Gabriel Bergeron.

Fowler was tall but bony. He had a thin oval face with a pointy chin and lobeless ears. A large nose dominated his face. His full lips were clamped onto a cigarette. He inhaled and then exhaled smoke through his nose.

His brows were scrunched together like he was staring into the sun. Vertical valleys ran from his nose half way to his hairline and deep furrows outlined each eyebrow.

"So who's the vic?"

Which was an odd question since the detective had already talked to Susan and Bradley.

Fowler was looking at Susan. He might be wrong but he believed the detective was cheered by staring at her, and she may have smiled wistfully back at Fowler.

"I don't know. I never saw him before."

Fowler glanced away from Susan and grimaced. "Is that so? What were you doing in that house?"

"Bradley asked me to come and take a look."

Another grimace. "And the kid is what to you?"

"Friend. Well, sort of. More an acquaintance really. And Susan asked me to come too."

"Is that right? Why?"

"That's a good question, Detective." Fowler focused on

him. "They thought I could help locate Lars Thorvaldsen who lives in that house. When he's in the country. They haven't seen him since Friday; he just returned from his latest voyage. He's a mariner, but I suppose they told you that?"

Fowler leaned in. His suit, hair, and skin reeked of smoke. "So you knew this Thorvaldsen?"

"Nope. Wouldn't know him if he walked up to me right now."

"Is that so? But you felt okay traipsing through his house?"

He tried smiling at Fowler while holding his breath. "Bradley and Susan came to my office to ask me to help. I should have told them no, but obviously I didn't"

"And what are you? Some kind of snoop?"

"No, I'm not. I'm an accountant."

Fowler let the cigarette fall from his lips and rubbed a hand over his face. He was probably more like thirty-five than forty. He stretched and grabbed another cigarette.

He lit it and took a deep drag. "So explain to me what an accountant was going to do to find this Duke guy?"

"I don't know. I don't think I could have helped. This time."

Fowler almost smiled at him and put an hand on his shoulder. "Bergeron, don't make me drag it out of you. I'm beat, and I get mean when I'm beat." He glanced at Fuchs. "Don't I, Fuchs?"

Fuchs just stared for a second. "Like a pit viper."

Fowler laughed. "What have I ever done to you, Fuchs?" Fowler looked back at him; the bony hand was stroking the back of his neck.

"Okay. Last year I helped out on a case with Bradley, and he may have gotten the idea that I'm a sort of amateur detective."

Fowler blinked. "Bradley's FBI. Well, a crime scene tech. Or so he says. I hate the FBI. Don't I Fuchs?"

Fuchs sniffed. "Like your mother-in-law."

Fowler laughed. "Fuchs, for a depressing sonofabitch, you crack me up. And she's my former mother-in-law." Fowler squeezed his neck a little harder like he wanted to wring the truth out of Gabe Bergeron. "Are you telling me that you worked on a case for the FBI?"

"Yes. As a consultant."

Fowler puffed on his cigarette as the street light above them hummed. He shook his head. "Okay. I want the truth, Bergeron. Is the FBI involved...in any freaking way...with this Duke Thorvaldsen?"

"Not to the best of my knowledge, Detective."

Which Fowler might have accepted, or not, but a black SUV screeched to a halt, and Cory leaped out at that precise moment.

Fowler said, "And who the Hell is this, Fuchs?"

Fuchs cast an appraising eye over Cory and his suit. "FBI."

"I hope you're wrong, Fuchs."

Cory flashed his badge at Fowler. "Special Agent Poirier of the FBI. And you are?"

Fowler clamped down on his cigarette raising it to an acute angle. "Detective Fowler of the Philadelphia Police Department."

They shook grudgingly.

Cory said, "Hi, Gabe."

"Cory." He smiled his very best smile but both Cory and Fowler were glaring at him.

Cory said, "I'm not here to interfere in your investigation, Detective."

Fowler glanced at Fuchs and snorted. "Is that so? So you were just cruising through West Philly on an April night and happened upon my crime scene?"

He thought Fuchs smiled.

Cory shook his head. "No. Gabe called me. Continue with what you were doing. Don't let me stop you."

But Fowler was flummoxed just a tad. He cleared his throat and ejected his half-smoked cigarette. "So, Bergeron, you don't know the vic. You don't know this Duke Thorvaldsen. Basically you don't know anything, but you found the body?"

"That's right."

Nobody believed him; not Fowler, Fuchs, or Cory.

Fowler said, "Stay right here." He looked at Cory. "You have a problem with that?"

"No, Detective. He's yours as long as you want him."

Fowler nodded aggressively and marched off toward Duke's house. He may have looked at Fuchs and then at the Bergeron perp. Fuchs moved closer.

Cory said, "So is there anything I should know?"

He had no idea so he told Cory everything that had happened since Bradley had walked into Garst, Bauer & Hartmann.

Cory and Fuchs listened attentively.

Cory said, "And that's it?"

"Yes. I know how it sounds."

Cory smiled at him. Well, he showed his pearly white canines and incisors. "No, you don't. Nigerian pirates?"

Fuchs snorted.

"Talk to Bradley, Cory, if you don't believe me."

"No. He's Fowler's witness or perp or whatever the Hell he is." Fuchs nodded in agreement. "And I'm not stepping on his toes for no good reason."

So they waited as the moon rose. Bradley and Susan had gone inside at some point with an officer trailing them.

"I'm sorry, Cory. This is all my fault. I should have known better."

Cory looked at him. "But?"

"No buts. I was wrong to come here."

"You were." Cory put an arm across his shoulder. "You were curious, weren't you?"

"If I admit it, will you punch me?"

Cory punched his arm.

"I deserve that. But Bradley and Susan were so worried about Duke and that was before I heard anything about the merchant marine and pirates and the dead captain...."

Cory said, "What dead captain?"

"Didn't I tell you?"

Fuchs muttered, "No."

"Duke was the second mate on the SS Kerkyra, and the captain of the ship was killed after being taken off the ship to be held for ransom."

Fowler emerged from Duke's house as the body was brought out. He was talking softly to the medical examiner. "Are you sure?"

That individual gave Fowler a how-dumb-are-you look and walked away.

Fowler spit out his current cigarette and ground it into Duke's lawn like it was a dandelion, and he was a lawn fanatic. From the set of his shoulders, he was feeling put upon and ill-used. This case was shaping up to being complicated if not bizarre.

And that was before Fuchs whispered in his lobeless ear about the Nigerian pirates and the dead captain of the SS Kerkyra,

Fowler stared. "You made that shit up, Fuchs."

Fuchs just stood there but his whole body said that he couldn't be bothered.

Fowler spied them and marched over. He ignored Cory and got so close they could have passed a cigarette from mouth to mouth...if the passee didn't mind taking the burning end.

"Where were you late Friday night to early Saturday morning, Bergeron?"

"I was asleep in my apartment."

"Can anybody corroborate that?"

He looked at Cory, but the special agent was looking off into the distance. He resisted the urge to punch him. "Cory can."

Fowler pulled back shaking his head. "Is that right, Special Agent?"

Cory didn't say a word for far too long but eventually he said, "Yes. He was with me all night, Detective."

Fowler was disappointed. Fuchs would have been too if he could have summoned up enough interest.

"He couldn't have slipped out?"

"No. I'm a light sleeper."

Which was a total fib. The bed could be carried out of the apartment, down the stairs, dumped in the back of a pickup, and driven across Philly, and Cory wouldn't rouse.

Fowler looked at Fuchs but Fuchs ignored him this time.

Cory said, "Is there something you want to ask, Detective?"

There was, and there wasn't.

Cory said, "If Gabe had gotten out of our bed, I would have known it."

Fowler absorbed that. "Right. Thanks for your help. You're free to go, Mr. Bergeron. But I might have more questions later on." Fowler glared at Fuchs. "What are you standing around for? Haven't you got something you should be doing?"

Fuchs didn't dignify that with an answer as he trudged to his patrol car.

Cory escorted him to his Jeep. "We're going to talk when we get home, Bergeron."

He didn't doubt it for second. He got into his Jeep and followed Cory to Arch Street.

Friday Noon

At the apartment, Cory had relented only after he had made a solemn vow not to have any contact with Bradley and Susan for the rest of his natural life.

Which seemed a bit excessive, but Cory had provided him with a rock solid alibi. Had Cory been embarrassed at all? He wasn't any longer. He loved Cory and didn't care who knew it.

He had come in to work early each day and had been working exceedingly hard. He was a pitiful shell of his former self, but he thought he might actually have to come in on Saturday.

Which was just wrong, but Jennifer hadn't been able to work on her clients even from home.

He sighed. He was just too goodhearted.

His phone rang. If it was a client, anybody's client, he or she or they were going to wish they hadn't called.

"Hello?"

"Bergeron?"

It was Detective Fowler.

Shit. "Yes, Detective?"

"Need to speak to you ASAP."

Shit. Shit. He cast a wary eye at Dana who was lolling in her chair reading a magazine. She knew nothing about Bradley or Susan or Bathtub Guy so far and hadn't been able to rat him out to Andy.

"Okay. Can we meet at CoffeeXtra? It's on South 16th Street not far from my office?"

"Fine. When?"

"Fifteen minutes?"

"Okay."

He looked around. Harry had brought Carla to work but had left mid-morning for some reason. Carla was trying to work, but she was looking unwell.

"Carla? I'm going out to lunch. Can I bring you anything?"

She was shaking out her hands; she had been doing it throughout the morning. She turned to glare at him. "No! Where is Harry? He said he'd be back by now?"

"I don't know. Did you call him?"

"Of course, I called him! He said he'd be back soon." Her voice was just a wee bit petulant.

"Okay? Is there anything I can do?"

She heaved herself out of her chair. "Sure! Go to the freaking bathroom for me."

He ran for the elevator as she waddled off.

He was eating a sandwich and drinking a calming milkshake when he spotted Fowler outside. He dumped a cigarette and walked in.

In the clear light of day, the detective wouldn't be unattractive if the furrows in his face could be smoothed out with the careful application of a bucket of Spackle.

His suit was very nice; his tie gorgeous. He looked at the no-smoking signs and shook his head. He glared at Martin and ordered coffee.

"Bergeron."

"Detective Fowler."

He sucked up the last of his milkshake. He debated getting another one, but he had gained two pounds since Monday.

Fowler was staring at him. "I talked to some people."

"I do that too, Detective. About anything in particular?" He may have been a bit cranky with the prospect of working on Saturday looming.

Fowler's furrows deepened. "Don't be a smart-ass. About you."

"People in the police department? Who? Golczewski?

Eads? Czerwinski?" He just hoped he hadn't talked to Oscuro.

"Eads and then Golczewski. They say you aren't an idiot. Or a nutcase."

"High praise indeed."

Fowler leaned over the table. "Do I need to smack you?"

"No, Sir, you do not. I'm sorry. How may I help you?"

The detective rubbed his face and then his hair which had been reduced to blond stubble. "I don't know. I hate this case."

"Yeah. I can imagine. So any sign of Duke? Have you identified the dead guy?"

Fowler stared at his coffee. "No sign of Duke. He flew in from Paris on Friday three weeks ago. Must have taken a flight from Nigeria but we haven't tied that down yet."

"But he was on the SS Kerkyra when the pirates came on board?"

Fowler nodded. "Probably."

"Does he have a criminal record?"

Fowler shook his head. "Not that we've dug up."

"And the dead man?"

Fowler had no idea who he was, but he was reluctant to own up to that.

Fowler said, "So Poirier isn't interested in this case? Because if he's going to swoop in, I'm forgetting about this...mess right now."

"No, Detective, he isn't. He works in art theft. Nothing about this ties into fine art."

Fowler nodded. "Yeah, I found out that much about him. But anybody else? According to Golczewski, you know half the agents in the area."

Fowler was looking hopeful.

"I'm sorry, but I don't know of any FBI interest in Bathtub Guy."

Fowler scowled ferociously at his coffee. "Shit. I was hoping...."

He chugged the rest of his coffee and stood up looking frustrated and perplexed. "Okay."

A tall, raven-tressed young lady was admiring the cut of

Fowler's trousers or something. She caught Fowler's eye, and they smiled at each other. Fowler admired her back for a bit.

Fowler focused. He planted his big hands on the table and leaned in. "Any ideas?"

"Have you called the Nigerian Police? In Port Harcourt?"

"Port Harcourt?"

"City of over a million on the coast of Nigeria...near where the piracy and murder of the captain occurred. Of course, you might want to start with the national police in Abuja, the capital."

He may have done a little harmless research.

"Yeah?" Fowler nodded. "You do taxes?"

"What?" He didn't want any more clients. He gave a noncommittal nod as he took a bite of his sandwich.

Fowler said, "Nan says I should get somebody this year."

"Is that so?"

Fowler nodded. "I'll tell her about you." And out he strutted with a certain loose-limbed, nicotine-coated grace. It wasn't impossible that he was hot on the trail of the tall young lady and not the killer of Bathtub Guy, but it was no concern of his.

He sighed. With his luck, Nan, whoever she was, or Fowler would be coming to see him. O frabjus day. He trudged back to work.

Carla was sitting in Dana's chair with her bag at her feet. Dana was flapping around, Uselessness personified.

"What?"

Carla really looked unwell now. "I need to go home, Gabe."

"Right. Absolutely. Wait. You want me to take you? I can do that."

He helped Carla into the elevator and got her seated in the lobby. "I'll get my Jeep." He tried smiling. "Won't be gone two seconds, and we'll get you home."

Carla didn't have the strength to glare at him. He ran to the parking garage and took the steps three at a time up to the fourth level. Where the Hell was Baldacci?

He shot out of the parking garage and proceeded to the Mahr Building at an unsafe speed. He may have braked too hard and skidded a bit. He might have laid rubber? He took a deep breath and ran into the lobby.

Dana was sitting beside Carla on the bench. Carla had her arms wrapped around her abdomen. She groaned and rocked a bit. Shit! He was feeling light-headed, and the floor was no longer horizontal. He closed his eyes and counted to ten taking deep breaths.

Carla said, "Bergeron! Don't you dare faint on me!"

His eyes popped open. "Right! No, I won't! I can do this!"

He had no chance in Hell of coping with this.

He really didn't, but he helped Carla to her feet and guided her out the door with Dana fluttering her nearly naked limbs in the background. They traversed the sidewalk. She still had to negotiate the curb, walk around the Jeep, and climb up into the passenger seat.

She had her eyes closed and was gritting her teeth.

He swept her up in his arms and carried her around the Jeep. He wasn't sure who was more shocked that he dared take such liberties, but he was going with Carla.

She wasn't really that heavy. Which was good, because he was pretty sure Carla was terrified that he was going to drop her. Which would be very bad.

He realized he should have opened the door before picking her up, but he managed to get it open without banging her head.

He deposited her gently into the seat. He may have been smiling at this demonstration of his manly strength and deft mastery of the situation when Carla grabbed him by the throat.

"Take me to the hospital, Bergeron! Now!"

He reassessed the situation. "So not home then?"

"No, idiot! Drive!"

And he did. Like the wind. Like a tempest. Like a typhoon. Like someone who should never ever have been given a driver's license. He whipped around the block and across the city bound for South 11th Street and the Thomas Jefferson University Hospital.

Strangely, they arrived at their destination unbroken and unbloodied.

When the Jeep stopped all forward motion, he looked over at Carla. She had her eyes closed.

He ran around the Jeep and picked her up again. He may have run screaming into the ER but his memory was a bit foggy.

In any case, Carla was on a gurney and being whisked away before his bellows stopped echoing off the walls.

Someone asked him if he was the father; he shook his head so hard he almost induced whiplash. Someone gave him a funny look. Someone guided him into a chair.

He sat and thought nothing at all for a remarkably long time.

A bright, fluty voice said, "Sir? Sir! She wants to see you. Sir!"

One of his eyes focused. A strange looking woman was talking to him. She had a very square face, a beak-like nose, and big bright eyes. He felt sure she was at least half chickadee.

She was fluttering around him like a mother bird trying to get her fledgling into the air.

"What?"

She leaned in close. "She wants to see you, Sir."

"Carla? Carla Baldacci? Okay."

He was exhausted but he followed the nurse until he was beside Carla's bed. She had her eyes open and actually looked better.

"Did you call my mother?"

"Your mother?" He had no knowledge of Carla's mother other than the generic knowledge that she probably had one. Since Carla never talked about her family.

Harry. Shit. But he could have called Harry. He should do that right now.

Carla grabbed him by the throat again. "Call my mother!"

"And Harry too? Right?"

"My mother!"

The avian nurse unlocked Carla's hands from his throat as she warbled, "Please don't excite yourself, Dear. I'm sure the...nice man will call your mother." She gave him a look that said she had doubts as to whether he was even sentient.

And then she shoved him from the bedside and pulled the curtain. Which was fine. He was happy, nay delighted and overcome with joy to be expelled. Which made him think about the baby. Wasn't it much too early for the baby to be born?

And then he realized he had not a clue as to the name or phone number of Carla's mother. He called Harry as he walked back to the ER waiting room; it went to voicemail. He left a terse, semi-scathing message for Mr. Baldacci.

Maybe Jennifer knew how to reach Carla's mother? And then he realized Carla's purse was hanging around his neck. He had no idea how it had gotten there.

Under ordinary circumstances, he would never touch it. He would sooner rip open a Chinese diplomatic pouch containing naughty photos of Xi Jinping. Or the briefcase with the nuclear launch codes.

He found Carla's phone.

He further found an number for "Mom."

A deep, raspy voice said something in what was likely Mandarin.

"Mrs. Wong?" Silence, palpable silence. "Is this Mrs. Wong? Carla Wong's mother?"

"Who are you and what have you done with my daughter!"

This was said in a tone that managed to be both gruff and screechy...like Tuvan throat singing.

"Nothing! I like Carla, and, to tell you the truth, I'm a teensy bit intimidated by her so I would never presume...."

"Where is my daughter!"

This was all screech.

"In the hospital. I brought her here since we couldn't find Baldacci."

There was some harsh sounding Mandarin, and then, "Which hospital, you idiot?"

"Thomas Jefferson University Hospital. The ER, at present. I think she's doing okay?"

And she was gone. He put Carla's phone back into her bag and sat there gradually returning to a semi-calm state. He had gotten Carla to the hospital just as fast as he could, and nobody could blame him if things went south. Well, they could but it wouldn't be fair.

He was wondering just how bad the hospital coffee would be when he saw two Asian ladies rush in; one older, one younger. Neither looked much like Carla. He remained in his chair as a nurse took them back.

Baldacci finally returned his call.

"Gabe! How is she? Where is she?"

He had forgotten to give Harry some vital info in the message. "Shit! Sorry. Thomas Jefferson University Hospital. I called her mother. She may or may not be here already."

But Harry was gone.

He sat some more. He paced a bit.

Harry arrived at a run. "How is she, Gabe?"

"I don't know. She seemed better the last time I saw her."

"Her mother's here...somewhere."

Two women arrived; again one older, one younger. One was known to him; Harry's mother, Rita. They other one must be his younger sister?

This supposed sister zeroed in on Harry. She had an oval face, long black hair with a streak or two of gray, and eyes that were identical to Harry's only not as happy. Well, Harry's eyes weren't happy now but in general.

Harry's sister said, "How is she?"

Harry said, "I just got here, Adriana."

Sister Adriana shook her head.

Rita was sixtyish with a sweet, round, almost cherubic face. She said, "Go ask at the desk, Adriana."

And Adriana marched off cutting a swath through the crowd like a Soviet tank army with Stalin in attendance.

Harry's mother hugged her son. "She'll be okay, Harry."

Rita looked at him. "Hi, Gabe."

"Hello, Mrs. Baldacci."

And then Adriana waved at them, and Harry and Rita followed Adriana heading, no doubt, for Carla.

He sat back down and awaited news. His phone rang. "Hello?"

Cory said, "Gabe?"

"Oh. Hi, Cory." He took a long pause as he pondered his

life choices. "So how are you?"

"What's wrong, Gabe?"

"Nothing. Well, I'm in the hospital...as a visitor. I brought Carla here. I'm not sure why or how she is now, but Harry's here. And her family. Probably."

Cory said, "You sound weird."

"Do not. Well, I've had a rousing afternoon. What's up with you?"

"I'm sorry, Gabe."

"You're going far away for an indefinite period."

"Yes."

"Well, that's okay. Is Bornheimer going with you?"

"Sure."

"Well, have fun."

Cory said, "It's my job, Gabe."

Cory sounded upset. He had to pull himself together. "I know, and it's fine. I'm just frazzled from driving Carla across town. I was afraid something bad was going to happen...like on my watch. You know? And what would I have told Harry?"

"I understand. Okay. I'll call you later tonight."

"Thanks, Cory."

He pocketed his phone and got to his feet.

He went searching for coffee. He found something that looked like sludge and smelled even worse. He dumped it and purchased a can of ginger ale which was better for his tummy anyway.

He was hungry. He was stuffing his face with potato chips when the younger Chinese-American lady came back through the double doors.

She spotted him and walked over. He stood up hoping she wouldn't want to shake hands since his were greasy.

"Are you Mr. Bergeron?"

"Yes, I am, and you're Carla's sister?"

She smiled. She had a round face like her mother; Carla's was more oval. Her hair was black like Carla's but silky and not frizzy-curly, and it was cut in a short bob.

"Yes, I'm Yvonne Wong. Carla has told us so much about

you, Mr. Bergeron."

"Really? It's very nice to meet you. Wait. How is Carla doing? I got her here as fast as I could."

Yvonne tried to smile again but it was as if the first smile had exhausted her smile banks. "The doctor wants her to stay overnight but she thinks she'll be fine."

"And the baby?"

"Also fine."

So she wasn't going to have it now? Or if she did, it would be okay? He wasn't going to ask.

"That's great. Please call me Gabe."

"Of course. And thank you for bringing Carla." A weak smile drifted across her face. "She told us all about it!"

He had doubts that he had come off as heroic in Carla's version.

And then Carla's mother popped out. She fired a burst of Mandarin at Yvonne from twenty yards. Yvonne nodded and said soothing sounding things as she hugged her mother.

Neither had Carla's big, beautiful eyes which were her best feature...unless you were a heterosexual male.

Yvonne said, "This is Gabe Bergeron, Mom."

Mom looked him over from stem to stern and back again.

It was a bit uncomfortable-making. "Hello, Mrs. Wong."

He was about to ask Yvonne if her mother spoke English when that lady demonstrated a firm grasp.

"Mr. Bergeron! I'm so happy to meet you. Sorry if I snapped at you on the phone but it's my first grandchild." Yvonne got a disparaging look before she continued, "Carla has entertained us with so many stories about you."

"Really? Wait. Good stories or bad stories? I mean am I the hero, the villain, or the comic relief in these apocryphal tales?"

Mrs. Wong smiled a smile that was the original of Yvonne's pale copy. "Never the villain, Mr. Bergeron."

Which was the best he could hope for.

"Call me Winnie, Mr. Bergeron."

"Okay. And I'm Gabe."

Winnie glanced at Yvonne. "I'm going to stay with her."

She held up a hand before Yvonne could utter. "I couldn't sleep at home, Yvonne, but I'll need a few things."

Yvonne's sigh was so subtle that three molecules of air were displaced; tops. "Of course, Mom."

Winnie looked back at him. He was beginning to feel a bit uncomfortable again when she said, "When things get back to normal, Gabe...."

"Yes?"

She smiled and shook her head. She said something to Yvonne in Mandarin and walked away heading for Carla's bedside.

He glanced at Yvonne but she just stared at him. "It was nice to meet you, Gabe."

And she was gone too but heading out the door.

He sat back down. He was starving but he should call the office. He grabbed his phone; it was just past 4:00 pm.

He dialed. Dana said, in one breathless burst, "Garst, Bauer & Hartmann, how may I direct your call?"

"Dana, it's Gabe."

"How is she, Gabe?"

"Okay. I think. I mean they're keeping her overnight but her sister says she and the baby are going to be okay."

Dana repeated his message in a loud voice. There was a murmur of relief from the cubicle dwellers still present.

He said, "Can you turn my computer off, Dana? And stuff the papers in my middle drawer?"

"Sure, Gabe. That was scary."

"It was." He wondered if Dana were thinking of her own baby? He didn't actually know that Dana was pregnant. Still.

"Night, Gabe."

He hung up. He wanted to talk to Cory but that wasn't happening. Did he have any food in his apartment?

He looked up, and Harry was smiling at him. He stood up. "So how is she?"

Harry hugged him.

Wednesday
8:00 am

The days, since the Carla crisis, had been uneventful, except that somebody had been in his apartment yesterday. Which was unsettling.

Nothing had been taken as far as he could tell but things had been moved around while he had been at work.

Maybe Cory had stopped by to get something?

He hoped that was it but he had to focus. Jennifer was officially out of the office until the birth. Carla wasn't back but might return today. Harry had taken Carla to a doctor's appointment yesterday to get the okay.

And he was currently talking to one of Carla's clients. "Yes, Sir. I understand, but Ms. Wong-Baldacci is not in the office right now. I can have her call you when she comes in...."

The bass voice was turning a bit acidic. "And when is that going to be?"

"Later today. Possibly. Or I could help you?"

"And who are you?"

"I'm Gabe Bergeron, a colleague of Ms. Wong-Baldacci. She has brought me up to speed on your account, Sir."

Which was a grievous falsehood. It was possible but not likely that Carla had talked to Harry about Elliott Construction.

"I don't think so!"

And Mr. Elliott was gone. He checked to see if he was sorry about that, and he was not. "May his life be full of splinters, and all his buildings be so out of plumb that they fall over."

Paul Hearne was passing nearby. "An unhappy client, Gabe?"

He spun in his chair. "Not even my client, Paul."

Paul Hearne was soft and gray and sixty with vacant, blue-glass, teddy-bear eyes. Or so it appeared.

"How is Carla doing?"

"Okay. As far as I know. Harry said that she might come in today." Paul looked doubtful. "What? Do you know something?"

Paul shrugged. "Stella and I were talking."

Stella Rook was another coworker. She was somewhere between forty and seventy with suspiciously red hair but real freckles. She favored pink lipstick and pink blush, and her face had a faintly, doll-like appearance.

"About Carla?"

Paul nodded and drifted off as was his wont. What did Stella know about Carla?

He sighed. He didn't have time to inquire. Not only was he fielding calls from Carla and Harry's clients but it was the start of the annual running of the tax filers; those who eschewed arithmetic and paperwork until they heard the heavy tread of the approaching April tax filing deadline.

April was the cruelest month, and not only for T.S. Eliot.

Tomorrow was the 15th of April, and if history were any guide, the frenzied hordes would storm the Mahr Building. He personally felt they should barricade the doors and warm up the boiling oil but nobody consulted him.

He went back to his spreadsheet but his phone rang.

It might be Cory. "GBH Accounting, Gabriel Bergeron here." He tried to inject a lilt in his voice.

Jennifer said, "Bergeron? What's wrong with you? You never answer the phone like that!"

"Nothing is wrong with me, and I am deeply offended, Jennifer. Wait. How are you feeling? Better, I hope?"

"I'm okay. But I won't be coming in."

"No, and you shouldn't. Take it easy. Everything is fine here!" He tried the lilt again but even he could hear how fake it sounded.

"That's why I'm calling."

Dark, ominous forebodings. Imagine Bach organ music in the background.

"Bergeron?"

"Still here."

Jennifer said, "Harry just called me, and Carla won't be back for at least a week."

Shit! Shit! Shit! "Can't she work from home?" Which was unfeeling and self-serving. "Sorry. I know she would if she could. But can't she?"

"She's going to try. Later on. Gabe?"

"Yes, Jennifer?"

"I need you to step up."

He sighed. "Right." There was no way. No way in Hell. "Wait. Harry's coming in, right?"

"Yes, but he'll need to take time off. He won't be in today. He's going to try to put in a few hours tomorrow."

He thought very bad thoughts about Harry. And Carla. And Jennifer and Andy. Their runaway, sexual appetites were impinging on his life in a very negative manner.

"I want to help, but I can't take on Carla and Harry's clients and some of yours too."

"I know, Gabe. Stella is willing to help out as needed with my clients. And Chatterjee will take over most of Carla's."

"And young Dhruva is welcome to the scurvy lot of them. Wait again. Does Carla know about this?"

"No. Please call her and tell her, Gabe. I'll talk to you tomorrow. I know you can handle this, Gabe. Do your best."

He stared at the phone. He hadn't voiced his doubts about Stella, but they were Jennifer's clients after all.

He sat there and stewed and fretted and bubbled about all this work like a witch's cauldron or one of Ezmeralda's experimental soups.

Well, he would have but he spotted Stella heading for her cubicle, which was three cubicles down from Paul's and also had a window.

He smiled his best smiled though his heart wasn't in it. "Hi,

Stella. Jennifer has talked to you about her clients?"

She smiled. It was a nice smile but it didn't quite make up for the vacant, blue eyes peering at him through the bangs. He reminded himself that he'd thought the same thing about Paul and been utterly wrong about Mr. Hearne's intelligence. And sense of humor.

She waved at her client chair. "Yes, Gabriel. I'm happy to help. Jennifer should never have pushed herself to work so late in her pregnancy. The poor thing is worn out."

Which he couldn't disagree with.

Stella had tiny opal earrings and a wisp of a gold necklace hung with tiny opal pendants. Her dress was russet and generously cut.

"Right. She did look worn out. So about her clients. I have a list of some that you could take a look at?"

He was finding it hard to focus on Stella and the clients because every square inch of the cubicle was plastered with photos of puppies. He had been led to believe that many of them were hers.

She smiled again. "Sure, Gabriel. Just send them to me, and I'll go over them right now."

"Thanks, Stella."

He would have asked her about Carla but the puppies were getting to him; too many eyes, too many lolling tongues.

He trotted back to his cubicle and reunited rump and chair. He had keyed one number into his spreadsheet when he noted that Dana was waving at him. He would have ignored her utterly, but she came over trailing two large guys behind her.

She simpered at the handsomer of the pair of troglodytes. "This is Mr. Bergeron. He'll tell you what to do." She stood there smiling at him.

He was too upset. "Who are you?"

They were wearing matching khaki ensembles with khaki baseball caps. The caps were decorated with an oval, blue and white logo, that featured "SJR" bisected by a red lightening bolt.

Guy One said in a monotone, "We're here to install a monitor."

Guy Two had a work order. "Some Jennifer placed the order."

He read the work order. Jennifer had been babbling about this last week? "Right. A big, flat-screen monitor...for conferences and Zoom meetings."

Guy One looked at him. "Where do you want it?"

He focused. "Oh. In the conference room." He led the way. "On that wall."

Guy Two said, "The wiring?"

He had no clue, but Dana was waving at him. "Should I call Devon for you?"

"Devon?"

Dana was being way too helpful. "IT? Devon Mahoney."

"Right. Good idea. Do that."

This thing needed an internet connection and power. He looked at the guys. "I'll find out. You get set up. Fetch your tools and take measurements. Strategize. Limber up. Deep knee bends and jumping jacks. I'll be back in a jiffy."

Guy One, who had a head shaped like a diseased turnip, shook that head at Guy Two, who had ears that looked like they'd been molded by a two year old. He cared not one whit.

His phone was ringing. "Hello?"

A voice said, "IT."

He'd had zero contact with the new IT guy who'd come onboard after the Telyn and Nemec debacle.

"The guys to install the wall monitor are here."

"Who is this?"

"What? Oh, Gabe Bergeron. Garst, Bauer & Hartmann. 11th Floor, the conference room. Jennifer probably told you?"

"Yeah. You say they're in the office now?"

"Yes. Can you come? Jennifer is out with the baby, and I didn't know they were coming." Why was he explaining?

"I guess so. Yeah, I'll be there in about a half hour."

"Okay. Good."

He told Guy One and Guy Two.

Guy Two said, "We can't wait around all day, you know."

He smiled hard enough to show all of his teeth which

seemed to give them pause.

He left them and went to find Chatterjee. Young Dhruva was not at his desk and not in the breakroom. He headed for the Men's Room.

"Chatterjee?"

"What?"

He was in a stall. "I got a call from Jennifer...about you taking over some of Carla's clients? Are you up to speed about that?"

Chatterjee sprang from the stall and began scrubbing his hands. "Jennifer called me."

He was tiny and dark and had a crown of shiny, gorgeous black tresses. His hair was as beautiful as Bradley's only curlier.

Chatterjee dried his hands and came back to the mirror to admire himself. Well, he leaned forward and tossed his head back so his curls were optimally disarranged.

"Something else, Gabe?"

"How old are you?"

Chatterjee gave him side eye. "Twenty-five. Why?"

"No reason."

Chatterjee turned and focused the big, brown eyes upon him. "Gabe."

Young Chatterjee was older than he looked despite his flawless skin and his attire. He had adopted scuffed combat boots and wore the same pair every day. He wore brown shirts, buttoned to the throat, camouflage green pants, and a black vest that looked thick enough to stop bullets.

His tie, which was lovely, was worn more as a scarf.

"You don't mind taking on some of Carla's clients?"

"No?"

"Okay. Right. Well I'm calling her to let her know."

Chatterjee nodded and swaggered out of the Men's Room. It was hard for someone who might weigh one thirty to swagger but he did his best.

Why wasn't he terrified? He shook his head and called Carla."

"Bergeron? Did you screw up one of my clients?"

"Hello, Carla. So good to hear your voice. How are things at home? I hope you're well. Chatterjee is taking over most of your clients until you come back."

He held the phone well away from his ear and awaited the storm.

Carla said, "Chatterjee?"

"Yes." He awaited thunder and lightning on a Wagnerian scale; *Götterdämmerung* as staged by Cecil B. DeMille.

"Good."

He took a pause himself. He closed his eyes. "What?"

"He's good. Is he at his desk?"

"I believe so."

"I'll call him. Gabe?"

"Yes, Carla?"

"Thanks for taking me to the hospital."

He opened his eyes. "You're very welcome. It was my pleasure. Well, not pleasure exactly...."

"Bergeron."

"Yes, Carla?"

"Don't ever pick me up again."

And she was gone. He sat at his desk. Chatterjee's cubicle was at the end of the row, and he could see him talking on the phone and smiling. So it was okay for Dhruva Chatterjee to work on her clients but not her close friend and crack accountant Gabe Bergeron?

He let it go and focused on the freaking spreadsheet for about the tenth time.

And Mahoney, the IT guy, got off the elevator. He was tall, thin, and about thirty with long, brown, frizzy hair that was bouffant but asymmetrical, having failed to coalesce into a spherical ball like Carla's.

Mahoney strolled over. "Bergeron?"

"Yep. Do you know what Jennifer wants?"

Mahoney nodded, and he pointed to Guys One & Two who were sitting on the conference room table looking like lumps of ill-formed clay.

Mahoney wandered in their direction with a little side trip

to talk to Dana before entering the conference room.

Mahoney was soon laughing and chatting with Guy One and Guy Two, and everyone was having just a splendid time.

And then Guy One began drilling holes through the partition wall separating the conference room from the breakroom.

The drill seemed a bit too robust for the task? He waved at Mahoney as he left.

Dana was behind him.

"Gabe. I have to leave the office."

"Okay?"

"Jennifer has some paperwork she wants me to pick up so you can take a look at it."

"Fine. Excellent."

He focused with every bit of concentration he could muster but the drilling didn't stop.

Until it did.

Guy Two was looking at the wall. He was taking measurements. He looked at Guy One. He donned safety glasses and began to drill more holes.

It wasn't his wall. It wasn't his monitor. He didn't care if they created a space-time vortex that sucked up the entire Earth and belched it out into the Gamma Quadrant of the Milky Way.

But the drill shrieking was boring into his brain, and he was seconds from doing his own shrieking when it stopped.

He stayed hunkered down and finished his spreadsheet. It was a lovely spreadsheet with cascades of links and functions and look-ups and pivot tables.

He had been refining it for years and adapted it to each client; none of them would ever appreciate its elegance and power.

He may have been smiling to himself when he noticed Guy One and Guy Two were exiting.

"Are you finished already?"

They ignored him and marched stolidly with their knuckles dragging on the carpet. Well, not dragging; they were a good two inches off the carpet.

He looked at the conference room. It was hard to see anything for the cloud of dust but the monitor wasn't on the wall.

He raced over in time to stop the elevator door from closing. "Hey! Where are you going?"

Guy One put a large calloused hand on his chest and pushed him back.

As the door shut, Guy Two said, "We'll be back."

"Yeah? You and the killer android from the future!"

But he was talking to the elevator door.

He went into the conference room and surveyed the scene. There were lots of holes in the wall in various places. There were spots that were more hole than wall. The monitor bracket was on the floor along with lots of bolts and screws and a few coils of cable scattered around it like the detritus of a robot homicide. The monitor was still in the box.

He was pretty sure Jennifer would not be pleased if she saw this in its current state, but it would be a month or more before she did.

He counted the holes in the bracket. There were way too many holes in the wall. And lots of them didn't line up?

Maybe they were for the cable? Maybe they would fill up the holes if any of them were surplus?

And maybe the Easter Bunny would bring him a chocolate rabbit and some Peeps. He wasn't sanguine about Guy One and Guy Two.

He could call SJR and complain? Not his job.

He needed coffee. The breakroom wall was a holey mess too. Why had they drilled through the wall?

He shook his head, dusted the breakroom and made a fresh pot of coffee. He was sad to see that it wasn't yet 11:00 am.

He sat down. He took a sip of coffee.

He may have shut his eyes.

Wednesday
11:00 am

The elevator dinged.
There was a time when that hadn't caused his heart to freeze up. He wasn't going to look. If he didn't see it, whatever the Hell it was couldn't see him. It was cubicle magic; a variant of blanket magic.
He continued punching in numbers.
"Gabe?"
It was Stella. He didn't look up. "Yes?"
"Someone here to see you."
And he sensed that Stella was walking back to her puppy-wallpapered cubicle. He still didn't turn.
Maybe it would go away.
A baritone voice with precise diction said, "Are you Gabriel Henri Bergeron?"
He sighed. "No."
A mellifluous baritone chuckle. "I think you are."
"I was, but I'm not any longer."
The owner of the sexy voice sat in his one client chair and rolled closer; the scent of his cologne wafting around them. He gave up and turned.
The guy was about his size and build; maybe a few years older. He had an olive complexion and an oval face graced with a finely-formed nose and perfect lips and ears. His brown hair was the correct length for tousling.
He had arched brows over big, brown eyes that could suck

the will to resist from the most stalwart of men...or women; in all likelihood.

He may have smiled. "Okay, I'm Gabe. Who are you?"

He resisted being sucked into the depths of the visitor's eyes and noted the great suit, tie, shoes and the tie tack which appeared to be a ruby.

Which went well with his navy suit.

And then he spoiled it all by pulling out an FBI badge.

"I'm Special Agent Aronson, Mr. Bergeron."

"Of course, you are." He looked around, and nobody seemed to be taking note of Aronson. "Let's go into the conference room."

Aronson smiled and followed.

He pulled out a chair for the special agent and dusted it with his handkerchief. Which he realized too late was something that the courtiers of Elizabeth I, the Virgin Queen, might have done for her.

"It's dusty in here. From the drilling."

Aronson smiled.

"These guys came in and drilled all these holes. Which I think was excessive. And I have no idea if they're coming back but I sort of doubt it."

Aronson alighted upon the chair prepared for him.

He grabbed a chair and sat; he didn't care what happened to the seat of his pants.

"I don't know anything, Special Agent."

Aronson laughed. "They told me about you, and I have to say that you do not disappoint."

"They who?" Aronson ignored the question. "Right. I should probably be offended by that, but I'm too tired." He straightened. "So why don't you tell me why you're here, and I can get back to work."

"You know Lars Thorvaldsen."

"Nope. Never seen him. You could be Lars for all I know. Talk to Steven Bradley and his mother, Susan. Well, she's Steven's mother not Lars'. Her feelings for Lars aren't maternal."

"Steven Bradley?"

"He lives across the street. He's a friend of Thorvaldsen."

Aronson was smiling again. "So you're looking for Thorvaldsen? For Bradley?"

He shook his head. "No, no, no."

"Are you sure?"

He smiled back at Aronson. He couldn't help himself; the eye vortex thing was too strong. He reminded himself that this guy wasn't Cory. "I will admit that it sounds like something I might do, but not this time. Honest. I haven't given him a single thought since we found Bathtub Guy."

Aronson lost the smile which was disappointing. "So you aren't helping Detective Fowler?"

"No. He doesn't want my help. Not that I offered it. So you are taking over the case?"

Aronson just stared into his eyes for a long time which was equal parts arousing and terrifying. If Aronson told him to jump out the window, he wouldn't reject the idea out of hand.

He tore his eyes away. "So if there's nothing else, Special Agent?"

Aronson said, "What do you know about the Nigerian connection?"

He shook his head and looked puzzled, since he was. "Nothing? And I don't want to know anything. I'm not involved...even a little bit."

Aronson stood up, and he did too. He was waiting for the guy to turn for the door, but he moved closer enveloping them both in the heady scent of that damn fine cologne.

"You know who 'Bathtub Guy' was, don't you, Gabriel?"

"No!"

"Shall I tell you then?"

He shook his head and put his hands over his ears. Aronson smiled and grabbed his wrists. They play struggled and then put some muscle into it, smiling at each other; he thought he was stronger than Aronson and could take him in a wrestling match.

Which wasn't going to happen.

Aronson said, "He was Clive Whalen, 52 years old, American, and lately first mate of the SS Kerkyra."

Aronson released his wrists and handed him a card. "If there are any developments, Gabriel, call me."

And Aronson exited.

Maybe Aronson had been in his apartment? Looking for clues to the mystery of Lars "Duke" Thorvaldsen?

And why had the special agent, if that's what he was, flirted with him? He was reasonably sure that the guy was straight?

Wednesday
4:00 pm

Dana had been at Jennifer's and hadn't seen Aronson. It appeared that no one was the wiser, and he was in a much better mood.

He should have asked Aronson for the name of his cologne...to buy some for Cory. It was sandalwood and something else?

He realized he was thinking about Aronson and smiling in an inappropriate manner. He chided himself. He should get back to work.

The elevator dinged again. He was going to go up on the roof and blow up the motors that raised and lowered the elevators. He had been up there and knew just where they were.

Explosives might be a bit much? Maybe he could just find the breaker box and cut off the power?

Or maybe just string some razor wire across the doors?

He was thinking happy thoughts about being safe from clients when he realized Dana was fast approaching.

He was raising his hand to ward off evil when he realized that he knew the family group surrounding Dana.

He stood up. Pete Lang was his client and Harry's brother-in-law. He assumed a quizzical expression as he shook Pete's hand since the personal taxes for Pete and his wife, Chiara, had been filed, and the corporate taxes for his trucking business were in hand.

Pete was taller and much rounder than he was. His face was

also round and generally as happy-looking as it was now. He had brown hair and a brown beard and little blue eyes.

"Hi, Gabe. I don't think you know Taz or Adriana?"

"We haven't exactly met but I know who you all are. How can I help you?"

Mother Rita of the cherubic face smiled at him and then hugged him. "Thank you for taking Carla to the hospital, Gabe."

He smiled at Rita. "Of course. I was happy to do it. So let's go into the conference room?"

Rita was wearing a gray blouse and slacks with a little red jacket and a necklace of red beads. "This is Taz."

He shook Taz's hand; Taz was staring at him without any expression on his face.

He was sixty but still rugged looking and putting off a don't-mess-with-me air. His hair was black on top but silver-white at the temples and on the sides.

He was outfitted in jeans, a blue-striped shirt, and a gray sports coat that had been purchased sometime before Y2K had been a thing. He seemed to be glaring at the cubicle dwellers now.

Rita said, "And this is Adriana."

Adriana was still looking somber; the gray dress was dark enough to be appropriate funeral wear. She was two years younger than Harry but she looked older. He knew she was divorced with two kids.

She wasn't wearing lipstick or any makeup that he could see. She was eyeing him; he wasn't sure just what emotion was bubbling up inside her?

He had dusted all the chairs and the table.

"Please have a seat and tell me how I can help?"

They sat except for Taz who examined the wall. "Who the Hell did this?"

He smiled at Taz. "Two guys came in. They were supposed to install the flat-screen monitor."

Taz tapped the box with the toe of his boot. "This one?"

He nodded.

Taz grabbed the monitor bracket and tried it against the holes in the wall; no combination of holes matched.

Taz looked at him. Taz was disappointed.

Rita said, "Sit down and quit messing with that thing." Taz complied. He made a little groan as he lowered his stocky body into the chair.

Rita was frowning at her husband. "Do you want one of your pills?"

He shook his head. Rita shook hers too and sighed before turning to him. "Our taxes aren't done, Gabe."

Adriana said, "Harry's been promising for two weeks. Didn't he call you and ask if we could come in?"

Rita said, "We have an accountant for a son and we have to come begging." She sighed again. Taz may have rolled his eyes ever so slightly.

He smiled his very best smile. "No problem, Mrs. Baldacci. I'm happy to help out."

"Rita."

"Right. So this is for you and Taz; a joint return?"

Rita nodded. "And Adriana's taxes too."

"Of course. I'll be happy to take care of that for you." Rita and Adriana had enormous purses so maybe the tax related papers were in them? "So do you have your information? Income, deductions?"

Rita said, "It's all in Harry's computer."

Adriana pulled a laptop from her bag.

"Right. May I take a look?"

He fired up Harry's computer. As he did, Adriana got her phone and dialed a number.

"Hey, Dumbass! You didn't call him, did you?" She glared at the phone. "Yeah, he's looking at it now. Tell him what he needs to know. What? So let her wait for her tea." She made a face.

Rita said, "He's worried about her."

"Yeah? So the doctor said she's okay. She's a lot tougher than Harry thinks."

She shoved the phone at him. "Harry?"

"Gabe! I'm so sorry. I meant to call you, but things have been crazy here. Did they all just barge in?"

"Not to worry. I see the files. Have you looked over this

year? Anything different from last year?"

"Shouldn't be. But could you double check me?"

"Will do."

He paged through the schedules from the last five years. It looked straightforward. He scanned all the documents from the current year.

Harry said, "I have to go, Gabe. Call me with any questions. Okay?"

"Sure, Harry."

He gave Adriana back her phone.

There were a couple of things he might change from last year, but he'd talk to Harry about that later.

"Okay. I can get these done and have them ready for signing tomorrow."

Rita said, "But tomorrow is the deadline, Gabe!"

"I know, but it's okay. Worst case, we could file for an extension...."

Taz was staring at him like an Easter Island statue. "No freaking extensions."

Adriana rolled her eyes. "Dad."

Taz stared at her. "What?"

Taz did not trust him. Rita wasn't too sure. Adriana? He had no idea.

Okay. I can get these done today and drop them by the house."

Taz said, "We'll wait."

Taz was a man of few words; Taz was getting on his last nerve.

"Okay. Right. I'll leave you here then." He stopped. These were Harry's nearest and dearest. "Would you like coffee? Sodas? I think there's tea?"

Taz said, "Coffee."

Rita smiled. "Please don't go to any trouble, Gabe."

Taz and Adriana did a father-daughter, double eye roll.

He got them coffee; he pillaged the breakroom and came up with an assortment of cookies. "Please help yourselves."

He took Harry's laptop to his desk and whipped through

their returns before going back to the conference room.

"You could e-file?" Taz gave him a terrible look. "Right. Good ole paper it is."

He printed the returns and got the signatures. He was going to offer to mail them with the company's mail, but Rita took the return. "Thank you, Gabe." She hugged him again. "I don't see why Harry couldn't have finished them."

Adriana took her return and shook his hand. She was his height, and she was staring into his eyes. "Bill Harry. It's his fault we had to bother you."

She kicked brother-in-law Pete's chair since he had nodded off during the wait.

"I won't bill Harry. He's my best friend."

She snorted. "Don't have many friends, do you?"

"Scads." He was weary of Adriana Baldacci.

She stuffed Harry's laptop and her return into her bag and headed with Rita and Pete for the elevator.

Taz was still standing there. He wasn't sure why?

Rita yelled across the office. "The elevator's here, Taz!"

He yelled back. "Go on. I'll catch up."

So she did.

Taz was staring at him. It was making him uncomfortable.

"You and Harry are buddies?"

"We are."

Taz nodded casting his eyes over the office. "He told me. You got kidnapped or something last year?"

"Right. By Frisian art thieves."

"But you caught the bastards."

"The FBI did. Well, I helped a little."

Taz nodded. "Where's Harry's desk?"

"Over there. Do you want to see it?"

A nod.

He conducted Taz to Harry's cubicle which was plastered with almost as many photos as Stella's but Harry's were Baldacci family photos. And photos of Carla. And there were a few of his vehicles, past and present.

"And this is mine." He pointed across the aisle. "And that's

Carla's"

Taz nodded. "Computers." He shook his head and was looking at a photo of Rita and himself. He reached out a large, rough hand and patted the back of Harry's chair gently.

"Gabe?"

"Yes, Mr. Baldacci?"

"Taz."

"Right, Taz."

"Is Harry a good accountant?"

"Very good. Meticulous, careful, conscientious, efficient...."

Taz actually smiled at him.

"Right. I talk too much. Sorry."

Taz shook his head.

They stood there a while longer. He was beginning to think that Taz had taken a spontaneous vow of silence when his lips parted. "Is he happy with Carla?"

"Very. Absolutely. Ecstatic. Over the moon...."

He shut his mouth when Taz smiled again, but he had to add, "Harry dated a lot of women but Carla is the only one he's ever really loved. And Carla feels the same about Harry...though it's hard to tell with Carla. She's not as outgoing as he is."

"He got that from his mother."

And Taz marched to the elevator.

He followed unsure of what was expected of him.

Taz shook his hand. "It the idiots who messed up your wall don't fix it right, give me a call."

And Taz got on the elevator.

Saturday
10:00 am

He thought that he might be on top of things. He smiled to himself in the empty office as he turned off his computer and cleared his desk.

Why was he smiling?

He was in the office on a Saturday. Cory had gone off somewhere. He was doing Jennifer's, Harry's, and even some of Carla's work since Chatterjee was swamped with Carla's monstrous and unnatural client load.

Shit. He should be in a foul mood; he should be raging against his sorry lot in life. He waved a fist lackadaisically.

He wasn't.

And then the elevator dinged. "Ask not for whom the bell tolls" was his motto so he ducked under his desk.

The elevator doors closed. No one said anything. He wanted to peek, but he didn't think he should. He stayed put.

He could have locked the doors into the office, but it was Saturday, and there was another new security guard on duty. He thought this one was day shift?

His name was Chase, and he had reddish-brown hair twisted into tight, corkscrew curls and little brown eyes. He wasn't handsome but he sported jaws and cheekbones every bit as square and impressive as Andy Boltukaev's.

And he had definitely looked sturdy enough to handle the defense of Fortress Mahr. Had he let someone come up on the elevator? Someone authorized?

He didn't hear anything but the carpet, though threadbare, would still muffle footsteps if one were stealthy.

He should just look.

He stayed put.

More silence but not your standard no-noise silence but silence filled with import and menace.

He heard the sound of Jennifer's office door being opened. Shit!

Of course, it could be Andy picking up something for Jennifer? But he didn't think so. He raised his head millimeter by millimeter. The large man in Jennifer's office was a head taller than Andy.

It was time to beat a retreat. He ran for the stairs as fast as his adrenaline-soaked muscles would carry him. He was in the stairwell and whipping down the flights of stairs.

Above him, the large individual was giving chase.

He ran down eleven floors and burst out of the stairwell and ran down the hall toward the front of the building and the security station.

It appeared that the large individual was gaining on him as he slid around the empty security desk and scrambled to the front doors.

Which were locked.

He grabbed his phone and was dialing 911 when the large individual caught up to him and took his phone.

Large Individual was seven feet tall and black. Well, he wasn't that tall though he was undeniably black. He had to weigh in just shy of three hundred pounds and very little of that was fat.

"Bergeron?"

"No!" He sucked in some more air as his heart pounded barely contained by his chest. "I'm Calvin Coolidge." Large intake of air. "Who are you? And give me back my phone!"

"Do not be stupid." Large Individual took a breath. "You know who I am."

He shook his head with determination. Large Individual had an accent; a bit British and a bit something African?

Large Individual said, "I am Okocha." He looked at the

phone. "You were dialing 911. There is no need for that."

He'd be the judge of that, and then he remembered Aronson mentioning a Nigerian connection. Mr. Okocha could be that?

Okocha was very large as previously established. He was also very dark. His hair and beard were trimmed close; his face was oval and could boast noble, angular features and big, brown eyes.

The eyes and their neighboring brows were drawn into a fierce expression that was not reassuring.

"Give me my phone back. What do you want?"

"No dialing." He returned the phone.

Okocha adjusted the drape of his suit after their brief footrace. It was silk. It and the matching vest were charcoal. He had accessorized with a striped silver tie, and matching hankie and just the right amount of silver bling.

It reminded him of an ensemble Carla might wear. Though Okocha filled it out better.

"Who are you working for?"

"Garst, Bauer & Hartmann." Okocha didn't swat him but glowered more fiercely.

"Stupid. I saw you at the house." And he showed him a couple of photos on his phone: Gabe Bergeron, Bradley, and Susan on her porch, and Gabe and Bradley going into Duke's house.

He tried smiling at Okocha. It didn't help.

Okocha said, "I spoke to the woman. And the boy. They knew nothing."

Shit. The boy was Bradley, and Susan was the woman. "What did you do to them?"

Okocha paused mid-glare and looked briefly surprised. "Nothing. Susan and the boy spoke freely to me."

And then Okocha smiled. "But I am quite intimidating. Or so I have been told."

And then Okocha grabbed his tie and pulled him close. "Who are you working for? I will not ask nicely again."

He put on his bravest face. "I'm not working for anybody...in the matter of Mr. Thorvaldsen. Who are you working for? And why do you want to find Duke?"

Okocha lifted him up on his toes a couple of times like he was trying out a defective yo-yo.

"You know who I am working for. You should stay out of this matter. This does not concern you or your countrymen. Or Monroe."

"Monroe? Shit! Don't tell me Monroe's involved in this?"

"As you know!"

This was said in a roar, and things might have taken a nasty turn for Gabriel Bergeron, but the new security guard entered the lobby at a run.

Chase was young and fit but half the size of Okocha. Well, three quarters. He suddenly had a truncheon in his hand. "What the Hell is going on here?"

Okocha sighed probably at the thought of cleaning up two bodies instead of one.

Chase was in a fighting stance that bespoke some martial arts training.

As Chase moved closer, Okocha sighed again, let go of his tie, and stepped back. "I will be going now." He pointed at the doors. "Open those. Please."

Chase said, "How did you get in here?"

Okocha ignored the question. There were two semi-massive, concrete urns planted with ersatz bonsai trees. Okocha hefted one of them off the floor and advanced toward the glass doors

Chase waved his hands. "Okay! I'll unlock the doors."

Okocha stood there with the urn in his arms until the doors were open. He put the urn down, dusted his hands and his suit, and stepped out.

He and Chase followed at a respectful distance. He said, "I'm really not involved in whatever this is, Mr. Okocha."

Okocha just stared at him and then he said, "It is a waste of time calling the police."

Chase said, "The Hell it is."

Okocha shook his head. "I have diplomatic immunity."

As Okocha was striding off into the weak April sun, he took photos.

He was shaking; Chase was too but he looked more jazzed than scared. Chase said, "What just happened, Bergeron?"

"No idea."

Chase smiled at him with a gleam in his eyes. "They told me about you so I know that's bullshit."

Chase had a bit of a southern accent; not deep South or a Texas twang but maybe North Carolina or Virginia? Cory had an accent like that on occasion.

"Is not." He massaged his neck and throat. "I know his name might be Okocha, but that's all. How did he get in?"

Chase shook his head. "Don't know."

He may have glared at Chase. "Not a good answer, Mr. Security Guard."

Chase nodded. "Yeah, I know. Shit."

They stood there mulling over recent events. Chase made a point of repositioning the urn without his help, but he had to drag it more than lift it. He said, "So what do we do?"

"I don't know. Thanks for scaring him off."

Chase shook his head. "Shit. He wanted to go or he would have taken both of us out."

"Well, thanks for trying to scare him off."

They smiled at each other, and he shook Chase's hand.

"So the police?"

"I have a feeling he was telling the truth about that diplomatic immunity thing."

Chase said, "So it would be a waste of time then?"

"Right."

Of course, he could find out a lot more about Mr. Okocha or the police could if they were called in, but he'd just get sucked in more than he already was.

And then he thought about Bradley and Susan. "Shit squared." He tried calling Bradley's number but it went to voicemail.

Chase was looking over his shoulder. "What's up?"

"I have to go!"

"Okay. Bergeron?"

He stopped at the door. "Yeah?"

"I'll find out how that character got in, and it won't happen again."

"Do that."

"And I'll have something with more stopping power if he ever comes back." His steely jaws were set. "Shit like this isn't going to happen in my building."

Which was cheering.

He ran for his Jeep and was parking in front of Susan's house in a trice.

He knocked on the door half expecting to find it unlocked and the front room strewn with bodies.

But she came to the door. She smiled. "Gabe? I didn't expect to see you again? But come in."

And then he remembered that he had sworn a mighty oath to Cory to never, ever have any contact with her or Bradley again.

He sighed, but he was already here. "Where is Bradley?"

She looked at him. "Is something wrong?"

He gave her a sickly smile. "I just need to know where he is."

"He's home, Gabe. Should I call him?"

He wanted to see him whole and not mangled even a little bit. "Please."

She called Bradley, and he popped in the front door a minute later with all of his limbs intact.

"Gabe? What's up?"

"Did you...either of you...talk to a large, black man who might have called himself Okocha?"

Susan was looking worn out as if she hadn't gotten a full night's sleep in a week. She started to shake her head, but he showed them the photos he'd taken.

She brightened up. "We both did. But he said his name was Johnson. Such a lovely man and so well dressed. He had such lovely manners, didn't he, Stevie?"

He was going to guess that his face currently looked dumbfounded and flabbergasted. He collected himself. "So he asked about Duke?"

They nodded. Susan said, "He said he was a private

detective hired by the shipping company to find Duke...he's a valued employee."

She smiled. "Oh. Would you like something to drink, Gabe? I just made coffee?"

He exchanged a look with Bradley. "That would be lovely, Susan."

He had good manners too.

Bradley said, "He showed up while I was gone, and she bought his story. By the time I got home, they were having tea. I knew it was bogus. So his name is Okocha. That's got to be Nigerian, right?"

"Maybe. Okay. Thank your mother for the coffee but tell her I had to go. And this time, I'm going to disappear from your lives. Forever."

Bradley swept the hair out of his eyes and glared at him. He was roughly a tenth of a percent as scary as Okocha. "Why did you even bother coming?"

"He came to see me and said he talked to you and Susan, and I was worried about you."

"Why?"

"I just was." Did Bradley know who Bathtub Man really was? He wasn't going to tell him. It could only lead to trouble.

"What did he say when he talked to you? Come on, Gabe?"

He looked at Okocha's photo on his phone. "Just wanted to know if I knew where Duke was."

Which he hadn't really asked? Because he already knew? Or could find him on his own? It was more about discouraging another player in this freaking game, whatever it was.

Was Detective Fowler still involved? Or was he out, and Aronson had tagged in?

It was Aronson, Okocha, and Monroe; that he knew about.

But not Gabriel Bergeron. Definitely, positively not Gabriel Bergeron.

Tuesday
10:00 am

He had considered and dismissed the idea of trying to find Monroe. Even if Penelope knew how to reach him.

Penelope had been Monroe's girlfriend a while back. She was Billy's mother and co-owner of CoffeeXtra.

So Billy might be able to contact Penelope Chernov aka Penelope Black who might be able to contact Mr. Monroe.

Did he really want to talk to the spy and crook and utterly untrustworthy dude known as Monroe?

The question answered itself.

Harry was looking at him. "What?"

"You were muttering to yourself. Again."

"Was not."

Harry smiled at him. "Were to." Harry stretched and smiled some more.

"Happy to be here, Baldacci?" He was going to add "and away from Carla" but he didn't have to.

"God, yes!" Harry looked shocked at the words that he had vocalized. "Gabe!"

"I will not tell Carla what you said under pain of death. So how bad is it?"

"Bad. I get that she's uncomfortable and even miserable and that this is all new to her, but it's not my fault!"

He may have raised an eyebrow while checking out Harry's groin.

Harry closed his legs. "Quit looking at my junk, Bergeron!

And you know what I mean. You're enjoying this, aren't you?"

"Absolutely not. I weep for you three times a day."

"Right."

"But she's doing all right?"

Harry nodded. "Yeah. But she goes back to the doctor on Friday so we'll know more then. She's coming in for an hour to go over some questions Chatterjee had."

And then the elevator dinged.

He had checked to see how expensive razor wire was just for fun over the weekend. It wasn't that bad, but you couldn't buy just ten feet of it.

And Carla and her mother, Winnie, stepped out accompanied by another lady. She was svelte and beautiful and looked younger than Carla, but, factoring in Carla's present condition, might be older?

He looked at Harry.

Harry closed his eyes and then opened them very wide while plastering a smile on his face.

He whispered, "Who's the other lady?"

Harry whispered, "Sister. Francine." He rose to his feet still smiling manically. "Her mother and one or other of the sisters are at the house twenty-four/seven."

And Harry sallied forth to greet his beloved.

He waved at Carla and Winnie and Francine. He may have felt a twinge of sympathy for his best friend before going back to work.

Harry escorted Carla to Chatterjee's cubicle and got her settled, and then ushered Winnie and Francine into the conference room where he plied them with coffee and donuts.

And ditched them as quickly as possible.

Harry sighed as he sat in his chair.

Carla called across the office, "Harry!"

Harry popped out of his chair smiling and attended her before running to the breakroom. He went back. "We don't have ginger ale, Carla."

"That's okay, Harry. I understand."

"I could go get some?"

"Would you do that for me?"

"Absolutely."

"And see if Mom and Francine want anything."

And Harry did, and then he left the office and possibly the state.

He went to check on Carla and Chatterjee. They were working away and smiling. Which was fine.

Well, he might have been happier to find Carla whipping a cowering Chatterjee, but his happiness wasn't paramount.

"So how are things going?"

Carla said, "Dhruva's doing great, but I knew he would."

This wasn't a dagger to his heart but it felt very like. "I'm so happy to hear that. Dhruva? You think you can handle this?"

Dhruva smirked. "Sure, Gabe."

He ambled back to his desk. So he wasn't to have Carla beg him to save her clients from Dhruva's incompetence? He could live with that. Probably.

Harry had been gone thirty minutes, and he was starting to doubt that he would return, but he did.

He gave Carla her ginger ale and went into the conference room with a bag for Winnie and Francine.

Harry came back and plopped in his chair. "They want you, Gabe."

"What?"

"You're up."

He was not at the beck and call of the Wong family like Harry, but he needed coffee. So he got some and sauntered casually into the conference room.

Winnie was wearing mocha slacks and a tan knit top that was almost a sweater; her tan raincoat was draped over the back of a chair. She smiled at him. "Hello, Gabe. This is my second daughter, Francine."

"Right. So Yvonne is the first. And Carla is the third?"

Winnie nodded. Francine offered her hand.

Francine had her mother's round face and tiny eyes, but the hair cascading to her shoulders was of a black ebony that existed magically in a state neither solid nor liquid but a bit of both.

She had red earrings, red lipstick and nails, and a cream suit that was hourglass perfect. She was, hands down, the fairest of them all.

She smiled at him. "It's so nice to meet you, Gabe. You don't mind if I call you Gabe, do you?" She tittered and stroked her meta-material hair.

"Not at all. So Harry said you wanted to see me?"

Francine said, "Why don't you sit down, Gabe."

It was a new experience for Francine having to ask a gentlemen to sit next to her. She didn't care for it.

He sat anyway and looked quizzically from Francine to Winnie.

Winnie said, "Carla's told us so much about you."

"Right? About my work ethic? My devilish charm and savoir-faire?"

Francine giggled. Winnie said, "About your...adventures, Gabe."

"Ah." They looked at him. "And you want to see if I'm as goofy as she made me out to be?"

Winnie and Francine tittered.

Winnie shook her head. "No, Gabe. I might have a job for you. A small one. I know you could do it."

This was a shock to Francine and most unwelcome. As it was to him, but he didn't run out of the room. Mainly because he liked Carla, prickly as she could be, and this was her mother.

"I'm not really an investigator, Winnie, and I'm really, really busy...."

He was spared from further babbling by Paul opening the conference room door.

"Sorry to bother you, Gabe, but Jennifer's on the line."

He could have lunged at Paul and kissed him on the lips but he chose the more normal option of nodding and getting to his feet.

He smiled at Winnie and Francine. "I have to take this. Paul? Can you entertain the ladies until I get back?"

Paul did not look shocked or rent with consternation or even slightly unwilling. "Sure, Gabe."

And he gave Paul an appraising look as he ran out the door:

Paul had lost weight, and his skin was more flesh-colored and less gray. His hair had been coiffed by someone who didn't use a bowl as a template. His suit wasn't shabby.

There was something else but he couldn't put his finger on it as he jogged to his desk.

He picked up the phone. "Paul's eyes are all sparkly!"

Jennifer said, "Are you high, Bergeron?"

"Never. Paul looks happy. Or excited. Have you called for a status update?"

"How are things going, Gabe."

She sounded like she was bracing for the worst. "Good, actually. The work is getting done. Stella is working away. Even Chatterjee might not be screwing up Carla's clients beyond all salvaging."

He wasn't mentioning the monitor situation.

Or anything Thorvaldsen related.

Jennifer said, "Are you sure, Gabe?"

"I am. You can ask Bauer. He walked through a while ago. I know I might tend to gild the lily on occasion but all is well. And how are you feeling?"

"Awful."

He had no idea how to respond to that.

"I'm sorry? I could take Andy out for a night on the town and get him a vasectomy while he's drunk? I know people, Jennifer."

She laughed. "And how are my clients?"

"They are ecstatic, one and all. Actually, I've had no complaints."

"Thank you, Gabe. This means a lot to me. And to Max."

Max was Maximilian Adolphus Bauer, head of the firm.

"Happy to do it. I hope the baby comes soon."

She groaned. "Now would be good. Bye, Gabe."

He almost had an attack of the warm, fuzzies.

Carla was behind him. "I'm going now, Gabe. Chatterjee is okay." She smiled at him. "I told him to check with you if he has any problems."

Which was very nice to hear.

"Right. Okay." He looked at Harry who was packing up. "So anything I need to work on?" Harry looked guilty. "Anything? I'm caught up. With Stella's help."

"What about your clients, Gabe?"

"Scum of the earth. They're fine."

Harry looked at Carla. "I need to talk to Gabe."

Carla smiled. "No problem. Mom's coming home with us. And Yvonne might stop over."

So Carla made her laborious way to the conference room where her mother appeared to be yukking it up with Paul.

Francine was glaring at Paul? But Winnie was all smiles. And Paul Bright-eyes escorted the Wongs into the elevator and apparently rode down with them.

When he wasn't so freaking busy, he was going to think about Paul 2.0.

Harry said, "I have to run to the little boys' room."

"Right."

But Harry was gone a long time...even if he were sterilizing his hands for an appendectomy. He may have walked over.

Harry was standing there staring at his haggard image in the mirror. "Harry? What's wrong?"

Harry tried to smile. "It's hard, Gabe. I know it's harder...a thousand times harder on Carla. I know that."

"What is it?"

"It doesn't help that her mother and sister have moved in. I mean I like them, and they help out."

"Right?"

"It's like I'm being tested, and I'm failing no matter which choice I make. I mean today I asked if it was okay if I came to work for a few hours, and Carla said it was fine. But then she and her mother were talking. And I got the feeling that it wasn't fine so I said I was staying home, and Carla said I'd just be in the way."

Harry looked at him.

"Sorry. I have no words of wisdom to impart. What about your dad? He's been through this three times?"

Harry smiled. "I love my dad, and I'm pretty sure he loves me, but have you ever tried to have a conversation with him?"

He was absolutely sure that Taz loved his son. "A grunt here and a noncommittal shrug there?"

Harry laughed. "Exactly."

"You might try him, Harry. Get him alone and be prepared to spend a good hour in near total silence but he might surprise you."

Harry was looking at him. "Really? What did he say to you?"

"Almost nothing." Harry smiled again. "But try him. He did offer to fix the monitor."

Harry nodded. "Now that sounds like my dad."

"You'll get through this, Harry. Carla may be able to come back to work, and things will return to how it was before."

"Which wasn't so great but I'd take it."

"Right. So stiff upper lip and keep on carrying on. Do you want a hug?"

"Get near me, and I'll punch you in the face, Bergeron."

But he hugged him anyway.

Harry said, "Thanks, Gabe. Now let go of me before somebody comes in!"

"Are you ashamed of our love, Harry?"

Harry punched him in the gut but he was expecting it.

He smiled at Harry and sent the pitiful soul on his way. How did couples who had large families do this?

Tuesday
4:00 pm

Stella and Chatterjee were looking at him. "What?"

Stella said, "I have an appointment, Gabe, but I can come in early tomorrow?"

He looked at Stella. How old was she exactly? Not that it was any concern of his but still. Her face said forty-five but the backs of her hands screamed seventy. And what was that perfume she wore? It was nice but cloying.

"Okay." She certainly had the work with Jennifer's clients.

She nodded. "I'm helping Dhruva with a couple of Carla's clients too." She smiled at young Chatterjee like he was one of her puppies.

Chatterjee said, "I have a problem, Gabe. Can you take a look?"

He pretended that he didn't want to, but he so did. He just had to find some way to let Carla know that he had worked on her clients. "I guess."

He followed Chatterjee who toiled in the last cubicle in Carla's row; it was Spartan, bare, and sterile.

He took the opportunity to review all the clients Dhruva had taken on, and he was actually doing a good job.

He strolled back to his own cubicle but Dana was waiting for him. "We have two new clients who want to make appointments. Who do I give them to?"

He looked at Dana askance. She twisted her fire engine red lips into a smile. Which made the hairs of the back of his neck stand up. "Who are they?"

She handed him two folders which summarized the essentials of the prospective clients in an unnaturally efficient manner. More hairs leaped to attention.

"Okay. Give this one to Paul. He can do this in his sleep. And this one...."

He cast an eye around the office. Matthews was in the breakroom again. He would teach him the error of his ways.

"Give this one to Matthews."

He may have smiled as he got back to work, and then a thought occurred.

Why was everyone coming to him with questions? And not just accounting questions either!

He looked around. Most of the cubicle dwellers were sort of working but no noses were near any grindstones.

He got to his feet, squared his shoulders, adjusted his tie, and went to the breakroom. He imagined that Matthews and his fellow slouchers had dented his Jeep and called Cory a faithless cad as he stared without a word. He was appalled to see that they quailed and scurried back to their desks.

He shook his head and made a grand tour of the office passing by each and every cubicle, peering in, looking knowingly at the papers and the screens, occasionally shaking his head as he had seen Bauer and Jennifer do a thousand times.

At the end of his tour, every head was bent as a feverish clicking of keys rose like a paean to toil and drudgery.

He stood there aghast. He was in charge.

And no one had told him!

He closed his eyes and took a deep breath. Where was Harry when he needed him? With his wife, the faithless dog.

Paul!

He strode over to Paul's cubicle. He smiled a fake, pleasant smile just like Bauer. "Paul? May I see you in the conference room please?"

And he walked away still channeling Bauer and Jennifer for some reason?

He closed the door and looked at Paul. "Why does

everyone think I'm in charge?"

Paul stood there gathering his wits for a long time. "Because you're a natural leader, Gabe."

"I am not! I'm the exact opposite...the...the antithesis of a leader...whatever that is. A follower? A half-assed follower who only follows some of the time."

He stopped talking; the smile that had flitted across Paul's placid face had finally clued him in. "Bastard! Wait. Jennifer told you that I'm in charge? Didn't she, Paul? Out with it, Man!"

Paul smiled; there might have been some chuckling. "Yes, Gabe."

"And she didn't tell me?"

"No."

"Why not? Why didn't you tell me? Or somebody?"

Paul was just this side of gleeful. "She swore us to secrecy. The whole office."

"But why?"

Paul patted his shoulder. "Her exact words were 'Bergeron would freak if he knew.'"

"I would not." Well, he would have freaked. He had freaked. He was still freaking. He would freak in the immediate future.

Paul smiled. "You're fine, Gabe. Just do what you were doing before you knew."

He looked out at the office. A hundred pairs of eyes were peering at him over cubicle walls. Well, there weren't that many but a lot.

"I don't want to be in charge."

"But we need you, and you've been doing fine for a week. Just continue on, but you don't have to pretend to be Jennifer or Bauer."

"Right. Okay. Wait. So I can give them all my work, and they'll have to do it? I can stride around like a colossus...."

Paul was holding up a hand. "She also said 'if he finds out and gets drunk with power, call me.'"

"Right. Jennifer's no dummy. So I do what I've been doing. Okay. I can do that."

He was thinking about the elevator. He could be out of the freaking Mahr Building in thirty seconds tops.

Paul grabbed his arm and guided him back to his cubicle. "Just answer any accounting questions. Send the Human Resources stuff to Charlene." Paul may have patted his head. "It will be fine, Gabe."

He muttered under his breath. "Will not."

Chatterjee was walking by; he smiled. "So he finally figured it out?"

He looked at Paul. "Can I fire him?"

Paul shook his head and smiled but didn't walk away. He waited. "Was there something else, Paul?"

"Gunpowder tea."

He waited some more. "Yes? Ned and Gary carry it. Aunt Flo loves it but I'm not such a big fan."

"Can you get some? A tin?"

"Sure, Paul. No problem. Why?"

But Paul was back on course for his cubicle.

He should get back to work. But he took a moment to fret over being the boss; the temporary boss. He didn't like it, and what was the point of being the boss if you couldn't fire somebody?

Jennifer was going to owe him big time for this.

Tuesday 11:30 am
A Week Later

Carla was still not back, and Jennifer was still pregnant.

But Harry had returned to work on a more regular schedule and was working away in his cubicle.

And Gabe Bergeron was getting used to the workload. It had occurred to him when his eyes had popped open at 5:00 am, that this was not good.

If he demonstrated that he could handle so many clients so well, then it was not impossible that Bauer and Jennifer...when she got over being grateful for his help...would see no reason he couldn't continue to work at this backbreaking pace.

This was obviously unacceptable and an outrage. Well, it would be an outrage should it come to pass.

He had been ruminating about how he could prevent this from happening.

It was a pretty problem since he took pride in his work no matter what Jennifer might think so he couldn't do a bad job.

But he might slow down. Or outsource his work to the cubicle dwellers who bowed to his will.

Not that they did.

He was leaning back in cogitation mode when the freaking elevator dinged, and Winnie Wong stepped out.

He smiled at Harry. "Baldacci! Up and at 'em. Mother-in-law inbound."

Harry's sigh was heartbreaking, but he twisted his features into a smile and met the enemy on neutral ground, which was just south of Dana's desk.

"Hi, Winnie?"

Winnie was wearing a pale green suit and had applied lipstick which looked like Francine's shade of red. She smiled. "Hi, Harry. Could you tell Paul that I'm here?" She looked nervous. "I'm a little early."

Harry transitioned from shock to relief to curiosity in the blink of an eye. "Sure, I'll get him for you."

He and Harry semaphored to each other with their eyebrows as Harry marched over to Paul's cubicle beside the windows.

Harry said, "Paul? Winnie Wong is here to see you?"

He was straining to hear along with the rest of the cubicle dwellers in the profound silence of naked office nosiness.

He heard nothing.

Harry came back and took his seat.

Paul did not drift by like a cloud; his gait was almost a stride. He was wearing a new suit; a navy pin stripe that might be tailored. His hair was darker; the gray was more like a frosting.

Paul smiled at him. He may have given Paul a thumb's up. "Hi, Winnie."

Winnie smiled. "Hi, Paul. I'm a little early?"

"That's okay. Come sit in my cubicle while I finish this email. Do you want some coffee? Tea? We have gunpowder tea?"

Winnie smiled. "Did you get that for me, Paul?"

"No, we have it all the time." But he gave her his wispy, I'm-up-to-something smile.

Winnie said, "I'd love some."

And Paul offered his arm, and they progressed to the breakroom.

Everyone was smiling. Stella had tears running down her face but she was an accomplished lachrymist.

He stood up and looked around the office. He made get-back-to-work and leave-them-alone hand signals. Heads began to sink behind cubicle walls. Stella could be heard blowing her nose.

He was smiling to himself when the elevator from Hell dinged.

Two Asian gentlemen in suits appeared. He was pondering whether they could be more of Carla's relatives when they asked Dana for him.

He sighed and got to his feet. "I'm Gabriel Bergeron. How may I help you?"

The older gentleman was closing in on fifty. His hair might still be coal black, but the wrinkles and a bit of neck wattle gave it away. "I am Mr. Chen, and this is Mr. Ma. Is there somewhere more private?"

He smiled and shook their hands. "Of course. Come into the conference room."

Chen and Ma weren't smiling. He was developing a sixth sense that caused his right eye to twitch in the presence of pseudo-clients. These guys were a total twitch attack but he was going to treat them like clients as long as he could.

Mr. Ma was probably twenty. He had an oval face and symmetrical features; perfect lips, glowing skin, and lovely eyes. He was bigger than Mr. Chen and filled out his suit nicely; the suit cost probably ten times what Chen's had.

As fetching as the packaging was, there was something about Ma; an indefinable air of smugness and entitlement.

Ma lounged in the chair and looked around the room. He waved a hand at Chen to get on with it.

Chen said, "We have a matter to discuss with you, Mr. Bergeron."

"Of course." He had grabbed a new client form. "May I get your full names?"

Chen frowned but Ma said something in Chinese and laughed. Chen said something back which had a finely wrought edge to it forged of exasperation annealed with deference.

Ma frowned at Chen and waved his manicured hand again as he said things. He had known Young Ma for ten seconds, and he wanted to break that hand already. He looked at Chen who was carefully blank as Ma rattled on.

Chen gave a shrug so tiny that it belonged in the quantum realm.

He wondered what the deal was with their names?

Ma said, "I am Ma Ying-jeou." He smirked at Chen. "And he is Chen Shui-bian. We are from Taiwan."

His English was understandable but he had an accent unlike Mr. Chen.

"Thank you. And you need an accountant?"

The question was proforma. No way in Hell these guys wanted a bookkeeper.

Ma laughed. It was a very irritating sound. Chen thought so too; probably.

Chen said, "It is a matter that should not concern you or those you are working for."

Ma nodded.

He smiled at Ma and Chen. "So you're here to tell me to keep my nose out of your business?"

Ma nodded vigorously. "Americans." He managed to pack a hefty dose of venom and contempt into those syllables.

Chen ignored Ma. "There could be an...incentive for allowing this matter to proceed naturally?"

"Ah. An incentive."

Ma managed to look even more contemptuous. Would it cause an international incident if he punched Ma in his smirky mouth?

Chen must have read his face. "Please, Mr. Bergeron, conflict is best avoided."

"Right. That's one of my mottoes. Along with 'let sleeping dogs lie' and 'fish and visitors stink after three minutes'."

He thought that was house guests and three days but he'd consult Aunt Flo later.

Chen said, "I don't understand?"

"I don't either, Mr. Chen. I'm an accountant. I work here. I don't work for anyone else in any other capacity. Whatever you think I'm doing, I'm not."

Ma's paper thin patience was shredded. "Lies! We know who you work for! And the Nigerian has been here!"

Chen said possibly calming, cautionary words to Ma, but Ma was vexed and seethed.

"You mean Mr. Okocha? Yes, he came here...with the same

mistaken idea that you seem to have. So I told him the same thing I'm telling you. I am not involved. In anything."

Ma was muttering in Mandarin.

Chen said, "Surely we could come to some arrangement, Mr. Bergeron?"

He could ask Chen for a hundred thousand dollars just to see what he'd do? Probably very unwise.

"I promise to do absolutely nothing."

Chen nodded.

Ma looked confused. "You do?"

"I do. And now I think it's time for you to depart."

Ma was still confused. "You won't look for him?"

"Him who?"

Chen wasn't quick enough to slap a hand over Ma's mouth. "The thief; this seaman? Lars Thorvaldsen?" Ma got what he probably thought was a crafty look on his face. "You know where he is."

Chen closed his eyes and shook his head.

"I do not know where he is, and I won't look for him."

Ma was unconvinced. "But you went to his house?"

Did everyone know that he'd gone to that stupid Victorian house in West Philly? Maybe Okocha had told them?

"A momentary lapse." He stood up. "Won't happen again. I promise."

He walked out of the conference room at a brisk clip because, as Chen and Ma had stood up, he'd noticed telltale bulges...under their jackets.

His Taiwanese friends were packing heat.

Chen would only shoot somebody after careful reflection and consideration of the ramifications; Ma would shoot if he had a hangnail.

He escorted them to the elevator. Ma was pissed and was probably going to take it out on Chen.

He should tell Chase to put these two on the no admission list.

Paul was at the breakroom door. "Gabe?"

"Yes, Paul?"

He followed Paul into the room, and he closed the door. "Winnie has something to tell you, Gabe."

Winnie smiled. "Carla told me but I thought she exaggerated."

"Told you what?"

Winnie said, "Your visitors weren't Taiwanese, and the names they gave were fake." She frowned. "And meant to be insulting."

He leaned against the counter. "I am all ears."

She smiled again. "I heard them...through the wall, through all these holes. I'm a teacher, Gabe. Has Carla told you?"

He shook his head.

"At Temple University. And I've had many students from Taiwan and mainland China. These men didn't speak Taiwanese Mandarin. They're both from northern China. 'Mr. Ma' spoke the Beijing dialect I have heard from students who were the children of high party officials."

"Really? High party as in the Chinese Communist Party?"

She smiled. "There is only one party in Beijing, Gabe."

Which he knew. "Right! But why would they pretend to be Taiwanese?" She shook her head. "But what did they say?"

"'Chen' tried to calm 'Ma' down. 'Ma' said that you were lying to them and that they had to find the seaman. They had been searching for three weeks already, and that his father would be disappointed in them both. 'Ma' used terrible language. Vulgar."

"Right. Okay. Thanks, Winnie. Wait. How do you know the names are fake?"

"Because, Gabe, Chen Shui-bian was the fifth president of Taiwan, and Ma Ying-jeou was the sixth. 'Mr. Ma' was sure you wouldn't know that."

Which had been correct. Ma, or whatever his name really was, had slapped him in the face for no reason at all other than he was an arrogant bastard.

He smiled at Winnie and Paul. "Thanks. But you should go have lunch."

Paul smiled at Winnie.

He went back to his desk. Should he tell somebody about

all this? And if so, who? He called Cory and got his voicemail.

He left a message that he missed him and would like to hear from him. There was no way he was telling Aunt Flo about any of this. Well, not yet.

Paul and Winnie waved to him as they left for lunch. He hoped Paul was taking her some place nice.

Paul gave him a look and would probably circle back to the fake Taiwanese thing in due course.

Wednesday
7:30 am

He knocked on the glass doors, and Chase came over to let him in. Chase was wearing light gray slacks; a dark sports coat had been tossed across the security desk. He had a red tie in his hand.

"Good morning, Chase." He stepped inside; Chase was an inch taller and maybe twenty pounds heavier than he was.

Chase smiled absently while looking at the red tie. "Morning, Bergeron."

"What's up?"

Chase glanced at him. "I'm supposed to wear a tie."

"Right?"

Chase had on a white long-sleeved shirt with the creases straight from the package. It was already buttoned to the throat. The shirt needed an extra inch in the neck. His chest and arms filled the rest of the shirt nicely. He had a truncheon and a ring of keys hanging from his belt.

He also had muscular thighs and a butt you could bounce quarters on...if that's what you were into.

"And what? You don't know how to knot a tie?"

Chase shook his head and smiled at him. "Not something I learned in the Marines."

Chase had a very nice smile. He was quite nice all over. He reminded himself that Cory was his one true love.

"I can show you how to tie it?"

Chase shook his head. "Just tie this one for me."

"You want a Windsor knot?"

Chase leaned in close. He had nice brown eyes but he had ladled on cologne that he'd bought by the gallon. "Is that what you've got?"

"It is."

"Looks good."

He cranked out the knot and handed the tie to Chase. He could have tied it on Chase but that would have required way too much contact.

Chase said, "Damn! Could you maybe do another one for me?"

"Do it a thousand times, and you get fast. Give me all of your ties."

Chase reached over the security desk and pulled out three more ties which might hail from a second-hand shop.

"Did you see the two Chinese guys who came in yesterday around noon?"

Chase said, "An older gentleman and a young punk?"

"That's them."

"Is there a problem?"

"Maybe. Can you give me a head's up if you spot them again?"

"That's affirmative."

"Don't try to stop them or anything. They were armed."

Chase smiled. "So am I."

He shouldn't have said anything. Now he was going to worry about Chase.

Chase seemed to know what he was thinking. "I can take care of myself, Bergeron, and they weren't that formidable."

The "formidable" had been enunciated most carefully.

"'Formidable'?" He may have raised an eyebrow

Chase smiled again. "My word of the day."

"Right."

Chase put on his red tie. "How do I look?"

"Very professional."

He headed for the elevator. That shirt needed the button moved so it wouldn't choke him. He was handy enough with a needle and thread to do that but it could lead to Chase taking off his shirt. He didn't need to see Chase without his shirt.

He unlocked the office doors while praying that only accounting clients showed up.

His phone played Cory's song.

"Cory?"

"Hi, Gabe. What's up?"

He was going to ease into Okocha, Aronson, and the fake Taiwanese. "Nothing much. Jennifer's out due to the imminent birth of her baby. She put me in charge of the office but she didn't tell me. Paul is dating Carla's mother. She's out too...also baby related. Harry's going crazy. How is your case going?"

There was a silence. "You're in charge of the office?"

"My domain encompasses the entire eleventh floor."

"Have you tried to fire anyone yet?"

"I have not! Well, I thought about firing Chatterjee, but Paul told me I couldn't. Well, he said I had to call Jennifer first, and I didn't think I should bother her. You didn't say about your case?"

"We've hit a brick wall."

"You don't sound upset about that?"

"I need to take some time off."

Cory was leading up to something that Gabe Bergeron wasn't going to like. "Rip off the bandage, Special Agent."

"Mother called me."

"Right. And what did Laura have to say for herself?"

"The house in Costa Rica burned down or was damaged at least. I'm not sure Mother really knows."

"The place they rent for the annual winter vacation?"

"They bought it two years ago and have been renting it out when they're not down there."

"I see. Well, no, I don't?"

"She wants me to go with them to help Dad get it sorted out. I was going to ask you to come with us, but it sounds like you're busy?"

"I am. Crazy busy." He sighed. "I would love to go to Costa Rica with you, but Jennifer and Carla are both out, Cory."

"You told me. Okay. I don't know how long I'll be down there. Maybe you can take a few days at least before I come back?"

"That would be divine. Wait. How much leave are you asking for?"

"Two weeks. I have a lot of time accumulated."

"And Danielle is okay with that?"

"Yeah. She knows I'll be back as soon as I can."

"Okay. So will I see you before you fly out?"

"We're flying out soon."

"Today soon?"

"Sorry."

"No, go help your Dad." The state of Hugh's health was still a closely guarded secret. He wasn't sure that even Hugh knew the details.

Cory said, "So anything else going on with you?"

"Not a thing." Dana was arriving. Her body was diverging from her normal columnar form more and more. He thought? Maybe her chartreuse mini-skirt and wide belt were just too tight? He lowered his voice. "I think Dana might be pregnant."

Cory laughed. "You think?"

"Yes. I can't very well ask. It would be awkward if she isn't...or if she is."

Cory said, "When has awkward ever stopped you, Henri? I'll call you when we land in San José."

"Okay. Have a good flight. Does Laura expect you to rebuild the house?"

"I have no idea. It may be much ado about nothing. Bye, Gabe."

"Bye. I love you."

But Cory was gone. He sighed. It was well known that he made Cory's life a lot more complicated that it needed to be. Hopefully, he made up for it by being an exceptional boyfriend?

He wasn't going to tell him about Okocha et al. He would hunker down and weather the storm on his own. He might want to put the Glock in his briefcase?

He wasn't going to get involved in the Thorvaldsen affair, and that was final.

He sniffed. He still smelled like Chase's cologne. He washed his face in the Men's Room, made a pot of coffee, and settled into work.

There was some kind of commotion when Stella arrived involving her and Dana and Paul, but he had too much work. He may have glared at them.

It was almost 4:00 pm when Dana got excited again which mostly involved hugging Stella and waving her spindly arms over her head.

Stella was crying profusely which was hardly remarkable; cute pictures of puppies, kittens, or babies or any combination thereof could set her off. There was a video of a soldier being welcomed home from Afghanistan by his dog that could prostrate her for hours. Well, he may have teared up over that one too.

But Paul was smiling.

"What?"

Paul said, "Jennifer has had her baby. Another boy."

"Yes? And she's okay? And the baby is too?"

Paul nodded.

"Good. Excellent." He'd have to get a card. "Wait. How much did he weigh? Aunt Flo and Ezmeralda will want to know."

From the limited information he had accumulated over the years, it seemed that having a big baby was better? But didn't a smaller baby mean an easier birth?

Stella said, "Nine pounds three ounces!" This was said with joy and vicarious triumph.

He smiled his third best smile. "Right."

Well, he was tired, and he would be properly enthusiastic when Jennifer and Andy brought the baby to the office.

But Dana and Stella were looking at him with something akin to loathing. He smiled at them and went back to work.

He would call Jennifer tomorrow and congratulate her and Andy.

Three sons. He couldn't imagine.

But maybe Jennifer would come back to the office soon? She did have Nina the nanny to look after her brood.

He hoped she still had Nina?

Wednesday
6:00 pm

Cory had called. He and his parents had landed safely in Costa Rica. They were probably nearing the house by now.

He was beat and starving. He had ignored all the notes on the snacks in the breakroom and eaten everything, but pickings had been sparse, and now the sun was westering low.

He was leaning back in his chair pondering the life choices that had led him to being the last one out of the office.

The last cubicle dweller had cleared out at 5:00 pm, and he had locked the office doors. Just in case. But he heard the elevator's ding anyway.

"Bergeron? It's Chase."

He unlocked and peeked out. Chase was smiling at him. "My shift ended a few minutes ago. The other guy hasn't shown up yet. Maybe you shouldn't be here by yourself?"

"Right. Thanks, Chase. I can be packed up in thirty seconds?"

Chase nodded. "I'll wait."

He shut off his computer and grabbed his briefcase. Chase was leaning against the office door, arms folded, dripping machismo. The butt of a pistol was visible above his belt.

Which was nice if Chase was intent on protecting him. He really knew nothing about him but he got into the elevator anyway.

"You weren't kidding about being armed."

Chase smiled. "No." Chase pulled it out.

"What kind of pistol is that?" It was blue-steeled and

stubbier than his Glock 22.

"A Walther PPK. A semi-automatic." Chase was looking at him. "Ever fired a gun, Bergeron?"

"Once or twice. A Glock 22."

Chase smiled.

When they got to the lobby, Doug, the ratty, night shift security guy, had arrived, and Chase exited the building at his side.

They walked to the parking garage which was poorly lit and creepy even in the middle of the day.

He was going to be glad of Chase's company until Chase did something to make him reevaluate that.

Chase said, "There's your Jeep. I'm down here."

Chase hopped into a very red Toyota Tacoma pickup. The hopping was necessary because the body was floating far above the giant, muscular tires installed on sparkly, eight-spoked rims.

Chase smiled as he roared past and out of the parking garage. He followed at a more sedate pace.

He pulled up in front of his apartment building. He'd get a ticket if he parked there but the alternative was to park in the garage down the block.

Ordinarily, that would be fine. It wasn't like he was a big fraidy-cat, but he had a bad feeling about the garage tonight.

He was sitting there trying to decide what to do when a black van cruised by slowly.

It didn't stop but it slowed menacingly. Or somebody was looking for an address and was as dangerous as Mary Poppins.

Or it could have been Jennifer's husband, Andy?

He shut off the Jeep and sprinted into his building. He ran up the stairs. He inspected his door.

It was still locked and didn't seem to have been tampered with. He entered stealthily.

His Glock was in the gun safe in his bedroom closet. He grabbed one of Cory's weights and searched the apartment.

It was empty. And there was no sign that anyone had gotten in.

He may have double locked and chained his door.

Thursday
7:00 am

By a stroke of luck or inefficiency, he hadn't gotten a ticket, and now he was looking at Chase who was standing at the security desk and smiling. "Bergeron."

"Chase."

"I had a buddy check out the lock on the back door."

Chase's jacket was too snug and didn't hide the bulge under his left armpit. He had gotten a holster for that Walther PPK.

"Want to see?"

He wanted to get to work and avoid all human contact but Chase was looking at him like a puppy with a ball in its mouth.

"Sure."

He followed Chase down the long, windowless hall to the back of the building. They passed the stairwell and went into the boiler room.

He had been there before with Augie and Buddy, two thirds of the building maintenance team. It was just as cold and noisy as he remembered.

The monstrous green boilers were still nestled in a maze of wires, pipes, and conduits. Only one bank of the fluorescent lights was on, and a platoon of serial killers could easily hide in the shadows.

He yelled over the ambient roar of the one boiler that was running, "You were in the Marines?"

The lights gave Chase's face an alien glow. "Yeah. Six years."

"But you didn't stay in?"

Chase shook his head, smile waning and waxing. "No."

It occurred to him again that he'd known Chase for less than two weeks, and he was facing him in a very dark, very private space that was noisy enough to drown out the loudest screams.

Chase's smile got broader as he seemed to pick up on his thoughts. "This place is kinda scary."

"No. It's okay." It so wasn't.

Chase ditched the smile and pointed to the back door. Heavy brackets had been installed to hold an equally heavy steel bar in place across the door. Bar and brackets were shiny and new.

Chase said something but it was hard to hear. He leaned closer. "He picked the lock."

"Okocha?"

Chase nodded. "It's not that great a lock but now with the bar in place nobody's getting through this door unless I let them in."

He heaved on the bar; he wasn't sure why but it seemed to be the thing to do. "Very sturdy. This is great, Chase."

Chase gave him a big smile.

"And quick. How did you do it?"

The building manager never moved that fast for Bauer or even Jennifer.

Chase shook his head. He lifted the bar out of the way and stepped out into the tiny alleyway wedged between the Mahr Building and the warehouse behind it. The alleyway was a hundred decibels quieter.

He followed, and the door slammed shut. The only exits were back through that door or out the gate at the end of the alley that let onto Windsor Street.

The alleyway was narrow, and the only light was from a slice of sky overhead and through the gate. It was a less ideal place to kill someone than the boiler room but not by much.

Chase said, "A buddy of mine owed me a favor. He installed the bar."

"But the building owners should pay for security upgrades, not you?"

"I didn't pay...it was a barter arrangement, Bergeron."
"Call me Gabe. So what's your name?"
"People call me LC, but Chase is fine."
"Okay, Chase it is."

They stood there. He wanted to get to work, and he wanted to get out of the alley, but Chase had something to say.

He waited. He may have noticed that the gate was chained and had spikes on the top which would make climbing over it difficult and possibly life-threatening.

Chase said, "So what's going on, Gabe?"
"With Okocha and the fake Taiwanese?"
"Yeah."

He was absolutely sure that Chase would be a deadly opponent in a fight. Even without the truncheon or the Walther PPK.

He took a deep breath. "Why do you want to know?"
Chase nodded. "I want intelligence on the enemy, Gabe. Who else might come after you?"

Which was certainly reasonable. "Okay. I know you didn't sign on for Okocha or any of my craziness. I could help you find another job? I'm sorry about this, Chase."

Chase smiled. "Hell, no! I thought this was going to be boring, but I can see it's not. So?"

If Chase wasn't who he claimed to be, he probably knew all about Duke anyway.

"Okay. I don't know much. It seems to concern a merchant seaman named Lars Thorvaldsen aka Duke. And some pirates."

He told Chase everything. Well, not about Cory being in fair Costa Rica. Or about Aronson. Or Monroe."

Chase shook his head. "Half."
"Half what?"
"You left out about half, Gabe."
"Did not. Well, there's a FBI agent who might show up."
"Not Cory." A little smile.
"No. Dark. Maybe forty and about my size. His name is Aronson." How did Chase know about Cory?
"And?"

"Okay, there's another guy. I'm not sure what he is: spy or agent of some sort who appears to freelance. He's tall and lanky with silver-gray hair and an angular face...with cheekbones and a jawline something like yours but more cadaverous."

Chase was having a splendid time. "'Cadaverous'?"

"Right. Gaunt, corpse-like. Cheeks sunken in just a bit; kind of pale. But pale doesn't mean weak; I think Monroe is very dangerous."

Chase pulled a notepad out of his jacket pocket and wrote down "cadaverous" and "gaunt" though his spelling was off.

"Anyway, he's talked about wanting my help a couple of times and hasn't actually threatened me, but I am sure he is capable of violence."

Chase nodded. "Black ops guy?"

"Totally."

Chase nodded again. "That's it?"

"Isn't that enough?"

Chase was excited. "So we could have Nigerian pirates show up?"

"No! Why would they?"

"Good question. But Okocha came. Think he's Nigerian?"

"Probably. I don't know for sure."

Chase nodded. "So is this Thorvaldsen friend or foe?"

"He doesn't even know me."

"But if he wants to stay lost and thinks you're after him?"

"Right! Shit. I hadn't thought of that. I have to get to work."

And Chase walked with him back to the elevators. Two of the flock of young women who worked on the 5th Floor stopped to fling themselves on top of Chase and ravish him.

Well, they flirted with him, and Chase certainly flirted back.

When they were in the elevator and Chase's virtue safe, he said, "Another perk of the job?"

Chase gave him a big smile. "Yeah."

Chase was looking at him. "What?"

"How did you and Cory get together?"

"Why?"

"Curious."

"He thought my great-aunt was an art thief, and he investigated us. That's his job at the FBI, recovering stolen art and putting the thieves behind bars."

Chase was looking at him. "But she wasn't?"

"No. She was a spy not an art thief."

Chase chuckled. "So cool. Are you serious?"

"Always. So how did you know about Cory and me?"

"Everybody in the building has at least one story about you, Gabe, and some of them are about him too."

Friday
7:00 am

He smiled at Chase who was standing at attention beside the security desk. "How goes it, Marine?" Chase's smile dimmed. "Sorry? Did I say something wrong?"

"It's okay, Gabe."

He went to work. He couldn't even greet someone without putting his foot in his mouth. Somehow?

Harry came in just after 11:00 am.

"Harry! How is Carla?"

"Better. The doctor was pleased."

"So did you find out if she can come back?"

Harry shrugged. "I don't think she wants to, Gabe."

"Really?" Which didn't sound like Carla? But pregnancy was obviously life altering. "So she can work from home. If she feels up to it?"

Harry nodded. "Yeah."

The only person in the office who seemed serene was Paul. He wanted to ask about Paul and Winnie, but Harry wasn't in a talkative mood.

And Chatterjee was stomping around the office and muttering. Even Stella seemed upset.

It could be client related? He wasn't going to inquire until he had gotten some work done. He sighed and hunkered down. He had called and congratulated Jennifer yesterday, but he needed to talk to her about one of her clients if she felt up to it. This client was setting off his hinky alarm. Which was different than his pseudo-client twitch. This was more a prickling of his scalp.

He toddled over to Dana's desk. She looked up from actual work. "Gabe?"

"Have you talked to Jennifer today?"

"No, I haven't."

"Okay."

"Gabe? These men are here...about the monitor."

He spun round ready to berate Guy One and Guy Two, but these were not they.

These were dressed identically to G1 and G2 from the soles of their work boots to the peaks of their SJR caps. These were equally large.

The major difference was that these two were sentient, and seemed to be giving everyone in the office, especially one Gabe Bergeron, probing stares.

He may have raised an eyebrow. "You're here about the monitor? To finish installing it?"

New Guy One said, "Yes, Sir." And after inspecting the humble cubicle of Gabe Bergeron, he strode across the office to the conference room.

He looked at New Guy Two. "I'll call our IT guy...."

New Guy Two smiled. "We've called him, Sir. Mr. Mahoney is on his way."

And Mahoney popped out of the elevator as if summoned by wizardry.

He considered. It was nice that these installers were efficient. Could installers be too efficient?

He shook his head. He called Jennifer but her grandmother answered. "Hello, Mrs. Garst. Congratulations on the new grandson! May I speak to Jennifer?"

"Hold on, Gabe." He heard her say, "Estelle? Is Jennifer awake?"

Estelle was Jennifer's mother whom he'd never met because she and Jennifer's father, Thaddeus Alexander Garst, Jr., always seemed to be vacationing somewhere in a far distant land.

A voice that sounded a bit like Jennifer's said, "She's asleep, Mother. What is it?"

"The office. Shall I tell them Jennifer will call when she can?"

"Yes, Mother!"

Which sounded a bit cranky.

Mrs. Garst said, "Did you hear that, Gabe?"

"I did, and there's no rush. It can wait. But if Jennifer feels up to it?"

"Of course, Gabe."

And she hung up.

He knew what Jennifer and her grandmother looked like; he was trying to merge them to come up with an approximation of Estelle.

He realized that a large shadow was being cast over him. He debated reaching for his Glock.

"Mr. Bergeron?"

He spun slowly around. New Guys One and Two were standing behind him forming a new cubicle wall taller than the others. Also more solid, sexy, and possibly dangerous.

"Yes?"

"We're done, Sir. If you'd like to check it out."

He let himself be herded into the conference room like the fatted calf but unless NG1 & NG2 planned on killing Mahoney too, he was safe.

The monitor was working, and Mahoney was chatting with a young lady with her hair braided into two plaits. She was sitting at a desk in an office somewhere.

Mahoney was leaning back in a chair. He had brown eyes. His mound of matching frizzy curls was massed on the left side of his head today.

He was wearing muted, gray-plaid slacks, a white t-shirt, and an ecru, suede shirt-jacket that was unbuttoned and untucked.

Mahoney said, "Up and running, Mr. Bergeron." Mahoney's sweet smile made his eyes crinkle to slits. "This is Kayla from my office."

He waved at Kayla, and Kayla waved back.

"Great."

And NG1 held out a piece of paper. "If you could sign, Sir,

on the line indicating the job has been completed to your satisfaction?"

He smiled at NG1 & NG2. They smiled back. They were rugged and virile and appeared totally trustworthy.

He signed the work order. This one lacked the brown stains that had marked the one that Old Guy Two had showed him.

And they and Mahoney exited.

He examined the wall. All the holes had been filled and were invisible unless you knew just where to look.

He wasn't going to indulge in suspicions about NG1 & NG2. He had enough going on as it was.

He went back to work. Well, he tried but his computer kept freezing up. He was about to call Mahoney when it resumed normal functioning.

His office phone had developed a click.

Nothing suspicious about any of those things.

Friday
1:00 pm

He had gone to lunch at CoffeeXtra. It was a lovely day, and Cory wasn't pissed with him...mostly because he had neglected to tell him heaps of stuff. He walked back to work thinking about visiting Aunt Flo on the weekend.

He was enjoying that happy thought when he entered the Mahr Building.

Chase had a ready smile but this was too much.
"What?"
"Step over here, Sir."
"Not happening."
Chase chuckled. "Relax."
He whipped out a vaguely club shaped object. It was about sixteen inches long including the handle; it had a strap to go around the wrist. It was black with yellow letters: "CYZ Ltd."

"What is that? A metal detector wand thingee?" Chase smiled. Chase was really getting into this. "Let me guess? You have a buddy who sold it to you cheap?"

"It's more of a loaner."

And Chase swept the wand across his groin. It beeped and LED lights lit up.

"Hey! Do not wand my private areas!"

"Nothing to worry about, Gabe. It's reading a smallish object."

"I'll have you know, Sir, that any objects I have are not 'smallish'."

Chase grinned. "Sorry. A smallish metal object. In your right pocket." Chase was studying the wand readouts. "Keys?"

He ran the wand from his chest to his ankles. "And something else? A cellphone?"

"Yes." Chase was very happy. "I know you're enjoying this, but please be careful. Okay?"

"Roger that."

"And I don't know how the staff and visitors are going to react to being wanded?"

Chase said, "Not going to wand anyone who works here...except maybe the nubile females...if they smile at me first."

"Let me guess? 'Nubile' is the word of the day."

Chase smiled. "A cool word too."

Chase switched off the smile to wand a guy who said he wanted to go to the 10th Floor. The guy didn't seem to mind.

He had been back in his cubicle for a good ten minutes when he got a call.

"Hello?"

"Gabe. You have two visitors on the way up. I wanded both, and they aren't packing."

"Chase?"

"Affirmative."

"Visitors?"

"Right. One is maybe too old for a Nigerian pirate but very cool."

He shut his eyes and shook his head. He may have moaned softly to the tune of "Nobody Knows the Trouble I've Seen."

The elevator bell tolled and out stepped a prince with his uniformed retainer two steps behind.

Dana stood up; she didn't actually curtsy but she made a little dip with an incline of the head.

"May I help you, Sir?"

The Prince handed Dana a card. The lovely bass voice resonated from the farthest walls like a mighty aria from *Boris Godunov*. "I am here to see Gabriel Bergeron."

His visitor had been trained in public speaking; nobody sounded like that right out of the box. The accent was from somewhere between Cambridge and Oxford and unabashedly plummy.

He rose to his feet. He tried to make his suit fit better as he walked over, but it was hopeless. He had only thought he'd seen beautiful suits before, and the Prince's tie was a thing of beauty.

The Prince was about sixty and black; he was dark though not as dark as Okocha. His once black hair and beard were frosted with silver; he wore dark-rimmed glasses. His face was oval and handsome enough.

Around his neck he wore a gold chain which was needed to hold a big, gold medallion. His scepter was probably out being polished.

"I'm Gabriel Bergeron. How may I help you?"

The Prince smiled. "I am Chinedum Onyewu." Smile. "I am the Second Secretary of the Embassy of the Federal Republic of Nigeria." He paused to let this Bergeron fellow realized the honor being paid him.

He extended his hand and waited to see if Secretary Onyewu would shake it?

He did.

"Please come into the conference room, Mr. Secretary."

Before the secretary followed, he made a little hand gesture to his retainer, and the tall guy in a green uniform halted. Was it a chauffeur's uniform?

The chauffeur was tall and slender. He was also black and fitted out with dark-rimmed glasses like Onyewu's, but he was around thirty with an oval face that seemed happy even in repose. His little mustache and goatee were neatly trimmed. He had a green cap in his hands.

He got Secretary Onyewu seated. He smiled his very best smile. "I'll be right back, Mr. Secretary."

He ran to his cubicle. Cory was in Costa Rica. He could call Aronson? But he knew nothing about the guy. Not even if he was a real FBI agent.

He shook his head; he would wing it. As he stood up, he noticed that the chauffeur had gone.

He waggled his fingers at Secretary Onyewu as he

whispered to Dana, "Where did the other guy go? Elevator?"

Dana nodded.

He pulled out his phone and casually called Chase. "Hey, if the chauffeur guy is around, engage him in conversation."

Chase said, "Roger that! Got any topics in mind?"

"His current boss, Chinedum Onyewu. Anything and everything."

He entered the conference room; Onyewu was on his feet again. "I'm dreadfully sorry to keep you waiting, Secretary Onyewu. The press of affairs. I'm sure you can understand."

The secretary roared. "I do not! It is outrageous, that I, a Secretary of the Embassy of the Federal Republic of Nigeria, should be kept waiting like this."

He just smiled and took a seat. He didn't like being yelled at. He didn't like the secretary. He should just kick him out, but he was too damn curious.

It was impossible for him to be otherwise. Which was probably an epiphany that he should have had ages ago.

He may have folded his hands and gotten more comfortable in his chair.

"Who were you talking to? Your superiors? I wish to speak to them at once. I will not waste my time with underlings."

"That isn't possible, Mr. Secretary."

"Make it possible!"

"Nope."

"What?"

"If you have something you'd like to discuss with me, please proceed. My time is also valuable, Onyewu, and I can't waste it on blather and bombast."

Two words he might mention to Chase.

The secretary sat down. "Who are you?" He waved at the humble offices of Garst, Bauer & Hartmann. "All this is charade. Obviously."

"Obviously." He smiled deprecatingly. "Who I am is unimportant. Tell me why you're here."

"I am on a fact-finding mission to your great country." Big smile.

"And do these facts concern a certain Mr. Chen and Mr. Ma?"

He had just thrown the fake Taiwanese out there, but Chinedum's big smile collapsed.

"Have you met them?"

"Mr. Ma occupied the very chair that you're sitting in, Onyewu."

"Ma was here by himself?"

That seemed to rattle Onyewu so he went with it. "Yes, he was. A very interesting young man. So well connected." He had no idea.

"What did he tell you? He's not...he's very young and headstrong. You shouldn't believe everything he says, Mr. Bergeron."

"No?" What was he doing? He should get rid of this guy.

Chinedum shook his head. "What did he want from you?"

"The same thing you want."

Chinedum laughed. "You have no idea what I want."

"So you wouldn't be interested in Thorvaldsen?"

"Where is he? Okocha has searched.... You can't know where he is?"

He got to his feet. "No, I don't."

"You don't?"

"No, Mr. Secretary. It's been a real treat meeting you, and I mean that, but I'm just an accountant, and I work here. In a little cubicle due south from our current location. Day in and day out; toiling ceaselessly. I don't know anything about Thorvaldsen, and I'm very happy about that. So if you could just run along, that would be great."

The secretary smiled and smiled. "All this pretense is silly, Bergeron, but I am aware that such information has value. How much?"

"How much for Thorvaldsen?"

Onyewu smiled some more.

He wanted to ask for a million dollars just to see how the guy would react, but he shook his head.

"I don't know where he is."

Onyewu was fingering his gold necklace. "A hundred thousand dollars? American."

"I don't know where he is, and I don't want to know. Please leave."

Onyewu frowned. "I could double that? But I would need a few days."

"Go away."

Onyewu got to his feet. "If I could come up with that amount, I would need assurances that this Thorvaldsen will be at the location you give me."

"Listen to me very carefully: I do NOT have a location to give you. I will NEVER have a location."

The second secretary smiled some more and took his leave. He counted to twenty. Dana was looking at him as he headed for the elevator.

"What are you doing, Gabe?"

"Nothing! I'm exploring opening a GBH branch office in Nigeria. I hear Abuja is lovely, and Jennifer is always saying I don't have enough clients."

She shook her head. If she called Andy, she did, but Jennifer had given birth so maybe it would be okay.

The elevator door opened on the ground floor. He peered out cautiously but Chase spotted him and waved him over.

"Stay down, Gabe."

He crawled to the security desk and peered over.

Chinedum Onyewu was getting in a limo. The chauffeur was holding the door.

Chase said, "That's Mr. Babalola. He drives for the embassy. Not this guy in particular. Limo has diplomatic plates."

"So he really came from the embassy?"

Chase nodded, and they watched Onyewu and Babalola motor off.

Chase said, "Babalola drove this guy from New York. He said this guy...."

"Onyewu."

"Yeah, him. Just arrived from Nigeria. Some kind of politician back home."

"So not second secretary of the embassy?"

Chase shrugged.

He sighed, but Chase was smiling. At least somebody was having fun. He went back to his desk.

He looked at Aronson's card. He wasn't calling him. He wasn't calling Cory.

He could call Cory's boss, Danielle, but she might tell Cory.

He could call Brunetti? She was less likely to tell Cory on him.

He dialed the number she'd given him but the voice on the line seemed uncertain that such a person existed. Or that people of Italian ancestry had ever come to America. He left his name and number anyway.

Nadia Brunetti was Danielle's boss, and had used his services in getting to the bottom of an FBI case involving fine art, fancy brooches, and a gang of Frisian thieves.

He was pretty sure that had actually happened and hadn't been a finely detailed delusion. She had even suggested that she might employ his special talents in the future.

Even so, he was almost certain he would regret calling her.

And then he called Aunt Flo and asked if he could visit before he drowned in obsessing about the whole affair.

Friday
6:00 pm

His phone played Cory's tune.

"Cory! I'm so glad you called!"

"Hi, Gabe. Are you behaving yourself?"

"Absolutely! I am still at work."

"Really?"

"Really. You believe me, right?"

"Yes, Gabe. Though it is out of character. Past six on a Friday? Totally unheard of."

"Well, that is true."

"Do you need to be working so hard?"

"Yes and no. I mean I could just ignore the wailing of my clients and Carla's and Jennifer's, but I'd feel bad. Not that I'm doing it all: Chatterjee and Stella are helping too."

"So how are they doing: Jennifer and Carla?"

"I forgot! Jennifer had the baby on Wednesday. A boy. Nine pounds three ounces. I talked to her, and she sounded weary to the bone but it's over. Harry says Carla is feeling a little better but may or may not return in the near future. So how are you, the parents, and the burnt-out shell of a residence?"

"We're fine. The house isn't a shell; the damage was mostly confined to the kitchen. One wall and a bit of the roof were damaged. Plus all the smoke and water damage. Dad tried to find someone to get it closed in before the rainy season really starts."

"Tried?"

"Yeah. Nobody was available. We couldn't wait so I did the

work myself. It's rough but it will keep the rain from ruining everything."

"Then it's really good that you could go with your parents."

"Yeah. Dad would have tried to do it himself."

"He would. Absolutely. So how long are you going to stay down there?"

"Not sure."

"Because?"

"Bornheimer called me."

"About the case. He's found a lead."

Cory was jazzed. "A good one, Gabe."

"So you're flying back?"

"Not yet. He's checking on some stuff. If it doesn't pan out, I was thinking maybe you could fly down and help me?"

"I would love that. Really. If Carla comes back or starts working from home then I could take off a few days. Maybe. I'd love to help you."

"And I'd love to have you here. Mother is trying to nag Judd into coming down too."

Judd was Cory's older brother. He was tall, dark, and slender. He was also a librarian and pianist; neither calling lent itself to nailing 2x4's or putting up Sheetrock.

"Has he building experience, Corentin?"

Cory laughed. "Even less than you."

"I'm quite handy. Did we not rebuild Aunt Flo's dock?"

"We did. Which is why you would be welcome on my job site."

"I would love to be on your job site and play with your tools."

Cory laughed. "Well, let's hope we can make that happen. I have to go, Gabe."

"Right. Say hi to Hugh and Laura."

"Will do."

Saturday
9:00 am

His eyes had popped open at 3:00 am. He had tossed and turned for a while before getting up. He had set out for Aunt Flo's house at a truly ungodly hour.

Her house was on the Eastern Shore of Maryland just south of Snow Hill on the banks of the Pocomoke River.

Florence Barnes was really his great-aunt, and she lived in the home built by her grandparents, Elijah and Rachel Barnes. The enormous, three-story Victorian pile was mostly white except for the six trim colors. And a slate roof.

It was a beautiful day, and he was thinking about kayaking on the river. Or taking a long nap.

He turned off Nassawango Road and drove up the lane. The gate was open, but the parking lot was full so he put his Jeep on the lawn.

Aunt Flo had turned her home into a bed and breakfast a year and a half ago, and she was still enjoying having the guests gamboling about the place. Her partners, Ute and Annika, did all the work. Along with Ezmeralda.

He marched to the side door and entered into Ezmeralda's kitchen. It might belong to Aunt Flo, being part of her house, but that was just legalistic piffle.

Aunt Flo met him at the door and hugged him. She was eighty-five or so; elfin tiny, but still erect. She had a delicate cap of silky, white hair and large, all-knowing, silver-gray eyes that sometimes looked teal.

She was staring at him and reading his deepest thoughts and plumbing his soul. "How are you, Aunt Flo?"

"I'm well, Gabriel." She gave him a look. "How are you?"

"Never better. Well, I'm tired. I didn't sleep very well last night. I'm really happy to be here."

"And we're happy to have you here, Dear."

Ezmeralda was cooking on her range which again might legally belong to Aunt Flo. She made a snorting sound.

She and Aunt Flo had been comrades and friends for fifty years and had been spies together until they'd escaped from Cuba. Well, Aunt Flo said they hadn't been actual operatives but more like support staff. Not that he was sure he believed that.

Ezmeralda turned and glared at them before turning back to the range. Well, not at Aunt Flo. She flexed a mighty forearm and smacked the cast iron skillet down on the range for no apparent reason making her gray curls jiggle.

Ezmeralda Gutierrez was dark, with a Roman nose and black, almond-shaped eyes. Her body mass was equal to his and Aunt Flo's times two.

He smiled at Aunt Flo. He walked over to the range. "Is there anything I can do to help?"

She glared at him but he hugged her anyway. "How are you, Ezmeralda? And how is Danilo?"

Danilo was her husband whom she had married with much pomp and circumstance two years previously. Danilo had once been Major Ochoa of the Dirección de Inteligencia; the Cuban KGB.

She softened the glare a bit. "Fine. Now, help! Make toast. I know you can do that."

"Indeed I can." He winked at Aunt Flo who smiled.

"Wait! Jennifer had her baby."

Ezmeralda spun round. "So?"

"A boy. Nine pounds three ounces. I don't know his name. Yet. I will inform you when I do."

Aunt Flo said, "And Carla?"

"Feeling better but may work from home for a while."

Aunt Flo nodded but didn't comment. She was looking at

Ezmeralda who had lost her baby almost forty years earlier; her first and only pregnancy had been when she was in her mid-thirties like Carla.

He smiled his very best smile and set to work making mounds of toast for the horde in the dining room above them. And when breakfast was finished, he washed the dishes.

He finished scrubbing the last dish and went outside strolling along with the guests across the lawn.

Aunt Flo's property was mostly wooded and bounded on the east by the Pocomoke River.

The dock was empty and he sat at the end and dipped his feet in the water. It was a bit chilly still. The river flowed serenely south; on the banks and in the shallow depths, bald cypress trees squatted.

The water lapping at their odd, flaring bases was stained brown from the tannic acid in their needles and bark.

The sun was shining brightly, and the temperature was probably eighty. It would be very nice to kayak with Cory, but not by himself.

He got to his feet and walked back to the house. The kitchen was empty, and he ran up the stairs and down the hall to the front of the house.

He knocked on Aunt Flo's parlor door. "Aunt Flo?"

"Come in, Gabriel." She smiled at him "Come sit beside me and tell me what's wrong."

He almost told her everything Thorvaldsen related, but he stopped himself. "I'm just tired, Aunt Flo. Jennifer has been out for a month and Carla for almost that long. And everyone has pitched in to get the work done, but it's a lot."

He smiled. "And Jennifer put me in charge."

Aunt Flo nodded. "Of course, Dear. Why wouldn't she?"

He would suspect sarcasm if he heard that from anyone else. "Right. I am trustworthy and diligent."

"And?"

"But she didn't tell me I was in charge. Something about me freaking out if I knew."

Aunt Flo smiled. "How long was it before you realized,

Gabriel?"

"Mere minutes."

More smiling.

"It might have been a week or so."

"And did you freak out?"

He smiled his very best smile. "Just a little. But then I wanted to fire Chatterjee but Paul told me I couldn't without calling Jennifer first."

Aunt Flo giggle-cackled. "Jennifer knows you very well, Gabriel."

"Maybe yes, maybe no. And on top of all the work I'm doing...and I'm shouldering most of the burden, Aunt Flo...Cory had to go to Costa Rica with his parents."

"At this time of year?"

"Right. His mother told him that their house down there had burned to the ground which was an exaggeration. He asked me to come down, but I don't think I can unless Carla comes back."

"She's six months? And she's having problems?"

"Going on seven. I think? No idea what type of problem but Harry was off somewhere, and I had to rush her to the hospital, but the doctor let her go home after a few days."

"You have had a lot of excitement, Gabriel."

"I know!" He sat there trying not to let errant thoughts zip through his brain. "I think I'll go take a nap, Aunt Flo."

"Go ahead, Dear."

"But maybe I can take you and Ezmeralda out to dinner? And Danilo, if he's around?"

"That would be very nice. I'll call, Ezmeralda."

And he ran up to the turret bedroom on the third floor which had been his since he'd come to live with Aunt Flo twenty years earlier.

He took his boots off and lay down.

He was telling himself that Aunt Flo would only worry if she knew about the Thorvaldsen affair when he fell asleep.

Saturday
5:00 pm

He might have slept right through dinner if his phone hadn't rung. The phone was baffled as to the identity of the caller, but he answered anyway.

Brunetti said, "What is it, Gabriel."

He sat up in bed. "Thanks for calling me back. I hate to bother you." He heard music in the background. It was polka music unless he was very much mistaken.

Nadia Brunetti had dark eyes in a narrow, elliptical face framed with long black hair. He could imagine her with Italian opera playing in the background. Cory used "Va, pensiero" for her ringtone. But not polka music.

Darth Vader's leitmotif would also work but definitely not polka music.

"Gabriel?"

"Still here. Sorry."

"What is it?"

"I may have gotten myself into something."

She made a sound best described as a smothered snicker. "Just tell me."

"Well, I need to know if a man calling himself Special Agent Aronson of the FBI is in fact one of your colleagues?"

"I can check, Gabriel, but why has he approached you?"

"It has to do with Nigerian pirates, a dead captain and first mate, a pair of fake Taiwanese, and a man calling himself Chinedum Onyewu, who also claims to be the Second Secretary of

119

the Nigerian Embassy. In New York."

Of course he couldn't see her but he was pretty sure Brunetti was smiling.

"Give me all that again; slowly and with details."

So he did his best to organize his thoughts.

When he was done, she said, "That was the SS Kerkyra? And the first mate was Whalen?"

"Right. You could call Detective Fowler of the PPD about Whalen. I don't know if Aronson took the case or left it with Fowler."

She said, "And Steven Bradley, one of our crime scene techs, brought you in on the disappearance of Lars Thorvaldsen?"

"He did. And his mother, Susan Bradley."

She was silent for a while. "I'll look into this, Gabriel. Don't speak to anyone about any of this."

"Okay. Cory is in Costa Rica with his parents so I don't want to bother him." And Cory would yell at him anyway.

"So you bothered me instead?"

"After careful consideration, I thought this required the discretion and finesse of upper management."

She laughed. "And don't go babbling to that great-aunt of yours either."

"I won't. Wait. Why did you mention her?"

"Because you're in her house, Bergeron."

He looked at his phone; the traitorous chips were shouting his location to all the world.

"I won't. And Aronson?"

"Especially him. Don't speak to him until I know more."

And she was gone.

Back to her polka music? There was surely a story there, and he was trying to envision Brunetti polka dancing when his phone chimed.

It was a text message from Cory: "Bornheimer has lead. Flying back to US. Out of touch for few days." With smiley faces.

So he'd left his parents in Costa Rica? But maybe Judd was with them to help with the clean up? He hit Cory's number, but it went to voicemail.

He had so been wanting to help Cory build something again, but on the other hand, the rainy season in Costa Rica might not be fun.

He would have to see if Aunt Flo needed a gazebo or something and get Cory to help.

He ran down to the second floor bathroom, washed his face, and ambled innocently to Aunt Flo's parlor.

Aunt Flo was looking at him. Brunetti was not the boss of him, and he could tell Aunt Flo anything he wanted to. And he had to find out how to make his phone un-trackable? Would taking the battery out do that? If that was possible?

Aunt Flo shook her head. "Tell me everything, Gabriel."

"You don't have to worry, Aunt Flo."

She held up a paper-thin hand. "Ezmeralda will want to hear this too."

Ezmeralda was also shaking her head, gray curls thrashing, eyes flashing like a summer storm. "Again?"

"I know. I don't know why it keeps happening?"

"Nosy!"

"I resent that. Well, I would but it's true. And I seem to have gotten a certain reputation."

Aunt Flo said, "Tell us the whole story, Gabriel."

"Well, I was working, and Steve Bradley came to see me. I don't think I told you about him? He works for the FBI as a crime scene tech, and we met on the Frisian thing...after Sieta and Wout and Kees kidnapped me."

Aunt Flo glared at him "I remember, Gabriel. And this Bradley came to see you?"

"Yes, and his mother Susan. And they implored me to find this guy."

Ezmeralda and Aunt Flo exchanged looks.

"His name is Lars Thorvaldsen, aka 'Duke', and he had gone missing. This was in early April... a month ago. He was Susan's boyfriend and had become a father-figure for Steve after his putative father died. They were both upset and worried about Duke so I agreed to look through his house...he lives across the street from Susan and Steve...just to see if I could find a clue as to where or why he'd disappeared."

He could just omit Whalen, but Aunt Flo would know. She said, "And it went wrong at the very beginning."

"Well, we found the body of First Mate Clive Whalen in Duke's bathtub. Whalen had worked on the SS Kerkyra, a merchant ship, bound from Hamburg to Nigeria."

Aunt Flo said, "I don't understand, Dear?"

"Well, you see Duke was the second mate on the SS Kerkyra. Which may have gotten taken over by pirates in the Gulf of Guinea. And Whalen and the captain had been held by the pirates for ransom. Duke had piloted the ship into port and then flown home as fast as he could. And Whalen had followed him after escaping from the pirates. Or being released? I'm not too clear about that part."

Aunt Flo and Ezmeralda were staring at him.

"But I called the police and Cory. Because Cory was my alibi for the time when Whalen was murdered. And I promised Cory I wouldn't get involved in anything to do with Thorvaldsen."

Ezmeralda said, "But you have broken your promise!"

"Not I! Really. I have resisted everything but it's been hard."

Aunt Flo arched an almost invisible eyebrow. "Explain 'everything' for me, Gabriel."

"That would be visits from a Special Agent Aronson, a large fellow call Okocha, a Mr. Ma and Mr. Chen, who claim to be Taiwanese but aren't, and lastly his Excellency Chinedum Onyewu, the Second Secretary of the Embassy of the Federal Republic of Nigeria."

Aunt Flo took a moment. "And what did they want?"

"Ah! Lars Thorvaldsen."

Ezmeralda said, "And what did you tell all these people?"

"That I didn't know where he was, and that I was not looking for him, and hoped never to see him." He shook his head. "But I'm not sure they believed me."

Monday
11:00 am

He had told Aunt Flo and Ezmeralda everything about the whole Thorvaldsen mess, and he was pretty sure they believed that he was sincere about not getting involved.

They had gone out to dinner.

He had done nothing at all for most of Sunday except go for a ten mile run, which wasn't so much fun without Cory.

And he had come to work and hadn't given a single thought to Thorvaldsen for hours. He had talked to Jennifer about her possibly hinky client and been given a tentative okay to dig deeper.

And he was doing that like a happy terrier when the elevator dinged. He was going to disable that bell.

Of course, it had been ding-donging merrily all morning, but he felt a sudden shadow pass over him.

Which was Dana standing behind him. "A client, Gabe."

He spun and stopped.

Special Agent Aronson was smiling at him. He hadn't heard back from Brunetti. Shit.

Dana hadn't seen Aronson the first time so he had a good shot at passing him off as a client. He had no idea what she'd made of Secretary Onyewu, but she hadn't told Jennifer.

Dana was staring at him so he got to his feet, smiling madly, and ushered Aronson into the conference room.

"What?"

"Tell me all about your recent visitors, Gabriel."

"No."

Aronson looked disappointed. "Why not. I thought we were friends, and you would keep me abreast of developments?"

"I talked to Brunetti."

Aronson smiled a very nasty smile. "So did I. She was supposed to call you. Why don't you give her a ring?"

He had been hoping that Brunetti would make Aronson disappear but that didn't seem to be the way it was playing out. He wondered why?

He dialed. There was a fair amount of clicking but Brunetti answered. "Hello, Gabriel."

"Hi there. I have a visitor."

"I'm sure you do. Aronson is FBI." She sounded appalled at the thought. He was sure her lip was curling. "In Counterespionage. Okocha is an inspector in the Nigerian police seconded to their embassy in New York. Chinedum Onyewu is a Nigerian businessman and politician. I have no information about Chen and Ma."

"So what do I do?"

"I can't say."

Which was passing strange. "Because?" Aronson was smirking again. "Because the case belongs to the Dark Prince?"

She laughed. "What is it you say, Gabriel? 'Just so'?"

"That is what I say. So you aren't telling me to work with him?"

"No."

"Or even suggesting it?"

"I have to go, Gabriel. Please don't call me again about this."

And she was gone. He looked at his phone. "Well shiver me timbers and shower me with pieces of eight."

He looked at Aronson.

Aronson smiled a slightly less triumphant smile. "So let's go over your visitors."

"Which ones?"

"All of them."

"Don't you have the whole place under video surveillance?"

Cute little smile. "Not the whole place."

"Okay. I guess. But after this meeting, I want you to take a hike and take your spies and bugs with you."

"Spies? Has someone been telling tales?"

"No! Absolutely not." He shook his head. "Okay. Inspector Okocha stopped by. Asking about Lars Thorvaldsen."

"I suspected he would." Smug smile and eye twinkle.

"And then two gentlemen who were pretending to be Taiwanese showed up, They said they were Chen Shui-bian and Ma Ying-jeou but those names were obviously fake."

Smug smile drained away, and eye twinkle morphed into something scary. "Why did they come here, Gabriel?"

"Don't you already know?"

Aronson did not. Which was interesting.

The Dark Prince said, "Tell me how you know they weren't who they said they were?"

"I have a friend who said they were from northern China, and Ma spoke a Beijing dialect favored by the well-connected. As for the names, anyone would know they weren't former presidents of Taiwan." Of course he hadn't but Aronson didn't need to know that.

"What friend?" Aronson frowned. "Carla Wong?"

"That's need to know."

Aronson managed to look very, very dangerous without moving a muscle. "I'm not amused, Bergeron."

"You and Queen Victoria. Get over it. I say again: take your spies and get ye hence." He needed silver bullets and garlic and a crucifix.

Aronson smiled. "Let's not have a falling out. What did they want?"

"Well, they wanted me not to look for Thorvaldsen. Financial incentives might be forthcoming if I heeled. And they knew that Inspector Okocha had been here."

"They told you they were looking for Thorvaldsen?"

"Ma did. I think Mr. Ma's well shaped skull is largely empty of brain cells."

Aronson smiled. "And how did Chen react to that?"

"He wasn't happy but he didn't seem able to do anything

about it."

"And is that it?"

The special agent knew it was not.

"And Second Secretary Onyewu of the Nigerian Embassy honored us by his presence. But you knew that?"

"What did he say?"

"He might be able to lay his hands on two hundred grand for the current location of one Lars Thorvaldsen."

Aronson was looking at him. "And do you know where he is?"

He shut his eyes and shook his head. "I do not know where he is. I have never even seen this man. I am exceedingly sorry that I was ever stupid enough to step foot in his accursed house."

Aronson nodded. Whether he believed him was another matter.

Aronson said, "One thing. Onyewu is not the second secretary. Or a diplomat. He was granted some sort of attaché status; just enough to confer diplomatic immunity."

"Right. So does Inspector Okocha also have diplomatic immunity?"

"Possibly."

"So what is Onyewu? If he isn't a diplomat?"

"A politician. With fingers in many pies and some interesting associates."

"Chen and Ma?" Aronson just smiled at him. "Does Onyewu have any pirate type associates?"

"Unlikely but not impossible. He has offices in Port Harcourt."

"Right. I have to get back to work."

Aronson stood up and shook his hand. "What will you do next?"

He shook his head. "You are just as thick as Chinedum Onyewu. I am not going to do anything."

Aronson nodded and smiled. "Why change what has worked so well in the past."

And he was out the conference room door.

Brunetti had cast him adrift on a parlous sea infested with

pirates and spies and a smirky FBI agent.

This too would pass. Maybe?

But he wasn't going to do anything or talk to anyone. If this mess didn't go away before Cory got back, he would have to tell him.

He called Aunt Flo. "News. Brunetti tells me that Aronson is indeed FBI, and that Okocha is an inspector in the Nigerian police."

She said, "Please stay out of this, Gabriel."

"I am doing my very best."

He didn't tell her that Aronson was in Counterespionage.

And he realized he hadn't told the special agent that Ma had called Thorvaldsen a thief. He probably should have?

Monday
5:00 pm

He was sitting in Stella's cubicle, and they had finished going over Jennifer's clients. Stella had them well in hand.

"Everything looks good to me, Stella. Even Smethhurst-Gillin. Have they called you?"

She nodded. "Twice today. But I think I calmed them down."

"Excellent. Just hold on until Jennifer gets back."

She smiled. "Oh, I don't mind."

Stella was looking at him funny. A new photo had appeared; it did not feature a canine though the subject did have lots of fluffy, brown hair and winsome teeth.

The smiling, vigorous, young man also had big, green eyes.

Stella was fiddling with the photo again.

He could take a hint...if it was really hammered home. "So who's that, Stella?"

Stella gave him a coy smile. "That's my nephew, Aaron. Isn't he handsome?"

"He is."

"You'd like him, Gabriel. And I'm sure he'd like you."

Which meant that Aaron was gay. And would be mortified if he knew his aunt was trying to fix him up.

"I'm sure. He looks like a sterling fellow. Okay. I have to get back to work, Stella. I'm expecting a call from Cory."

She smiled. "He left on one of his cases a month ago, didn't he?"

"Not quite that long. And we talk. And his job's important."

She smiled sympathetically. "I'm sure it is but you're all alone."

He gave her his third best smile and didn't kick her in the shins. He walked back to his cubicle and sat at his desk.

He was not quite shaking with anger. He picked up Cory's photo and studied it. He loved Cory, and Cory loved him, but he had a job which he also loved. More than Gabriel Bergeron?

He wasn't going to think about that. And Stella's nephew looked like a sheep dog.

He took a few cleansing breaths and was able to get back to work.

Stella had left a few minutes later.

And now it was almost 6:00 pm, and he was "alone, alone, all, all alone, alone on a wide wide sea!" Well, he was in his cubicle and a goodly number of nautical miles from the sea but the office was empty.

He put the final touches on some forms for one of Jennifer's clients, and now he could go home well satisfied with the day's labors. He shut off his computer and took the elevator to the lobby.

Neither Chase nor the rattish delinquent who worked nights were at the security desk.

But the doors weren't locked. Should he call Chase to tell him? He tried but the call went to voicemail.

He stepped out into the gloom. The clouds were thick enough to blot out the sun, but it wasn't dark enough for the street lights to flicker on. A black van was idling at the curb a few car lengths down the street toward the parking garage.

Andy had a van like that but it wasn't his; this van had no windows on the side.

He stopped.

He had a very bad feeling; something akin to what a distant ancestor might have felt upon scenting a leopard circling his tree. He was turning around when two guys in Ninja black erupted from the van.

He may have sprinted back inside. Chase was still AWOL

He couldn't lock the door; he punched the elevator button

savagely, but the guys were entering the lobby.

He ran down the long hall. The door to the stairwell was locked. He may have said bad words as he continued to the boiler room door.

If it was locked, he was screwed. Well, he had his Glock but there were two of them, and he had seen the flash of pistols in their hands as they'd come into the lobby.

The door wasn't locked.

The place was dungeon dark. One fluorescent light bulb was humming and flickering as if it were not long for this world.

He hid behind the second boiler and tore open his briefcase to get his Glock.

He chambered a bullet and set himself. He took a deep breath and held it.

The door was flung open; someone yelled something. A large guy was perfectly silhouetted by the hall lights.

Including the pistol in his right hand.

He slowly squeezed off a shot.

The guy screamed and cradled his right hand with his left, still standing there.

Arms grabbed the first guy and pulled him back. He fired twice more before the door slowly shut.

He waited.

No one seemed eager to barrel through the door a second time. Which was good since he was trapped. Even if he got into the alley, the gate was probably chained.

He waited some more.

He marched over to the door. It was metal sheathed and looked potentially bullet proof. He took a deep breath and pulled it open staying behind it.

Nothing.

He waited some more, holding the door open. He didn't have a hat to shove into view so he used a clipboard. Nothing.

He got on his knees and peered around the door with one eye.

The portion of the hall he could see was empty, but it zigzagged around the stairwell before running straight to the lobby.

He offered the clipboard as a potential target again.

Nothing.

He peered. The hall was empty.

He extended the Glock in front of him and walked to the lobby. It was also empty, and the black van was gone.

Walking back to the mechanical room to get his briefcase, he saw the blood on the floor. Not a lot; just drops on the worn tile.

He got his briefcase.

What was he going to do? Call the police? And what would they do? Keep him half the night, asking lots of questions, and not believing any of his answers.

Well, Vonda might. Detective Golczewski was a pal. Or Eads.

He was shaking. And cold.

Adrenaline.

He slid down the wall and sat on the floor. He couldn't think. He was taking deep breaths when he heard the elevator's ding from the lobby.

He aimed the Glock. If anybody came down the hall, they were going to regret it.

And then he heard Chase's drawl and giggling of the female variety.

He put the gun down and got to his knees. And then carefully to his feet leaning against the wall.

When he thought he wouldn't fall over, he picked up the gun and his briefcase. He shoved the gun into his belt making sure his jacket covered it and started down the hall.

"Chase?"

The talking and giggling stopped. Chase looked down the hall and spotted him coming. "Gabe?"

He just nodded.

Chase said something to his companion. A blonde young lady was exiting when he made it to the lobby.

Chase was standing by the door. "Shit. What happened to you?"

"I'm fine. Or I will be."

Chase said, "Why was the door unlocked? And where the

Hell is Doug? He came in, Gabe."

He collapsed on a bench in the lobby. He tried smiling at Chase. "Who was your friend?"

Chase sat beside him. He smiled. "That was Micaela."

"From the 5th Floor?"

More smiling. "She was helping me with my math homework."

Chase did have a text book on the security desk, but he was disheveled and flushed.

"Right. I see. And what were you helping her with?"

Chase laughed. "I like her." He stopped smiling. "Now tell me what happened to you, Bergeron?"

"Two masked guys chased me to the boiler room. They were armed. I shot the first one in the hand. They decided they didn't want to talk to me after all."

Or grab him and throw him in the back of the van. Which was an old song that he'd heard before.

Chase shook his head. "Shit. The door was open. Shit. Doug came in and said he had it."

"So you went up the fifth floor to study with Micaela. Not your fault, Chase."

"Doug went back out and left the door open? I'm going to teach him to do better if I have to twist his dumb head off." Chase looked at him. "But this is on me."

"I don't see how?"

"I could have made sure he locked the door before I went to see Micaela."

"No. This is all Doug. And the guys who chased me. And you aren't my bodyguard, Chase."

"Building security is my job."

"And you're doing better than anyone who ever worked here before. Hands down."

Chase said, "Are you calling the police?"

"I don't know. I'm trying to think."

Chase got up and locked the door and went down the hallway. He came back. "There's blood on the floor. Two slugs in the wall outside the boiler room."

"Yeah. After I shot his hand, I fired twice more to discourage his friend from coming through the door."

"I'd say you did that." Chase smiled. "You're not too shabby with the Glock, are you?"

"I'm fair. Cory's better."

"So?"

He had to call somebody. He pulled out his phone and dialed Aronson. He didn't know if he'd even answer.

But he did. "Gabriel? Is there a problem?"

"Yes. I'm at the Mahr Building. I don't suppose you could drop by? Doesn't have to be tonight. I'll save a blood sample for you."

Aronson said, "Are you hurt?"

"Nope. Some guys tried to grab me."

"Are you secure now?"

"Moderately."

"Stay there. We're on the way."

"Okay. See you soon."

Chase looked at him. "Aronson. He's FBI."

Chase nodded. "You told me."

"Right. But I verified that he really, truly is FBI." Not a nice FBI agent but FBI.

Chase nodded and sat on the bench beside him.

"You could go home?"

Chase smiled at him. "Oh, Hell no. I wouldn't miss this for the world."

He smiled at Chase. "Then I suggest you tuck your shirt in, don your tie, and wipe the lipstick from your cheek."

Monday
7:00 pm

The first person to arrive was not Aronson.

He said his name was Collins, and he did not want to show his badge so they didn't let him in.

Mr. Collins was vexed.

He was wearing a gray t-shirt with a stretched out neck, jeans, and a thin, navy jacket. His blond hair was long and hadn't been washed for some time. He parted it on the left, and a greasy hank stretched over his head covering his right ear and giving him a lopsided look. He had little brown eyes and uneven teeth. He needed a shave too.

"I work with Aronson."

"So you say."

"He's going to be pissed."

"When he gets here, I will beg his forgiveness. Until then, I don't know you."

Collins laughed. "I've been following your dumb ass for days."

"Really? Well, kudos to you. Stellar undercover work. Where were you when the two guys jumped out of the van?"

Collins shook his head and went back to a vehicle as unprepossessing as its owner; it was a tan pickup with a rusting camper top strapped onto it.

Chase said, "Think he's really FBI?"

"Who can say? I'm going to err on the side of caution."

But Aronson arrived soon enough. He let Collins speak for

about ten seconds before holding up a hand.

He walked over to the doors. "Going to let me in, Gabriel?"

He was having serious second thoughts about calling this guy. "I suppose. Is Collins FBI?"

"He works for me, Gabriel."

Which didn't really answer the question, but he nodded to Chase who unlocked the door.

Aronson came in. He was in a suit but no tie.

He glanced at Chase. "Tell me everything that happened, Gabriel."

"This is Mr. Chase, building security."

"I know who he is. I'm waiting." Aronson was smiling but he wasn't any happier than Collins who was glaring at everyone including Aronson.

"There was a black van idling over there when I was leaving at about 6:10 pm."

Collins said, "Make and model?"

He looked at Collins. "A black, Nissan cargo van. It didn't have any windows except for the driver and passenger-side doors. And the windshield, of course."

Collins wanted to smack him or possibly shoot him. "And you didn't get a license number? Not even a partial?"

"Nope." He looked back to Aronson. "I turned around to come back inside, and two guys dressed in black from head to toe jumped out and gave chase."

And he told Aronson the rest.

Aronson said, "Why shoot for the hand?"

"I didn't want to kill him." Collins snorted. "I suppose I would have aimed center mass if they hadn't cleared out."

Aronson finally looked at Chase. "And what did you see?"

"Nothing, Sir. It was over before I came down...."

"From doing his rounds on the upper floors." Aronson didn't need to know about Micaela.

Aronson frowned. "All right. Give Collins your information, and you can go...."

Collins said, "We need fingerprints and a DNA sample."

Aronson smiled like that was a private joke between him

and Collins.

Chase squared himself and came to attention. "The night shift guard hasn't arrived, Sir, and I'm not going anywhere until he does."

Aronson shrugged. "Just stay out of the way then."

Chase took his seat behind the security desk.

Aronson said, "With me, Gabriel."

And they walked through the whole incident from lobby to boiler room. By the time they were done, two guys who made Collins look overdressed were taking blood samples and digging out the slugs he'd fired.

They found the first attacker's gun where it had slid after being smashed from his hand.

Aronson said, "You're sure you didn't see his face?"

"No. He was just a silhouette."

"So no idea who he was?"

He had been thinking about it, and it wasn't impossible that it could have been Mr. Ma. The shape had been right.

Aronson was staring at him hard, eyes willing him to comply. "Are you sure?"

"Bigger than you. Not fat. The shape was right for Mr. Ma. But that's all I can say."

Aronson exchanged a look with Collins.

He followed them back to the lobby. The crime scene techs, if that's what they were, had gone.

Chase was reading his text book.

"Night, Chase."

"Night, Gabe."

And he stepped out into the night with Aronson and Collins. It was misting and chilly.

"So what now?"

Aronson said, "What do you mean?"

"Are you going to try to find the guys?"

"Of course, but we don't have much to go on."

"You have his DNA and his gun, and maybe his fingerprints on the gun."

Collins said, "Which will be worth nothing if he's not in

one of the databases."

"Right."

Collins said, "We don't even know if this is connected with our case."

He looked at the guy. "Of course it is. Wait. What is your case?"

But he just smirked. "This could be somebody else you pissed off."

He looked at Aronson who was getting into his big, black Ford SUV. "You don't believe that, do you?"

Aronson shrugged.

"So I'm working with you on the case now?"

Aronson smiled at him, face lit my the dome light. "No, Gabriel."

"No?"

He closed the door and the light went out, but he powered down the window.

His baritone voice came out of the dark. "I don't know what Brunetti allowed you to believe, but you're a civilian and have no standing whatsoever in my investigation."

He stood there as the rain started to pelt down.

Aronson said, "But call me if there are further developments."

"I just want this to go away."

"Then start asking questions and find this Thorvaldsen. Just a suggestion."

And the special agent pulled off, leaving him standing there with rain running down his face.

Collins was about his size but pudgy and out of shape and was smirking at him again. He was seriously tempted to see if he could rearrange his nose and mouth.

Collins stepped back. "Easy, Bergeron."

He was heading for his pitiful truck. It occurred to him that Cory sometimes looked as grungy as Collins when he was undercover.

"So what am I?"

Collins slammed the door and started the engine. "To us?

You're bait, Bergeron. Live bait. Or maybe of no further use to us at all? It's unclear at this point." And he pulled off smirking again.

He didn't empty his clip into Collins. Or his camper.

He should have called Vonda. Or Eads. Even Oscuro would have been a better choice.

He was in deep shit.

He called Cory.

And got his voicemail.

He certainly wasn't sharing any of this with Aunt Flo.

Tuesday
8:00 am

He had walked to the parking garage and retrieved his Jeep Glock in hand. He had been mentally daring anybody to jump out at him.

He had regained a little perspective by the morning, and he may have slunk to his Jeep keeping to the shadows. But no one had approached him.

Cory hadn't called him back.

Chase was at his post. "Hi, Gabe."

"Hi to you too. Have you been here all night?" He looked remarkably bright-eyed and bushy-tailed but he was young and a Marine.

"No. Doug crawled in a couple of hours later after I called him a dozen times. He said he went out to grab some food. When he got back, he heard the gun shots and took off."

Chase smiled, "But we had a little discussion, and Dougie promised to do better." Chase stopped smiling. "I'm going to keep an eye on him from now on, Gabe."

"I appreciate that, Chase." But that wasn't Chase's job. Maybe he should just leave earlier? While Chase was still on duty.

"So what are those guys going to do? Aronson?"

He shrugged. "A good question. I'm thinking nothing."

And he took the elevator skyward.

He made coffee. He sat at his desk sighing audibly, but Harry and Carla weren't there to hear him; not yet. But Harry was supposed to come in.

So he tried to look at the elevator with a hopeful expression when it dinged at 8:35 am.

Harry, Carla, Winnie, and Yvonne debouched.

He may have shut his eyes to blink back tears. He was smiling madly at them as Winnie and Yvonne guided Carla to her chair.

He hugged Harry. "Welcome back!" He leaned over Carla and patted her shoulders. "And an extra welcome back to you!"

He even hugged Winnie who was taken aback but he didn't care.

Carla said, "Get off my mother, Bergeron! I'm not staying long. Just so you know."

Yvonne was too light on her feet or he would have hugged her too.

"No. I understand. How are you feeling? Much better I hope? Is there anything I can get you?"

Carla glared at him as she patted her nimbus of black hair. "No! Why are you so hyper? Where's Chatterjee? And how are my clients?"

"Your clients are excellent. Chatterjee and I have seen to that." Where was young Dhruva? "I'm sure Chatterjee will be with us momentarily."

The intensity of his smile was almost certainly scary, but he couldn't help it. He was exhausted from working long hours...well, long for him...and getting shot at wasn't the pick-me-up that some people might think.

Winnie waved at Paul who strode over exuding a startling amount of manliness drawn from some well that had been capped decades earlier.

"Hi, Winnie."

"Hi, Paul."

"Tea?"

She smiled at him, and they skipped to the breakroom hand-in-hand. Well, it was implied.

Carla and Yvonne were giving them a look. It wasn't exactly a glare. Concern? For their mother?

A wisp of a smile crossed Harry's face. "So Jennifer put

you in charge?" Big smile. "And didn't tell you?"

"Yes and no! It's been Hell, Harry. Pure Hell."

Carla was gazing at her monitor raptly. "Man up, Bergeron. Now be quiet so I can focus. And find Chatterjee for me."

"Yes, your majesty. By your command, your highness."

Carla gave him a surprised look. "Are you okay, Gabe?"

"Sure." Harry was looking at him too. "Right as rain."

As luck would have it, Chatterjee appeared and distracted them. As much as he wanted to tell them everything, they had problems enough.

He smothered a sigh. What was he going to do about Aronson and Thorvaldsen et al?

He was going to get to work.

Winnie and Paul were laughing in the breakroom and sipping Gunpowder tea.

He realized that Yvonne was standing next to him. She was watching them. He spun around. "Yvonne?"

She smiled a faint smile which seemed the best she could do. "Mr. Bergeron, may I come back to see you? Around 11:00 am?"

Carla said something in Chinese.

Yvonne said, "About a tax matter."

"Of course." He experienced a Level 5, pseudo-client twitch. He looked at Carla but she and Chatterjee were hunched over her computer. Winnie and Yvonne departed.

He went back to work. The task was all. Nothing else existed: not mean FBI agents or Nigerians or Chinese...other Chinese or Chinese-Americans...non-Wong Chinese.

Carla made a sound, half groan, half squeak, He spun. "Carla?"

Carla was looking very tired.

"What, Bergeron?"

"Shouldn't you go home, Carla?" Harry spun around. "I'll drive you if Harry's tied up?"

Carla was patting her belly. She shook her head. "I'm fine." She grabbed her phone and had a short conversation in Chinese.

And presently Yvonne and Francine, Carla's older sisters

emerged from the elevator with two younger Chinese-American ladies.

They all locked onto him. He wasn't scared; he had enough bullets to shoot them all.

Carla said, "Let's go into the conference room, Gabe."

She was standing right behind him. When he had been more robust, he would have shrieked and jumped into the air.

"Okay."

And Carla led the way. He looked at Harry who avoided his gaze and appeared rooted to his chair.

They all sat.

Carla said, "You've met Yvonne and Francine. These two..." Carla smiled. "...are the twins, the babies of the family."

They looked alike but not twin alike; fraternal twins?

Carla said, "This is Hui-ting." She patted her sister's arm.

Hui-ting had an oval face like Carla's, but her hair was long and brown and straight. Her eyes were lovely but not the equal of Carla's. She was wearing a casual yellow dress with long sleeves.

Hui-ting smiled. "It's a pleasure to meet you, Mr. Bergeron."

"Nice to meet you too. Please call me Gabe."

Carla looked across the table at the other twin. "The one with the hair is Hui-wen."

She should have said "the one without the hair" since Hui-wen's hair was shorter than his and spiky and mostly black. It reminded him of Martin's hair, the head barista at CoffeeXtra, or Astrid's, his girlfriend, except for the random patches of purple.

Her face was oval like Hui-ting's but her mouth and eyes were smaller. She was wearing a white t-shirt and what looked like gray flannel plus-fours; pants that ended four inches below the knee for no particular reason and hadn't been fashionable in a century.

"It's nice to meet you, Hui-wen. And call me Gabe."

She gave him side eye, a grimace-smile, and a nod.

Yvonne sighed.

He tried smiling at all the Wongs as he scanned their faces for some clue as to what the Hell was going on; no joy. But he did note that they all had Winnie's nose.

Carla nodded to Yvonne, who said, "As you've probably guessed, Mr. Bergeron, we aren't here to talk about accounting." Weak smile. "Carla said you would help us."

Carla looked at her older sister. "Carla said no such thing. Carla said that you...that we could ask him."

He closed his eyes and counted to ten, but they were all still there when he opened them. "Something about your mother?"

Yvonne drew on energy reserved for dire emergencies and gave him a full smile. "Yes."

He may have glared at Carla who looked abashed for the first time since he'd met her. "What exactly, Yvonne?"

But Francine said, "Is this a good idea? Really? And what is he going to charge?"

He smiled at beautiful Francine. "My standard fee is ten thousand dollars plus expenses."

They all looked nonplussed except for Hui-wen of the purple spiky hair; a smile flitted across her stolid features.

And Carla, who said, "He's kidding."

"Am I, Carla? Am I?"

"Yes, Gabe, you are. Go ahead, Yvonne."

"Our father died fifteen years ago, and our mother has been alone since then. She was only forty-eight at the time."

Carla said, "She's dated a few men over the years."

Yvonne said, "One asked her to marry him."

Hui-ting said, "He was a very nice man."

Hui-wen finally spoke. "You don't remember him."

"Do too." Hui-wen shook her spiky head.

Yvonne said, "We believe it is because of her first love."

Francine said, "That's silly. She loved our father."

Carla said, "Of course, she did, but she loved Gavin Sommer first. He was in her class in high school, Gabe. He was very handsome...from the yearbook photos."

Hui-wen said, "And very blond."

Yvonne said, "That had nothing to do with it, Hui-wen."

Hui-wen was smiling at her sisters.

Yvonne said, "He asked her to marry him on the night they

graduated."

He looked at the sisters. "And she said no?"

Yvonne said, "Our family was very traditional, Mr. Bergeron. She couldn't marry him without her parents permission."

"And they said no?"

Yvonne nodded.

Spiky Hui-wen smiled. "Grandmother Wu said no! She called him a white devil."

Which caused a ruckus that began in English and spilled over into Chinese. Yvonne, Francine, and Carla were yelling at Hui-wen who was laughing and yelling back.

Her twin, Hui-ting, just fiddled with her long, brown hair looking profoundly uncomfortable.

The tumult eased eventually. Carla said, "You have no idea what Grandmother Wu said or thought, Hui-wen. You were a year old when she died!"

Hui-wen sat there looking proud of herself. "I bet she did. Why else would they have forbidden her to marry Gavin?"

Yvonne said, "Because they were too young, and he had no job. And he was poor." Yvonne looked at him. "His father had died, and the family was almost destitute, Mr. Bergeron."

Hui-wen smiled. "I prefer my version."

Hui-ting said, "Behave. I didn't have to call you." Hui-wen frowned.

He raised a hand before Hui-wen could rouse the rabble again. "What do you want me to do? And is this the same job Winnie started to talk about?"

Yvonne nodded. "Yes. She seems to have changed her mind...again, but we want you to find out what happened to Gavin so she can get on with her life."

Carla said, "He disappeared after graduation."

Yvonne said, "We think she looked for him...after father died."

Francine shook her head. "She wouldn't have."

Hui-wen said, "Why not? Father was gone, Francine. She deserved to be happy back then, and she deserves to be happy now." She had an impish smile on her face. "I want to see this Paul stud before we go."

Amid the bedlam, he left the conference room. He also considered leaving the building or possibly the continent.

But he was still standing around when they all trooped out.

Hui-wen was smiling at him. "Which one is he, Dude?"

Carla was glaring at him, but Paul came drifting out of the breakroom, and he may have nodded at Mr. Hearne as he sailed back to his cubicle.

Francine grabbed Hui-wen's arm to keep her from following.

Carla said, "I'm going home, Gabe. His full name was Gavin Alexander Sommer, Jr.; he was born on April 2, 1963, in Philadelphia."

She gave him Gavin's parents address and handed him a grainy enlargement of his yearbook photo. And with her sisters forming a phalanx around her, she proceeded to the elevator.

Nobody seemed to care that he hadn't actually agreed to find this Gavin. He went back to his desk and sat down. He looked over at Harry. "Wow."

Harry snorted. "Welcome to my world." Harry spun in his chair. "Though usually I don't have all five of them together. Hui-wen is a firecracker, isn't she?"

Agitator was closer. He waved Gavin's photo at Harry. "Yeah. Why are they asking me to track down Gavin? Not that I can."

Harry rolled over for a tête-à-tête. "I'm sorry, Gabe. Carla likes Paul, and she thinks Winnie does too, but Yvonne seems to feel that Winnie won't seal the deal until she knows that Gavin is unavailable."

"Seal the deal? No, don't explain. But she hasn't seen this guy in how many years?"

"Carla figures he disappeared in 1982."

"Shit, Harry. Maybe he got a job in Texas and has twelve blond children? Or he became a merchant seaman and is living in Tasmania. Or he died in 1982! And his body was buried in a landfill in Jersey!"

Harry held up his hands. "Don't yell at me, Bergeron."

"You have to tell Carla that this is hopeless."

Harry laughed and laughed. "The only things I say to Carla are 'yes, dear' and 'what can I do' but mostly I keep my head down." Harry was looking at him. "What's up with you?"

"You don't want to know." He wanted to tell Harry so bad, but the guy looked exhausted.

And he had too much work to do.

And he was adopting an ostrich strategy toward all things Thorvaldsen until he could think of a better way to cope.

Tuesday Noon

Harry had asked him to go to lunch. And since his Glock was fully loaded, and he had three extra clips ruining the drape of his suit, he had felt confident enough to go with him to CoffeeXtra.

The coffee shop was on a corner, and two walls of floor-to-ceiling glass let in an eye-searing amount of light on lovely May days such as this one.

Billy, the owner of CoffeeXtra, was behind the counter; his motley crew of baristas, Martin, Selena, Astrid et al, were not in view.

Billy was in point of fact Dr. Vilim Stanko, PhD, who had been known to author papers on differential geometry. He wasn't quite clear what that was, and he was happy to leave it that way. Apparently, it was possible to be a doctor of mathematics and to starve to death, hence Billy's coffee shop ownership.

Billy was looking sad, forlorn, doleful. Which was perfectly normal. He was tall, skinny, extremely hairy and had big brown eyes; only two of them. If he'd had six, there would have been a definite spider vibe about him.

"Hi, Billy."

"Gabe. The usual?"

"Sure."

After Harry ordered they grabbed a table in the front half of the shop. Harry was staring at him. "What, Baldacci?"

"After we get our food."

If Harry was going to be weird, he would just go back to

work. Billy was filling their order. He may have stared at Billy as intently as Harry was staring at him.

Monroe?

Billy was bringing their order. He alternated between wearing tank tops and shorts and gorgeous, embassy-worthy suits for reasons never made clear.

He was currently in a deep burgundy number with a cream stripe, a cream shirt, a paler burgundy silk tie figured with black fleur-de-lis, and four silver rings. The suit hid his furriness except for the backs of his hands.

Billy set their food on the little table. "Something else, Gabe?"

"How are you, Billy? How are Martin and Selena and Astrid?"

"Okay. They're off today." Billy was looking at him.

"And how is Penelope? Heard from her recently?"

Billy sat down, ignoring his customers. "What's up, Gabe?"

"Nothing! Just making polite conversation. Is she around?"

Billy shook his head and went back to work.

Harry said, "Okay, Bergeron, tell me what the Hell is going on with you. Why do you need to find Penelope? And why are you so jumpy?"

"I'm not jumpy!"

Harry smiled at him; Harry had a great smile. "Gabe, you were looking behind you the whole way here."

Which was true. He'd been looking for Collins or Ma. The more he thought about it, the more certain he was that it had been Ma who had tried to grab him.

Harry was staring at him. "Wait a second! What's that bulge?"

"Just never you mind my bulge, Baldacci."

But Harry grabbed the lapel of his jacket and looked for himself. "Shit, Gabe! You're wearing the Glock!"

He had found one of Cory's shoulder holsters. If he needed the Glock, he wanted it to be at hand and not in his briefcase.

The Glock felt funny against his ribs, and the shoulder straps were uncomfortable, but maybe he'd get used to them?

"It's nothing."

"Is Cory still in Costa Rica?"

"No. But he's out of touch."

"And he has no idea that you've gotten yourself in deep shit, does he?"

"Not really."

"Tell me everything, Bergeron."

"It's better if I don't."

But Harry was shaking his head. "Tell me."

And he did. Maybe he shouldn't have but it all sort of spilled out once he'd started.

Harry looked shocked. "So nobody knows about this except for this Aronson jerk?"

"No. Well, except for the Nigerians and the fake Taiwanese. And Aunt Flo and Ezmeralda."

"You should call Cory."

"I tried. He isn't picking up. He probably won't for days or weeks."

"So call his boss."

"That's the last resort, Harry."

Harry was shaking his head again. "And we aren't there yet? With armed guys trying to grab you off the street?"

"They won't try that again." He had no idea. "And I'll just wait this out. It isn't like I'm going to get more involved or anything crazy like that."

"Gabe, I've heard you say shit exactly like that before."

Which was absolutely true. He sipped his coffee but it was cold. He trotted to the counter where Billy was standing with a vacant look on his face. "Can you nuke this for me?"

But Billy poured it out and gave him fresh.

"Thanks, Billy."

Billy's big brown eyes locked onto him and were boring in. "You need to speak to Mom, don't you?"

"No." He gave Billy his very best smile; he wondered if Billy still had a thing for him? "I might need to speak to Monroe."

Billy's eyes widened. "She doesn't know where he is."

"Okay. But she might know how to get him a message?"

Billy shook his head.

"Can you ask her?" He broke out his ultimate smile unleashed only when extinction level events were imminent. "For me?"

If he'd known he was going to use his awesome sex appeal, he would have dressed better and combed his hair. And whitened his teeth.

Billy smiled at him but by the time the light from Billy's lips reached his eyes, the smile was already gone.

"I can call her."

He may have reached over the counter and hugged Billy. "Just have her ask him to call me. I'll be eternally grateful."

Unless it all went horribly wrong.

He took his seat across from Harry. "What are you doing, Gabe?"

"Nothing."

Harry said, "I can't help you. I'd love to, but I have Carla to take care of. And I have to think of my son."

"Carla's having a boy?"

Harry nodded as his eyes and lips and cheeks united in a glorious smile.

He hugged Harry again. "Congratulations, Baldacci! And I don't want you to do anything. This will just go away if I sit tight."

They walked back to the Mahr Building.

It might. Or it might not.

He wasn't sure how Monroe was involved? Would Monroe call? Again, no idea.

Tuesday
5:00 pm

He was on his way home when his phone rang. He was praying that it was Cory but it wasn't.

"Hello?"

Bradley said, "Gabe! They've kidnapped her!"

"Her who?"

"My mother!"

"Are you sure? Why do you think that?"

"Of course, I'm sure! I just got home, and she's gone! The backdoor was kicked in, and the bastards left a note."

"Right. Have you called the police?"

"Of course!"

"Have they arrived?"

"Not yet. Can you come? Please?"

"What does the note say?"

"'Where is Lars Thorvaldsen? Tell us if you want the woman back. Be in the house tomorrow.' And that's it, Gabe. How am I suppose to tell them? I have no idea."

"I don't know, Bradley."

Bradley said, "The police are here, Gabe."

"Go talk to them."

And Bradley was gone. He kept motoring in the direction of home. He sighed and dialed Aronson's number.

And it just rang and rang.

He said bad words about Aronson as he altered course and drove across the bridge into West Philly.

He had sworn he would never come within a country mile of Thorvaldsen's house again but there it was.

And there was Officer Fuchs still tall, wide, and depressed.

Fuchs looked him over as he got out of the Jeep. "Bergeron?"

"That's me. How are you doing, Officer Fuchs?"

With a glint of schadenfreude in his tired eyes, Fuchs said, "Fowler will be tickled to see you."

"So he's here?"

Fuchs nodded toward Bradley's house. "In the back. The FBI guy coming?"

"Nope. Just me. Wait. Have you seen a Special Agent Aronson? About my size, dark, smirky?"

"They're all smirky." And Fuchs planted his rump against his patrol car ready to wait until a superior yelled at him or he expired.

Susan's row house was the end unit so he jogged around to the little backyard; a crime scene tech was dusting the busted door.

There was a covered patio with a couple of chaise lounges like Aunt Flo had. "Bradley? Detective Fowler?"

Fowler stood up, a cigarette pendant from his lips. "What the Hell are you doing here?"

"Bradley called me."

"Why?"

He shrugged. "He thought I could help."

Fowler glared at him. He tossed his cigarette on the ground and rubbed a hand down his thin face from furrowed brow to pointy chin. His well-cut, gray suit couldn't disguise how bony he was.

Fowler turned back to the patio. "What the Hell."

He was going to take that as an invitation. Bradley was sitting on the other chaise lounge. He was leaning over, and his hair had flopped into his face. His eyes were red when he looked up.

"Gabe! Thanks for coming."

Fowler sat down and fired up another cigarette. "So when did you last see Susan?"

"This morning. About 8:00 am. She was fine then."

Fowler looked at a slip of paper in an evidence bag. "And you're sure she couldn't be off shopping or gabbing with a girlfriend or off with this Thorvaldsen?"

"I'm sure. Her phone and purse and her keys are on the kitchen table. Go look. And I called all her friends while I was waiting for you."

"Relatives?"

"Uncle Brian hasn't seen her! The only other person is a cousin in Wyoming." Bradley was staring at Fowler. "What do I do now?"

"Nothing. Her picture has gone out. Every cop in the city is looking for her." The detective smiled at Bradley. "Your mom is a nice lady, and we're going to do everything we can to find her."

Bradley nodded.

Fowler was glaring at him now. "I suppose you have an alibi, Bergeron?"

He glared back. "For the whole day from 7:00 am up until Bradley called me; a dozen people can vouch for me at work. I thought you talked to Vonda?"

"I did." Fowler snorted. "Any idea what the Hell is going on here?"

"People really want to find Thorvaldsen."

Bradley said, "What people?"

So he told Bradley and Fowler about everyone who'd expressed an interest in the seaman. He sent Fowler the photos he'd taken of Inspector Okocha.

Bradley said, "Why didn't you tell me?"

"Because I didn't want to get in any deeper, and I didn't want you to get sucked in either."

Fowler was shaking his head. "Shit. Tell me about this FBI agent, Aronson."

"You haven't talked to him? He didn't take over the Whalen murder?"

Fowler said, "How do you know the name of the vic?"

"Aronson told me." Fowler was looking pissed and suspicious and put-upon. "Honest. He did. He said the guy had been the first mate on the SS Kerkyra."

"And I suppose you can contact him?"

He tried to smile but it was a poor effort. "I have a number but he didn't answer when I tried it a little while ago."

Fowler growled as he stood up. He was going to be arrested. Fowler would invent a charge if he had to.

"But you could call Nadia Brunetti of the FBI's Art Theft Team. She has an office in the Hoover Building. I talked to her about Aronson, and she checked him out."

True she had told him not to call her about Aronson again but he didn't care at this point.

"So she'll back up what you're saying?"

"Yes." He calculated his chances to be no better than one in ten. "But let me try Aronson again?"

The phone rang twice. Aronson said, "Gabriel? Developments?"

"You could say that...."

Fowler took the phone out of his hand. "This is Detective Fowler of the Philadelphia police. Identify yourself."

Fowler listened while chewing on his cigarette. "Is that right? Look I need to talk to you. Why the Hell not?"

More listening and cigarette masticating.

Fowler said, "I need to talk to you." He spit out the cigarette and was going to crush his phone. "Because Susan Bradley's been abducted, Jerk Off!"

Fowler listened for a while, and then he handed the phone back.

"Aronson?"

"Detective Fowler isn't very agreeable, is he?"

"Susan Bradley's been kidnapped!"

"Yes, he told me."

"So what are you going to do?"

"Nothing at present. I am very busy. Sorry, Gabriel, but you and Fowler are on your own."

And Aronson was gone. "Shit." Fowler was staring at him. "He said we're on our own."

"Bastard. We don't need him."

But he was pretty sure that was bravado.

Fowler looked at Bradley. "Maybe you should take a walk, Kid."

Bradley shook his head. "I have a right to hear. She's my mother, and I am FBI."

Fowler shrugged. "Any idea what's going on, Gabe?"

"I don't know. But from what Ma said...."

"The fake Taiwanese?"

"Right. He called Thorvaldsen a thief. So maybe Thorvaldsen swiped something that belonged to Ma...or to this Chinedum Onyewu...and they followed him from Nigeria?"

Fowler said, "But what were Ma and Chen doing in Nigeria? And what did the guy steal? And did he bring it back here? Or stash it over there somewhere?"

"Not a clue. Wait. Brunetti told me that Aronson is in the Counterespionage Division."

Fowler rolled his eyes to heaven. "A spy chaser? Just shoot me here and now."

Fuchs was suddenly behind them. How long had he been there? He looked at Fowler with a hand resting on his gun. "If you say so, Detective. Where do you want it?"

Fowler smiled at Fuchs. "You'd enjoy it too much. What?"

"The guys want to know if you want to monitor the landline and both cellphones?"

"Hell, yes. Bradley's and Susan's."

Fuchs nodded and stood there.

"What?"

Fuchs said, "The guys have canvassed the block and are spreading out. One old lady may have seen something."

Fowler said, "If I have to drag it out of you piece by piece, I'll shoot you!"

Fuchs looked almost happy momentarily. "She says she saw a black van parked out front. Around 2:00 pm."

He said, "Ma might be driving a black, Nissan cargo van." Fowler looked at him. "I thought I saw him outside the Mahr Building with another guy yesterday after work."

He hadn't told Fowler about the gun battle, and he wasn't

sure he should. Fowler might take his Glock. "I'm not sure about this, but his right hand may have been bandaged."

Fowler and Fuchs were staring at him. Fowler said, "Anything else, Bergeron?"

"Nothing comes to mind. So what now?"

Fowler had no idea, but he rallied. He was staring at the photo of Okocha. "So this Inspector Okocha and the other Nigerian...."

"Chinedum Onyewu."

"Yeah, him. The embassy should have numbers for them?"

"They should. If they'll give them out?"

Fowler said, "So what? I go to New York and bang on their freaking door?"

Fuchs smiled. "He hates New York."

"Lay off, Fuchs! If I really try, I can make your life more miserable than it already is."

Fuchs snorted at the empty threat.

Fowler said, "Got any photos of Ma and Chen?"

"No, sorry. I can describe them for a sketch artist?"

Fowler nodded. "First thing tomorrow." He looked at Bradley. "When the tech guys are done, I want you to stay here in case the call comes in on the landline. Somebody will stay with you."

Bradley said, "But what do I say if they call? I don't know where Duke is!"

Nobody had a good answer to that.

Wednesday Noon

He had done his best with the sketch artist, and the drawings looked sort of like Ma and Chen.

Of course, they didn't know if Susan had been abducted by them but the black van pointed that way.

Fowler had called the Nigerian embassy, but they hadn't been helpful in getting in contact with Okocha, and they had totally stone-walled him about the very existence of Chinedum Onyewu.

So Attaché Onyewu didn't want to talk to police, and his embassy was okay with that. Which didn't mean they approved of him, of course.

He had planned to lunch al desko but he had to get out of the office. So he was sitting at a table in CoffeeXtra and trying not to think about Susan and what she might be going through.

He looked at Billy. Had Billy told Penelope that he wanted to speak to Monroe?

He shook his head. Monroe wouldn't help even if they talked. But he wondered about Inspector Okocha?

He placed a call to the embassy. A lady with a lovely accent and mellifluous voice answered.

"Hello, I'm Gabriel Bergeron. I wonder if you can help me?"

"I will do my best, Sir."

"I need to speak to Inspector Okocha. I don't know his first name, but he's quite large and impressive."

There was a decided pause.

"Maybe you could just take a message for me?"

"I suppose I could do that, Sir."

"Just tell him that I need to speak to him about Susan Bradley, and it is most urgent. A person with a more dramatic flare might say it's a matter of life and death."

Miss Mellifluous said, "I have the message, Sir. May I be of further assistance?"

"No. Thank you."

"Thank you, Sir."

And he drained his cup. He wanted to help Susan and Bradley. He sauntered over to the counter. "Hi, Billy."

Billy flashed him a smile. "Hi, Gabe. Get you something else?"

"Monroe."

Billy shook his head. "I don't know where he is."

"Did you speak to your mother?"

Billy nodded, big brown eyes looking sad. Lugubrious; another word for Chase.

"Yes, Gabe. She said she'd text him. She didn't want to but she did it for me."

"Thanks, Billy. I appreciate it. Wait. So she has a number for him?"

Billy smiled. "No way. She knew you'd ask. She won't give you his number. She made that very clear."

"Right. Okay. Thanks, Billy."

Well, he would likely never hear from the rogue agent, sometime spy, whose name was certainly not Monroe, but no stone unturned.

He called Fowler. "Detective? Any news? Did they call?"

Fowler said, "Bergeron? Not now. I'm a little busy here."

And Fowler hung up on him. Was being busy a good thing? Maybe. He wandered back to work.

Wednesday
5:00 pm

Carla was working from home which was just as well because he didn't want to talk to her about this Gavin guy.

And he had helped Chatterjee with one of her more persnickety clients along with everything else on his plate.

And now it was time to go home. He washed out his mug and peered out. The clouds had massed and were launching an assault on Philly with wind and rain and the occasional flash of lightning with thunder accompaniment.

He stepped off the elevator and froze.

Inspector Okocha was glaring at Chase who was aiming his Walther PPK at the inspector's heart.

"Gabe! He's back."

"Right. I see that. I sort of asked him to come. Well, to call me anyway."

Chase glanced at him. "Say again?"

"But that doesn't mean I trust him." He pulled out his Glock and got a bead on Okocha. "It might be a good idea to wand him, Chase."

Chase smiled. "Can do."

And he relieved the inspector of his very own Glock and a knife.

Okocha shook his head; his eyes and brows drawn into attack formation. "Unnecessary."

He said, "Maybe yes, maybe no. Why don't we sit down?"

He took a bench and waved Okocha at one across the lobby.

"I feel better knowing you aren't armed. Ignoring what you could do bare-handed to us, of course. So do you know what happened to Susan Bradley?"

Lightning flashed beyond the glass walls of the lobby an instant before the thunder rattled them.

Okocha said, "Yes. When I received your message, I investigated. Is there any news?"

"Are you concerned for her?"

Okocha frowned. "Of course." He looked at Chase. "Should he be here?"

He smiled at Chase. "It's up to him."

Chase just smiled, and Okocha shrugged. "I do not know who has taken her."

Chase said, "She was kidnapped?"

He nodded. "Yesterday." He looked back to Okocha. "So it wasn't Chinedum Onyewu or someone he hired?"

"No. In Nigeria, I would suspect him immediately, but here, he knows no one."

"And just to be clear, you didn't take her?"

"No! I would not!"

"Not even if Onyewu asked you...or offered incentives?"

Okocha stood up. "I am going. I want my gun."

He said, "I had to ask. Please sit down. I have a few more questions. Please."

He sat

"Do you know why Attaché Onyewu wants to find Lars Thorvaldsen?"

He shook his head. "He would not tell me. What do you know about this?"

"He came to see me and offered me a respectable sum of money for Thorvaldsen's location. Which I don't know! Though he wouldn't believe me."

"He doesn't deal with honest people, Mr. Bergeron."

"No. I sort of gathered that. I think that Thorvaldsen stole something that may have belonged to him or that he wants."

"What?"

"No idea. Not yet. But two other men came to see me also

looking for Thorvaldsen. The stolen item might belong to them."

He had Okocha's attention.

"A Mr. Ma and a Mr. Chen."

Okocha sat back on the bench leaning against the glass wall. "And who are they?"

"I only know that they pretended to be from Taiwan but actually were from a bit farther north...from the Beijing area."

Okocha's face achieved a sculptural stillness.

"Do you know them? I think they might have Susan."

"I do not." He was looking at his large, dangerous hands. "If I knew where she was, I would tell you. Or go find her myself."

"I hoped you'd feel that way."

"What have you heard of Susan?"

"Nothing today. But I haven't been able to talk to Detective Fowler yet."

Inspector Okocha snorted. "The smoker? I fear for her if he is in charge."

"So you've seen him?"

"Yes."

"While you were watching Thorvaldsen's house?"

Okocha said nothing.

"Right. Would Mr. Onyewu know how to find Ma and Chen?"

He shook his head. "I am not sure. I will look into this, Mr. Bergeron. Is there anything else?"

"What happened after the captain and first mate of the SS Kerkyra were abducted by pirates? How was the captain killed? And why? And how did the first mate, Whalen, escape?"

He shook his head. "I knew that Thorvaldsen had been the second mate on the ship. You think the piracy connects him to Onyewu and to the Chinese in some way?"

"Maybe."

Okocha stood up. "I must go."

"Wait." He pulled out copies of the sketches of Ma and Chen. "These are the guys who came to see me. They might have Susan. They might be driving a black, Nissan cargo van."

Okocha flexed his eyebrows as he glanced at the sketches.

He looked at Chase and held out his hand.. "My gun, please."

He nodded to Chase who popped the clip and handed it over. Chase kept the knife.

Okocha said, "I may call you, Mr. Bergeron."

And he stalked out into the storm like Frankenstein's monster complete with lightning bolts slashing around him.

Chase said, "Can I help?"

"Thanks, Chase, but I don't see how? I have no idea what to do myself, and the police are doing all they can."

And he went out into the downpour.

Wednesday
6:00 pm

He had done everything he could think of, but he didn't feel right just going home.

He pulled in two blocks away from Susan's house. He didn't see any police presence near her house, but he didn't want to go barging in. He called Fowler.

"Detective."

"What?"

"Did they call?"

"Where are you?"

"Two blocks east of Susan's house."

Fowler sighed. "Stay there."

He sat. The storm had passed over. The western sky was blue, and the sun was sparkling off the raindrops hanging from the trees and shrubbery.

He sighed. He was really tired, but he saw Fowler marching toward him.

Fowler got in. He had a cigarette in his mouth; he raised an eyebrow. "I'll put the window down, Detective. Exhale outside."

Fowler sucked in a lungful of smoke and blew it out the window. "The bastards called."

"And?"

"And what do you think? Bradley couldn't tell them anything they wanted to hear. He did good keeping them on the line but it wasn't long enough."

"What did they say?"

Fowler's eyebrows were scrunched, his forehead crumpled like used tin foil. "They said they'd kill her if Bradley didn't tell them where Thorvaldsen is."

"Do we know for sure that they have her?"

"Yeah. They let her say a few words."

"Well, that's good."

Fowler glared at him. "And then they smacked her around so we could hear her scream."

He shut his eyes. "Shit. Poor Susan. Poor Bradley."

"Yeah. They said they call tomorrow, and then they were going to send her back in pieces; one finger each day."

He didn't know what to say to that. They sat there with Fowler puffing away.

Fowler said, "They weren't American. The guy who did most of the talking had a trace of an accent, but the other guy, the one who was yelling and freaking out when Bradley couldn't tell him anything, his was a lot stronger."

"What kind of accent?" Fowler shrugged and tossed his butt and lit another cigarette. "Chinese?" Another shrug.

"Right. So I talked to Inspector Okocha."

Fowler looked at him. "They gave you his number?"

"Nope. I left a message, and he came to see me at work. He claims he doesn't know anything about Susan. He says that Attaché Onyewu doesn't either."

Fowler said, "You believe him?"

"I think so. He seemed interested when I told him about Ma and Chen. He said he'd call me."

Fowler was unimpressed. He got out of the Jeep and leaned in through the window. "So any other ideas?"

"None. Well, I reached out to Monroe."

Fowler gave his face a rubdown and massaged the bridge of his large nose. "Monroe?"

"Didn't I tell you about Monroe?"

"No, Bergeron, you didn't."

"Sorry. My bad. When I first met Okocha, he told me that I should stay out of this mess, and that Monroe should too. So Monroe might be involved or not." Fowler was losing patience.

"He's a free lance agent or spy or political operative. He has sources and knows people, but he's sort of a phantom."

"But he's a buddy of yours?"

"No! But he might help for reasons of his own. Anyway, I'm trying to contact him."

Fowler shrugged. "Go home, Bergeron." And he walked off.

He wanted to go home, and there was nothing he could say or do for Bradley.

He rolled up his window and put the A/C on max hoping to exhaust the smoke as he set sail for Arch Street.

He had collapsed onto his sofa the second he'd gotten inside his apartment. It was dark now, and he had no idea what time it was.

He was feeling his way to the light switch in the kitchenette when a voice said, "Why am I here, Gabriel?"

He flicked the switch and pulled his Glock in one semi-coordinated motion. Monroe was stretched out in a chair and had been inches away as he'd gotten off the sofa in the dark.

"What the Hell, Monroe!"

"Put that down, Gabriel."

"You couldn't just knock like an ordinary person?"

Monroe smiled. He wasn't handsome or pretty but the bastard was striking. How old was he? Not that it mattered. But he couldn't help perusing the silver-gray hair, the ice-gray eyes, the cubist cheekbones, and the long, lean body.

Monroe said, "Keep looking at me like that, and I may blush, Gabriel. And please put the gun away. I could have taken it from you if I'd wanted to."

Which was absolutely true. He holstered his gun and his libido. "I'm sorry, but you scared the shit out of me. Thanks for coming. Are you going to help?"

"Help? Specify, Gabriel. And quickly. I'm always happy to see you, but I'm pressed for time."

"Would you like refreshment?"

"I assume you're offering me coffee since you don't have anything else."

"Wrong! I have gunpowder tea. And stay out of my cabinets."

Monroe smiled. "Coffee, please."

He poured water into the coffee maker and set it brewing.

He splashed more cold water into his face and dried off with the last paper towel on the roll. He sat across from Monroe.

"So how long did you sit there in the dark?"

"Not long. You need better locks."

"Like any locks would keep you out."

Monroe smiled at the compliment.

"So are you aware of Lars Thorvaldsen, Inspector Okocha, Attaché Chinedum Onyewu, Mr. Ma, Mr. Chen, Stephen and Susan Bradley? All of them or any of the above?"

"I've run into Okocha."

"And that's it?" An elegant shrug. "What about the SS Kerkyra?"

Monroe's face was always carved from granite but he thought there had been an eye blink.

"So what do you know about that good ship?"

"Nothing."

"Please. It's important, and I can keep a secret."

Monroe rolled on the floor. Well, he didn't but he made a little sniffing sound that passed for laughter with him. "I would never tell you anything that I didn't want to read on the front page of the New York Times."

"That's a vile calumny. The SS Kerkyra?"

"Why?"

He got two cups of coffee; Monroe sipped his. His long, elegant fingers were drumming on the arm of the chair.

"Okay. I'll try to be brief."

And he told Monroe everything that had happened in more or less chronological order.

Monroe blinked.

He shook his head. "Gabriel, Gabriel."

"That's me."

"Every word of that was true, wasn't it?"

"Sure?"

He shook his head. "There ought to be a way to weaponize you. Drop you into a hot spot and let you wreak havoc."

"Just help me out here, Monroe."

"And why would I do that?"

"Because you like me? Because you might have a use for me in the future? Because Susan Bradley doesn't deserve to have her fingers cut off?"

Monroe sipped his coffee.

"Come on, Monroe. What do you know about the SS Kerkyra?"

"Very little."

"But you know that Lars Thorvaldsen was the second mate on a voyage from Hamburg to Nigeria?"

"Not until now."

"So what is your interest in the ship?"

"I have none." Monroe held up a hand. "Before you have a tantrum, I will tell you that I may have an interest in the Greek company that owns that ship."

And Monroe settled back in his chair; his face a fair copy of the bust of Ramses II...only leaner and less forthcoming.

"Shit, Monroe! But why does Okocha think you're messing with this?"

"I can only guess that he learned that I made some inquiries about various ships owned by the company...nothing to do with the hijacking. And that is all I have to say, Gabriel. Thank you for the coffee." He stood up. "Always a pleasure."

And he was out the door.

He could have chased after him, yapping at his heels, but that would be pointless and undignified.

He did go to the stairwell and yell. "Thanks for coming, Monroe."

There was a faint rustle of laughter.

He went back inside and locked every lock and engaged the chains. He resisted the idea of pushing the sofa in front of the door.

He picked up Monroe's cup. There was a business card beneath it which bore a single phone number and the word, "Emergency."

Maybe Monroe did like him? No. That wasn't it. Someday he might find out why, but today was not that day.

Wednesday
11:00 pm

He dropped his clothes on the floor and fell into bed with his eyes already closed.

He was bound for the Land of Nod when his phone rang. He may have ignored it, but it started ringing again.

"What?"

Inspector Okocha said, "Bergeron?"

He sat up. He may have slapped his face. "Yes?"

"I shouldn't do this."

"Yes, you should! The proud people of Nigeria expect no less of you." He had no idea.

Okocha grunted. "You are such a silly man."

"Am not. Wait. Do you know something about Susan? Or Ma and Chen?"

"It is not my job to protect Americans."

"It should be. Innocent Americans like Susan." He had the feeling that Okocha shrugged. "Inspector? Isn't it your job to prevent crime if you can? And kidnapping and cutting off fingers are certainly crimes."

"They are."

Silence.

"Please, Okocha. If you know something? I will never say where I got the information. I promise."

More silence.

"Please. You talked to Susan. You know she's a sweet, gentle lady."

"Never tell anyone that I told you this."

"Never. My lips are sealed and...."

"Please stop talking. She may be at 1125 Hampden Avenue in West Philadelphia"

And the inspector was gone.

He called Fowler.

"What the Hell, Bergeron?" Fowler sounded only half awake.

"Hello, Detective. I may know where Susan is being held."

There was a slight pause as Fowler was silently girding his loins and possibly lighting a cigarette. "Where? And how do you know?"

"1125 Hampden Avenue in West Philly."

"And?"

He had known that the detective was going to ask the how question. "Monroe told me."

Monroe would not be pleased to have his name used in vain, but it was for a good cause. Monroe would understand. Probably.

"Monroe? The phantom spy?"

"Yes."

"And you think this might be real?"

"I do. I'm sure of it. Well, mostly sure. Look, I can go scout out the area if you want...."

"No! Stay in your apartment. I will handle this."

And Fowler was gone.

So he sat there for a good thirty seconds before jumping into his pants, retrieving his Glock, and sprinting for the door.

But he wasn't a cowboy or a total idiot no matter what some might think, and he parked blocks away from the address which was over a mile from Susan's home.

He consulted all available maps as he waited. The address was in the middle of a block of row houses. Or it had been when the ground photos had been taken. It had looked abandoned even then.

And desolate. And a suitable spot to hold a kidnap victim.

He sat. He discovered that he was starving. What was open

at midnight? Bars were open. But he didn't want bar food which consisted of pretzels as far as he knew.

He sighed. And then he watched two patrol cars speed by as stealthily as they could. They were heading in the right direction.

He resisted the urge to follow.

He sat some more. He could call Fowler but the detective was no doubt busy and would yell at him and make hurtful comments about his intelligence.

He fired up his Jeep. He was weak from hunger, and there might be a twenty-four hour market somewhere nearby.

He waited for another patrol car to pass before he pulled out. This patrol car halted in a violent manner and reversed taking a year's worth of rubber off its tires.

Officer Fuchs was staring at him as he rolled down his window. He did the same.

Having a bright yellow Jeep had its drawbacks. "Hi there."

Fuchs gave him his normal despairing glare with a dollop of exhaustion thrown in for good measure. "Bergeron, what do you think you're doing?"

"I wanted to be close by if you found Susan."

Fuchs looked straight ahead. "If I tell you to go home, can I trust you to do that?"

He may have smiled at Officer Fuchs.

Fuchs beckoned him with a finger; not the middle finger either. "What?"

"Turn off your Jeep and get in the patrol car. Do it now."

"Okay. In the back?"

But Fuchs leaned over and pushed open the front passenger door.

He got in.

Fuchs engaged his warp drive, and they shot down the nearly empty street.

"Have you heard anything?"

"Shut up."

"Yes, Sir."

And they proceeded in a comradely silence to a gathering of squad cars. Was there a collective noun for police cars? It was a swarm of bees, a flock of sheep, a murder of crows.

He realized Fuchs was looking at him.

"Yes, Officer Fuchs?" Fuchs eye-rolled him. Which made him think of Jennifer. He should call and see how she and the baby were doing. Where was Fowler? He looked back to Fuchs.

"Space cadet."

"I resent that."

Fuchs got out of the car and walked around the vehicle. "Out."

He exited.

Fuchs opened the rear door. He sighed. It wasn't unexpected. He got in, and Fuchs locked him inside.

By his reckoning, they were four blocks from the address Okocha had given him. How did Okocha know? He'd followed the Chinese? They didn't seem like very good spies?

Or maybe Okocha was just a lot better?

He was peering out the window when Fowler walked by. He waved. Fowler paused long enough to light a cigarette while ignoring him.

Fowler made eye contact briefly. He was upset and not with Gabriel Bergeron either.

He settled in and tried to get comfortable but Fuchs' patrol car had a certain odor. It was faint. No doubt heavy duty cleaning agents like bleach and carbolic acid had been applied in attempting to expunge it, but it had clung on and was coating his nasal passages and throat.

Even so, he was drifting off when he heard a burst of gunfire. And then another. And then a full-scale fusillade.

And then silence.

He sat there. Had they found Susan? Who had been shooting? Besides Fowler and Fuchs et al?

He saw Fuchs coming looking no worse for wear. He opened the door and started back the way he'd come.

Which was an invitation if he'd ever seen one.

He caught up to Fuchs. "So?"

"Three guys. Two down. One on the run."

"Susan?"

"Fowler's looking for her."

Fuchs had long legs, and he trotted to keep up. There were guys in army style uniforms with helmets and night-vision goggles. Some had long, lethal looking rifles with sniper scopes.

Fuchs marched through them to 1125 Hampden and halted. He looked at Fuchs.

"Forensics has to go in."

"Right. I understand. Susan?"

Fuchs growled at him. So they waited.

1125 Hampden was past its glory days. It was in the middle of the block with ten or more row houses on its right.

Each pair of houses shared a porch and a central set of stairs. Centered over those stairs was a pediment supported by columns. Half the porch and thus half of the pediment belonged to each house. Each owner had painted his half of the triangle a color to match his house or personalized it in other creative ways. It gave an overall harlequin look to the place.

Or it had because all that house-proud effort was long past. All the houses on the left of #1125 had been reduced to rubble.

And then he noticed the end of the black, Nissan van sticking out. It had been tucked in beside the house on a bit of flattened rubble.

And then the lump beside the van resolved into a body.

"She's here. She has to be. Right?"

Fuchs looked at him but didn't vocalize.

And then Fowler came out of the door of the next house down carrying Susan in his arms.

He looked around. "Hey! Where the Hell are the freaking paramedics?"

And two of those individuals rushed over, gurney in tow.

Fowler laid her down. "You're safe now, Susan."

Susan patted his face. "Please call Stevie. Please, Mitch."

Fowler smiled at her. "Will do. He'll be at the hospital by the time you get there."

Her face was bruised, and her lip cut but she seemed otherwise whole.

Fowler spotted Fuchs. "Go get Stevie and take him to the

hospital."

Fuchs turned and stalked off making a sub-sonic growling sound like the vibrations of a bass amplifier.

Fowler said, "Gabe!"

He smiled at Fowler. The detective locked arms around him and lifted him off the ground.

"Golczewski was right about you! Crazy bastard!"

The SWAT guys were smiling. "Let go of me, Detective."

Fowler was still grinning as he released him from the bearhug. "I'm jazzed, Gabe."

"I can see that. I am too!"

"This could have gone so wrong. We might never have found her, or she could have been killed when the firing started."

"But she's safe now."

Fowler nodded. "How did Monroe know?"

"I don't know. He wouldn't tell me if I asked him."

"Can you find this guy?"

He shook his head. "No way. I'd like to go to the hospital."

Fowler nodded.

"So your name is Mitch?" Another nod. "Can I call you Mitch?"

"You can call me whatever the Hell you want, but there's something you need to do before we head for the hospital."

Fowler's glance had shifted to the body beside the van.

"Right. Okay." He really didn't like looking a dead people...and these two might be in a condition best described as open-casket-challenging. "Let's get it over with."

But the guy beside the van looked like he was napping on the concrete block rubble. He had been short and stocky with a round, plump face, tiny ears, and dark hair buzzed short. He had been in his mid twenties.

And he looked like he'd been a pleasant fellow before a dozen bullets had stitched his sweatshirt to his chest. The blood looked very dark and shiny.

"I've never seen him before."

Fowler said, "Take a good look, Gabe."

He did. "He's Asian but he's not Ma or Chen. He looks

nothing like them."

Fowler nodded and walked to the third house down. He climbed the steps; the door had been kicked open.

This guy was also on his back but his arms were thrown wide. Fowler focused his flashlight on the face.

He glanced and looked away.

"Gabe?" Fowler shone the light in his eyes which were firmly closed. "Come on, Bergeron. You've seen bodies before."

Which was true. But still.

It appeared this guy had only been shot twice; once in the center of his chest. His white t-shirt had gained a red, after-market circle. And his head had been clipped. So he was missing part of his forehead. He focused on the ninety percent of his face that was left.

He had an oval face with a wide nose and dark hair. He had been older; maybe thirty-five or so.

His dark eyes were open and staring up at them. Well, they weren't really.

"Not Chen. Not Ma."

Fowler said, "Shit. So are these guys connected to your guys?"

"Unless there are two separate Asian groups after Duke Thorvaldsen."

Fowler nodded. "Yeah. That wouldn't make much sense."

"No, it wouldn't." But who knew at this point?

"Can you close his eyes?"

"They'll do it at the morgue. Let's get out of here, Gabe."

Thursday
2:00 am

Susan had been taken to Mercy Philadelphia Hospital on South 54th Street which had transitioned to something called PHMC since he'd last visited. He hadn't spotted Physician Assistant Ian of the cranberry scrubs in the ER.

Susan had been checked over and pronounced in decent physical shape. As far as mentally, he knew what it was like to be kidnapped, and it wasn't fun.

She was still in the ER, and Bradley was at her bedside.

Fuchs and Fowler and Gabriel Bergeron were drinking vile coffee and generally smiling. Even Fuchs; a flicker here and there.

Fowler smiled. "I thought you were full of shit when you called me, Bergeron. I was hoping I was wrong."

Fuchs said, "That was a safe bet."

Fowler smiled at Fuchs. "Even you can't bring me down."

He said, "So what happened? I was locked in Officer Fuch's patrol car at the time."

Fowler said, "And I was hiding behind a stone wall when World War III kicked off."

"So?"

"The SWAT guys had the place locked down, and they were gathering intell when this big guy walked out the front door. He took one look and started blasting away at anything that moved as he scrambled back inside."

Fuchs said, "Then it got messy."

Fowler laughed. "If you mean that two other perps opened

fire with automatic weapons, and our guys returned fire, it got very messy. The commander tried to get our guys to stop firing, but the perps kept shooting."

Fuchs said, "One dumbass ran for the van."

He said, "The plump guy."

Fuchs nodded. "Big mistake."

Fowler said, "Snipers shot through the window to take out the second guy as he ran past."

"Have they been identified? Any documents on them?"

"Not yet. Neither had any I.D., but a team is searching the row houses. We've got prints and DNA."

"I have a feeling that might not be so helpful with these guys. And one guy got away?"

Fowler nodded with his usual exasperated expression returning. "Yeah. Somebody had taken the trouble to break through the walls of the adjoining units one after the other, connecting all the houses. And the third guy crawled through the holes to the end unit. A couple of guys chased him but he was fast. But we'll catch him."

"Maybe Susan can help? When she's up to it."

Fowler nodded. "Maybe." Fowler was looking less cheery. "I want to talk to Monroe, Gabe."

"I don't have any way of contacting him."

Fowler and Fuchs were staring at him. "Sure about that?"

"Yes. Absolutely sure." He wasn't going to share Monroe's phone number since he was sure it was a one use only number, and Monroe couldn't help them anyway.

Did Inspector Okocha know where Ma and Chen were? It wouldn't hurt to ask if he could reach him. He wondered if the number he had was any good?

Fowler was looking at him. "We'll revisit that. But I want them."

He nodded. "Me too, Mitch. But Monroe is not the way to go." He smiled his very best smile. "So somebody's going to take me to my Jeep, right?"

Fowler said, "I'm staying here with Susan." But he smiled and pointed a finger at Fuchs.

More sub-sonic growling.

Thursday
11:00 am

He had set his alarm which he may have ignored the first few times it went off, but he had been at his desk with both eyes open by 9:00 am.

And now he was feeling more human.

Carla and Harry were working away. Chatterjee said that all of his own clients were current.

He decided to call Jennifer. "Good morning, Jennifer."

"What did you do?"

He was momentarily nonplussed. And a bit hurt. "Everything is fine, Jennifer! I'm calling to see how you're feeling and how the baby is doing. Have you named him?"

"I'm feeling better. His name is Adam Ruslan Boltukaev...after Andy's grandfathers."

"Lovely."

She laughed. "Don't let Andy hear you say his son's name is 'lovely'."

"Right. Point taken. It's very manly. Suited to a warrior prince."

"Are you sure everything is okay, Bergeron?"

"Yes! That's why I'm calling. To put your mind at ease. All is well."

Doubt and trepidation were shooting through the copper and fiber optic cables and pelting him in the face.

"It really is." He spun around and rolled over to Carla's cubicle. "Carla, tell Jennifer that all is well at Garst, Bauer &

Hartmann." Carla gave him a look that would make wolverines soil themselves. "Please?"

Carla took the phone. "Hi, Jennifer. How are you feeling?"

Apparently the answer required a thousand well-chosen words. And then Carla described her own travails...in exquisite detail.

He covered his ears during most of it. Harry was laughing at him, or at least, his mouth was making laughing motions.

Carla smacked him on the back.

He uncovered his left ear. "What?"

Carla said, "Everything is under control, Jennifer. Bergeron is doing a good job and has worked more hours since you left than all of last year."

"That is not true!"

Carla wouldn't give him back his phone. "I have worked very hard but I worked hard last year too. I always work hard. I am dedicated and loyal and...."

Carla was smiling at him. "What?"

"She's gone, Bergeron."

"Really?" She was. "Wait. Did she hang up before or after you told her I was doing a good job?"

Carla smiled a truly evil smile. "After."

He wasn't sure he believed her.

He had wanted to subtly ask if Jennifer was thinking of coming back to work in the near term. Maybe next week?

He got to his feet and departed. He felt he deserved an early lunch after being treated so shabbily, but mostly he wanted to talk to Susan and Bradley.

He parked behind the patrol car in front of Susan's house. Bradley popped out and told the officer that he was okay or he would have been sent on his way.

Bradley was smiling at him and shaking his hand as he pulled him inside. "Fowler told me! You did it, Gabe. I knew you could."

Susan was in the front room. She got off the sofa and moved toward him.

Bradley said, "You should rest, Mom."

"I'm fine, Stevie."

And then she hugged him. "Thank you, Gabe. You saved me."

"Well, Detective Fowler and a whole lot of police and SWAT guys did more than I did, Susan."

But they both shook their heads.

Susan said, "Mitch said that you told him where I was being held."

Bradley said, "If you hadn't...."

He knew they were thinking about the finger-cutting thing. "Two giants, Roy and Dale, once threatened to remove my fingers with lopping shears."

Susan looked at Bradley, and they burst out laughing.

He didn't see what was funny?

Bradley sobered first; Susan was having small, giggle fits which were kind of cute. "Giants, Gabe?"

"Well, they weren't actually giants but they topped out at six feet eight. And they brought their lopping shears in a cello case."

More riotous laughter.

Susan took a deep breath. "I'm sorry for laughing, Gabe."

"That's okay. You've been through a lot. How are you feeling?"

"I'm fine. The nasty one slapped me a few times, but the others treated me decently. I don't think they liked him."

"Did Detective Fowler show you the sketches of Ma and Chen?"

She nodded. "The nasty one could have been Ma, but I only got one glimpse of his face. They made me wear a hood for most of the time."

He pulled out a copy and showed it to her.

She shivered just a bit. "I think it was him."

He said, "He was very smug and well pleased with himself."

Susan nodded. "Smug. Yes, that describes him. But I never saw the other man. I was kept in that abandoned house most of the time, and I think it was just the three of them with me but I could be wrong. Mitch showed me photos of the dead men. I had never seen any of them until they broke in here and grabbed me." She was looking at her front door. "I always felt safe here, Gabe. I don't know if I ever will again."

"It will take some time."

Bradley said, "How did you know where they were keeping her?"

"I asked a guy I know."

"And how did he know?"

He sighed. "I should tell you the whole story."

And he did. He was tempted to leave out huge chunks but Susan deserved to know it all; Bradley had heard most of it already. He didn't rat out Okocha though.

Bradley was looking lost and dejected when he finished, but there was no way to make Duke look innocent.

Susan said, "So Ma and Chen came to see you to persuade you to give up looking for Duke?"

"Yes. I tried to tell them I wasn't but they didn't listen."

Bradley said, "And you think they tried to kidnap you?"

"Yes."

Bradley said, "I shouldn't have come to see you. Maybe none of this would have happened if I hadn't?"

Susan stroked his hair. "We don't know that, Stevie." She smiled. "Where are my manners? Would you like some coffee or something, Gabe?"

It was lunchtime.

Bradley said, "I'll get it, Mom."

As soon as he was out the door, she said, "Are you going to help Mitch with this, Gabe. He thinks you are?"

"I am now."

She nodded. "Then there are some things I should tell you. About Duke. Stevie doesn't know, and I'd rather he didn't find out."

"I won't tell him."

She smiled, and allowing for the bruises and busted lip, she was very pretty. She smoothed her hair.

"I'm sure you'll think I'm an idiot."

"No, I won't!"

"You should hear the story first. I've been dating Duke Thorvaldsen for ten years. It began after Robert, Stevie's father, died in 2007, and I think that Duke was going to end it on the last date that never happened...that weekend getaway, over a month ago now. We went to dinner that Thursday, and Duke was circling around telling me then, but he never did. And then he disappeared."

"Do you know why?"

"He was so happy; the happiest I think I'd ever seen him. He wanted to tell me what was making him so happy. He kept hinting and almost coming out with it. It had to do with money."

"Why do you think that?"

"He was tired of his life. He had been working on ships since he was sixteen; almost thirty years. And he had nothing to show for it. He wanted to escape, and he said that his voyage on the SS Kerkyra was going to be his last."

"And he needed money if he was giving up his job? Maybe he had another job lined up?"

She shook her head. "I don't think so. He's handsome and strong, but he's barely literate, Gabe. He's good with math...with maps and the navigating part of his job and with machines. He can repair them, and I think hefakes the rest. And he's never done anything else."

"He could be a mechanic?"

She shook her head. "I suggested that once, but he said that would be worse than being a merchant seaman."

"So he had come into money?"

"I'm sure of it."

"And this Whalen, the first mate on the Kerkyra, knew about it and came to take it from him. And Duke killed him?"

She nodded. "It might have been in self-defense?"

"But if he robbed someone, wouldn't he know they might come after him?"

She smiled. "He isn't great on planning ahead or seeing the consequences. He probably thought no one would suspect him."

So Duke had robbed the Chinese? And Attaché Chinedum Onyewu knew about it? Somehow? And had co-opted Inspector

Okocha into helping him take whatever it was?

"So where do you think he is now?"

She shook her head. "I have no idea. He should be a thousand miles from here."

"Right. This is a freaking hornet's nest. Do you know of anyone he'd go to?"

She shook her head. She didn't want to tell him something. "Susan?"

"This is the idiot part, Gabe."

"I won't tell anyone."

"In the ten years I've dated Duke, he's probably had dozens of other girlfriends. Here and across the world. I told myself that I had no claim on him, and I could take what he offered...which was an occasional good time." She smiled. "A very good time. Or I could ask for more and lose him."

"So he has other girlfriends in Philly?"

"I know he has, but I think all of them are former girlfriends because they have more self-respect than I do. Except for the latest one: Gianna Bonacci. She works at Mack's Market. It isn't far from here."

"And you think she might know where Duke is?"

"Or he might be staying with her? I couldn't bring myself to go to her house." She sighed. "But please don't tell Stevie about this, Gabe. He wouldn't understand. He's loved Duke since the first time he brought him a souvenir from Singapore; a little carved dragon. Stevie was lost after Robert died, and Duke was exciting and happy to play at fatherhood as long as it didn't put any demands on him. They watched sports together, and he taught Stevie how to throw a football. Stevie practiced for hours and hours so he could show Duke how good he was when he came home the next time."

"And he was a real swashbuckler sailing the seven seas."

She nodded. "He was sort of that for me too. But I don't want Stevie to lose that...if it can be helped."

He had no idea but he didn't see how Duke could be the hero in all this. The best that could be hoped for was that Duke would never be seen again, and Stevie could tamp down his doubts and keep his memories.

"Okay. Any other thoughts?"

"If you can...."

"Can what?"

"If you can help Duke, please do it? I think he's all alone and needs help. From somebody."

She still loved the jerk.

She shook her head as Stevie...Bradley...brought in the coffee and a homemade pound cake.

Bradley said, "I can make sandwiches, Gabe?"

"No. This is great."

They talked until the coffee and cake were gone.

Bradley said, "We should get going, Mom."

She nodded. "I'll get my suitcase."

"I'll get it."

She smiled at Bradley. "I'm fine." And she went up the stairs.

He looked at Bradley. "Where are you going?"

"To stay with Uncle Brian, Mom's brother, for a few days. She doesn't want to stay here right now."

"No, I wouldn't either. So do you have any idea where Duke could be?"

He shook his head. "No."

"I'm sorry about Duke."

Bradley squeezed his eyes shut. "Maybe he got into this by accident? Maybe he's a victim too, Gabe?"

"He could be." And the Nazis had a secret base on the far side of the Moon laying the foundations for the Fourth Reich.

He was on the porch when Bradley said, "You could check out the bar."

He spun. "What bar?"

"Tiny's Bar. It's about ten blocks that way." Bradley pointed due west. "Duke goes there sometimes when he's home. He has some buddies there."

"Buddies who would let him stay with them for over a month?"

Bradley shook his head. "Maybe. You could check it out?"

He smiled and nodded at Bradley and got into his Jeep.
A working class bar in West Philly. He'd fit in like one of Cinderella's wicked stepsisters' big feet fit into that glass slipper.

Thursday
1:00 pm

He was parked outside of Mack's Market which was in a converted, corner row house. The second story looked unchanged from the outside, but all the windows on the ground floor had been bricked up. The one remaining window beside the front door was barred.

A big, stainless steel, restaurant-style, exhaust fan stuck out of the wall toward the back of the building like the jet engine of a 747.

The sign over the entrance advertised PA lottery tickets, soda, candy, hoagies, milk, eggs, frozen food, cold cuts, cigarettes, and PA lottery tickets a second time.

He could talk to Gianna Bonacci about Duke, but he really wanted to find Ma and Chen and associates. Well, he wanted to discover their location and turn the actual finding over to Fowler and his SWAT guys.

And it was not impossible that Inspector Okocha knew where Ma and Chen were. He dialed the number.

It rang and rang. He sighed. He should have known it wouldn't be that easy.

He walked into Mack's Market. The proprietor didn't look like a Mack but more like a Mukerjee or a Masood. He inhabited a cage-like structure just inside the door. In front of Mr. Mack, there was a small counter with a cash register. Every square inch of the walls around the counter and behind the proprietor held every candy known to man in a riotous display of screaming marketing.

He nodded to Mr. Mack and grabbed a basket.

There were three narrow isles. The floor was a checkerboard of worn blue and white vinyl tiles. Sagging, discolored acoustic panels made up the ceiling; the lighting was provided by naked fluorescent bulbs over each aisle.

But it was spotless. The shelves were jammed floor to ceiling with goods, and not a speck of dust adorned any of those thousands of items.

It appeared that Mr. Mack had cornered the market on Goya beans, condensed milk, and a brand of peas he'd never heard of; they were stacked like a step pyramid at the end of an aisle.

"Gandules Verdes" certainly looked like peas; he grabbed a couple of cans anyway since there was nothing in his cupboards. He added ketchup and a few cans of tuna.

And cheek-by-jowl was a shelf of laundry detergents: Tide with "*Eau Froide*" emblazoned across the box.

Where was the cereal aisle? He needed toaster pastries and some of the cereal that Cory liked. He may have grabbed a bag of chocolate chip cookies.

He shopped as casually as he could while looking for Gianna. The walls were lined with freezers and coolers stocked with beer and wine and frozen foods.

He looked up and realized he was being watched by a scaled down version of Mr. Mack. He tried smiling but the young man vanished behind a rack of chips.

It was probably the suit that marked him as alien.

He had completed a circuit of the store; no Gianna. But there was a door in the back which looked sturdy enough to hold off any invading force.

He was reaching for toaster pastries when he spied a cat gazing down upon him. Said cat was black and white and perched on paper towels stacked almost to the ceiling, she was surveying her domain.

He set his purchases on the counter next to a gallon jar of giant pickles.

Mr. Mack gave him a smile; he was wearing a thin blue sweater over a white dress shirt with the collar splayed out. "Did you find everything you were looking for, Sir?"

A couple of candy bars may have jumped off the rack.

He paid. He smiled at Mr. Mack. "Is Gianna here today?"

Mr. Mack looked him up and down and shook his head, disappointment writ large.

"She isn't?" Mr. Mack nodded. "She is?"

Mr. Mack said, "She's in the back. Working." And Mr. Mack looked pointedly at the door.

He hefted his groceries and took the hint.

He got into his Jeep. When did Gianna get off work? He wasn't going to wait around; work was piling up as he dawdled in West Philly.

He strolled innocently along the block. There was an alleyway with an open gate. The back door of Mr. Mack's establishment was propped open with a concrete block, and a youngish woman with long, black hair with blonde streaks was seated on the threshold smoking.

She gave him side eye.

He smiled his very best smile. She was unimpressed.

"Gianna Bonacci?"

"Who wants to know?"

"I'm Gabriel Bergeron." He gave her a card; he wasn't sure why?

She glared at his innocent card. "So? I'm not buying...." She looked him over and maybe noted his suit which happened to be his best one. "...whatever you're selling, Bud."

"I'm not selling anything."

She let his card fall on the ground. "You've got until I finish my cig."

"I understand you're Duke Thorvaldsen's girlfriend?"

Gianna had a long face with a chin sharp enough to score glass. Her big brown eyes were outlined with magic marker or something similar, and the thin lips were painted pink. A smock covered her white blouse and modest endowment.

She stood up and brushed the seat of jeans stretched tight across a big butt. She was an inch taller than he was.

She was looking down at him as if he were a new and

potentially nasty species of vermin.

"What do you want?"

"I'm just wondering if you know where Duke is?"

"Hell, no!"

"Right. So when is the last time you saw him?"

"I don't have to talk to you!"

"No, you don't, but I'm trying to help Duke."

"Says you!"

"You can talk to me or to Detective Fowler, and I'm much nicer than he is."

She stood there. He was beginning to fear that her brain had locked up and might need to be rebooted, and he wasn't sure how to do that. She didn't appear to have a power cord.

But her processor struggled through the conundrum. "Who cares? I don't know where he is...the bastard!"

"I'm sorry to hear that. When is the last time you saw him?"

She placed a hand on hip and struck a pose. "What's it worth to you?"

He didn't usually carry cash...mostly because he had so little, but he thought he had two hundred bucks.

He pulled out his wallet and selected two twenties.

She grabbed them and then laughed; it was not a nice laugh. She held out her hand and tapped her foot as she took a last drag on her cigarette.

He took out a hundred and proffered it.

She snatched it. She stuffed his money down her bosom and held out her hand for more; her nails were aqua and dagger shaped.

He shook his head. "When did you last see him?"

She looked him up and down and snorted. "Two weeks ago."

"Where?"

"At my place. The bastard thought he could move in and not pay anything! I was supposed to feed him and clean up after him! Got old real quick, but he kept begging me to stay just a few more days."

"So you kicked him out?"

"Hell, yeah, I did!"

"Why did he say that he needed to stay with you?" She waved a hand at her bod. "Right. Okay, I'm sure he appreciated your...what you had to offer, but that wasn't it, was it?"

"Hell, no. He was scared. Big, dumb sailor was wetting his pants any time a car slowed down in front of my place."

"Did he tell you who was looking for him?"

She shook her head. "My break's over."

"Did he tell you or even hint why someone was after him?"

She shook her head tossing her long hair.

"Right. Did you see anyone suspicious around your place?"

She laughed. "Yeah."

"Who?"

"He didn't give me his card." More very unpleasant laughter.

"Can you describe him?"

"Big, black, scary looking."

"Did he have an accent? Sort of British but not quite?"

She nodded. "Who is he?"

He showed her Okocha's photo. "Is this him? Another nod. "He's a cop."

"Yeah. I can believe that. So Duke is in deep shit? No. I don't want to know what that idiot did."

She shook her head. "Look, I told the British cop that Duke took off, and I had no idea where he would go, and I'm telling you the same thing."

And she shoved the concrete block out of the way and slammed the door of Mack's Market.

He marched back to his Jeep. So Okocha was ahead of him. What would Okocha do if he found Duke?

Or maybe he'd found him, and Duke's fate had already been decided.

No. Okocha was still watching. And luckily he was watching the Chinese too.

He had work to do, but on his trip back to the Mahr Building, he drove past Tiny's Bar.

It was another corner row house. The ground floor had two

tiny windows in the front which were taken up with neon beer signs. The door was steel clad and inset diagonally into the corner of the building. Two air conditioners sprouted from the otherwise blank yellow walls.

A sign with "Tiny's Bar" was bracketed above the door. In front of the building, an incongruous tree was clinging to life in soil as hard as the sidewalk around it.

He sighed. He didn't think he wanted to walk through that door. Not even with his Glock.

Thursday
4:00 pm

He had called Fowler on the way back to work and left a message, and now his phone was ringing.

He ducked into the break room. "Detective?"

Fowler said, "Give me some good news, Gabe?"

"Sorry. I talked to Gianna Bonacci."

Fowler said, "Am I suppose to know who that is?" He sounded a bit cranky.

"Sorry. She's Duke's latest girlfriend."

"What? The bastard's got somebody on the side?"

"He does. Or he did. I think Gianna's done with him. Susan gave me her name."

He processed that. "She knows?"

"About her and a bevy of others spanning the globe and the twenty-first century."

"Shit."

"Right. I feel much the same way. But Gianna says that Duke was staying with her until two weeks ago. She says she kicked him out. Maybe you could have a chat with Miss Bonacci and verify that? Or have somebody stake out her place?"

Fowler sighed. "Where is it?"

"No idea but she works at Mack's Market."

"Yeah. I know the place. I'll see what I can do, but I don't have unlimited manpower, Bergeron."

"I know. And Duke also hung out at Tiny's Bar. I was wondering if you could go with me to ask some questions?"

Fowler laughed. "Not your kind of place."

"Not so much."

"I would but nobody is going to talk to a cop, Gabe. Not in a blue collar place like Tiny's."

"Right. I should have thought of that. Okay. Any other news?"

"Not much. The van had a tracking device, but we don't know who tagged the Chinese. Think it was this Monroe?"

"I don't know." It was likely Inspector Okocha.

"And we haven't ID'ed the bodies."

"Not Americans?"

"Or not in the system." He paused probably for a long drag on his cigarette. "I want this Ma, Gabe."

"Me too. And Chen and whoever else is working with them."

"Yeah. Okay. Call me if you get any ideas."

"Will do."

He couldn't ask Harry to go with him to Tiny's Bar. Who else did he know who would be comfortable in a blue collar bar? Maybe Stan?

Stan had been fixing his vehicles for years but he had no idea if the guy frequented bars. Or really much about Stan at all. He would have to remedy this. Was he married?

He considered dialing good ole Stan, but he'd seen the bullet holes in various vehicles. Stan might say no, and then things might be awkward.

He pocketed his phone. Paul was smiling at him from the doorway. He liked Paul but it was just a tad creepy how he could move like fog.

"Hi, Paul?"

"Hi, Gabe. Can we talk?"

"Sure."

Paul closed the breakroom door. "You know that Winnie and I are dating."

"Sure, and I'm very happy for you. For both of you! Though having Carla as an in-law does sort of give me pause...."

Paul was smiling so he stopped.

"We aren't at that stage, Gabe. I'm not sure we will ever get there."

He had no idea what to say. "I'm sorry?"

Paul said, "I think Winnie likes me, but there seems to be a problem."

Paul was looking at him with a neutral face. "What kind of problem?" Why the Hell had he asked that? Paul might tell him things he didn't want to know.

A sad little smile. "I was hoping you could tell me? You had that meeting with all of her daughters, Gabe?"

Shit. "I did."

Paul said, "I'm sorry to put you in an awkward position but I really like Winnie. Was it about me?"

"No! It was about someone else...someone from the past...the distant past." Paul just looked at him. "They wanted me to find this someone, but I don't think I can, and I don't think it's as important as they think anyway. But I guess I can try...but not right now."

Paul smiled. "No. You're busy. With non-accounting stuff too. Want to tell me about that?"

He poured two cups of coffee and told Paul the saga of Lars "Duke" Thorvaldsen.

Paul was smiling even before he was half way through. "This is a good one, Gabe. Can I tell Chatterjee?"

"I'd rather you didn't. I don't want Jennifer to find out and get upset. I really tried to stay out of this, Paul."

Paul nodded. "Sure. I understand. But you couldn't after they took Susan Bradley. So can I help?"

"At the moment I don't see how?"

Paul said, "I like bars, Gabe. I've spent a good portion of my free time in bars...all kinds of bars."

"Really? So you'd go with me to Tiny's?"

Paul smiled. "I couldn't let you go alone. After work?"

It was probably good to do this as soon as possible. "Okay. In an hour or so? I have some stuff to finish up."

Paul was fingering the lapel of his very nice suit. "We need to change, Gabe."

"Dress down? Right. So jeans and a sweatshirt?"
"That should be okay. I'll meet you at your apartment?"
"That would be great, Paul. I appreciate this."
Paul nodded.
"About Winnie? Maybe you should just ask her if there's a problem?" Why was he giving romantic advice? He had no idea what he was talking about.
Paul nodded and drifted away.
He went back to work. Did Paul think that the daughters had asked for information about his background? And if so, was there something to find?
He knew nothing about Paul except that his wife had passed away three years ago, and that Carla had liked her.
How long had Paul worked at GBH? He was pretty sure he'd started before that sterling accountant, Gabe Bergeron, had been hired? But how long before that?
He turned off his computer. He had to go home and find some blue-collar-bar-appropriate garb. Cory had lots of ratty undercover stuff but it was too big for him.
He would find something.

Thursday
6:30 pm

Paul smiled when he saw him.
"What?"
"Turn your cap around, Gabe."
He had thought he looked good with the Philadelphia Phillies baseball cap worn backwards, but maybe not? "Okay. But the jeans and the sweatshirt are good?"
Paul nodded. "I can drive, Gabe."
Paul's car was a Volvo; the color and vintage were uncertain. It might have been green or a greenish-yellow at one point. It had two doors and a general break-down-at-any-moment air.
"How old is this car, Paul?"
Paul smiled as he motored along. "Younger than me."
Which wasn't reassuring.
Paul looked as worn as his car with nondescript pants, a baggy, rusty t-shirt, and a thin army jacket. It had been army green a long time ago, but it still had the patches: "US Army" above the left breast pocket and "Hearne" above the right.
"Were you in the army, Paul?
"A century ago." Paul smiled at some private joke.
They parked down the street from Tiny's.
"I guess we should go in."
Paul nodded. "Or I could go in, Gabe?"
Which was an idea. "Wait. You don't want me to come with you?" Paul smiled. The smile was getting old. "I won't embarrass

you."

"No. I know. Just be...."

"Be what?"

"A little less Gabe than usual."

Paul got out and was ambling toward Tiny's. How the Hell was he supposed to be less "Gabe"? Maybe keep his mouth shut?

He caught up to Paul. "I never go into bars. Even gay ones. I don't drink, but I'll be okay."

Paul said, "You can't just walk in and start asking questions about this Duke."

"No? What then?"

"We need to settle in and let his name come up naturally."

He stopped dead. And how would that happen? Paul should have told him sooner, and he could have crafted a clever stratagem. Maybe Paul had a plan?

Paul kept plodding forward. "What are you going to order?"

"I don't know? A diet cola?"

Paul didn't smile. "No."

He'd gotten far too few hours sleep so what he really needed was a gallon of coffee . At least if he fell asleep, Paul would see that he got home.

"No? Then what? I got drunk on champagne once...."

Paul made a snorting sound; it was most unattractive. "Order a draft beer. Or just get what I get."

But what if they asked him which draft beer? He would just pick one. How hard could it be?

"Just sip it, Gabe."

"Right. I can do that. Will they have pretzels?"

But Paul was through the door into Tiny's.

He stepped from the May sunshine into a cave. Well, more like a subway tunnel...that had been abandoned for so long that even the rats had left.

It smelled like beer and floor polish with hints of disinfectant and urinal cakes.

There were two ceiling fans with low wattage bulbs, a scattering of advertising signage glowing mostly in the red area of the spectrum, and two, flat screen TVs.

The TVs were carrying most of the load of illuminating the place. They were tuned to a baseball game.

The bar itself was on the left; a row of tables with black spidery chairs were on the right. Lost in the gloom beyond the end of the bar, he thought he spied booths.

There were four men at the bar. A woman of uncertain age was at one of the tables and a horde of goblins were occupying the booths. Well, there could be goblins in that gloom.

The stools at the bar had been fashioned from telephone poles. At least, that's what they looked like. The seats were square and covered in cracked, red vinyl. The black tar coating on the poles had been worn away in spots by ten thousand heels rubbing against them.

Paul took a stool. He tried to achieve the same natural air as he slid into position beside him.

The bartender could be thirty or fifty given the ambient lighting, but he was probably young. He was wearing a Philadelphia Flyers cap and an unbuttoned, striped dress shirt over a black t-shirt with a red, spiky design that looked like a bundle of barbed wire that might be animate.

"What'll it be?"

Paul ordered Michelob, and he did the same. There was a neon sign above the cash register with letters six inches tall: "Cash Only".

He had sixty bucks, but he wasn't planning on any heavy drinking.

He sipped the beer. It wasn't bad, but there were no pretzels in sight. Paul sat there nursing his beer like he had been born in this bar and had never found a reason to leave.

He looked at Paul but Paul ignored him.

He sipped his beer; he watched a good three minutes of baseball. Being less Gabe probably meant a modicum of patience.

He observed his fellow bar mates.

The two closest guys were about Paul's age and had graying beards and bellies that rivaled Jennifer's before she gave birth.

Duke was by all reports fit and more like the other two

guys whose silhouettes were certainly not svelte but boasted shoulders wider than their guts.

He thought the lady of uncertain age was the best bet. Duke was by every report a stud and likely to attract the attention of the fair sex.

He watched more baseball. The batter hit a home run which cheered the tiny crowd.

Paul finished his beer and ordered another.

He sipped his beer. Except for the baseball game, the place was deathly still. He tried to watch the game.

The bartender was glaring at him. "Something wrong with your beer?"

"What? Oh. No, it's okay." He didn't think he should say it was refreshing, delicious, or that the hops gave it a fruity bouquet? He took a bigger drink.

He was torn between smiling at the bartender and glaring at him. The general, no-nonsense air seemed to require a glare. He imagined that the bartender had blackened the teeth and drawn devil's horns on his favorite photo of Cory.

He may have overdone it a bit.

Paul said, "He's just pissed because he thinks his girlfriend is going out on him."

There were some supportive grunts. The bartender nodded and moved off.

The lady of uncertain age got to her feet. She crossed the floor like it was canted at a thirty degree angle. She shoved her way between him and Paul and banged her empty glass on the bar.

She smiled and winked at Paul. She might be younger than Aunt Flo.

She turned her attention to Gabe Bergeron; she pinched his butt cheek while massaging his chest. "Why would anybody go out on a cutie like you?"

The bartender was giving her side eye. He refilled her glass and banged it on the counter. He stood there glaring at her.

She frowned. "What's your problem, Harold?"

"You got your drink."

She stuck out her tongue at Harold, but she went back to

her table.

He had no idea how to bring up Duke's name so he just watched the game. He had done this plenty of times with Cory without whining so this was in his wheelhouse.

More guys came in, and the sound of human interaction rose above the level of a Quaker meeting.

Paul was talking to the guy next to him about the pitcher; Paul was not a fan. The guy was trying to defend him.

The pitcher was tall and bearded and balletic as his lean body unfurled to release the ball and send it screaming toward the catcher's glove. Or more often the bat of the opposing player.

The manager strode out to the mound. The baseball uniform was not flattering to a man of his build and age.

Paul said, "He's done."

The other guy nodded. "Yeah. I hope they don't put Stettner in."

Paul and the guy groaned as Stettner got the nod and chugged to the mound. Mr. Stettner was chunky...not to say obese, but he appeared to be able to throw the ball; hard.

But the batters sent it back at him with remarkable frequency. Paul and his new friend, Dave, were shaking their heads.

Obviously Stettner was doing something wrong. He wanted to ask Paul what that was, but that would be Gabe-like.

He sat on his stool and endured. He had drunk two beers over the course of however many hours they had been trapped in this pit of despair, and Harold was eyeing his empty glass with a jaundiced eye.

"Another, Harold." And Harold responded with an ennui almost as intense as Officer Fuchs. "I'm Gabe."

Harold was profoundly uninterested. He was tall and slender and had a prominent nose and dark hair. His eyes were large and could be almost any color hidden beneath the brim of his cap.

At some point, the baseball game ended, and now the Vegas Golden Knights were doing battle with the Minnesota Wild in a live NHL match.

Hockey was more fun to watch than baseball. He realized he had drunk his beer, and Harold had given him another. He should slow down.

Men had been entering in greater numbers; there might be two dozen now. The lady of indeterminate age looked each one over and made suggestive comments to some.

Those individuals stepped quickly past her.

Harold was not best pleased. "Lily!" She smirked at him; she may have given him the finger. "Just keep pushing it. Go ahead."

She ignored him.

And then two youngish ladies bounced in. They were wearing tight t-shirts and jeans. They had pony tails, black baseball caps, dangly silver earrings, and purses that could double as luggage in a pinch.

One had donned an orange t-shirt and one wore pink. They marched past Lily like she was a waxworks figure. It wouldn't be untrue to say that every eye was briefly aimed their way; Harold included.

They bosomed up to the bar to order beers.

Orange T-shirt smiled at Harold. "Hi Harold. Looking good." Pink T-shirt giggled.

Harold said, "Cut that out, Julia."

She fluttered her eyelashes at him. "But it's true, Harold. You're a real stud."

Pink T-shirt was giggling too hard to stay on her stool.

Harold poured two beers. "Denny will kick my ass if you keep that shit up, Julia."

He wasn't sure but he thought Denny might be the large individual who was glaring at Harold from a booth in the back.

Julia laughed and arched her back so that her mammary artillery was locked and loaded. Harold tried to tear his eyes away but he was frozen until she and her boon companion strutted to the aforementioned large individual, who might be Denny, and sat in his booth.

Julia may have lip-locked with him and then stroked his chest and shoulders like he was her Brahma bull who had just won a blue ribbon at the county fair.

Harold was shaking his head.

And then Julia and Pink T-shirt headed through a the door in the back only to return thirty seconds later.

Julia and Pink T-shirt marched back to the bar and Harold. "The freaking door still won't close, Harold."

Denny was hulking behind his love.

Julia said, "You promised to get it fixed!"

"Sorry, Julia. I've been trying to find somebody."

Pink T-shirt said, "And the floor is sagging worse and worse, Harold. If I fall through and wind up in the freaking basement, I'll sue your skinny ass!"

He smiled as inspiration struck; Paul who was eyeing him might have looked uneasy for the first time since he'd known him.

He said, "Harold?"

Harold glared at him. "What?"

"I can fix it for you."

"What?"

"I'm a builder. Me and my partner Cory. Want me to take a look?" Which was not an outright lie since he and Cory had rebuilt Aunt Flo's dock.

Harold said, "Who the Hell are you?"

"Gabe Bergeron." He held out his hand which Harold was loathe to shake but he did. "It can't hurt to let me take a look?"

Lily said, "Let the cutie look at the crap floor in your crap Ladies' Room, Harold."

Lily had a square face that was curiously unlined, tiny eyes, and a red scarf tied around her head; mostly, he thought, to cover her lack of hair.

Julia said, "How about it, Harold?"

Harold waved a hand in defeat.

He hopped off his telephone pole stool; Pink T-shirt grabbed his arm. "I'm Hannah."

Hannah and Julia and Denny escorted him to the Ladies' Room which was indeed crap. Not that it was dirty.

But the floor had sagged and pulled away from the wall creating a dark void. The door jamb was out of plumb. The plaster above the door was cracked, and the door lacked six inches of closing. He got down on his knees and peered into the void which had a distinct mildew, mold, and damp earth aroma.

"Shit. How long has it been like this?"

Julia said, "Months."

"I need a flashlight."

Hannah said, "Harold's got one." And she came back with it.

There was a store room below. He smiled his best smile at Hannah being careful not to look at Julia and rile Denny. "How do I get into the basement?"

But it was Denny who said, "Back here." Denny had a voice suited to his barrel chest.

And they all trooped down into the basement. He assessed the situation in a thoroughly professional manner, nodding sagely, poking and tapping the main beam and the floor joists.

He nodded confidently for the benefit of Denny, Julia, and Hannah.

He went back to his seat. "The floor joists are resting on a rotten beam. You had termites?"

Harold nodded.

"You should do something about that beam, Harold."

Julia said, "Yeah, Harold."

Lily nodded. "Before we're all drinking in the freaking basement, Harold. Tiny would never have let it get so bad."

Harold glared at Lily. "Mom's gone, Lily, and I'm doing the best I can. Is that okay with you? Cause if it isn't, you can take your sorry ass to another bar."

Lily smiled at Harold. "Take a pill, Harold." And she sipped her drink.

Harold closed his eyes and shook his head. "It's bad, isn't it?" Harold looked at him. "But I don't know you. Got any references?"

He smiled his very best smile at Harold. "Sure. I can give you the names of satisfied customers.... Hey, wait. You know Duke Thorvaldsen? Talk to him. I did some work on that old Victorian for him."

Harold looked happier. "You know Duke?"

"Sure. I was hoping I'd run into him tonight. Susan said that he hangs out here?"

Lily said, "Now, there's a man."

He thought Julia wanted to second that emotion, but Denny was standing next to her.

Harold said, "Haven't seen him for a week. But he'll turn up. About these repairs...."

"I can check everything out and write up an estimate tomorrow."

Harold said, "Okay, but I can't afford to spend a fortune. What was your name again?"

"Gabe. Gabe Bergeron. I understand, but we need to shore up that beam at least or the floor back there could collapse. That can't wait, Harold."

Julia said, "Yeah, Harold."

Poor Harold nodded. "Okay. Come by tomorrow."

"Right. I'll be here." He had his first construction job; he couldn't wait to tell Cory. "So about Duke? I tried calling his number, but the message said his phone was unreachable or some shit like that?"

He had finished his fifth beer...or sixth? He was feeling pretty good. He might be smiling too much so he tried to press his lips together as he fought the urge to giggle.

Harold shrugged, but big Denny said, "Why?"

He managed to focus both eyes on Denny and consolidate his image into a unified whole. Denny was a little taller than Cory. He had on jeans, boots, and a tight, white t-shirt that molded to his pecs and belly. His arms were big; maybe as big as Cory's.

Denny was fast approaching fifty. His hair was buzzed; the sides had gone gray. He had a square face, little gray eyes, fat cheeks and jowls. It wasn't an ugly face but not even his mother would think it handsome.

He was currently glaring at Gabe Bergeron.

"Why do I want to talk to him?" Denny nodded flexing fingers that could crush wheat into flour. "He sent me a message. No idea what he wanted."

Denny processed that.

"Is he a buddy of yours, Denny?"

A nod.

"Right. Me too." He held out his hand. "Gabe Bergeron. I didn't catch your name, but happy to meet a buddy of Duke's."

Denny shook without pulverizing his bones. "Denny Krueger."

"Right. If you see him, let him know I tried to call him? He's got my number if it's important."

Denny stood there looking like he was in a coma, which was probably his thoughtful, introspective look.

Julia was looking at him. "Denny?"

But Mr. Krueger shook his head. "No, Julia."

She rolled her eyes and stomped off to talk to Hannah. She and Hannah hugged and then Julia was marching toward the door.

"We're leaving."

Denny followed her.

He looked over at Paul who smiled at him. "Are you tipsy, Gabe?"

"Sure am. I have zero tolerance for alcohol."

Paul said, "So Denny knows where Duke is?"

He leaned over to whisper into Paul's ear and almost fell off the stool but Paul caught him. "I believe so."

Paul said, "Should we leave now, Gabe?"

"That might be wise."

He did his very best not to stagger out the door. With Paul's guidance he located the viridescent Volvo.

He was climbing in very carefully when Denny and Julia drove past. She was speaking to Mr. Krueger in a forceful manner.

Paul said, "Did you get the tag number, Gabe?"

"Maybe yes, maybe no. Did you?"

Paul nodded.

"Hold on." He called Fowler. "Detective, is that you?" He may have giggled. "Gabriel Bergeron here."

"What the Hell's wrong with you?"

"Not a thing. I am right as rain, as fine as frog's hair. I am at the very pinnacle of my intellectual and physical prowess."

"Are you drunk? You went to Tiny's?"

"I did. Attend. It is likely that Duke is bunking with one Denny Krueger who resides in West Philly." He giggled again but he focused on Paul. "My associate will give you Mr. Krueger's tag number."

He handed the phone to Paul who rattled it off.

Paul was smiling. "Yes, Detective."

Paul handed the phone back to him.

Fowler said, "Tell me you aren't driving?"

"In my condition? I resent that, Detective. I take umbrage. I am deeply offended."

"Go home, Bergeron."

And Fowler was gone.

He looked at Paul. "I'd like to go home now."

Friday
8:00 am

He had gotten up the stairs to his apartment. He thought there had been singing on the way.

Fifteen men on the dead man's chest—
...Yo-ho-ho, and a bottle of rum!
Drink and the devil had done for the rest—
...Yo-ho-ho, and a bottle of rum!

He didn't believe that he'd known the words so it seemed likely that Paul had supplied them and had joined in. He wondered what else he'd done?

He wasn't going to think about that.

He was sitting in his cubicle wondering if he should call Fowler when Dana said, "Gabe?"

He wasn't feeling so good; he was developing a stabbing pain above his left eye.

It had been years since he'd gotten drunk on champagne and eaten lots of chocolate, Smith Island cake. Which wasn't a combination he'd recommend.

He thought this was worse, and he was in no mood to tolerate some scummy client.

He turned teeth bared.

Hui-wen with her purple spiked hair was smiling at him. "What's wrong with you, Dude?"

"Nothing." He may have glared at Carla who gave her

sister a nod and him a get-over-it look. "What may I do for you, Hui-wen?"

Hui-wen smiled her *enfant terrible* smile as she looked over the cubicle wall. "Be right back." She tripped lightly to Paul's desk.

She stuck out a delicate hand with chipped green nails. "I'm Hui-wen Wong. Winnie's daughter."

Paul stood up. "I know. Nice to meet you, Hui-wen."

She was grinning at Paul. "What are your intentions toward my mother, Sir?"

Paul smiled back at her as calm as the Pocomoke River on a sunny day. "Semi-honorable, Ms. Wong."

"What does that mean?"

"That's for your mother to discover for herself."

Hui-wen smiled at Paul. "Good. Don't wait too long, Mr. Hearne."

"I'm not in control of the timetable."

Hui-wen nodded vigorously. "Too right. Okay. Nice to meet you."

And she spun on her heel. "Bergeron. Conference room."

He sat at his desk. He wasn't going to be ordered around by another Wong. He just wasn't. The pain above his left eye had shifted; the back of his head felt like a jack hammer had been jammed against his skull.

Carla said, "You might want to put your rear in gear, Bergeron. You don't want to see Hui-wen pissed."

"I fear no woman and no man either.

Carla and Harry snickered at him, but he joined the firecracker sister in the conference room.

She was sitting on the table with her legs crossed in a modified Lotus position. She was a vision in olive drab.

Her t-shirt had the trilobed radiation warning symbol set on a mottled, brownish background. Her long shorts were also olive drab with buckles and pockets and random stitching. She had girded her loins with a black leather belt four inches wide and twice as long as it needed to be.

He may have given her a jaundiced look. "What?"

"You're hungover?"

"I am no such thing, Young Lady. You have thirty seconds."

She stared at him. "Carla said you were funny."

"What? I am funny. Wait. No, I'm not. Just tell me why you're here, Hui-wen, and leave me to die in peace."

She was smiling at him. He wanted to tell her to get off the freaking table.

She hopped off. "Chill, Dude."

He sat down and massaged the back of his head. The conference room smelled funny but he couldn't place the scent.

She said, "I just want you to try to find this dude, this Gavin. I mean really try."

"Why?"

"Because I think my sisters are right...for once...and Mom won't give big Paul a real chance until she knows...one way or the other...about Gavin."

Hui-wen was motionless with a thoughtful look on her face for a good five seconds. "I think she really loved this Gavin. Really."

"It sounds like she did...probably still does, Hui-wen. Right. I can try to find him. Not today! Maybe not this week. But as soon as I can."

She smiled and held out her hand. "Deal."

He shook her hand. "What about you? Have you ever loved someone that much?"

She looked flustered and then pissed off. "No way, Dude!"

But then she smiled and bounced out the door. She ran over to Carla, hugged her, and said something in Mandarin.

She and Carla stared at him smiling. And then Miss Hui-wen tripped lightly to the elevator like a post-apocalyptic elf.

So he was cranky. He needed aspirin. And coffee. Dana was looking at him.

"She's a client."

Dana nodded and went back to her magazine. Neither of them believed that for a second, but Dana hadn't ratted him out to Jennifer or Andy about anything. So far.

He went into the breakroom.

Paul appeared at the door. "Hi, Gabe."

"Hi, Paul. Thanks for going with me to Tiny's! And for helping me up the stairs. Did we sing?"

Paul smiled. "You're welcome. I had a good time, Gabe. And we did sing."

"Not well as I remember?"

"Well enough. Are you going to fix Harold's beam?"

"Nope. But I could."

Paul smiled at him. "You did really good, Gabe, getting them to talk about Duke."

"Thanks."

Paul nodded and stood there like a statue in a nice gray suit.

"About Winnie's visit here. And Hui-wen's. They want me to find out something...."

Paul said, "You don't have to tell me, Gabe."

"Right. I want to, but I can't really. Though I can tell you it's nothing about you. It's about something from Winnie's past. Nothing bad. Just something she'd like to know."

Paul nodded. "But you're busy."

"Yeah, but I'll make time."

Paul smiled and drifted away.

Why the Hell had he told Paul that? He had no time to find Gavin, and no idea how to go about it.

Well, he could search online? Or ask Fowler?

He sighed. He had too much accounting work to get done before the day ended. He wasn't working Saturday.

But he had calls to make.

He dialed. Harold said, "Tiny's Bar."

"Hi, This is Gabe Bergeron."

"Yeah? You coming?"

"Sorry, Harold, but something's come up, and I won't be able to take on your job."

"Okay. I couldn't pay you anyway."

"Harold, you need to have that beam fixed."

"I know. Gotta go."

He sighed. Tiny's Bar was an accident waiting to happen. He dialed again.

"Detective Fowler. It's Gabe."

Fowler didn't say anything.

"Mitch?"

"Yeah. I'm busy, Gabe."

"Right. I just wondered if you caught Duke?" Fowler grunted. "Is that a no?"

"The slippery bastard was there."

"But he got away?"

"Sorry, Gabe. We screwed up. He was at Krueger's house. We arrested Krueger for assaulting an officer."

"Not you?"

"Fuchs."

"Is Fuchs okay?"

"He looks about the same. Anyway, the girlfriend told me that Duke had been there for over a week, and she was glad he was gone."

"Julia."

"Yeah. The bastard left some clothes but nothing that tells me where he is now. I couldn't stake out the place...use plainclothes guys...too freaking much is going on right now."

"I understand."

"Look, I appreciate your help. If you come up with anything else, call me."

"I will. There is one thing."

"Talk faster, Bergeron."

"There's a guy: Gavin Alexander Sommer, Jr." He gave Fowler all the info that Carla had given him. "So he may be connected...in some way."

Which was a lie so egregious that he felt his nose to see if it had lengthened.

"How?"

"I'm not sure. Can you see what you can find about him?"

Fowler sighed. "No address but his parent's? You're killing me, Bergeron. Later."

Well, he hadn't said no.

He called Cory and left an I-was-thinking-of-you message. He took some more aspirins and applied himself to his actual job which paid him the pittance which kept body and soul together.

And it was suddenly noon. He met Harry in the elevator coming back from taking Carla to a doctor's appointment.

"Want to come to CoffeeXtra with me? I'll pay?"

Harry smiled. "Sorry. I have to get some work done and then get some groceries and take Winnie home since Francine is busy."

Harry looked exhausted.

"Okay. I went to a bar last night with Paul."

Harry brightened. "No? And what? You drank sarsaparilla and embarrassed the Hell out of Paul?"

"I don't even know what that is. I'll have you know I drank enough beer to render me quite giddy and giggly." He patted Harry on the shoulder. "I'll tell you all about it when you have time to savor all the nuances."

"Can't wait." Harry smiled. "I'm sorry Hui-wen is bothering you about Gavin."

"It's okay, Harry. Nothing you can do!"

He moseyed along to CoffeeXtra. He tried to exercise what Cory called situational awareness, but it was a pretty day, and his headache had eased up, and he didn't want to see anyone remotely connected to Duke Thorvaldsen even if they were lurking everywhere.

He ordered and sat and zoned out.

Until his phone rang: Aunt Flo. "Hello, Aunt Flo?"

"How are you feeling, Gabriel?"

"Fine. Well, I've been better."

"You have a hangover, Dear, in case you don't know."

"Wait. How do you know..." And the memory of a late night call came back to him in bits and pieces. "Shit. I called you. I'm sorry, Aunt Flo."

"Not at all, Gabriel. Tell me about Susan. Is she all right?"

"Did I mention the kidnapping?"

She laughed. "You did."

"Right. Okay. And Gianna Bonacci?"

"And Paul going with you to Tiny's Bar. Did they catch Thorvaldsen, Gabriel?"

"No. They didn't. Almost, but no cigar."

"So this is still ongoing? And you are still in danger."

"I'm being very careful, Aunt Flo."

"I'm sure you think you are. Please call Cory and ask him to come home, Gabriel."

"I'll try, Aunt Flo. I'll call him, but he may not answer."

"Then come here until he does."

"I'll call him as soon as I hang up, Aunt Flo. I promise."

She didn't say anything. "Call me every day, Gabriel."

"I will."

He hung up and rang Cory. And left another message. He was looking at the stupid phone when it rang again: Harry this time.

"Yes, Harry?"

"A 'client' just walked in. If you could see me, you'd see the air quotes I'm putting around client."

"Shit. Shit. Shit. Tell me."

Harry said, "This has to be the guy who said he was the second secretary from the embassy?

"Of course, it is. Chinedum Onyewu to his best buds. What does he want?"

"You, and he's getting loud about it."

"Tell him I'm at CoffeeXtra. He can come here. If he objects, get Chase to shoot him."

And he hung up. It was possible that he was still a smidgen grumpy.

The limo pulled up in front, and the chauffeur hopped out and came inside. They locked eyes.

"Mr. Bergeron?"

"Yes, it is I."

"Mr. Onyewu would like to speak to you in the limousine, Sir."

"No. I'm having my lunch, and I'm not budging from this spot. You're Mr. Babalola?"

Mr. Babalola was still tall and still wearing black-rimmed glasses.

"I am, Sir?"

"What do you think of Mr. Onyewu?"

Mr. Babalola smiled. "He is a fine gentleman, Sir."

He smiled back. "I'm sure he is. Totally untouched by the slightest hint of corruption and racketeering and a host of other unsavory matters."

Mr. Babalola grinned. "Totally, Sir."

"I don't doubt it for a second. Why is he in the U.S.?"

"Who can say, Mr. Bergeron?"

"Something was taken from him? Something very valuable? Something he hopes Inspector Okocha will find?"

"I do not know. Truly. I will give him your message."

And in due course, the fake second secretary entered CoffeeXtra. His sniff was audible to the farthest reaches of the establishment.

Billy and his band of baristas were agog; partly due to the suit and the gold bling, but also to the man himself. Onyewu really did carry himself like a prince.

He could make a sumptuous living separating little old ladies from their life savings if he ever decided to give up whatever criminal enterprise he was currently engaged in.

He marched over.

"Have a seat, Mr. Attaché."

Onyewu raised a single eyebrow and declaimed, "I am the second secretary...."

"You are not."

Onyewu smiled and sat. He may have examined the seat before depositing his elegantly-clad bottom.

"Have you considered my offer? It has been a week, Mr. Bergeron."

Astrid came over. "What can I get you?"

Onyewu didn't even look at her. "Go away, Woman."

Astrid was a large, sturdy woman with black, spiky hair, and the personality of a snapping turtle.

He got between her and the Attaché before she beat him senseless with the chair she was clutching...or even her large fists heavy with spiky rings.

"He's not worth it, Astrid!"

Astrid thought he was worth at least a mild concussion or a bloody nose, but Martin and Selena grabbed her arms.

She could, of course, have flung them off like Godzilla stomping through the Japanese army, but Attaché Onyewu was already out the door and diving into his limo.

Astrid still wanted to inflict damage on the attaché or at least his limo, but Martin was whispering into her ear and gradually calmed her down.

Martin and Astrid and Selena were an item. He couldn't fathom it, and he didn't want to think about it.

He strolled out to the limo.

Onyewu rolled the window down. "That woman is insane!"

"No. She's just Astrid...well, I will admit she has a short fuse."

Onyewu shook his head. "Have you considered my offer?"

"I don't know where Thorvaldsen is. Truly. What did he steal? Was it yours? Or Ma's?"

Onyewu wasn't looking at him when he hit the button to roll up the window. He was beating on the partition to let Mr. Babalola know that he wished to leave.

He was watching the limo disappear when he got the feeling that someone was watching him.

He spun around, and an elderly, medium-sized, black man was staring at him from ten feet away. He was wearing tan jeans, a black polo shirt with a red and white stripe across the chest. And a brown pork pie hat.

He would have put it down to an interest in the limo and Onyewu's antics, but there was something about the guy's eyes and his face

His hand was creeping toward his Glock when the guy turned and hobbled into the crowd.

He went back inside but he wasn't really hungry any more.

Friday
5:00 pm

He had left promptly at 5:00 pm. Well, maybe a half hour early.

Chase was standing at his security desk reading something on his laptop. "Good night, Chase. Have a good weekend."

"Roger that, Gabe. I'm hopeful it will be."

Chase had a really nice smile, and the rest of him was pleasing to the eye; very pleasing. Well, he could look. Where was Cory now? He sighed and walked toward the parking garage.

He wasn't as alert as he could have been, but the guy following him was kinda obvious.

Well, to be fair, it was hard for someone his height to be inconspicuous. He was black and had shaved the sides of his head.

He stopped.

They stared at each other. The guy looked like a cat on finding that the mouse was running at it and not away.

Younger Gabe would have fled.

Older Gabe, whose headache was back, was made of sterner stuff, but his shadow turned and loped off.

He didn't feel like giving chase. He got into his Jeep and drove home. If anyone followed him, he didn't spot them.

He may have been napping when his phone rang. When his eyes focused, he sighed. "Bradley? What's happened?"

"Nothing, Gabe."

Bradley sounded a little funny. "Sure about that?"

"Yes, Gabe."

"Are you and your mom still with your uncle?"

"Yeah. Look, I just called to tell you...to ask you not to bother trying to find Duke."

He sat up and focused. "And why is that?"

"I just think it would be best if we forgot about Duke. He's gone and isn't coming back, and the sooner Mom and I get used to that, the better it will be."

"So Susan's onboard with this one hundred eighty degree course correction?"

"Yes, Gabe."

"Wait. Have you heard from him?"

"No! Nothing like that. It's just better if we forget about Duke. Mom and I really appreciate everything you've done. I'll pay you whatever you think is fair for your time and any expenses you've had. I want to do that, Gabe."

"Right. I don't think so. If I had actually found him, then maybe we could discuss a small sum...a modest remuneration...but with things still up in the air like this...."

"Please, Gabe. And please stop looking for Duke. I'll call you next week."

And Master Bradley was gone.

This was an unexpected turn of events.

He sat and pondered.

And then he woke up again. It was now past midnight, and he headed for his lonely bed.

What was he going to do in the morning? He was going to do laundry, clean his apartment, and definitely get groceries.

And when that was done, he was going to watch TV and read a few chapters of his new book. He wasn't going to even think about Lars Thorvaldsen, aka "Duke" since no one wanted him to find this gentleman.

Well, except for Fowler.

And Chinedum Onyewu who didn't count.

Saturday 11:00 am

He had done his laundry and vacuumed in a desultory fashion. He had to get groceries, and he'd left his Jeep in front of the building. He was watching TV and eating a slice of cold pizza before venturing out into the temperate May day.

And then a knock came on his door.

This was not a good sign. Usually.

"Who is it?"

"Aronson." He shook his head and debated letting him in. "Open up, Gabriel."

"Or you'll huff and puff and blow my house down?"

"Something like that."

"Is Collins with you?"

"No, he isn't."

He opened the door, and Aronson strolled in. He took a seat on his sofa and crossed his legs. "How have you been, Gabriel?"

"Peachy. Why are you here?"

"Any chance of some coffee? Or tea?"

Aronson was smiling at him, and the dark eyes were sapping his will to resist.

But he was stronger than that. "Stop smiling at me." He frowned at the agent. "You left me high and dry, Aronson. I'm pissed with you."

"I'm very sorry, but I had critical developments in another, parallel case. There was nothing I could do. And you found Susan without my help. Tea?"

"Do you like gunpowder tea?"

Aronson smiled at him.

"I'm still pissed with you."

He made tea and a pot of coffee. Gunpowder tea was not what he needed.

Aronson sipped. "Very good, Gabriel. Where did you get this?"

"Excelsior Tea; a client of mine. An accounting client. You can have the tin?"

"I'd appreciate that, Gabriel. How did you find Susan?"

"Detective Fowler found her."

Aronson smiled and shook his head. "Don't make me laugh. Some of the locals are marginally competent but he's bottom rung."

"He's okay."

"How?"

"Fowler found her." He could mention Monroe just to see if Aronson would react but he didn't want him to know.

Aronson shook his head more hurt than angry. "You don't trust me, Gabriel."

"Hell, no!"

"I see. So tell me about any other developments. Please."

"Nothing really."

"Sure about that?"

"What developments would interest you, Special Agent" Thorvaldsen developments? Or Nigerian or Chinese developments?"

"Any of the above."

He didn't believe that for a second. "We almost caught Thorvaldsen."

"Really?" Aronson was all but yawning but he played along.

"He'd been staying with his girlfriend, Gianna Bonacci, until she kicked him out, and then he was bunking with his buddy, Denny Krueger. They almost caught him at Denny's place."

Aronson sighed. "Fowler let him slip away."

"Not at all." Well, he had, but he kind of liked Fowler and

felt a need to defend him.

"But you don't give a shit about Thorvaldsen. It's the Nigerian-Chinese connection that puts some lead in your pencil."

The special agent laughed and laughed until he just cut it off. "So nothing for me then? Are you sure, Gabriel?"

"Yes, I am."

Aronson got to his feet in one lithe movement and came closer and closer until he could have numbered his long eyelashes.

Aronson put a hand on his shoulder while staring into his eyes. "I guess I'll have to find my own leads to fortify my pencil, won't I?"

The aroma of his cologne was imprinted on his brain forever as Aronson's hand massaged his chest. "Call me if you find out anything, Gabriel."

He may have been rooted to the spot as Aronson turned and headed for the door. He thought there was something he wanted to ask the guy?

"Wait." He tossed the tin of tea to him. "If you really want it?"

"I do. Thank you, Gabriel." Aronson looked at him; one eyebrow raised above a big, brown eye. "Something else?"

"I want to look inside Thorvaldsen's house again."

"What's stopping you?"

"I don't have a key."

Aronson laughed at him and patted his face. He didn't get punched in the mouth only because he had great reflexes.

"Sorry, Gabriel." He put up his hands. "It's just that you are so...."

"Choose your next word carefully, Special Agent."

"Capable of remarkable lateral thinking and yet dense at the same time."

"Meaning what? I should break in? Pick the lock?"

"I'm sure you'll figure it out." And he was off down the stairs.

He didn't want to break in, and he didn't know how to pick a lock. And Bradley wasn't home. Not that he could ask him for the key since Bradley had asked him to stand down.

He could take a look? But he wasn't doing any breaking and entering. With his luck, Fuchs would drive by and arrest him.

And enjoy it. As much as Fuchs enjoyed anything.

He ran down the stairs.

Aronson's black SUV was parked behind his Jeep. The special agent wasn't in view but a red sports car was idling on the street.

He slipped between the SUV and Jeep. Aronson was in the passenger seat of the sports car next to the driver, a young lady with long, flowing hair.

He couldn't see her face because she and Aronson were snogging in a spirited manner.

He took a moment.

This was certainly an interesting development but not his current concern. He got into his Jeep and set off. He tried to see if anyone was following him after the two guys from yesterday, but he didn't spot any suspicious vehicles.

He parked down the block from Bradley's house. He was going to do this. And then a thought occurred. He grabbed a clipboard from his briefcase and walked confidently across the street.

On the right of Duke's house were two row houses; the remains of a line of them that had been torn down?

A commercial building of some kind was on the left. It had two, steel, roll up doors and looked like it had been a warehouse or car repair place? It was empty now.

He was a termite inspector, and Duke had hired him. He had every right to be on the front porch. The door was locked, of course, and short of breaking a window he wasn't getting in that way.

He walked around the house inspecting the eaves for termite damage and making inspector type notes on his clip-board.

He tried the back door in a pro forma way.

It swung wide.

Which was an interesting development.

And then his phone rang.

Aronson said, "Where are you?"

"On the back steps of Duke's house. The door is open."

"Go inside. And hide."

The special agent wasn't the boss of him, but there was something about the tone that got his feet moving. "Okay. I'm inside. Shit!" He drew his Glock.

"What?"

"Somebody has torn the place apart."

"Just find some place to hide. Help is on the way."

"Okay. And I need help because?"

"You were followed."

"From my apartment?"

"Yes, you idiot."

He was running upstairs. "I resent that." But he really didn't. He should have been more careful.

He found a closet in the front bedroom and ducked inside. "And you followed the followers?"

"More or less. I knew where you were going."

"What do I do?"

"Stay put."

"Will do. So who is following me?"

Aronson laughed. "Two vehicles. three men. I would guess that they're Nigerian."

"Shit. Wait. Is one of them wearing a brown, pork pie hat?"

Aronson said, "Yes?"

"He was following me yesterday."

"Idiot."

"Well, I didn't know he was following me, did I? Maybe I should have realized but people don't usually follow me."

And then he heard a vehicle screeched to a halt in front of the house. He peered out. Aronson got out of his SUV as another vehicle pulled in.

"Come out, Gabriel."

So he did.

Aronson was talking to two men who looked like agents and Collins who did not.

Aronson said, "Run the plates."

Collins said, "Probably stolen."

"Do it anyway."

Collins nodded. "Our resources are stretched thin, Sir."

Aronson just glared at Collins who scampered off.

And then Aronson glared at him. "You had no idea you were being followed?"

"No."

"You're lucky I spotted them."

"I am. Thank you." He looked at Aronson. He hadn't seen any guys following him. Was he going to take Aronson's word that three men had followed him here?

He thought he was.

Aronson smiled. "Skeptical and naive rolled up in a fuzzy ball."

"So any idea why they followed me?"

"Tell me about the guy in the pork pie hat."

He may have shivered just a bit. "I was standing outside of CoffeeXtra. Attaché Chinedum Onyewu had run out before a barista could beat him unconscious...Astrid is not someone to be trifled with...and Pork Pie Hat was staring at me as Mr. Babalola motored away."

Aronson was looking at him. "And he scared you?"

"He did. Something about the face. He would scare Astrid."

Aronson said, "What was that about the house being torn apart?"

"Come with me."

The lovely walnut wainscoting had been ripped off and holes punched in the walls. All the walls.

Someone had spent a lot of time systematically tearing Duke's house apart. The kitchen was a shambles.

He led Aronson into the bedroom; the mattress had been gutted. Some floorboards had been pried up.

He went back upstairs. The place still had a faint dead body odor. "The body...First Mate Whalen...was in there. The ancient medicine cabinet had been ripped out of the wall.

Every room they went in had been gutted.

He looked at Aronson. "What were they looking for?"

Aronson shrugged.

He didn't believe the shrug for a second. The shrug reeked of falsehood and deceit and secrets for which he would never have high enough clearance.

Aronson smiled. "I'm sorry, Gabriel."

And the special agent was tripping down the stairs and out the door. He followed.

Aronson got into his SUV. Most of his merry men had gone, but Collins was still hanging around.

Collins, who might or might not be FBI, had shaved his head and looked like an egg with freckles.

Aronson said, "You should go home, Gabriel."

"I will. Don't worry. Who was the woman with the long, brown hair?"

Aronson smiled at him and rolled up his window.

Which wasn't entirely unexpected. He got into his Jeep and started the engine. They rolled out, and he followed but he kept straight when Aronson and Collins turned. He pulled over as soon as he could.

He grabbed his phone. "Detective Fowler?"

Fowler said, "What now, Bergeron?"

"Are you working?"

"No, I am not working." There were background noises; maybe restaurant type noises.

"Are you having lunch?"

"Bergeron."

"Right. I might know where the Chinese are. Or have recently been."

"Yeah? Where are you?"

"Four blocks from Duke's house."

"Stay there. Are you sure about this, Gabe?"

"I am. Well, it makes sense. If I'm wrong, I'll pay for your lunch."

Saturday
1:00 pm

He pondered why Aronson was aggressively flirting with him while he waited for Fowler. Did he think a nice smile would render him pliant and cooperative? Or was it some sort of game?

He sighed and put Aronson out of his mind as Fuchs pulled up alongside the Jeep. "What now?"

Fuchs was looking particularly unenthusiastic but that may have been the black eye. "Sorry about your eye."

Fuchs' growl was in the infrasound range audible only to elephants and blue whales.

"I think I know where the Chinese are."

Fuchs looked at him. "Susan Bradley?"

"Yes, the guys who kidnapped her."

"Where?"

"In the abandoned warehouse, or whatever it was, next to Thorvaldsen's house."

Fuchs just looked at him and then got on his radio. More patrol cars arrived as the forces of law and order massed four blocks from the warehouse.

Fowler got out of his car. "Bergeron. Get over here."

He trotted over. "Yes, Detective?"

"Tell me why I'm here on my day off."

"Someone has ripped Thorvaldsen's house apart; every wall smashed open, the furniture taken apart, floorboards pulled up."

"Okay?"

"Someone has had easy access to the house for weeks.

Nobody has seen them coming and going."

Fuchs was standing by the car. "The warehouse."

"Just so, Officer Fuchs."

Fowler said, "And you parked in front of the house?"

"Well, a few houses down."

Fowler pointed at his very yellow Jeep. "In that?"

"I did. And there were some other cars there. Briefly."

Fowler's eyebrows were scrunched up, and his forehead was furrowed like someone was going to plant corn. His normal gray complexion was dotted with red spots.

"Who the Hell?"

"The FBI. Special Agent Aronson and three of his men. In suits and black SUVs."

The red dots on Fowler's face were connecting up. He wasn't sure but he thought Fuchs was laughing somewhere deep inside his large body.

"But they were only there for a few minutes."

Fowler said, "Well, that's okay then!"

"Look, I'm sorry but I didn't know I was going to find the house demolished, and the warehouse idea just occurred to me. Or I would have called you before I ever went near the place. Honest."

Fowler took a deep breath and then lit a cigarette. When he had a jag of nicotine in his lungs, he said, "So these bastards could be long gone?"

"They could. Absolutely."

Fuchs said, "Or not."

Fowler rubbed his forehead. "Shit."

Fuchs said, "SWAT."

Fowler nodded. "If the assholes aren't there, Bergeron...."

"What?"

But Fowler got on his radio.

He went and sat in his Jeep. He loved his Jeep but it was highly recognizable. If he ever decided to become a real detective, he would need to trade it in. Or have it painted. But he loved it just the way it was.

And Cory would have to teach him about disguises and the total undercover gestalt. Not that Cory would do that.

It appeared that this was going to take some time, but he had a book; a book about octopuses...and not octopi as the first page informed him.

He was starving. He got out and ambled over to Fuchs who had his butt planted against his patrol car.

"Any place around here to get some food?"

Fuchs shook his head. Which either meant there wasn't or that Gabe Bergeron wasn't going anywhere.

He leaned against Fuchs' patrol car. "Got a candy bar? Or some gum? Water even?"

Fuchs shook his head but he reached inside the car and handed him a water.

He was sipping when they heard the gunfire; a single burst.

And then silence. He looked at Fuchs who only added to the silence.

They stayed there, asses on car, for hours. Well, it was a good twenty minutes before Fowler came jogging back to them.

Fowler was glaring at him. "What? Did somebody get hurt? Did you catch anybody? Was it the Chinese? Did a SWAT guy trip and fire his weapon by accident?"

Fowler smiled. "We caught one of them."

"Yeah? Great! Who?"

Fowler said, "Not Ma or Chen. But four guys have been living there."

"So Ma and Chen and an unidentified henchman are still at large?" Which was kind of disappointing.

Fuchs said, "'Henchman'." And he smiled.

Fowler made his startled face as he looked at the officer.

"Can I talk to the guy?"

Fowler said, "Come with me."

And they marched shoulder to shoulder back to the warehouse. The perp had been handcuffed and was about to be tossed into the back of a patrol car. The SWAT guys were striding about seeming a bit disappointed that there was no reason to fire hundreds of rounds of bullets.

He and Fowler approached. The guy was maybe twenty and looked terrified. He had an oval face with spiky hair much like

Astrid's and little ears that stuck out like the handles of a jug.

Fowler glared. "Who are you?"

The guy shook his head, and then blurted something out in Mandarin. Well, it was probably Mandarin. He should get Carla to teach him some useful phrases in Mandarin.

"Do you speak English?"

The guy shook his head.

Fowler smiled at him. "But you understand English?"

Another vigorous head shake.

The guy was tall but he was hunched over like he expected to be slapped around.

Fowler said, "Bergeron? You want to take a shot?"

The guy looked up and stared at him. "Do you know who I am?"

Another head shake.

"I'm Gabe Bergeron. Did Ma and Chen tell you about me?"

Nothing.

"How do you feel about Ma?" There was just a flicker in Mr. Ears' eyes. "He's an idiot, isn't he? But his family is connected?"

Mr. Ears was studying his dirty running shoes. The knees of his jeans were muddy as if he'd been gardening.

"You're all here because of him. And the two men who were killed when Susan Bradley was rescued are dead because of him. He's the one who started shooting at the police. Did he tell you and Chen about that?"

Mr. Ears was staring at him now. "Where is he? He doesn't deserve your loyalty."

But Mr. Ears shook his head with finality.

Fowler said, "We'll have a lot of time to talk, Asshole."

And Mr. Ears was locked away in the back of a patrol car.

They searched the warehouse and found nothing; nothing useful.

"So I'm guessing Mr. Ears has no ID?"

Fowler smiled at him. "Mr. Ears?"

"Well, you saw them."

"Nothing on him. And I don't see anything here either."

He was right. There was nothing to indicate where Ma, Chen, and Henchman had gone.

"Somebody will stay here in case they come back."

"Right."

Fowler said, "Now tell me about the house?"

So he took the detective on a tour of Duke's house from attic to ground floor.

The was an access to the crawlspace in the back of the house which wasn't closed all the way. Mr. Ears had probably gotten his muddy knees from crawling under Duke's house but the scuff marks in the mud were just around the entrance.

Fowler said, "What are they looking for?"

"No idea. But Duke brought it home from Nigeria, and these guys...mainly Ma...want it back."

Fowler said, "Real bad."

The bathroom had damp towels draped over the shower curtain rod. "So no water or power in the warehouse?"

Fowler shrugged.

"So our Chinese friends have been bathing in Duke's tub."

Which was creepy, but they may not have known about Whalen's body being left there.

They had looked around some more but there didn't seem to be any clues to the mystery of Thorvaldsen and the Chinese and the Nigerians so he had gone home.

And Fowler had called him in the evening to let him know that Special Agent Aronson had swooped in and carried Mr. Ears back to his FBI aerie.

Monday
10:00 am

He had spent Sunday doing as little as possible. His brain had been as tired as his body, and he'd put off grocery shopping again.

But he had called Aronson to see if Mr. Ears had talked. He had also called Inspector Okocha to see if he knew where Ma might have flown.

Neither had deigned to answer their phones. Which was just rude.

He had called Aunt Flo and told her he was fine and was still trying to reach Cory.

And now he was sitting at his desk hard at work for all the world to see. Well, Harry and Dana.

Of course, Harry didn't care whether he worked or not. Within reason. But Dana could report to Jennifer that he was still being an exceptional employee. He was sort of happy about that.

He may have been smiling to himself when a voice said, "You're weird, Dude."

Hui-wen was standing beside him.

"You're the weird one."

Hui-wen smiled. "Nope. I'm your average American woman." And she flexed her arms in a double biceps display. Her arms were corded, and she had biceps with respectable peaks.

She was wearing a white, peasant blouse with a pleated front and poofy sleeves. The neck was so wide that the blouse was nearly sliding down her slender body. Her gray-striped pantaloons were also poofy but gathered at the ankles. She kicked off her sandals.

And she sat on his desk; on top of his papers. He really didn't like her or anyone sitting on his desk. He even gritted his teeth when Cory did it.

Harry said, "Hui-wen." She glanced at him. "You might want to get off his desk."

Hui-wen studied this weird Bergeron's face. "He looks like he's going to stroke out?"

Harry said, "If you want him to do something for you, sit in the client's chair."

She frowned at the silly men trying to bridle her with their obviously sexist rules but she got off the desk. She managed to scrunch her butt and feet onto the chair seat like a cat wedging itself into a box half the size of its body. She wrapped her arms around her legs and gave him a basilisk stare.

He took a deep breath. "Yes?"

"I went to his parent's house."

"The parents of Gavin Sommer?"

"Sure, Dude." She frowned at him.

"And what did you find there?"

"Some old lady."

"Gavin's mother?"

Hui-wen got her glower on. "I had to bang and bang before she answered the door. And then she said she wasn't! She said she'd never heard of Gavin. Father or son. Or Gail Sommer. Think she was lying?"

"What else did she say?"

"Some shit about owning the house for twenty years, and she couldn't even remember the names of the previous owners. I told her I wasn't buying any of that dreck, and she slammed the door in my face, Dude!'

"How rude of her!" He may have rolled his eyes at Harry.

Hui-wen caught it. "What?"

"I think that if a strange young woman came banging on my door and called me a liar, I might choose to terminate the conversation too."

"Yeah? Some people are just snowflakes, Dude. I always say what I think."

"I believe you."

She gave him a tiny smile. "Maybe you could talk to her? You're slick...when you aren't hung over or having a hissy fit over your desk."

He smiled while imagining burying her in the foundation of the nearest construction site. "I will talk to her. Not today. Have you done any other digging?"

She nodded. "Online. No obituary for Gavin Sommer, Jr. or Gail Sommer."

"What about the father?"

"Yeah. Gavin Sr. died in 1979, two years before Mom and Gavin graduated."

"Send it to me anyway."

She was glaring at him, disappointment clouding the air around them along with whatever scent he was picking up.

And then it hit him: sage. Like Aunt Flo's house before the coming of the B&B "guests" and the sundry odors clinging thereto.

"Okay." She was staring. "Do you love anybody as much as Mom loves this Gavin?"

"Yes, Hui-wen."

"Who?"

He pointed to Cory's picture on his desk.

She snatched it up. "He's hot." She looked at the photo and at the flesh and blood Gabe. She shook her head.

She uncoiled from his chair, slipped on her sandals, and loped to the elevator before he could ask what the head shake meant.

So he wasn't as handsome as Cory. So? Cory was lucky to have him. He was.

He shook his head and turned to Harry. "Baldacci, you are a saint. No, a martyr. Do you have to be a martyr before you can become a saint?"

Harry smiled. "It helps but it's not absolutely required." Harry rolled over. "Actually, I hardly ever see Hui-wen."

"Which is a good thing! What is with the sage scent?"

Harry shrugged. "Some kind of organic, Vegan, recycled, environmentally responsible soap. She gave Carla some; the bars weren't quite solid. Sort of gooey. Carla trashed it."

His phone pinged, and he took a second to read the obit for Gavin Sommer, beloved husband and father. Graveside service. The survived-by's were limited to Gavin, Jr. and his mother, Gail. Which didn't help.

He was about to return to the task at hand, but it was break time. He was thinking about updating Harry and Paul about the events of the weekend when he got a call.

"Mr. Bergeron!" Chase was a bit excited but trying for a calm, professional tone.

"Who's in the freaking lobby now?"

"A Mrs. Iwobi and party to see you, Sir."

"Did they pass the wand test?"

Yes, Sir."

"Right. And how many of them in total? Three?"

"No, Sir."

"Four?"

"Yes, Sir."

"Thanks, Chase. I'll update you afterwards."

"You bet you will. Sir."

Who the Hell was Mrs. Iwobi?

He had the Glock but he felt he should take additional measures. Harry was packing up to go somewhere to do something related to Carla. He took a tenth of a second to feel bad that he hadn't listened to Harry. He smiled and patted Harry on the back as he dashed over to Paul's cubicle.

"We have incoming. Don't know who or what their intentions are but if I give you the signal, dial 911."

Paul nodded and set his briefcase on his desk. Paul had been in the army. It was not impossible that he was armed?

He turned to get to the elevator.

"Gabe?"

"Yes, Paul?"

"What is the signal?"

He spun back and shared a smile with Paul. "Right. We'll

be in the conference room. I think. Anyway, if I yank on my left earlobe, send for the cavalry."

Paul nodded.

He stood beside Harry who was waiting for the elevator. Harry was looking at him funny. "Do I want to know?"

"New clients."

Harry just shook his head. "Don't tell me."

The elevator dinged.

And Mrs. Iwobi and party emerged. He smiled his very best smile and extended his hand. "Mrs. Iwobi? I'm Gabriel Bergeron."

She gave him back a lovely, gentle smile that extended to her big, brown eyes. She shook his hand. "I'm very pleased to meet you, Mr. Bergeron."

"Would you like to come into the conference room?"

Harry stood there holding the elevator door and looking back at him with eyes wide enough to hold a hundred questions.

He had to focus.

Mrs. Iwobi was wearing a slate gray dress topped by a jacket with muted pink flowers crossed with horizontal gray stripes; a strand of white chunky beads around her neck.

Was this what well dressed pirates wore?

Her hair was done in fine dreadlocks and reached below her shoulders. He was going to guess she was forty or fifty.

Pork Pie Hat was one of her party. He told himself to be calm and carry on.

"And who are your...associates?"

She smiled. "This is Mr. Enemkpali, a dear friend."

Mr. Enemkpali was Pork Pie Hat. Which he was wearing along with tan slacks and a black Nirvana t-shirt.

He hadn't really gotten a good look on the street but now he noted that Enemkpali's face sagged like it was made of wax set out in the tropical sun. But the left side was more pronounced with the left eyebrow drooping over the eye. The right side of his mouth was pulled higher than the left.

Had he had a stroke?

There were three slashes on his right cheek that had healed decades earlier. His hair and mustache were grizzled, and he moved slowly, carefully to shake his hand. Mr. Enemkpali was in his seventies; probably.

"And this is Mr. Melifonwu."

Mr. Melifonwu was in his mid-twenties and tallish. If you thought seven foot in sandals was tall. The sides of his head had been rigorously shaved and buffed. A garden of short, finely woven dreadlocks sprang from the top of his head and bent allwhither.

His face was square and striking; perfect skin pushed him over the handsome goal line. He had a pencil mustache.

Mr. Melifonwu shook his hand and gave him a nod. He had been the guy following him Friday night.

"And this is Mr. Obioma."

He was of medium build with a shaved head and an oval face. He might be mid-thirties. He was wearing blue jeans and a silky blue shirt with jumbled blocks containing words. Or names?

He looked perfectly ordinary but there was something about his expression. Appraising? Or predatory? Mr. Obioma just stared as they shook.

Everyone took a seat.

He sat across from Mrs. Iwobi. "And how may I help you?"

She had a round face and an serene expression that might come from an untroubled life or from overcoming the not so serene portions of said life.

"I am looking for someone, Mr. Bergeron."

"So you don't need accounting services then?"

She smiled. "No, no. I do not."

"And you think I know where this person is?"

She nodded. "You may."

"Who is this person, Mrs. Iwobi? And why do you think I know where he, or she, is?"

"Mr. Enemkpali saw you talking to someone on Friday."

He tried smiling at Enemkpali but it was like smiling at a sad sculpture. "And that would be Attaché Chinedum Onyewu."

The temperature of the room dropped to the daytime highs on Pluto. If Mrs. Iwobi had been a little bit less a lady, she would have spit on the floor at the mention of the attaché's name.

"Are you working for him?"

236

"No. He didn't strike me as very trustworthy. And I think Mr. Babalola agrees with me."

"Who is that?"

"The chauffeur. Mr. Enemkpali must have seen him?"

Mr. Enemkpali may have nodded.

"I don't know what Attaché Onyewu is up to, but I want no part of it. Or him." He wanted to ask her if there was a connection between Onyewu and Ma, but he kept his mouth shut.

Mrs. Iwobi said, "He is no diplomat. It is a disgrace that he is allowed to pretend to be one at our fine embassy."

"So you're all from Nigeria?" She nodded. "I know he's no diplomat. But you aren't looking for him. Who are you looking for?"

"We do not know his name...his real name."

"Can you describe him?"

A little smile. "I could. But why are you involved in this, Mr. Bergeron?"

"Why indeed? I've asked myself that a dozen times. The short answer is that a friend of mine was also looking for someone, and he asked me to help. I had no idea what I was getting into."

"Indeed? And you are a detective then?"

"Not really."

She was staring at him. "An agent of your government?"

"No! Never. They wouldn't have me. Not that I want to be an agent or a spy or anything like that. But I have helped solve mysteries in the past. Which my friend knew."

She looked at Mr. Enemkpali. If he had any sage words of advice he kept them to himself.

"Mrs. Iwobi? Tell me who you're looking for, and if I can help you, I will."

Mr. Obioma said something in a language he'd never heard before. She gave him a curt reply.

"Which one of the five hundred languages of Nigeria is that?"

She looked at him. "Why?"

"I'm just curious."

She nodded. "Igbo."

"Really? Thank you for telling me."

She sat back in her chair. "The man I am looking for is Chinese. He claims to be from Taiwan but that is a lie."

"One second, please. I'll be right back."

He hoofed it to his desk and found copies of the sketches. He unfolded the sketch of Mr. Ma in front of her. "Is this the man?"

She gazed at it and then looked at the tall Mr. Melifonwu. He looked at it, and his eyes popped open.

She said, "It is him."

Melifonwu looked frightened. "It might be. I am not sure, Mrs. Ama...."

He stopped speaking...mostly because Mr. Obioma had punched him savagely in the gut.

Young Melifonwu didn't offer any violence in response to Obioma; he barely glanced at him before focusing his eyes on the table and scrunching up as best he could. It mattered not a jot that Obioma was more than a foot shorter.

Mr. Enemkpali spoke for the first time; in Igbo possibly. His speech was halting, but Obioma stopped glaring at Melifonwu.

He tapped on the sketch of Ma. "This man called himself Ma Ying-jeou."

Ms. Iwobi said, "You met him?"

"I did. He was sitting where Mr. Enemkpali is currently sitting. And this man was with him." He unfolded the sketch of Chen. "He said his name was Chen Shui-bian. Both names are fake."

Ms. Iwobi's face was bright with hunger to know everything about Ma. "How do you know that?"

"Because the names belong to the fifth and sixth presidents of Taiwan. A friend told me."

She shoved the sketch over to Melifonwu who shook his head. "No, Ms. Iwobi."

She nodded. "And when did you see these men, Mr. Bergeron?"

"Almost two weeks ago now."

She frowned. "Do you have any idea where they could be?"

"No. But the Philadelphia police and other parties are looking for them."

"Why?"

"It's likely that Ma has committed crimes in the city."

"What kind of crimes?"

He smiled his very best smile. "Why are you looking for Ma?"

She smiled back at him. "It is likely he also committed crimes in Nigeria, Mr. Bergeron."

"I don't doubt it for a second. Ma is arrogant and stupid and thinks when he says jump, the world asks how high."

She laughed and spoke in Igbo to Mr. Enemkpali; the right side of his flaccid face may have tightened ever so slightly.

And then Enemkpali said something else; it seemed difficult for him to get it out. Or to get it organized?

She said, "Mr. Enemkpali wonders why they came to see you?"

"They wanted me to stop looking for someone. The someone my friend had asked me to find."

"And what did you tell them?"

"That I had already decided to stop looking."

"And was that true, Mr. Bergeron?"

"It was. But then Ma did some stupid things and pissed me off."

She smiled. "I understand. So you would like to find Ma?"

"I want the police to find him to punish him. I have no interest in him personally, but tell me this, Ms. Iwobi, are you looking for anyone else besides Ma?"

"Only him." Her face said that Ma would regret running into Ms. Iwobi for as long as he lived.

She could be lying about Duke but he believed her. She was laser focused on good ole Ma, She might have heard of Thorvaldsen but she had zero interest in him.

Which, if true, made her the only person in the greater Philadelphia area not trying to find Duke Thorvaldsen.

She forged a smile out of raw determination and slapped it over her face still hot from the furnace. "Is there anything else you can tell me?"

"Not at this time."

She nodded. "But if you should find Ma...."

"If I find him, I will call you. And if you find him or Chen, you will call me? Deal?"

Mrs. Iwobi said, "I thought you had no interest in him?"

"I would like to see him punished for his crimes...after you're finished with him. And I'm curious about all this. Though I doubt Ma would answer my questions but Chen might."

She nodded. "That is acceptable. And he will be punished, Mr. Bergeron."

He had been going to say that he didn't care what happened to Ma and Chen after he talked to them, but that might give Mrs. Iwobi the idea that he was down with whatever she wanted to do to them.

And Ms. Iwobi stood up. "Thank you, Mr. Bergeron."

He followed her and her band to the elevator. She said, "Do you believe that Ma is still in the city?"

"Yes. I'm not sure why but he seems determined to stay."

He wasn't going to tell her about Duke. Or Bradley and Susan. Or Inspector Okocha. Or Aronson.

She was smiling at him as the elevator door closed.

Paul's voice came from two inches behind his right ear. "Who were they, Gabe?"

"No freaking idea. Except they're from Nigeria. But if Mr. Ma had a brain, he'd be on the first flight to Beijing."

"Could they be the pirates?"

He stared at Paul. He smiled and shrugged.

Monday
7:00 pm

It occurred to him while eating a cheese sandwich made with the heels of a loaf of bread, which was all the bread he had, that Ms. Iwobi probably knew that he had gone into Duke's freaking house.

If her men had followed him that far before Aronson intervened? Which seemed well-nigh certain.

And what would she make of that? He had no idea.

What he did know was that he absolutely, positively had to go grocery shopping tomorrow. Or go on a fast.

And then his phone rang.

It was Okocha.

"Good evening, Inspector. Why don't you answer your phone when I call you?"

"You brought the police to the warehouse, didn't you? The Smoker would never have thought of it."

"I did. Was that bad for you? And if so, why? We did catch one of Ma's minions. Mr. Ears."

Okocha snorted. "Mr. Ears?"

"Yes, the guy with the prominent ears. Not that he can help that, but I guess he could have plastic surgery?"

"Shut up! He's a child who knows nothing. And now Ma and Chen are in the wind. I will have to track them down again."

"Oh. Sorry about that."

Okocha didn't say anything.

"They were tearing the house apart bit by bit, wall by wall, room by room. They were starting on the crawlspace."

"I knew this."

He was pretty sure Okocha was fibbing.

"So you want to find the Chinese or Thorvaldsen?"

Silence. "Thorvaldsen. The Chinese are secondary."

"Right. Until two weeks ago, he was living with Gianna Bonacci, his girlfriend. But you knew that."

Okocha said, "And now?"

"Until Friday, he was with his buddy, Denny Krueger."

"Where is he now?"

"No idea."

"You tracked him down, and the Smoker let him slip away!"

"I can neither confirm nor deny that supposition, Inspector."

"Stupid."

He wasn't sure if he or Fowler or both of them were being disparaged. "So I could call you the next time I have an idea. No, wait. That won't work because you don't answer your phone."

More silence, but this time it was because Okocha had no come back.

"Call me. If there is a next time."

Right. Maybe yes, maybe no."

"Where is the man the Smoker caught?"

"The Smoker's name is Detective Fowler, and the FBI took him."

"Aronson?"

"Yes. You are very well informed."

"Better than you Americans with all your resources."

"Is that so? Well, do you know that some more of your countrymen have arrived?"

"What?"

"A Ms. Iwobi came to see me. Attended by Mr. Enemkpali, Mr. Melifonwu, and Mr. Obioma."

A long silence.

Followed by bad words in a language that sounded like Igbo to him.

When the cussing stopped, he said, "Was that Igbo?"
"What do you know about Igbo?"
"Almost nothing. Except that Ms. Iwobi spoke it."
"Is that what she told you?"
"Yes. Wait. It wasn't true?"
Silence.
"Okocha? Do you know who they are?"
The silence went on so long he was about to hang up when Okocha said, "Stay away from these people. They are very, very dangerous."
And then Okocha was truly gone.
So he didn't know, but he thought that Ms. Iwobi et al were the pirates? Or related to the pirates? Either by blood or criminal association.
Everybody else remotely connected to the SS Kerkyra was in Philly or had been until their demise.
But she looked too gentle to be a pirate queen.
But what did he know? He'd seen Johnny Depp movies and "Captain Blood" with Errol Flynn and Olivia de Havilland; he had no idea what a real, modern pirate looked like.
He should visit Aunt Flo. They could watch "Captain Blood" again and enjoy the wonderful Korngold score.
He called Aunt Flo and told her he was fine. He didn't tell her about Ms. Iwobi because he didn't really know who she was. Maybe she was the pirate queen, maybe she wasn't.

Tuesday
8:00 am

He had parked the Jeep and was contemplating the work day ahead when Inspector Okocha knocked on his window.

He didn't shriek.

He did hit the floor and reach for his Glock. Okocha was glaring at him through the driver's side window. He thought that Okocha had smiled but he could be mistaken?

He sat erect and adjusted his jacket and straightened his tie; it was brand new and very lovely, and it wouldn't do to wrinkle it.

"What?"

Okocha did smile. "Did I frighten you?"

"Not a bit. You're just lucky I didn't shoot you."

He smiled a second time. "I do not think you should be armed, Gabriel."

What was up? All this smiling and using of his first name?

"How can I help you, Inspector?"

Okocha walked around and slid into the front seat. "I never spoke to you."

"Did too."

"No, I did not. And I never asked you to help me find this stupid sailor."

"And I never heard you ask and will not be helping you."

Okocha drew his eyebrows together and corrugated his forehead until he looked almost Klingon; Worf or maybe Gowron, though handsomer than either.

"Help me, and I will protect you." Okocha looked at him.

"From yourself."

"I do not need your protection, Sir."

Which might or might not be true. But he didn't trust Okocha. Well, he sorta did, but not enough to help him find Duke.

"But just say that I did find Thorvaldsen for you. What would you do to him?"

"Nothing."

He shook his head. "I'm not saying that I don't believe you, but do the words, 'Liar, liar, pant's on fire' mean anything to you?"

"Silly man."

"You want to present him to Chinedum Onyewu wrapped in a red ribbon. Which I guess is sort of your job?"

He shook his head. "But I have no choice in the matter."

"Do you even know what Onyewu wants with him? No, you do not. And I do not trust Chinedum Onyewu even a little bit."

Okocha was staring into space or at the concrete wall in front of them. "I told him about your latest visitors."

"You told Onyewu about Ms. Iwobi? And?"

"I thought he would return to Port Harcourt on the next flight."

"And be out of your hair. But he didn't. Which is interesting."

"There is nothing interesting about any of this."

"I mean Onyewu doesn't seem like a brave man." Okocha laughed. "And you said Ms. Iwobi and her companions were very dangerous, and I know they don't like the attaché. So whatever he wants from Thorvaldsen is very important to him; very, very important."

Well, he already knew that since Onyewu had offered him two hundred thousand for Thorvaldsen's location.

"What the Hell does Thorvaldsen have?" He had been thinking about something valuable but maybe that wasn't it? "Something incriminating? Something that would get Onyewu thrown in jail for years? Or something that would take down one of his rivals?"

Okocha shook his head.

"And Onyewu hasn't hinted?'

"He trusts no one."

"Right."

Okocha got out and came around to his window. "If you find him again, please call me first. I will not harm him or allow him to come to harm from Onyewu."

And the inspector strode off an unhappy man.

Tuesday
2:00 pm

He heard the elevator's ding but Chase hadn't warned him so he didn't even look up.

Not until the light from the windows was blotted out, and he was in the umbra.

He may have ducked and covered.

But it was Cory, and he was about as angry as he'd ever seen the special agent.

He didn't even try smiling. "Why don't we go into the conference room, Cory."

Cory nodded.

They sat; Cory was looking out the window.

"Did Aunt Flo call you?"

Cory sat there an angry lump of gorgeous. His cheeks were as red as his hair; big eyes a lethal blue. Muscles flexed. A vein throbbing on the side of his noble forehead.

"You could say that."

"So Aunt Flo called your mother who called Danielle who called you."

Cory nodded.

"I'm sorry."

Cory held up a hand. "Do you know how much I hate having my mother call my boss?"

"I do. I am very sorry. Did coming back to Philly ruin your case?"

Cory sat there a while. "No."

"Good."

They sat and didn't look at each other until Cory said, "Tell me about this freaking mess."

"How much do you know?"

Cory looked at him for the first time. "Assume I don't know anything after you promised me not to see Steven and Susan Bradley again. And don't leave anything out. Not the smallest detail."

"Right."

So he did just that.

"Monroe's in this too?"

"He says not but he isn't trustworthy."

"And Brunetti told you that Aronson is Counterespionage?"

"Yeah."

And you think this Ms. Iwobi is a pirate?"

"I don't have any hard evidence, but I do."

Cory took out his phone. "Poirier. I'd like to request two weeks leave. Yes. More convoluted than I could have ever imagined. Thank you, Ma'am."

Cory placed another call. "Mrs. Barnes? It's Cory. I'm with Gabe, and I'm not going to leave his side until this is over. No. Not at all. I'm very grateful that you contacted me. Yes, I will."

Cory put his phone down. "So what now?"

"I don't know."

Cory stared at him. "You don't know?"

"Not at the present time."

Cory said, "Give me the numbers for Aronson and Inspector Okocha. And your phone."

And he did. Cory nodded. "You can go back to work, Gabe."

He got to his feet. He was almost out the door when he said, "I didn't do anything until they kidnapped Susan, Cory."

Cory wouldn't look at him. "Is that the truth?"

"Of course it is!"

"Okay."

He went back to work. He was seesawing between guilt and semi-righteous anger. Harry and Carla were sneaking looks at him, but he didn't want to talk. He had no idea what would come out of his mouth.

Stella walked by and patted his shoulder.

Cory was on the phone. The first conversation lasted five minutes; the second five seconds. Cory was even more unhappy which hardly seemed possible.

He got up to get coffee and saw Paul talking to Cory. How had Paul gotten into the conference room without him seeing?

And what the Hell was Paul saying to Cory?

Paul shook Cory's hand and stepped out to catch the prevailing winds and be wafted soundlessly back to his cubicle.

He needed to see if Paul could teach him to move like that. He would also like to learn how to pick locks but Cory wasn't going to show him.

He tried to put Cory out of his mind and get some work done. When he looked up, the office had emptied out, and Cory was in Carla's chair looking at him.

"You really are working hard."

"I am, but I've done it before. It isn't like spotting Sasquatch."

Cory's smile was an uneasy tincture of good humor and residual anger. "Almost."

"I called you every day...sometimes twice...and I would have told you everything if you'd called back. It's been a week, and I couldn't have held it in." He smiled at Cory. "You know how I am."

Cory handed his phone back. "Yeah. My bad."

He looked at Cory. Did he mean that? It was 6:30 pm. "I think it's time to go home."

Cory nodded.

"Are you coming with me?"

"Yes. I have a vehicle."

He locked the office door and got into the elevator. "Did you talk to Aronson?"

A nod. "He warned me off."

"I think he did the same thing to Brunetti. Which is surprising?"

249

Another nod but no comment.

"And Okocha?"

"He wouldn't talk to me."

"Did you identify yourself as FBI?"

Cory said, "He never gave me a chance."

He drove home and parked in the garage. He never saw Cory but he showed up a half hour later.

"You were followed."

"Chinese or Nigerian?"

Cory almost smiled. "Two black guys. One had dreadlocks on just the top of his head."

"Ah. That would be Mr. Melifonwu."

Cory looked at him. "And he's a pirate?"

"I think so." He felt silly saying it, but he was pretty sure.

"What do they want from you?"

"They are hoping that I will lead them to Mr. Ma."

Cory said, "And what are they going to do to him when they find him?"

"I don't know, but I have a feeling it won't be pleasant."

"Why?"

"I have no freaking idea."

They watched TV and didn't speak of the accursed sailor again. Cory had started out on the sofa, but sometime during the night he had slipped into the bed.

But their first night together after a month apart was depressingly passionless and insipid.

Wednesday
5:00 pm

Cory had escorted him to work at 8:00 am and told him not to leave the building for any reason.

He had nodded. He had the feeling if he did it would not be good for the health of their relationship.

Cory had appeared at noon, and they had lunched together at CoffeeXtra. Cory had been taciturn but not openly angry.

Which was good.

And now he was waiting for Cory to escort him home.

His phone rang. "Hi, Cory?"

"I'm downstairs. Ready to go?"

"Sure. I'll be down in a second."

He had to do something to put an end to this chapter in their lives. Sure, Ms. Iwobi might find Ma and deal with him. Or Ma might find Thorvaldsen and also deal with him. Or Okocha might find Thorvaldsen for Chinedum Onyewu and deal with him.

Or all of them might give up and go home. But he couldn't count on it happening before Cory's two weeks of leave were up.

He would never tell Cory but he thought he could handle this. Was that just a fool's brew of vainglory, hubris, and stupidity?

He sighed as he shut off his computer.

He got in Cory's black SUV which was nicer than Aronson's. He smiled at Cory.

Cory shook his head. "I'm not going to like this, am I?"

"I don't see why not? I want to talk to Steve Bradley."

"Why?"

"I don't know yet."

Cory smiled at the steering wheel; it maintained a cool, insouciant air as inanimate objects often do.

"Okay. Is he still with the uncle?"

"I don't know. He could be home by now. I'd rather he didn't know we were coming. If he isn't home, we can look at Duke's house again and track Bradley down after."

And Cory set the vehicle in motion. Cory seemed to be driving normally.

"Are we being followed by anyone?"

"No."

"Are you sure, Cory?"

"Yes. Or they're very good."

"Are the Chinese and/or Nigerians very good?"

Cory shook his head.

Still, he kept looking behind them as Cory drove along, but they reached 9847 Williams Street without incident.

Cory parked in front of the warehouse across the street from the row houses. They surveyed the scene. A run-down, blue van was in front of Susan's house.

Cory said, "Is that Bradley or Susan's van?"

"I don't think so." He may have pulled out his Glock.

Cory got out. "Stay in the vehicle, Gabe." Cory had his Glock in hand.

The van had two small windows in the back, almost opaque with dirt. The driver's window was down. Cory was in a crouch as he crossed the street diagonally, Glock first.

And then Susan's front door slammed open.

With the roof and the green, aluminum awning, the porch was in deep shade, but he could see a shape.

The shape was too big to be Susan or Bradley. He rolled out of the SUV.

"Cory! Porch!"

And then Ma emerged out of the deep shade with an automatic weapon in his left hand. His right was bandaged.

Ma sprayed the area with bullets like he was watering Susan's hedge with a garden hose.

Cory was in the middle of the street and fired at Ma as the guy charged down the dozen stone steps.

Cory was running back but he wasn't safe yet.

He had to distract Ma. He yelled, "Ma! You stupid asshole!" And he fired a round that took out one of Susan's planters. Mr. Ma flattened to the ground. He kept firing at Ma until Cory reached the SUV.

Ma got to his feet and fired half a hundred rounds at them. He and Cory hunkered down. Cory said, "Stay down!"

Which was sound advice but he wanted to shoot Ma again. And in some more vital area than his hand.

And he had a flashback: he and Cory were huddled behind Cory's Jeep in Aunt Flo's lane, and Yuri Corzo was shooting at them. And he'd had no clue how to load a Glock.

That had been five years ago, not long after he'd met Cory.

He didn't have time to reminisce. He crawled around the end of the SUV and started firing at Ma who had paused at the foot of Susan's stairs and looked back.

The bullets pinging around him got the bastard moving again. Ma made it to the van. He thought he might have winged him?

The engine started up. He and Cory were both pumping the van full of lead when Chen dashed out of Susan's house running pell-mell.

He fired twice. He didn't want to kill Chen so he aimed low hoping to clip his leg, and Chen went down.

The van roared away. Cory fired a few more rounds. The van swerved but righted itself and continued on. Rapidly approaching sirens were wailing in the West Philly afternoon.

Chen was on the sidewalk; bleeding. His automatic weapon was beside him.

He looked at Cory. "That's Chen, but there's at least one henchman unaccounted for."

Cory smiled ever so briefly. "Chen! Kick the weapon away!"

Chen put up his hands. "Don't shoot!" He managed a feeble kick that moved the gun a few feet.

A voice yelled something in Mandarin from Susan's door.

Chen yelled something back as the sirens got louder.

The henchman yelled again.

Chen said, "Yun wants to surrender. Don't shoot him! Please, Mr. Bergeron."

"Tell him to leave any weapons inside. And to come out slowly with his empty hands in front."

Cory gave him a funny look, but he had to focus on Yun the Henchman who was just a dark shape on Susan's porch. He was going to shoot Mr. Yun if there was the slightest metallic flash as he stepped into the sun.

But Yun's hands were empty. He was shaking and almost fell down the steps.

Cory said, "Tell him to lock his fingers and put his hands behind his head."

Chen translated, and Yun obeyed with alacrity.

He was older than Ma or the others who had been killed or captured. He had an oval face and big, black eyes that reminded him of Carla.

Cory said, "Tell him to get down on his knees."

And Yun sank down; his wobbly legs barely up to the task of supporting his body anyway. Cory cuffed him.

And then he thought about Susan and Bradley. He looked at Chen. "Anyone else in the house? Susan? Or Bradley?"

Chen shook his head. "No one. The house was empty when we got here. I don't know where the girlfriend or her son are."

Cory still had his Glock in his hand, and Gabe Bergeron was holding Chen's automatic weapon when the first patrol car screeched to a halt. The officer was aiming at them when Fuchs pulled in and defused the situation.

Fuchs nodded. "Got'em all?"

He shook his head. "No! Ma got away. But I think he's on his own now. And I may have winged him."

Fuchs nodded looking less forlorn.

Cory gave Fuchs the van's tag number.

They were standing around as the paramedics assessed Chen when Detective Fowler pulled in.

Fowler smiled at him. "So you got the rest of them?"

"Not Ma. The main idiot."

Fuchs said, "Put out the van's number."

Fowler nodded. Cory was on the phone. Fowler smiled at him. "And just how did you find them? This time?"

"I wanted to talk to Steve Bradley, and they were inside Susan's house. Chen said that the house was empty when they arrived."

Fowler nodded. "I phoned her the second I got the call about shots fired at this address." He smiled. "She's cooking a thank-you dinner for her brother. And Stevie's with her."

Fuchs was giving Fowler a look. Fuchs had a nuanced face that could be as expressive as tree bark or a bit more transparent as it currently was.

He looked from Fuchs to Fowler. "What?"

Fuchs said, "He's invited."

"To Susan's thank-you dinner?"

Fuchs nodded.

Fowler blushed most becomingly. "What of it, Fuchs?"

Fuchs put up his extra-large hands and ambled off. There was a faint snickering noise but there was no way that was coming from Officer Fuchs.

Fowler said, "Thinks he's a comedian."

"Fuchs?" The mind boggled.

"Yeah. So back to the Chinese. So you pull up and...?"

"And Ma comes out guns blazing. Look at Cory's poor SUV."

"Yeah. And you returned fire, and Chen went down."

"Yes. But I think Ma was going to leave him behind anyway."

"Yeah? Guy's a real prince."

"Actually I think he is. A princeling of the Party. Okay if I talk to Chen before they haul him off?"

"Sure. Is that FBI jerk going to take these two?"

"Maybe yes. Aronson is a bit odd. Or so it seems to me."

And he and Fowler marched over to the ambulance; Cory and Fuchs tagged along.

Chen was on a gurney.

Fowler looked at the paramedic; he seemed to think that she filled out her uniform fetchingly. "How's he doing?"

"Through and through of the lower leg. Might have chipped a bone."

"So he's going to be okay? She nodded and smiled at Fuchs who may have winked at her. "Thanks, Janet."

Fowler waved at him. "Gabe."

He sat down next to Chen who was glaring at him. "You shot me!"

"I did. I'm very sorry. So what can you tell us about Mr. Ma?"

Chen said things in Mandarin.

"I'm sure that was all heartfelt. Could you do that in English? Please?"

"He is an idiot. I have often used that word to describe those who were slow to understand, but I was misusing the word. I see that now."

"So why do you want to find Thorvaldsen? Or rather what do you want to get from him?"

Chen shook his head. He looked like he'd aged ten years in a few weeks.

"But you did all this for Ma?"

He nodded. "I tried to rescue the situation. If I had known Ma even a little better, I wouldn't have tried."

"What went wrong? In Nigeria?" Chen shook his head. "Okay. In general terms, why did the situation need rescuing?"

Chen stared at him. "Ma was given a simple job. A blind donkey could have done it. And he had a Mr. Su to guide him."

"But he screwed it up."

"In a spectacular fashion. And Mr. Su was killed. He was a very capable young man. He would have done great things. But he's gone. And Ma just keeps making the situation worse."

"Right. So was kidnapping Susan your idea?"

Chen gave him an exhausted glare. "No! I had nothing to do with that. Nothing, Mr. Bergeron."

"So Ma got two of your men killed."

"I think they admired him. At first."

"Because he was daring. And connected to power. And a rising star."

Chen laughed. "His father and grandfather...."

"What about them?"

"Nothing. Please go away, Mr. Bergeron."

"I will. So where is Ma now? Where would he go?"

Chen shook his head. "I don't know. If I did, I would tell you. I hate that young man. Truly." Chen rallied enough to smile. "But not as much as he hates you!"

"Me?"

"Yes. He believes you brought the police to the house where he was keeping Susan. And he knows you brought them to the warehouse." Chen glanced out the back of the ambulance at that building. "He blames you for everything going wrong."

"I did what I could. So what the Hell does Duke have?"

But Chen closed his eyes.

"You thought it might be hidden in Susan's house? You couldn't find Duke, and you were desperate."

Chen shook his head. "It was a stupid idea! How could we hope to find...something so small? But Ma was the desperate one. If I hadn't gone along, he would have shot me and tried to blame me for all this. I'm sure of it, Mr. Bergeron."

Fowler questioned him for a bit, but Chen was done, and Yun was either pretending to speak only Mandarin or really had not a syllable of English.

He and Fowler and Cory were standing in the street. Fuchs was loitering nearby.

Fowler said, "So about the FBI jerk?" He looked at Cory. "No offense intended."

Cory smiled. "None taken. Aronson is a jerk."

"So is he on his way?"

He looked at Cory. "Should I call him?"

Cory shrugged. "Yeah."

And he dialed Special Agent Aronson. "Gabriel. Developments?"

"We caught Chen and a miscellaneous henchman named

Yun. Ma is in the wind but the police are straining every nerve and sinew in the search for him."

Aronson laughed. "Well done."

"Would you like to speak to Detective Fowler?"

Aronson sighed. "I suppose I should. Gabriel?"

"Yes?"

"Thank you."

He handed his phone to Fowler.

"You coming?" Fowler nodded. "Chen needs to be patched up. Yeah. Gabe shot him. Nothing serious. The other one is all yours if you want him?"

Fowler listened. "Right. You know where the station is."

Fowler handed back his phone.

Fuchs was heading for them. "They found the van. Abandoned."

Cory said, "Where?"

Fuchs looked at him. Fowler said, "You and Gabe going to help out, Special Agent?"

Cory nodded. "I am. I'll be back. Come on, Gabe."

"Wait. Where am I going?"

"Home." He walked off.

Fuchs was looking at him funny. And then Officer Fuchs patted his shoulder and nodded at Cory. He mumbled, "You did good no matter what the old ball and chain says."

He was too surprised to do more than give Fuchs a weird, half smile, and then he followed Cory like a lamb to the slaughtered SUV. It didn't seem to be bleeding any fluids, and it started.

He didn't think of Cory as "the old ball and chain" even a little bit. Cory was looking out for him. But still. "Why am I going home, Cory?"

"Because. And you're going to stay there."

"While you gambol about West Philly looking for Ma?"

Cory was smiling. "'Gambol'? I don't gambol, Henri."

"Why can't I come along?"

"Because Ma hates you."

"He's probably not too fond of you either, Poirier."

"This isn't up for discussion, Gabe."

"Oh, it so is! If I hadn't been with you, it would have been Ma and Chen and Yun against just you."

"No. I wouldn't have been at Susan's house to begin with."

Which was undeniably true.

"But we caught Chen and Yun! Come on, Cory!"

"No."

And Cory was obdurate and adamant and pigheaded. They walked up the stairs to his apartment, and Cory checked for unwelcome guests.

Cory leaned in and kissed him on the cheek. "I thought going to Susan's house would be safe enough." He shook his head. "Stay here. Lock and chain the door. Do not come out."

And Cory was off.

He sat on the sofa.

He was vexed.

Cory had done everything but tuck him into bed with his blankey and a bottle.

It was unfair.

And uncalled for. He wasn't scared of Ma.

Thursday
5:00 am

He had talked to Cory around 2:00 am, and he and Fowler were following up on some kind of lead. Not that Cory would tell him what or where.

He had fallen asleep on the sofa. He tried calling Cory, but it went to voicemail. He hated voicemail. He hated the man, woman, or precocious child who had first thought of it. He wished them harm and harm to all of their nearest and dearest.

He was making coffee when the phone played Cory's tune. "Cory! Where are you?"

But Ms. Iwobi said, "Mr. Bergeron. Come downstairs please. Mr. Enemkpali and I are out front. We need to speak to you."

"No. I don't think so. Wait. Why do you have Cory's phone?"

"That would be because we have Cory. Look out your windows, Mr. Bergeron."

He didn't want to, but he had to. And four stories below, he saw Cory, literally bound hand and foot, being held by the freakishly tall Melifonwu and the predatory Obioma. They dragged him into a gray van and motored down the street.

He grabbed his Glock and ran just as fast as he could down all those flights of stairs. He burst out the door, but the van was already far away. He ran after it. He would have fired but he knew he might hit Cory.

He didn't know what to do.

He stood there in the middle of the street, barefoot and in nothing but his briefs.

He thought he was going to pass out or his head explode, but he took a deep breath and turned.

Ms. Iwobi was standing on the sidewalk next to a blue Chevy Silverado pickup. He ran back.

Ms. Iwobi was smiling at him. He had never wanted to shoot someone so much before. He extended his arm and aimed very carefully at the center of her chest.

"He will be fine, Mr. Bergeron. They will not harm him in any way."

Mr. Enemkpali was sitting in the passenger seat. He rotated his body and extended his legs. He slid off the seat into a standing position. The jolt seemed to pain him, but he moved in front of Ms. Iwobi.

"You will see him soon."

"You speak English?"

He nodded. "Since before you were born, Mr. Bergeron. Lower the weapon. Please. It will do nothing for you."

His heart was pounding. He felt like he might pass out again but he couldn't wimp out. If he was ever going to man up, whatever that meant, now was the hour.

"Why did you take him?"

Enemkpali said, "To ensure your cooperation."

He aimed at Enemkpali. "I'm going to shoot you right here, right now, and then Ms. Iwobi is going to tell me how to find Cory. Or I'll shoot her too!"

Enemkpali tried to smile but most of the muscles of his face didn't get the message. "You are not a killer, Mr. Bergeron."

Ms. Iwobi said, "No, you are not but Obioma is."

Enemkpali sighed. "Sadly, that is all that he is. He is my nephew but he has no soul."

She said, "But he will not harm your Cory if you do what we ask."

Enemkpali said, "But he will kill Cory if you do not." He sighed. "He is not a patient man."

"I'm going to call the police...the FBI. You can't kidnap a

federal agent."

Ms. Iwobi smiled again. "I know your brain is whirling, Mr. Bergeron, but think. You don't have your phone."

Which was undeniably true since he was pocket-less being quite pants-less.

"We would be gone by the time you came back."

"I could shoot out your tires!"

She nodded. "But the police and the mighty FBI can do nothing. If we do not rejoin Obioma in ten minutes, he will kill your Cory."

Enemkpali said, "And we will find another way to reach Onyewu."

"Onyewu?"

She nodded. "He has grown very cautious. But he will come if you call him and arrange a meeting. That is all you need do. The instant we see Onyewu we will release your Cory. Unharmed in any way. I give you my word."

He may have laughed hysterically.

She and Enemkpali looked at him. It occurred to him that they had lots of practice in assessing how kidnap victims and the people who wanted them back were handling the ordeal.

"Why do you want Onyewu?"

She said, "He has dealt with the Chinese many times before. He will have some way of contacting this Ma."

"And you want Ma."

"We do."

"Why?"

Mr. Enemkpali said, "Because of Nwosu, my son."

Ms. Iwobi said, "Who was also my husband."

Shit. "And Ma did something to Nwosu."

She had tears in her eyes.

Mr. Enemkpali said, "Nwosu was a good man." He tried the smiling thing again. "He was also what you would call a pirate."

She said, "It was Nwosu who went on board the SS Kerkyra and took the captain and first mate and held them for ransom."

Enemkpali nodded. "He did. As he had done many times

before. Without harming anyone. The ship owners would pay the ransom and get back their crew. It was just a cost of doing business in the Gulf of Guinea."

She said, "And Nwosu shared the bounty with his men and their families and all the people of our compound."

He almost made a snide remark about the man being the Nigerian Robin Hood before he thought better of it.

"So what went wrong?"

She said, "Ma."

"I don't understand?"

Enemkpali said, "We don't know why he and his men came to our compound. Most of Nwosu's men were away or the outcome would have been very different."

She said, "They wanted something from Nwosu...or from the captain or first mate."

Something that Duke Thorvaldsen had brought back to Philly.

Enemkpali said, "He tortured my son, Mr. Bergeron, but Nwosu couldn't tell him what he didn't know."

She said, "He tortured Nwosu for hours. And then he started on the captain and would have done the same to the first mate but we returned with Nwosu's men. This Ma escaped...as did the first mate."

"And you've been looking for him ever since?"

She nodded. "We paid for information about this Ma and the Chinese."

Enemkpali said, "Information which pointed to Onyewu."

She said, "Who came to your city."

"And you followed. But maybe Onyewu doesn't know how to contact Ma? It doesn't seem that they are working together? I think they're competing...for whatever it is...for whatever they thought your Nwosu had."

She said, "We have to try."

"But I can find Ma. I've almost caught him twice before."

But they shook their heads.

Enemkpali said, "No. He is very stubborn, but even someone as stupid as he is may give up after all that has happened to him and return to China. We cannot take that chance ."

She said, "We know that Chen has been arrested." She smiled again which wasn't reassuring in the slightest. "Do what we ask. Please. And Cory will come back. If you do not you will never see his smile, never hear his voice, never feel his touch, and you will have had no time to prepare yourself for this."

"I can call Onyewu but I don't know if he'll come?"

Enemkpali was trying to get back into the truck. "You must try."

"Wait. Take me instead of Cory. I'll go with you, and we'll find Ma. I'll call Onyewu first but there are other ways. Please?"

Ms. Iwobi looked at Enemkpali, but he shook his head.

She said, "No. You are very clever but you need to be free to do whatever it is you do. Onyewu may not come with just a call, but you will find a way. For Cory's sake."

He looked at her. "And what will you do to Onyewu?"

"We will ask him for the information. He is not a brave man, and he will tell us. There will be no unpleasantness."

"And you'll let him go? Alive?"

Mr. Enemkpali said, "You are a good man but you shouldn't concern yourself about Onyewu. He has killed many times...with his own hands when he was younger and now through others."

She said, "He would kill us without hesitation. Or you. Or Cory to get what he wants."

"What does he want?"

She shrugged. "I do not know."

And he believed her.

She handed him a phone and got into the pickup. "Arrange to meet Onyewu at this coffee shop."

Enemkpali said, "CoffeeXtra. Where you met before."

She said, "I will call you later today. I hope you will have good news for me, Mr. Bergeron. We must go or Obioma will do something bad to Cory. Or to Melifonwu."

"What? Why would he do that?"

Enemkpali said, "Because Melifonwu ran away and left Nwosu to face the Chinese alone. He says he did not but he did."

She said, "He is alive now only because he saw Ma's face

before he ran."

Enemkpali said, "But Obioma is not a patient man. As I said."

Enemkpali was staring at him out of his half-dead face. "You must bring Onyewu to us."

And he watched them drive off. His feet were cold.

He was in his briefs.

He didn't care but there was no point in standing on the sidewalk.

He could call Fowler.

He could call Brunetti.

He could call Okocha.

Monroe wasn't a sensible option.

He called the Nigerian embassy and left an urgent message for Chinedum Onyewu with another lady with a voice almost as mellifluous as the first lady he'd talked to.

Thursday
6:00 am

He put some clothes on and called Aunt Flo.

"Aunt Flo, something bad's happened."

She said, "Tell me, Dear."

And he did as concisely as he could.

She said, "I see. Is there anything I can do? Or Ezmeralda or Danilo?"

"I don't think so? I could call Fowler or Brunetti. They would try to get Cory back, but neither can offer to trade a Nigerian attaché for Cory. They might want to, but it wouldn't be doable."

"No, Dear. It wouldn't. The state department would step in; the higher ranks of the FBI would make a risk-reward analysis. They would be very sorry."

"Yeah. And Okocha might not like Onyewu but he wouldn't help me hand him over to pirates."

"No, Dear. He wouldn't. I don't see that you have any options."

"That's what I thought. If I can lure Chinedum Onyewu to a meeting, and they kill him, then I'll have to live with that. Do you think Iwobi and Enemkpali will really let Cory go?"

"I don't know, Dear. You spoke to them?"

He shook his head. "I'm not sure. I think they might. She loved Nwosu very much."

"Then you have to proceed on that assumption. I don't want you to be alone. Let me talk to Ezmeralda and Danilo."

"Thanks, Aunt Flo, but I don't want to involve anyone else."

"I understand that, Dear. Call me as soon as you hear anything."

"Will do."

Ms. Iwobi called at 8:00 am. "Mr. Bergeron?"

"I called and left a message at the embassy. I don't have any other way to contact him."

"Yes, I understand. Let me see what we can do."

"Is Cory all right?"

But she was gone.

Aunt Flo called back. "Gabriel, I'm very sorry, but Raúl is in Texas visiting his father."

Raúl Gutierrez was Ezmeralda's nephew and big and semi-dangerous.

"And Mikhail and Kirill have gone off on a hunting trip. Danilo says he can't reach them."

They were Danilo's large sons and were full-on dangerous...if the occasion called for it.

"Thank you, Aunt Flo. I have to hang up. Ms. Iwobi is going to call me back. Aunt Flo?"

"Yes, Dear?"

"I love you."

"And I love you too, Gabriel. I'll use the landline the next time."

He sat and waited.

He wasn't good at waiting for even trivial things. He was cleaning his Glock and filling his briefcase with ammo clips when Ms. Iwobi called back at 9:30 am.

She gave him a cellphone number for Onyewu. "Call him, Mr. Bergeron."

"Okay. Wait. Won't he wonder where I got his number?"

"Perhaps. Call him."

She was not a chatty woman. He dialed the number, and Attaché Chinedum Onyewu said, "Hello?"

"Mr. Onyewu, this is Gabriel Bergeron."

He could hear Onyewu's brain spin up and his handsome

smile click into place. "Ah, Mr. Bergeron. Do you have information for me?"

"I do. I have the location of a certain sailor who was lost but now is found."

"Very good. And the price?"

"I believe a figure of two hundred thousand was mentioned?"

"It was, but I don't have that much on hand."

"That's unfortunate. How much do you have?"

"A hundred."

He sighed. "I am disappointed, Mr. Onyewu, but this information is time sensitive...as you can imagine, and a bird in the hand is worth two hundred thousand in the bush."

"What?"

"I mean that one hundred is acceptable. Meet me at CoffeeXtra ASAP. The coffee shop near my work."

"I know where it is, Mr. Bergeron. I will leave at once. I should be there in three hours."

"I'll meet you there. I'm very happy we can do business, Mr. Onyewu."

"As am I."

So if he was coming from New York City then three hours was reasonable, but if he pushed it he could get to Philly faster than that. If a vehicle was available?"

He called Ms. Iwobi. "He's on his way. He said three hours which would make it around 12:30 pm."

"You have done very well, Mr. Bergeron. You will be at the shop by 11:30 am."

"And you'll be there?"

"We will, but you will not see us."

"How is Cory? Let me speak to him!"

"That is not possible. Be at the coffee shop."

She was gone. He was staring at the freaking phone when it rang. Harry was calling him.

"I can't talk, Harry."

"Gabe? Jennifer's here with the new baby. Where are you?"

"I really can't talk now, Harry."

And he hung up, but then he thought better of it and called back. "Sorry, Harry. Listen...."

"What's up, Bergeron. Are you okay? Should I call the cops?"

"I'm fine. Just don't let anyone go near CoffeeXtra for the rest of the day. No one. Not for any reason."

He hung up and stared at the clock in the kitchenette. He wasn't going to wait; he was going now.

He was almost out the door.

He dialed Monroe's emergency number, and he answered. "Gabriel?"

"Hi. I need help. Cory's been kidnapped by Nigerian pirates."

Anyone but Monroe would have paused to parse that statement. "I see. That was very careless of him. I'd love to help but I'm in Athens, Gabriel."

"Athens, Greece? What the Hell are you doing there?"

"Business. I'm very sorry. What are they asking for Poirier?"

"They want to talk to Chinedum Onyewu."

"I see."

"Can't you call someone? You must have minions or henchmen?"

Monroe laughed. Well, there was a rustling sound more like the scales of a rattlesnake gliding across a hard scrabble desert. "No. Fresh out. I am sorry but I have every confidence that you can handle this. Bye, Gabriel."

He stood there in the doorway saying bad words. He had known it was a long shot.

He grabbed his briefcase and an umbrella and ran down the stairs. He was in the parking garage on South 16th Street well before time even with the rain and traffic.

He sat in his Jeep.

He didn't like the idea of sitting in CoffeeXtra behind those floor to ceiling windows like a guppy in a fish bowl.

Not with Iwobi and Onyewu and other felons outside waiting to scoop him up or shoot him dead.

And Onyewu hadn't asked where he'd gotten his number.

Because it really didn't matter? Because Gabriel Bergeron would soon be sleeping with the fishes. And not guppies either.

Shit. He put on his tie, grabbed his briefcase and umbrella, and checked to see that his Glock was loaded to the tippy-top with bullets.

And then he walked boldly north along South 16th Street for all the world and any lurking Nigerians to see.

It was misting but he wanted them to see him so he kept his bumpershoot furled.

He strode into CoffeeXtra smiling madly at Martin and his girlfriend, Astrid, and at Selena, his other girlfriend. The baristas were taken aback.

Well, Astrid was. Selena was just the personification of a sunbeam and not capable of thought. Martin was a hundred times smarter than he looked

He came over. "Is something wrong, Gabe?"

"Not a single thing. Coffee and banana bread, please."

Martin gave him his bone-breaking, tendon-ripping, well nigh impossible, double-wide smile and leaped to obey.

Shit squared. He hadn't given a thought to Martin and the customers, but he didn't see what he could do now?

He sipped his coffee and played with his banana bread. The smell of it was making him sick so he tossed it.

It was 11:45 am, and time to put his plan into effect.

It was a poor thing, his plan, but it was all he had come up with. He waved Martin over.

"Gabe?"

"I'm going out the back door."

Martin's big, dark eyes weren't as happy as his smile would indicate. "Okay. Why, Dude?"

"For reasons I'm not going to share right now. But, Martin."

"Yeah?"

"Should there be a small contretemps, you and Astrid and Selena and the customers should hit the floor."

Martin wanted to tease him about "contretemps" but Martin was wise enough to be uneasy.

"What kind of contretemps?"

"You'll know when you see it. And if anyone should ask where I went, direct them to the back door. Without hesitation."

Martin just stared at him for a bit. "Gotcha."

And then he had a confab with Astrid who kenned the concept of "danger."

He never wore hats unless the air temperature would freeze his ears in seconds, but he'd grabbed one before heading out.

He jammed it on his head and went out that backdoor into the alley heading south back toward the parking garage. He was able to stay in the alleys as far as the Conrad Building where his mother's boyfriend, Ted, had once had a lovely office.

It had its own parking under the building for a lucky few employees.

He put up his umbrella and hunched over and scurried onto South 17th Street for fifty feet before ducking into the parking garage under the Conrad Building.

He pretended he was an employee, and he looked the part well enough that the security guards ignored him.

He had to cross South 16th Street to get back to the commercial parking structure where he parked his Jeep every work day.

He didn't see anybody who looked even remotely like one of Ms. Iwobi's men so he ran across the street dodging between the cars speeding north.

Thursday Noon

He had picked a spot on the ground floor of the garage which was a block and a half from CoffeeXtra. He had a clear view of the street and shop. With any luck at all, Ms. Iwobi and company would believe that he was still in CoffeeXtra. And Attaché Onyewu too.

He hoped.

He was barely set when he saw the limo coming. The windows were tinted, and he couldn't see who was inside as it passed his position.

It slowed in the traffic still half a block from the shop. Mr. Ma jumped out of the limo with his automatic weapon in hand. He was running toward CoffeeXtra.

The gray van screeched to a stop behind the limo, and Mr. Obioma boiled out of the van also armed and chased Mr. Ma.

The limo was still moving with the traffic and was almost to CoffeeXtra when Ms. Iwobi's blue Chevy pickup roared past and pulled in front of the limo to block it in.

He had left the parking garage and started running toward the van the second he'd spotted it.

Ma was focused on the Chevy pickup until Obioma fired at him. Ma spun and fired back. They were at most thirty feet apart. Neither sought cover. They kept walking toward each other firing as they came. Ma's face was locked into a fright mask.

He reached the van. No one was in the front. He ran around to the side door.

Ma and Obioma were both on the sidewalk bleeding now. Ma was crawling toward the limo. Obioma was on his knees, his forehead resting on the sidewalk. He was still clutching his gun and trying to get up.

The limo was blocked in; the chauffeur, Mr. Babalola, being an intelligent person, exited and ran for cover.

He pulled open the van door. Melifonwu was tied in a large bundle clad only in his underwear. He held up his bound hands. "Don't shoot me!"

He ignored Mr. Melifonwu because Cory was sitting on the floor of the van next to him. Cory was smiling at him. Which was good.

Cory was still bound but he had brought a knife for just such an eventuality. He cut the ropes around Cory's wrists and peered out.

Ms. Iwobi was standing over Mr. Ma. She shot him three times and was obviously thinking of shooting him some more.

Attaché Onyewu chose that moment to make a break for CoffeeXtra, but Mr. Enemkpali shot him.

Onyewu went down.

He cut the ropes binding Cory's feet and looked out again. Mr. Enemkpali was standing over Ma. He put four more bullets into the already very dead Mr. Ma.

Pirates didn't ken the concept of "overkill" apparently.

And then he and Ms. Iwobi turned to Onyewu who was sitting on the sidewalk leaning against the building with his briefcase clutched in front of him.

Cory said, "My feet and hands are asleep, Gabe. I don't think I can walk."

"Just stay put." He could carry Cory if he had to, but they were safer in the van. He was dialing 911 when he heard the sirens coming from the south.

The Nigerians heard them too but they were still yelling at each other in Igbo. Onyewu pushed the briefcase across the sidewalk toward Ms. Iwobi, waving his hand at it.

She opened it. He caught a flash of green; his hundred thousand. Well, it wasn't really his since he had no idea where

Thorvaldsen was. But still.

She took the briefcase but she was still aiming at Onyewu who was pleading with her.

She looked at Enemkpali. He made a gesture of discarding something of no value.

Before she could look back, Onyewu pulled a pistol of his own and started shooting.

He was a very poor shot even by pre-training, Gabe Bergeron standards but Iwobi grabbed Enemkpali and dragged him toward the pickup. She looked back but Onyewu had crawled on his hands and knees into CoffeeXtra.

A squad car was coming.

Ms. Iwobi got Mr. Enemkpali into the pickup and jumped in herself. She ran up on the sidewalk rather than back up and then roared up South 16th Street under full power.

The police car slowed. The officer saw the bodies and pulled in. It was raining harder, and rivulets of blood from Ma and Obioma were streaking the sidewalk.

Officer Debby Tully rolled out of her patrol car. She was short and stocky; an unkind person might say she was shaped like a washing machine.

He smiled at her. "Hi there, Officer Tully."

"Bergeron?" She shook her head. "What the Hell?"

"The bad guys...well the bad woman and the bad man...are in the blue Chevy Silverado pickup, and they are escaping as we speak. I have the tag number?"

She was still shaking her head but she called it in.

"Are you armed? Hand it over."

"You will note that my weapon has not been discharged."

She snorted as she gazed at the bound Melifonwu and Cory. "And who are these two. If this is some kind of bondage thing gone wrong, I don't want to know about it."

"Certainly not. I am offended, Debby." He fished Cory's FBI credentials out of his pocket since Cory's hands still weren't working so good.

"And the other one?"

"This is Mr. Melifonwu. He's a pirate, and I'm not going to

cut him free."

Melifonwu was shaking his head. "I am not a pirate!"

She tried really hard not to laugh. She turned around and took deep breaths before turning back. "Just for fun. Tell me what happened here."

And he did. He didn't think that Debby believed a word he said, but she couldn't deny the bodies. Or the large, nearly-naked Mr. Melifonwu whose assets were on display.

"You're turning this neighborhood into a high crime area all by yourself, Bergeron."

"Am not." Well, he sort of was. It could be argued that he attracted an undesirable element.

"Stay put."

Cory was smiling at him. "So you and Officer Tully?"

"Ah. We have history. Peter Hahn tried to run over me, and of course, there was the incident with Eren Durmaz. Debby was present for both."

Cory shut his eyes. "Don't remind me."

He rubbed Cory's arms and hands trying to get the feeling back in them. He was looking at Debby; something was different?

"She's had her hair styled!"

Cory smiled again. "And you mention this because?"

"Well, she usually uses a bowl and hedge trimmers."

Cory laughed but then grabbed his stomach and groaned. "You need to go to the hospital, Cory."

"No."

Mr. Melifonwu said, "He does. Obioma was a very bad man. I tried to stop him from beating your friend. Please untie me?"

He shook his head.

Melifonwu leaned forward to peer at Obioma's body again. "Is he truly dead?"

More officers arrived; a detective he didn't know came. He could have saved the guy some work since this was surely going to be a FBI case.

They took Mr. Melifonwu away.

The first ambulance arrived. Onyewu was yelling louder

than Cory so they attended to him first. "They should look at you, Cory."

"I'm fine."

He shook his head. "I'm so very sorry this happened to you, Cory. It should have been me."

Cory said, "Not your fault. This time."

He didn't agree with the special agent. "I have to call Aunt Flo."

"Yes, you should. I'm okay."

He didn't look okay. He looked like he'd gone ten rounds with a mixed martial arts champion. With his arms tied behind his back.

"Aunt Flo. Cory and I are both safe."

There was a silence, and then she repeated his message. Ezmeralda said, "Where is he? Should we come?"

"Tell Ezmeralda that we're at a crime scene and won't be released for some time. I would love to see you both, but there's no need to come now."

Aunt Flo said, "Tell me what happened."

And he did. Cory was looking at him funny.

"I'm glad you're both safe, Gabriel. Is Cory there with you?"

" He is."

He handed the phone to Cory, and he managed to grip it. "I'm fine, Ms. Barnes. Your nephew is a special person." Cory listened. "Of course. But what he did could have gone so wrong...."

Cory smiled and handed the phone back. "I'll call you tomorrow, Aunt Flo, when the 'hurly-burly's done'."

He looked at Cory. "What did she say."

"'Never look a gift horse in the mouth'."

"Just so, Corentin."

Cory said, "You lured Onyewu here?"

"I did."

"They could have killed him."

"They could but he brought Ma who would have killed me so I'm not overly concerned. And he's not dead. Listen to him."

Cory said, "You should have called the FBI."

"Nope. They wouldn't have done whatever was necessary to get you back. Some foreign policy or legalistic shit or greater-good stupidity might have gotten in the way."

Cory hugged him.

"Should I call Aronson?"

"He's a jerk but yes."

He dialed. Aronson said, "Not more developments, Gabriel?"

"Mr. Ma is lying dead on the street in front of CoffeeXtra shot several dozen times. Ms. Iwobi and Mr. Enemkpali and Mr. Obioma all had a hand in that."

"Are the police on the scene?"

"They are."

"Tell them we're on the way."

He wasn't going to do that. The detective would be upset and would say mean things to him.

He called Fowler. "News. Ma is dead. The police are on the scene, and the FBI is coming fast."

"Gabe?"

"Who else?"

"I'm half asleep. Busy night. Ma is dead?"

"Yes, Detective."

"Thanks. I'll tell Susan and Stevie."

And then he called Inspector Okocha. "I still don't know where Thorvaldsen is, but Mr. Ma is dead, and Attaché Onyewu has been shot but he appears to be very much alive."

Onyewu was on a gurney yelling at the detective.

Okocha said, "Your doing?"

"I never fired a shot. I'll tell you all about it if you care to join us at CoffeeXtra."

And he hung up on Okocha for a change.

He looked at Cory. "I'm starving."

Cory nodded. "Me too."

"And you're really all right?"

Cory nodded.

He placed a call to CoffeeXtra. "Martin. Gabe here. Now

that the contretemps is over, could I get two coffees and a double order of banana bread. We're just down the street. By the gray van. Thanks ever so."

Thursday
1:00 pm

Inspector Okocha had arrived promptly. The Philly police looked askance at his credentials and wouldn't let him talk to Onyewu. Or to Melifonwu.

So he talked to Gabe Bergeron.

"What happened here?"

He smiled at Okocha. "Inspector Okocha of the Nigerian Police assigned to the embassy in New York meet Cory Poirier of the FBI."

They inspected each other like cats meeting at the boundary between their territories.

Okocha said,"You are with Bergeron?"

"I am."

"Very brave." Okocha may have smiled.

"He's very lucky. So Chinedum Onyewu brought Mr. Ma in his limo. You can ask him why?"

"Why did they come here? To meet you?"

"It's possible."

"You called Onyewu."

"No, I don't recall doing that. But then the pirates arrived. Mr. Obioma..." He pointed at the body without really looking at it. "...began shooting at Mr. Ma who shot back."

"Both of them went down. Ms. Iwobi shot Ma many times because he'd tortured and killed her husband, Nwosu. Who was also Mr. Enemkpali's son."

"And then Onyewu tried to run but Mr. Enemkpali shot

him. They would have finished him off too but the attaché stalled them long enough for the police to get close forcing Iwobi and Enemkpali to roar off thataway."

Okocha was frowning at him.

"In a blue, Chevy Silverado pickup."

"And Agent Poirier?"

"Him?" He smiled and patted Cory gently. "I have no idea how he got here."

Okocha said, "This is not the time or place for levity."

He gave Okocha his best smile as Aronson rolled up at the head of a small fleet of black SUVs. There was a collective groan from the police contingent.

Okocha marched toward Aronson.

His phone rang. It was Jennifer, but he couldn't talk to her just now. He would call her back later.

He and Cory were sipping coffee. Cory wasn't eating his banana bread which Martin had kindly delivered.

Martin said, "You knew this was going down, Dude?" Martin's willowy form was still shaking which wasn't helped by the confluence of blood from Ma and Obioma flowing past their shoes.

"No. Sit down, Martin, before you fall over. Take deep breaths." Martin nodded. "I knew something might happen."

Martin was leaning against the van. "You let it happen, Dude?"

"I had no control, Martin." Which was just a bit disingenuous.

Martin was looking at Cory. "What happened to him?"

"He had a contretemps of his own."

Martin managed a smile; it wasn't as wide as his normal, abnormal smile, but it was okay.

Aronson was talking to Attaché Chinedum Onyewu. "Can you stay with Cory for a bit?"

Martin nodded. "Sure, Dude."

He headed for Special Agent Aronson. He didn't look at the bodies; he was sure Ma must be a bloody mess, and he didn't need to see that.

But Aronson was looking fine. The rain may have dampened his tousled brown hair but the big, brown eyes were at full wattage. If you listened carefully, you could hear the throb and crackle of power.

The throbbing eyes were wasted on a petulant Onyewu. "I demand that you take me to the hospital! At once! I am a diplomat of the Federal Republic of Nigeria, and I will not be treated like this! Okocha, do something! It's your fault I had to come here. If you had done your job, none of this would have happened. You will pay for your incompetence!"

But Inspector Okocha was putting heart and soul into ignoring Onyewu.

But that was their problem. He smiled at Aronson who graciously waved him over.

And then he smiled at Onyewu who was ignoring him. "Treated like what? A criminal? Is that what you're bitching about, Your Excellency?"

"Go away, Bergeron!"

"You brought Ma. Why? To kill me?"

Onyewu looked at him. "No! To persuade you to help but he was insane. I see that now, but how was I to know? His family...."

He didn't give a shit about Ma's noble party birth. "You gave Ms. Iwobi the hundred grand."

Onyewu managed a smirk. "That is not her name."

"But that wasn't enough, was it? You told her what Thorvaldsen brought home from Nigeria."

Onyewu shook his head but he glanced at Okocha who was suddenly all rapt attention.

"You and Ma were willing to kill for it but you told her all about it to save your worthless hide."

"No."

"Yes. But Mr. Enemkpali was going to kill you anyway."

"I don't know what you are talking about."

But Mr. Onyewu knew very well. He had shared with Ms. Iwobi but not with Gabe Bergeron.

Onyewu looked at Aronson. "Let them take me to the

hospital. Please?"

Aronson said, "Any more questions, Gabriel?"

"No, I'm done."

He headed back to Cory. He may have snagged a paramedic on the way. "A patient for you."

Cory was still sitting in the open doorway of the van. "I'm fine. I don't need a paramedic."

"You haven't even tried to stand up, Poirier. Check him over. I think he was badly beaten." Cory was trying to shove the paramedic away. "Let him look you over, or I will call your mother."

Martin and the paramedic smiled but Cory stopped fussing.

The paramedic opened his shirt, and Cory was black and blue over most of his torso.

Martin said, "You should go to the hospital, Dude."

Cory may have groaned through gritted teeth when the paramedic touched his side. "Okay."

And the special agent was loaded into an ambulance. He leaned in. "I'm really sorry, Cory."

A voice behind him said, "Gabe?"

He spun but it was Harry. Paul and Chase were with him. "Hi, Guys."

Harry said, "What the Hell happened? Is Cory okay?"

"I think so but he's going to the hospital to be checked out. I can't talk now, but I'll call you. Tell Jennifer I'm okay, and I'll call her too."

Paul said, "Sure, Gabe. I hope he's okay."

Chase nodded.

Aronson was coming over. "I need to speak to Poirier."

"Yes, you do. At the hospital. After they check him over." He stared into Aronson's Svengali eyes. "But he doesn't know anything about the Chinese agents, Aronson, and that's the only thing that has ever interested you."

Aronson shunted more power to the luminous smile and the kaleidoscope eyes. Aronson leaned in, and it was like being in a forest of sandalwood. "Not the only thing, Gabriel. I want to thank you for your help in locating them."

Aronson was going back to the office, put his feet up, and collect a laurel wreath now that Chen and Ma and the supernumeraries were accounted for. He was pleasant to look upon...and smell...but he was a jerk. And not gay? Or bisexual?

"So who is the lady with the long, brown hair?"

Aronson smiled. "Let's not lose all of the mystery so early in our relationship, Gabriel."

"Right. Fine. Maybe you could take time out from her and track down Ms. Iwobi and any merry men she has left?"

She may not have had a hand in Cory's beating but she had kidnapped him and left him with Obioma. He wanted Aronson or somebody to find her and put her away for a hundred years or so.

Aronson nodded. "We at the FBI take the kidnapping of our agents very seriously, Gabriel."

"I'm glad to hear it."

He got into the ambulance with Cory. Aronson waved at him as the paramedic closed the door, and they were off.

Friday Noon

And he had called Cory's mother. Not only because Cory had become difficult once the doctor had mentioned keeping him overnight, but also because she needed to know that her son had been hurt.

She had not been in Costa Rica but on the family farm in Loudoun County, Virginia. Which was good.

And now he had sprung Cory from the hospital, and they were fast approaching Cory's D.C. condo since there was no way Cory could climb the stairs to his fourth floor apartment on Arch Street.

He parked. "I could find a wheelchair? Somewhere?"

Cory glared at him. "And I will punch you. I can walk."

He smiled at Cory. "For a short period, until you regain your legendary strength and vigor, I'm not really scared of your punches."

Cory smiled at him. "Okay. But I can walk. Is Mom going to be here?"

"Of course."

"Who else, Bergeron?"

"Hugh for now. Judd and Diane will be stopping by later."

"I don't need all this. I'm fine."

"You will be."

Cory was looking at him. "We need to talk. Later."

"About?"

"About what you did. This Onyewu could have been

killed."

"And he would have deserved it."

Cory nodded. "But the Nigerian government...not to mention our government...wouldn't have seen it that way, Gabe."

"I don't give a fig."

"A fig?"

"Just so. And if you can walk, then the time is now."

"You would have been arrested at the very least. You could have gone to prison. Other people...pedestrians, customers could have been killed. Civil and criminal charges...."

He put a hand over Cory's mouth. "Cory. I would have blown up CoffeeXtra and the Nigerian Embassy if that's what it took to get you back."

Cory smiled. "And where would you have gotten explosives, Bergeron?"

"I would have found some." He was pretty sure Aunt Flo and Ezmeralda could supply whatever he asked for. Of course, they might have talked him out of using it. Or not.

He got out of the Jeep and walked Cory to the elevator and to his apartment.

Cory's mother met them at the door. Laura had long, auburn hair, finely-wrought cheekbones, and blue eyes that were amazing unless they were compared to Cory's.

She was as supple and shapely as women half her age. She was also so patrician that Roman senators would have felt declassé in her presence and rent their togas.

She had seen Cory at the hospital but she patted his face gently. "What did those men do to you, Corentin?"

Cory was glaring at him. Did he think he wouldn't tell Laura? Silly special agent.

"I've been through worse, Mother."

She closed her eyes for a second. "I know. But you're home now and safe. Do you want something to eat?"

"No. Thank you, Mother. I just want to lie down."

"Of course, Corentin. Help him, Gabriel."

And he did. He may have taken some guilty pleasure from tucking Cory into his bed. "Are you really okay?"

"Fine, Bergeron."

"What happened?" Cory was glaring at him. "What?"

"You mean how did they grab me? Which you could have prevented if you'd been there?"

"That's not what I meant." Though he was sure he could have foiled Iwobi's evil plot. He wasn't going to say it now but Cory rushed into things, which his partner, Matt, tempered when he was around. "Why did they beat you?"

"The small guy was a psychopath."

"Mr. Obioma. I don't think that's his real name. So?"

"I think the woman...."

"Ms. Iwobi."

"If you say so. I think she told him to leave me alone but as soon as she left, he couldn't help himself. You could see it in his eyes."

Cory would never say but he had been scared.

"I thought he was going to kill the tall guy when he said something." Cory smiled. "And his name was?"

"Mr. Melifonwu. It seems they blamed him for the death of Nwosu. They thought that Melifonwu ran away when Ma and his men attacked their compound."

Cory was shaking his head. "Who the Hell is Nwosu? No. Start at the beginning, Bergeron."

And so he told Cory everything that Ms. Iwobi had shared with him.

Cory said, "Right. I'm going to take a nap and then we'll talk about all this at length."

"Absolutely. So if you're really okay?"

"I am."

"I'm gratified to hear it. So I can go back to Philly and explain to Jennifer? And put in a few hours?"

Cory smiled at him. "When I feel better, I'm going to take you to a doctor for a thorough examination." Cory patted his head. "A doctor who specializes in the area where you need help. Lots of help."

"What? Because I went to Duke's house? Or because I'm going to the office now?"

"Both."

The Duke thing was best forgotten. "I can be responsible."

"I know. I'm good."

He kissed Cory gently and went back to the living room. "I should go into the office to talk to Jennifer...if you guys are going to be here for a while?"

Laura said, "Hubert and I are spending the night."

Laura was giving him a look. It said that he was an incorrigible bastard who was always putting her darling boy at risk. Or something very like. And he couldn't even disagree with her.

Hugh/Hubert said, "If that's okay with you, Gabriel?"

Hugh was an older, less gym-obsessed version of Cory and still handsome.

"Absolutely. No need to ask. I wouldn't leave Cory if you weren't here, but Jennifer will be wondering where I am."

Laura tried to smile. "How is Jennifer?"

"She was just delivered of her third son. Two weeks ago. He was nine pounds and some ounces." He had no idea what the young man's name was.

"How wonderful for her, Gabriel!"

"Better her than me." He hadn't meant to say that out loud. "Sorry. I'm sure she's delighted."

Now that all the agony was over.

"So I'll be back later this evening."

Laura said, "We'll be here. And Gabriel, we need to talk about how Corentin was hurt."

"Sure. I hardly know any of the details."

He wasn't sure if she meant what had happened to Cory after he'd been grabbed by Iwobi or what madness of his had led to Cory being grabbed in the first place.

There was no upside to discussing either with her. Cory would tell her what he wanted her to know and wouldn't be pleased if he deviated from that script.

And he felt guilty enough as it was.

Hugh was looking at him. He couldn't even guess what Hugh was thinking, and then Hugh patted his arm.

"But I'm very sorry that he got hurt. He went off by himself..."

Laura said, "You're saying it was his fault?"

"No! It was all mine, and I'm very sorry."

He was out the door before anything else could be said. And then it hit him that Laura was feeling guilty too because she had called Cory and engineered his return...to watch over his ass. Shit.

He met Matt Bornheimer, Cory's partner, in the lobby. "How is he?"

He smiled. "He's okay. Well, he's going to be in time."

Matt said, "What happened, Gabe?"

"It's a long story. Which I'll be happy to tell you later. Do you know anything about the Chinese spies and Nigerian pirates? Cory can bring you up to speed."

"Not that. Tell me what happened to him."

"Ah. A Mr. Obioma beat him rather severely...for no particular reason except he enjoyed it. He's one of the pirates. Or he was until he had a gun battle with Ma. Both are now dead. Which is good because it means I won't have to go to Nigeria and track Obioma down."

Matt said, "And what would you have done if you'd found him?"

"Turn him over to the authorities. Or shoot him many, many times...in the pirate manner."

And he walked out with Matt staring at him.

Friday
3:00 pm

Chase was away from his security station when he breezed into the Mahr Building.

He didn't see Jennifer, and Harry and Carla were gone for the day, but he waved at Paul and walked over.

"I can't talk now. I need to find Jennifer, and then I have to get back to Cory. Of course, his mother is with him, but I think he'd rather have me."

Paul nodded. "The men who were shot?"

"Mr. Ma and Mr. Obioma were bad men and deserved what they got...or what they gave to each other."

Which was true, but he had still felt a chill walking over the sidewalk where they had fought to the death; so much latent rage erupting into fury.

Paul said, "Is it over, Gabe?"

"I think so. Maybe yes, maybe no. Is Jennifer here?" The lights were on in her office.

Paul nodded.

"Gabe?"

Jennifer was behind him. He spun and smiled his very best smile. "Jennifer. How wonderful to see you looking so well! Sorry I couldn't take your call yesterday. I was very busy. And congratulations on the birth of your son...."

He couldn't remember the name. Had somebody told him? Wait. Jennifer had told him.

"Adam Ruslan Boltukaev!"

Jennifer smiled. "Yes, Gabe."

"After Andy's grandfathers. So how is he doing?"

"He's wonderful." The smile said it all. Neither he nor any man would ever know that particular joy.

"So your clients are up-to-date and ship-shape. I can show you what I've done. If you're back? If not, I can soldier on."

She laughed. "Who are you and what have you done with Gabe?"

"Cory seems to agree with your assessment. I don't really understand it myself."

"Gabe, we can talk about my clients later."

"Right. But I haven't had a chance to really dig into the hinky one but I will. I fear he has abandoned the straight and narrow...for the crooked and broad?"

"Later. Come into my office."

She sat at her desk and twirled a lock of brown hair. "What's going on, Gabe? Harry said Cory was hurt? And two men were killed outside of CoffeeXtra?"

"I'm sorry I got involved. Tell Andy that. Please."

He gave her a highly bowdlerized version of Bradley, Duke Thorvaldsen, the SS Kerkyra et al.

"So you knew Bradley from when you were kidnapped?"

"Yes. And I thought he was harmless. Truly."

She shook her head. "But he wasn't."

"Well, he was but the guys after Duke were not. Which Bradley didn't know back then. He may have questions now."

He wanted to talk to Bradley. Ma was dead. Iwobi was probably on her way home? But Thorvaldsen was still out there, and he just wanted to know what had launched a thousand ships...so to speak.

"Is it over, Gabe?"

"Yes. I think it is."

She shook her head. "Be careful, Gabe."

"Absolutely." He smiled his most careful smile.

"So about your clients. Are you back, by the way?"

"On Monday. Half days for a couple of weeks."

"Very sensible. We can get you up to speed about your

clients then."

    They were a lot more high maintenance than his clients but Jennifer had spoiled them. They expected a lot of whim-catering, and he would be glad to be rid of them.

Monday
8:00 am

After the longest weekend of his life, he was happy to be back at work. He loved Cory, and he liked Laura and Hugh, but the four of them in one condo could not long be borne.

Hugh had realized that early on and had gone home on Saturday. Laura hadn't.

Which he could understand. She didn't get many chances to do things for her son, and she was determined to make the most of this window.

He had listened as Cory told her how he'd gotten snatched by pirates. Except Cory hadn't called them pirates. They had morphed into "white-collar criminals", and Ma and his band of spies had disappeared from the tale altogether. Susan had been kidnapped for inexplicable reasons by these almost gentlemanly criminals.

Laura had said, "The poor woman."

So she might be a little less furious with one Gabe Bergeron?

And Cory had fallen down a flight of stairs...apparently, repeatedly...and not been savaged by Obioma.

Well, she was his mother, and he was capable of doing the same thing with Aunt Flo. Except Aunt Flo always knew when he fibbed.

He thought Laura knew when Cory did too, but they both tacitly agreed to accept the fictional world they inhabited.

But they differed about him. At least, he hoped they did.

What had Cory said about him? Had he defended him?

He was sure that Laura would expel him from her son's life in an instant if she could. He wasn't going to think about that.

He had updated Chase, Harry, Carla, Paul, and Chatterjee about the events of Friday noon. He thought Chatterjee was pissed that he'd been out of the loop?

They kept asking him if this adventure was over. He had been wondering that himself when Jennifer had come in at 9:00 am.

They had worked together at bringing her up to speed with her clients until 1:00 pm. He and Stella had them in good shape, and she, being a bright lady, was ready to resume the reins.

Which was just wonderful.

Of course, Andy had come to pick her up and had looked at him funny. But he and Jennifer had made it through the birth...well, mostly Jennifer...and Andy probably wasn't harboring any grudges. He hoped not.

He realized he was too tired to care much.

After Jennifer left, he may have entered a coma-like state. When consciousness flowed back into his brain, his hand was resting on the keyboard and a million three's had been entered into the worksheet cell. And he had a paper stuck to his face.

He turned off his computer and staggered to his Jeep.

He shook his head and called Bradley.

Who didn't answer.

He called Susan at her home.

Detective Fowler said, "Hello?"

He may have smiled. "Fowler? Gabe Bergeron, here."

A long silence; the kind of silence that ensues between flicking the switch on a detonator and the actual explosion.

"What the Hell now, Bergeron?"

"Nothing much. So you and Susan are best buddies now?"

"Shut up, Bergeron."

"I bet Fuchs can tell me all about it. Well, a few well chosen grunts here and there."

"Why are you calling Susan?"

"I want to talk to Bradley. He's not answering his phone."

Fowler laughed. "Maybe he doesn't want to talk to you?"

"Why ever not?"

"What do you want with the kid? Ma is gone. The FBI is looking for these pirates. What's left?"

"Duke Thorvaldsen probably killed Clive Whalen."

"Yeah. I haven't forgotten."

"And we don't know what Duke brought back."

"And we probably never will. Look, Stevie is taking a training course. It'll be late before he gets back. After 8:00 pm."

"Tell Bradley that I called."

"Sure."

He didn't think Fowler was going to tell Bradley anything. He sighed. He called Cory.

"How are you feeling, Special Agent?"

"Better. Where are you and what are you doing?"

"I am at work doing work-type things: recording debits and credits, balancing balance sheets, constructing elegant cash flow and P&L statements. Those sorts of things."

Cory's baritone voice quivered with tones of disbelief. "Is that the truth, Gabe?"

"Yes. So is your mother still there?"

"Yes."

"Would you hate me if I stayed at my apartment tonight? I'm kinda beat."

"Can you come and rescue me?"

"And what would I tell your mother? Suck it up, Corentin. This too shall pass. It's always darkest before the dawn. The brave only die once."

"Idiot. But you'll come tomorrow?"

"Without fail."

He looked at his phone. He felt really bad about being less than truthful with Cory as he started his engine and headed for his apartment.

Monday
9:00 pm

He parked in front of Bradley's row house. No car. No lights on. He had taken a chance, and it hadn't worked out.

Light was issuing from Susan's house next door; as well as music, rock music. The structure was throbbing with the bass.

It appeared Susan was having a party.

He ran up the stairs and knocked on her door. He knocked harder on the door.

Susan threw it open. She wasn't naked but she wasn't fully clothed. It appeared she wasn't entirely sober either.

The music erupted from her house onto the porch. The vocalist was screaming, "Every day now! Every day now!"

Detective Fowler was playing air guitar in his underwear.

He hadn't found Bradley but this more than made up for it.

Fowler became aware of him as Susan smiled at him and said, "Gabe?"

"Hello, Susan, I was looking for Stevie?"

"What?"

"Stevie?"

Fowler had a silly grin on his face as he bounced over to the door. He was long and lean and fitter than he'd thought; sinewy. His face looked totally relaxed for once. "What now, Bergeron?"

"Stevie!"

Susan said, "Not home yet."

Or at least that's what he thought she said. "Thanks! Sorry to interrupt the party!"

She smiled at him. Fowler smiled at him. Something was different? Besides the nudity and the intoxication?

"You aren't smoking!"

Fowler cupped his ear. "What?"

He made smoking motions with his fingers and lips. Fowler thought that was just the funniest thing he'd ever seen.

"I quit!" He patted his arm. "The patch!"

And he did indeed have a nicotine patch on his arm.

"Good for you!"

Fowler smiled and shut the door. It appeared that something good had come out of the search for Thorvaldsen.

He was strolling back to his car when he thought he saw a light in Thorvaldsen's house.

He froze and stared at the window. He rocked his head from side to side in an owl-like fashion, but there was no light.

Until there was.

A definite flash of light.

He knew he should not go inside alone. Even if he could find a way.

But Fowler was not in any shape to go with him. Where was Fuchs? He had no way of calling him.

Well, he could dial 911.

But the light had only been for an instant. It could have been a reflection? From the car that had just passed by?

He knew he was talking himself into creeping up on Duke's front porch and peering into the windows. He knew he should not listen to himself.

He was at the foot of the stairs when Susan's music cut off. The steps creaked and groaned in the sudden silence of the night. The porch squeaked at every other step. He peered in and saw nothing. The house was properly black inside.

He shook his head. He was seeing things.

He had to pass the front door to get to the steps.

It was locked. He knew it was. It would be silly to try it but he did. And Lars "Duke" Thorvaldsen's front door swung wide.

Shit!

He flattened against the wall intent on slipping silently

down the steps and getting into his Jeep in a ninja-like fashion.

Monday
9:30 pm

But he had to close the door.

Still flattened against the wall, he reached his hand inside to grab the door handle.

A much larger hand reached out of the blackness and grabbed him. He may have produced a treble note so high that dogs pricked up their ears for blocks in every direction.

The hand pulled him inside. He was reaching for his Glock when the hand swatted him like a pesky horsefly and slammed the door shut.

He still might have gotten to his gun but a flashlight blazed in the darkness and burnt out his retinas.

The same big hand grabbed his Glock. He grabbed it but the hand was attached to an arm with lots of muscles, and he was lifted off the floor before the gun was wrenched out of his hand.

He scrambled to his feet as car headlights shone through the windows.

And he was face-to-face with a monstrously large stranger.

Well, the guy was six four at least. With shoulders as wide as your proverbial refrigerator.

He had on a sweatshirt with the hood pulled up. The light framed his face in radiance like Moses in a 1950's biblical epic; a Viking Moses with eyes so blue they radiated in the ultraviolet range and disinfected anything he gazed upon.

And he had a beard woven of gold and silver threads; well, his blond beard was streaked with a little gray.

He realized two things: he was holding his breath, and Viking Moses was aiming a large gun at his chest.

He put up his hands while sucking in some air. "Don't shoot!"

Viking Moses dragged him into the back hall and turned on another fifteen watt bulb.

And lo, he spake in a mighty voice, "Who the Hell are you? And why are you in my house?"

Actually his voice was a bit high for Moses. "You're Thorvaldsen? I'm Gabe Bergeron! I'm a friend of Bradley's...Steve is my good buddy."

Thorvaldsen shook his head; his hood fell back revealing long, golden locks. Thorvaldsen had the aforementioned, broad shoulders, a mighty chest, legs like tree trunks, and a full complement of manly charms. Thorvaldsen was saying something to him. Perhaps, he should cut out the gawking and attend?

"What?"

Thorvaldsen was giving him a look such as Thor might give Loki. "Are you deaf? You're lying. Stevie's never mentioned you."

"Well, I'm a recent friend. But we worked together last year...."

"FBI?"

Thorvaldsen shoved the barrel of his large pistol into his chest to make assurance doubly sure that he didn't miss the heart when he fired. It was a funny looking pistol but that was an inquiry for another time.

"No! Absolutely not! The FBI would never have me...not that I want them to! I don't like them at all." He smiled his very, very best smile. "And I know you were the second mate of the SS Kerkyra that was sailing to Nigeria when things went awry."

Thorvaldsen stared at him. ""Awry'? Went to Hell you mean!"

"Yes. The pirates. And Mr. Ma and Mr. Su."

Thorvaldsen grabbed him by the throat. "How the Hell do you know about them?"

"Well, you see Stevie hired me to find you. Mr. Ma is the one who tore up your house, by the way."

Thorvaldsen grunted. "Bastard did everything but bulldoze the place."

"I know. Terrible. The wainscoting was lovely. May I call you Duke? Stevie's been very worried after you disappeared. And so has Susan. Very worried."

Of course, she seemed to be recovering nicely with Fowler's help but Duke didn't need to know that.

"Stevie." Duke shook his head. "I let him down."

"You did?"

"Yeah. I needed his help, and the kid was happy to do what I asked. I was scared for him but I didn't see any other way."

"Really? So what did Stevie do for you? He didn't get hurt, did he?"

"No." Duke was looking sad; like a bear whose honey had been stolen. "He came to Tiny's but he found out about Gianna...and the others."

"And he got pissed with you."

Duke nodded like a very sad bear indeed. "Yeah."

He thought Duke's sad expression changed to a crafty one. "What?"

Duke said, "You aren't as small as Stevie, but you'll do."

He was absolutely certain he didn't want to know what use Duke was thinking about putting him to.

"What happened when Whalen came?"

"Whalen? Oh, yeah. Mean bastard."

"The alpha and the omega."

Duke said, "What?"

"His tattoos. That he had on his arms? He thought he was a fighter."

Duke shrugged off the tattoos. "He was a fighter! Tough bastard. He usually left me alone because I'm big."

"But he broke into your house?"

Duke's face suffused with anger. "I was in the freaking bathtub...naked...and I heard this noise on the stairs. I got out dripping water, and he pushed into the bathroom, shoving me back against the wall."

"And then what happened?"

"The bastard is leaning against me, smiling. He said, 'Give me the diamonds, or I'm going to beat the shit out of you.' He was still smiling. And then...."

Diamonds. He had to remain perfectly calm. "Then what?"

"He said he was going to take what he wanted."

"But you fought back."

Duke nodded. "Hell yeah! I pushed the bastard off me. I pushed him hard."

Duke nodded but then shook his head. "I just pushed him."

"And then what, Duke?"

"He slipped on the wet floor. And fell back. The asshole smacked his head on the bathtub...it's one of the old, cast iron ones. And then he was just on the floor, bleeding, with his eyes open. He made a sound in his throat."

"And he was dead. Which wasn't your fault."

Duke nodded and smiled a wondrous smile. He wanted to keep Duke happy just to see it again and to prevent Duke from shooting him.

"No. I just pushed him."

"Anybody would have. Totally self defense."

More nodding and smiling. He could see what had made Susan willing to put all the girls in all the ports out of her mind. And to make Bradley want to find him.

"So what did you do, Duke?"

"I tried to find his pulse but he was dead. And there was a lot of blood on the floor. And I was standing there buck naked. So I got dressed and then I put him in the tub...as a temporary thing until I could think...and I was cleaning up the blood when I heard more noises...from downstairs."

"So I went down, and a bunch of Chinese guys with guns were in my house! The guns had silencers. And I ran for it. Too much was happening too fast. I needed to think. The bastards chased me until they saw a cop car, and they backed off."

"But you couldn't get back in to get the diamonds? Because of Mr. Ma."

"Yeah! Him and the freaking cops were here every other day! And this big, black guy was always around."

"That's Inspector Okocha from Nigeria."

"Yeah? I figured. And the freaking Chinese were living in the old warehouse. I thought it was hopeless but I couldn't give up. The diamonds were my ticket out."

"Out of being a seaman for the rest of your life?"

Duke nodded. He didn't know what to do except to keep the guy talking. Duke had shoved the Glock into his belt but he wasn't going to win a test of strength with Mr. Thorvaldsen.

"So how did you get the diamonds in the first place?"

Duke smiled. "Well, the second we knew pirates were actually coming onboard, these two bogus Taiwanese hauled ass to their cabin."

"And you followed them?"

He nodded. "I knew those assholes were up to something from the second they came onboard. The Ma guy didn't even pretend to know shit about being a deck hand. And Su talked to the Captain too much. So they ran to their cabin, all panicky. I hid and watched and then followed them into the hold. They stuffed a small package into a crate."

Duke shook his head. "But one of the pirates was coming, and Ma, the stupid one, freaked and shot him dead."

"Ma was stupid. He's dead now."

"Yeah. Who got him?"

"One of the pirates."

Duke nodded. "Good. I saw the tall one, and I thought that was them. So anyway, Su seals the crate but more pirates came, and it was a freaking war zone. Su got shot and Ma ran for it. I guess he got away because I didn't hear any more shooting."

"And you grabbed the package?"

Duke smiled. "Like a shot. I had my own little hideyhole, and then I let myself be captured by the pirates and played dumb."

"And you came home as soon as you could?"

"Yeah. Which was probably a mistake? I should have played it cool...and maybe Whalen and the other bastards wouldn't have come to Philly?"

"It's possible."

Duke said, "So where are the pirates now? Gone back to

Nigeria?"

"Maybe. The wife of the leader of the pirates, Ms. Iwobi, shot Ma...many times. Which is why she came to America."

"Yeah?"

"Ma tortured and killed her husband, the pirate leader."

"For the diamonds? Yeah. I get that. So now I need you to do something for me. What was your name again?"

"Gabe. What exactly?"

Duke's eyes focused on him. "Hey. You're the guy Denny was talking about. The one who was in Tiny's asking about me! You told the cops I was at Denny's place!"

"No, I didn't! Really! Denny never said a word, and I had no idea where you were." Duke was mulling this over. "What was it you needed me for?"

Monday
10:00 pm

Duke nodded and gave him a big smile as he patted his shoulders. "You'll fit."

"Fit what exactly?"

"It's okay, Gabe."

He didn't believe that for a second but he had to keep Duke happy. He needed to get away or get help. Susan and Fowler had the music on again and wouldn't hear anything over that. What time was Bradley supposed to get home?

Duke ushered him to the hallway beside the front stairs and was looking at a small door built into the space beneath the stairs. He opened the door to a closet and turned on a light inside.

"What? You can get into the closet as well as I can." Which was almost true.

But Duke shook his head and pointed at the floor. "I don't fit through the hatch."

He wasn't sure that he'd fit through the hatch either.

Duke said, "Bradley can slip through with no problem. He got the diamonds for me."

"So why do you care if I fit through?"

"Cause Bradley put them back. After he got pissed with me." Duke opened the little hatch. "I was going to crawl all the way from the back of the house through the crawlspace but I've got you now."

"I'm not going in there." At the very least, there'd be spiders and mold and muck...he wasn't going to think about snakes. "And I could get stuck."

"I'll pull you out."

"No way."

Duke nodded. "If you won't then I don't need you."

Which was a point. "So why is this hatch here?"

"Used to be an old floor furnace here in the hall. Granny had it taken out, and I repaired the floor." Duke ran a hand over the hardwood. "Did a good job too. But they left the metal frame that held the burner and motor, and that's where I stashed the cash box."

Duke grabbed him by the throat again. It was very unsettling how well his throat fit within Duke's paw.

"And you're going to do me a favor and get the box."

He nodded. He didn't have much choice.

The hatch was tiny but if he extended his arms through first he thought his shoulders would just fit through.

"So where is this cash box?"

"You'll see the furnace frame." Duke pointed to the spot on the floor. "Just reach inside."

Duke gave him the flashlight. "Don't even think about trying to get away." Duke grabbed his ankle. "Unless you want to lose a leg."

Which wasn't a viable option.

The air coming from the hatch was cool and damp and smelled like a fungal, creepy-crawly, spider paradise. He switched on the flashlight and inspected the ground as far as he could see. He saw the furnace frame. It wasn't that far but he'd have to twist his body around.

Duke said, "Hurry up!"

He slid his arms through and twisted until his shoulders were diagonal to the hatch. He squirmed and popped through. He used his hands to walk to the frame.

Duke had a grip on his left ankle. He could kick with his right and maybe get loose but Duke had the guns.

His chest was on the mucky ground but he found the little, metal cash box and pulled it out.

And started to back up toward the hatch. He put his right

foot next to his left.

Duke grabbed both and yanked hard. He pulled him straight up by his ankles and through the hatch like he was tonging on Chesapeake Bay; Gabe Bergeron was the tong and the cash box was the harvest of oysters.

Duke dumped him on the hall floor and grabbed the box. He opened it and let out a long, slow sigh of relief.

He stood up and started backing away from Duke.

Duke stopped admiring the shiny things and aimed the gun at him again.

"No."

"But you have the diamonds."

"You'll tell the cops."

"No, I won't!"

He would never know but he was reasonably sure that Duke would have killed him if a car hadn't pulled in across the street.

He smashed his elbow against the window pane as hard as he could. It shattered, and shards of glass fell onto the porch. He could hear Susan's music clearly now.

Duke grabbed him again. He was certain that it was neck wringing time but Duke looked out the window.

"Shit."

And Bradley came through the front door. "Duke? What's going on? Gabe, are you in here?"

"Yes! Over here, Bradley!"

Bradley saw Duke. "So you got them?"

Duke nodded.

Bradley looked at him. "Did he make you go through the hatch, Gabe?"

"He did. I think I have cobwebs in my hair."

Bradley laughed and then stepped between them. "You got what you came for. Now leave. Gabe won't tell the police."

But Duke shook his head. "How do I know that, Stevie?"

"Because I'm telling you. Gabe's a friend, and he'll do what I ask. You'd better not hang around, Duke. It's not safe."

"Gabe says that Ma is dead."

"But the pirates are still in Philadelphia."

"Are you sure, Stevie?"

"Yes, and they want the diamonds. Move toward the door, Gabe."

He took a step but Duke was shaking his head.

He said, "I promise that I won't tell anyone I saw you. And I don't know anything about any diamonds, Duke."

He wasn't sure Duke was going to let them go.

Bradley said, "You aren't a killer, Duke. Whalen was an accident."

"It was, Stevie."

And then they heard Susan. "Stevie? Where did you go? Stevie!"

Bradley said, "You want her to come in here, Duke?"

Duke shook his head and marched down the hallway to disappear into the gloom. He and Bradley scooted out the front door and across the street.

Susan came out her door again tying a mom-type bathrobe around her. "Stevie?"

Bradley said, "I'm okay, Mom. Just talking to Gabe."

"There you are. Are you sure, Stevie?"

"I'm sure, Mom, but it's been a long day, and I need to sit down."

"Sure, Honey. Want me to fix you something to eat?"

"Thanks, Mom, but I got a pizza on the way home." And Bradley reached into his car to retrieve the box.

"That isn't a proper meal, Stevie."

"Mom."

"All right." And she swayed a bit going up the steps into her house.

Bradley turned to him. "Please come in, Gabe."

His heart was slowing to a more normal pace. "Are you sure he's gone?"

"Yes. He wouldn't have hurt you."

"Says you!"

"No, he wouldn't."

Bradley's front room looked a lot like his mother's. "Come

into the kitchen."

They sat at the kitchen table, and he gradually stopped shaking. The pizza smelled good.

He smiled at Bradley. "Thanks for saving my ass."

"I got you into this mess."

He was suddenly ravenous. "You did. Going to share your pizza?"

Bradley smiled. "Sure."

And when they were munching away like rabbits safe in their burrow, he said, "So Duke called you?"

"Yeah."

"And asked you to risk your life to get his diamonds."

"Yeah."

"And you took them to Tiny's Bar."

Bradley nodded. "I was there for hours with the stupid cash box under my arm. And I tried calling him and got no answer, and then Lily said I should call Gianna." Bradley was looking at him. "I guess I was stupid but I thought he loved Mom."

"He did. He probably still does. In his way." He didn't think Bradley bought that.

Bradley said, "And then his friend Denny told me what a player Duke is. And Lily said that Duke had banged every woman in the freaking bar. Including Denny's girl."

"I know it was a shock."

"You could say that! And Lily made sure I knew that she and Duke had...done it."

"Right."

"But she's so old, Gabe!"

"She wasn't always old, Bradley."

"No. I guess not. Anyway, I didn't want to see Duke by then, and I went outside...to get away from Lily. I sat in my car for a while and then I saw Duke with this woman hanging onto him."

"She yelled at him. She asked why he cared if Susan's kid saw them together. She asked him if he was ashamed of her. Duke just laughed at her and went into the bar alone. He was wasted. I left. And I called him the next day and told him his box was back under the house, and I didn't want to hear from him again. I guess it was childish putting the box back, but I don't care."

"I know. I would have done the same thing. So where will he go?"

"No idea. Did he steal the diamonds?"

He shrugged. "I guess? Technically. But they were payment to Chinedum Onyewu; a bribe to get him to do something for whoever or whatever agency Ma was working for. So not good guys. And Ma is very dead. Not that the diamonds were his anyway."

Bradley was looking at him. "Do you believe that Duke murdered Whalen?"

"No. I believe him when he says it was an accident."

"Then let him go, Gabe. I asked you to find him, and you did, but now I'm asking you to forget you saw him. Please?"

"Are you sure about this, Steve?"

"Yes. I know he isn't the guy I've always thought he was, but let him go."

"Okay. I can do that." He probably couldn't find the guy again anyway, and he was tired of the whole business. He finished his slice of pizza and walked out to his Jeep.

He was almost home when he remembered that Duke had taken his Glock. How the Hell would he explain the loss to Cory? And he had some bruises and scrapes on his arms and shoulders too.

He parked and closed his eyes. Those were problems for another day.

Tuesday Noon

He invited Harry and Paul and Chase to lunch at CoffeeXtra; Carla was working from home. He was even going to pay.

Paul and Chase had been there for him, and Harry was just pitiful. And he was his best friend in Philadelphia, now that Neal had gone off again.

But Harry was looking at him funny. "What's up, Bergeron?"

"Nothing."

Harry said, "You never pay."

"Look, Baldacci, do you want lunch or not? I was going to relate the exciting denouement of the Chinese-Nigerian Pirate Caper, but if you don't want to hear?"

Harry smiled at him.

So he told them almost everything.

Harry said, "You let him go?"

"Obviously, you weren't listening Baldacci. He let me go."

Paul was smiling. "Diamonds."

"Yes. I may have caught a glimpse of them glowing in the beam of the flashlight as a giant, possibly-murderous man fondled them."

Chase said, "You should have called me."

He smiled at Chase. "Thanks! But did I know I was going to need backup? No, I did not."

Harry said, "And you haven't told Cory? About the gun?"

He shook his head.

Chase said, "You have to report it stolen."

"I know. I'm going to."

Paul said, "But why was Ma carrying diamonds to Onyewu?"

"A most excellent question, Mr. Hearne. I'm certain that no one is ever going to share that with me; not Aronson if he knows. If Chen talked? Certainly not Monroe. Or Okocha."

"Oil?"

"I understand that Nigeria has lots of that but who knows?"

Paul said, "You did good, Gabe."

Which was nice to hear. If he could just magically summon his Glock out of the foul and filthy air, everything would be copacetic.

He needed to use the little boy's room which entailed walking innocently by the entrance to the back room of the coffee shop. It had a more intimate air with its distressed brick walls and overstuffed, black leather sofas..

He may have glanced...innocently...at the occupants lounging on those black leather sofas.

He would have missed them if not for a flash of lime green since they were snuggled down in the farthest sofa doing something. He wasn't going to speculate; that way upchucking lay.

Dana's spindly arms were locked around Mahoney; Devon Mahoney, the IT guy.

Well, he could say for sure that they were kissing and moaning. He knew he should turn away but he couldn't seem to do it.

And then they stopped kissing. Devon stood up and pulled Dana to her feet.

They weren't undressed in any way, and nothing unseemly had been going on. Well, except for the public kissing thing.

Devon reached out and patted Dana's tummy gently as they smiled and stared into each other's eyes. Their joy was potent enough to make him smile too.

And then he ducked behind the nearest sofa and crawled to the Men's Room. On the way, he may have passed Astrid who just looked at him and shook her head.

They were gone by the time he came out so he could return to his table upright.

He sat down.

Harry said, "What now, Bergeron?"

"Dana's pregnant, and IT Devon is the father!"

They all nodded; even Chase.

"Wait. You knew?"

They all smiled. No one told him anything. He should have never told them about Thorvaldsen and the pirates. The next time he had secrets he would keep them, locked away deep inside.

They were smiling at him again.

He was going to storm out of CoffeeXtra but he caught the scent of sage.

And Hui-wen was leaning over Harry's shoulder and glaring at Gabe Bergeron.

Except she wasn't. Her fearsome gaze was centered on Chase who was smiling at her.

Hui-wen said, "Dude."

Chase said, "I had to hear what happened with Thorvaldsen, Hui-wen."

Her frown mellowed. "All done?"

Chase nodded and got to his feet. He stood very close to her and leaned over her. She leaped into the air like a leopard, locked her arms around his neck, and kissed him. For a long time.

This public kissing thing was getting out of hand.

When she and Chase broke the vacuum seal of their kiss, she let go of his neck and slid down his body.

She locked onto his hand and was leading him to the door, but she stopped. "Bergeron."

"Hui-wen?"

"I'll talk to you later."

And she dragged Chase out the door. To be fair, he seemed more than willing to go.

He looked at Harry. "Don't look at me, Bergeron. I have enough on my plate reading Carla. And Winnie. I don't have energy for the rest of them. Though Hui-ting seems nice."

"Right."

Harry glanced at Paul and didn't mention Gavin. He got to his feet. "Thanks for lunch, Gabe." He smiled. "I'm sorry I wasn't more help with this one."

"Don't be. I understand."

"Good. I should get back. Before Carla calls."

He was about to make a comment about wives and babies and the sheer horror of it all when he looked at Paul. "Do you have kids, Paul?"

"Two boys and a girl. They're grown."

"So you've been through the birthing process?"

He was pretty sure Paul was laughing at him on the inside. "That was mostly Annie, Gabe."

"Right. I do know that. But you were there?"

"I was." Paul finished his tea. "It was wonderful."

He held the shudder deep within. What else didn't he know about Paul Hearne? Scads most likely.

"I should get back."

Paul nodded. Paul wasn't going to ask him about Hui-wen. So he said, "I'm glad the Thorvaldsen mess is over."

Paul nodded as they walked shoulder to shoulder along South 16th Street.

"I'll be able to focus on other stuff."

Another nod.

He had to figure out how to help Paul and Winnie.

Tuesday
3:00 pm

He may have used his computer for a none-work-related search for anything about Gavin, *père et fils*, and Gail.

He found nothing. Well, he found a death certificate for Gail Alice Sommer who had passed away in 1985. And where Gavin Sr. was buried.

He was determined enough to leave early and drive to Bala Cynwyd...to a cemetery.

He had to admit that he was lost and driving in circles but he wasn't ready to give up. He stopped by a guy making an afternoon out of trimming one puny tree like he was a bonsai master...on a grander scale.

The malingerer was bored enough to point him in the right direction and then to jump in his cart and lead him to the grave of Gavin Sommer, Sr.

It was in a corner of the cemetery. There were houses across the street. Some of the headstones had been vandalized.

Gavin's stone was modest and had just his name and "1930-1979" carved into it. There were two unmarked graves next to his; Gail and Gavin Jr.?

He had no idea.

But the three graves seemed to have been tucked into a plot belonging to a Riley family. Judging from proximity to a rather grand headstone for a David Eoghan Riley, born 1938 and departed in 1975, and Petra Emily Riley, his wife, born 1942.

But there was no departure date for Petra, nor was there any sign of a grave for her.

So Petra was still alive? And might be connected to Gavin? He needed to find this Petra; he pulled out his phone.

And found an address for a Petra Riley!

Of course, it might not be his Petra Riley but she didn't live that far away. He set his Jeep on a southerly course

Petra's house was an enormous Victorian that could give Aunt Flo's a run for its money size-wise.

It was brick with a central block with two stubby wings; pediments adorned arched windows replete with stain glass.

Seven foot Mr. Melifonwu could stand tall and proud and pass through the front door without ducking his head; even Mr. Hand would fit with no problem.

He ran up on the porch and knocked.

He was about to knock again when he spotted a form approaching down a long dark hallway.

She opened the door. "Yes?"

She was larger than Aunt Flo but not by much and possibly younger? She was wearing a dark suit, black or navy blue. It was hard to tell in the gloom of the hallway.

She had white hair, gray eyes, and delicate gold hoop earrings.

"Hello, I'm Gabriel Bergeron." He gave her a card. "Are you Ms. Petra Riley?"

Her face was square and unsmiling. Her features appeared to have set like concrete some decades earlier and couldn't or wouldn't admit of alteration now.

"I am, but I don't need an accountant, Mr. Bergeron."

"Right. No, I'm not here looking for work. Could I come in?"

She stared at him shaking her head. She was going to slam the door in his face and who could blame her?

"It's about Gavin and Gale Sommer."

"What?"

"Gavin and Gale Sommer." He pulled out Gavin's grainy yearbook photo. "Did you know them?"

"Are you asking me if I knew my own sister and nephew,

Mr. Bergeron?"

"I am."

"What is this about?" She had her hand on the door and was stepping back.

"A long time ago, in 1981, a girl named Winnie...." He realized he didn't know Winnie's maiden name. "Well, she's Winnie Wong now. Wait! Winnie Wu, that was her maiden name, and she and Gavin Sommer, Jr. fell in love, and he asked her to marry him on the night they graduated from high school, but her parents wouldn't allow it. And she being a traditional sort of girl obeyed them...."

"Winnie Wu?"

"Yes? Do you know the name?"

"Certainly not. You say that Gav asked her to marry him?"

"He did. And then Winnie got married to a Mr. Wong but he passed away in 2006, and she's been alone since then...."

"Are you quite sane, Young Man?"

He gave her his very best smile. "Mostly. I'm not sure I'd go so far as to say quite sane."

He thought there was a flicker of something that might have been a smile twenty years earlier.

"What do you want with me? My sister Gale had nothing after her husband died, and poor Gav had less so if this is about a love child...."

He may have giggled. "Sorry! It's just that Winnie is so respectable."

She snorted. "Presumably she was young and less respectable at one time."

"Presumably. No, I'm not telling this right, but I don't want you to slam the door in my face."

She nodded and walked down the hall leaving the door open. He followed her to the first parlor.

She sat on a brocaded settee and waved at a matching one. "And?"

"Right. So Winnie has always wondered what happened to Gavin....what might have been if she'd told her parents to get over themselves or had run off with him. I believe the phrase 'carry a torch' is apt for her state of mind...or heart."

Petra was coming perilously close to smiling. "So you're here to find out what happened to Gavin Alexander Sommer, Jr.? I see. But why did this Winnie Wong choose you?"

"Ah. Well, you see I work at Garst, Bauer & Hartmann, and her daughter, Carla Wong-Baldacci, works next to me. And I may have had some experience getting to the bottom of things. And Carla may have told her mother stories about me."

He smiled.

She smiled back. "And are the stories true?"

"Well, mostly true. Not that I've heard Carla's version of them so it's hard to give a definite answer."

"No, I can see that. But you want to know what happened to Gav?"

"I do. Very much."

She sighed and shook her head. "He died in 1985, Mr. Bergeron. He preceded my sister by a few weeks which devastated her, but she was never the same after what her husband did...."

She had her hands bunched up in delicate fists but she splayed out her fingers and smoothed her skirt. "I don't want to talk about him. He died, and that was the end of it."

He said, "A 'nothing in his life became him like the leaving it' sort of thing?"

She shook her head. "Not exactly, Mr. Bergeron."

"I see. Well, I don't really. But you had them all buried in the Riley plot."

"I did. Have you been out there? I should visit but it's been so long now. The truth is I don't think I'd remember what David looked like if I didn't have pictures of him."

"Well, it's been a long time."

"It has."

"So what happened to Gavin Jr.?"

Her face which had been thawing a bit locked up tighter than ever. "It was a hit-and-run.. He was only twenty-two."

"I'm sorry. Where did it happen?"

"Why?"

"Just curious."

She smirked at him. "No doubt. It was in North Carolina." She stood up. "If that's all, Mr. Bergeron."

He got to his feet. "What was he doing in North Carolina?"

"I have no idea."

Which was a fib.

"But you helped your sister bring the body home for burial?"

"I did. Gale couldn't cope."

"It was good that you could help your sister. I have a half-brother, Donnie. I should really call him more."

He may have stood there lost in thought for a second or two.

"Mr. Bergeron?"

"Right. Sorry. Do you have any photos of Gav? I know Winnie would love to see them."

"I can't give you my photos."

"No, of course not." He pulled out his phone. "I can take photos of the photos...would that be a meta-photo?"

She definitely smiled this time. "I'm sure I wouldn't know. Come on and then you have to go."

"Absolutely."

She had some in frames which she grudgingly let him take out, and she had some loose photos. One was of Gav with two other young men. Gav was in the center with his arms on the shoulders of his two friends; all were smiling.

"That's the last photo I have of Gav. It was in Gale's things."

He snapped a last photo of a last photo. "Thank you so much. What can I do to repay you? Do you want to go to dinner? Or lunch? Sometime?"

She came perilously close to blushing. "No! Thank you, but no. And now it's time for you to go."

"Okay. Thank you so much. This will be closure for Winnie. I'm sure she'll be very grateful."

Petra escorted him to the door. "Why was Gav in North Carolina? And what happened to his father?"

She shook her head and locked her face. "I've told you all I can tell you, Mr. Bergeron. The rest...the rest is a family matter and best forgotten. Don't come back and please be sure to make Mrs. Wong understand that I have nothing more to tell her about Gav; about his life or his death."

And then she did slam the door.

Wednesday
10:00 am

He had taken the train to D.C. Cory hadn't noticed his scrapes or he hadn't mentioned them.

Laura had gone home, and they had spent a quiet night alone together.

Matt was coming to take Cory into work for half a day. The fact that Cory had stayed out so long was an indication of just how badly he'd been hurt. And tried to hide from him.

And he had taken the train back to Philly and was now in his cubicle feeling very guilty about Cory again.

He hadn't told Carla about Gavin yet. He didn't have Hui-wen's phone number but he wouldn't have called her first anyway.

Did all the stuff that Petra wasn't saying matter to Winnie? He didn't think so, but he needed to talk to Carla.

But she and Harry were seeing the doctor.

He wanted to know more about Gavin's passing, and he had never met the guy. It wasn't impossible that Winnie might want to know more too.

He had spent two hours online and now knew far more about the governmental agencies of the state of North Carolina than anyone but a life-long resident would want to know.

There was, as far as he could tell, no record of the death of Gavin Sommer, Jr.

Which was odd? He even had the year. There should be something? Unless Petra had lied to him?

He didn't think so; omission not commission.

Cory had made it abundantly clear that the FBI was not a resource to be used by Gabe Bergeron to satisfy his curiosity.

He called Fowler.

"Bergeron? What now?"

"Hi, Detective. How are you doing? How is quitting smoking going? How is Susan?"

"I'm busy, Bergeron."

"Right. Okay. I asked about a Gavin Sommer, Jr.?"

"You still want that info?"

"I do. I would be ever so grateful."

"Hold on."

Which meant what? That Fowler had found something and neglected to inform him?

Of course, it was true that Fowler didn't work for Gabe Bergeron. But still.

"Bergeron?"

"Still here, Detective."

"Let's see."

And the pause went on and on. Was Fowler that slow a reader? "Yes? You found something?"

"Hold your pants on. I can't read Calder's handwriting."

He sat there. He may have clamped a hand over his mouth to keep unhelpful comments from spewing out.

"Yeah."

"Yeah, what?"

"He changed his name."

"What?"

"Don't yell at me, Bergeron!"

"Sorry! But Gavin Alexander Sommer, Jr. changed his name? To what?"

Fowler chuckled for far too long. It was good that this was over the phone; otherwise he might have lunged for Fowler's throat.

"The guy changed it to Gavin Alexander Winter. Isn't that a hoot?"

"Why would he do that?"

"Don't ask me, Bergeron. I can email you a copy of the

document. If you want?"

"That would be super, Detective."

"Okay. So how is this guy connected to Thorvaldsen?"

Shit. "I'm not sure. I'll call you if I come up with something. So how is quitting smoking really going?"

"It's Hell, Bergeron."

"But you can do it?"

"Yeah. Maybe. Bye."

And he hung up.

And knowing Gavin's new name, it was easy enough to find the death certificate.

Gavin Winter had died on the evening of July 3rd, 1985, in the tiny village of Buxton on Hatteras Island; part of North Carolina's outer banks.

What the Hell?

Wednesday
7:00 pm

They were sitting on the sofa in Cory's condo. He had just finished telling him all about Gavin Winter, né Sommer, and Cory was looking at him funny. Which seemed to be happening a lot lately.

"What?"

"You're going down the rabbit hole."

"Am not! I'm just curious."

Cory said, "That's how it always starts."

He probably shouldn't have told Cory about Petra and Gavin and North Carolina.

"Not this time. This is Winnie's mystery, and I don't have any agenda of my own. So what should I tell her? Or tell Carla first? Any suggestions or comments would be greatly appreciated, Special Agent?"

"Carla is your friend, right?"

"Sort of. Yes. A prickly, acidic, choleric friend."

Cory waved all his qualifications away. "She's your friend, and you should tell her everything and let her decide what her mother needs to hear."

"Good."

"Really?"

"Yes. That's what I was thinking."

Cory was still looking at him. "If I hear a whisper, a hint of a whisper about exhumation, I will put you in a facility."

"Not the one where your grandmother, Josephine, is a

'guest' at this time?"

"The very same. Mother knows the people who own it, and you could be admitted before you knew what was happening."

"Aunt Flo would get me out."

Cory laughed. "Well, that's true. But you wouldn't like it until she mounted a rescue."

"No, I wouldn't. It isn't very nice to threaten me, Corentin. I'm not going to dig up Gavin Jr."

"Just see that you don't."

He would never do that. Of course, Bradley owed him a favor, and Bradley didn't mind bodies. True, he wasn't a pathologist but he was a crime scene tech.

"But it's been thirty-six years, and there's probably nothing left to find...about the cause of death."

Cory jumped on top of him and pinned him to the sofa.

Which was very nice.

"Bad Gabe!"

"I'm not going to do it. You're the one who brought up exhumation. It had never crossed my mind."

"Liar!"

He smiled at Cory. "So how are your ribs and internal organs doing?"

"Getting better every day."

"I'm delighted to hear it." He slipped his hands under Cory's t-shirt and rubbed his side gently; Cory flinched ever so slightly. "But not action ready at the current moment."

"I'm always action ready, Henri."

"Nope. You might hurt yourself, or worse, I might hurt you with my tempestuous love making."

"I think I'll chance it."

Cory kissed him. One or both of them should be adult about this but they were well past that stage.

Thursday
9:00 am

Carla was cranky. Which was not a great surprise and totally understandable.

Sort of. He was trying to get his head around having a ten pound weight slung around his waist, forcing him to walk bow-legged, while pressing on his bladder and other areas; not to mention the plethora of other symptoms.

And to realize that this nightmare had been a choice.

Carla was glaring at him. "Earth to Gabe! What do you want, Bergeron?"

"This pregnancy was intentional? Right?"

She just stared.

"Of course, it was." He patted Harry's shoulder. "Harry'd be dead by now if it hadn't been."

Harry said, "Shut up, Bergeron."

Carla turned back to her desk. "Go away, or I will hurt you."

"I found out what happened to Gavin Alexander Sommer, Jr."

Carla and Harry spun back to gaze at him.

"So I can tell you first or I can call Hui-wen who seems more interested than the rest of you."

Carla got to her feet and waddled toward the conference room. He and Harry trotted after.

Carla sat. She glared. Harry was too cowardly to take a seat and hovered in the doorway.

He smiled his very best smile. "It's a strange tale which will take many hours to relate."

Carla picked up an errant stapler. "Right between the eyes, Bergeron."

"Calm yourself, Ms. Wong-Baldacci. Gavin, or Gav as his aunt calls him, was killed in a hit-and-run 'accident' on Hatteras Island in 1985."

Harry sat down. "Did I hear air quotes around 'accident', Gabe?"

"You did, but I have no idea if they're justified or not."

Carla said, "So he's been dead all this time? He was what? Twenty-two when he died?"

"He was. I have no idea why he was in North Carolina on July 3rd, or why he had changed his name from Sommer to Winter."

Their reaction was all that he could have hoped for. He wanted to take a picture of their dumbfounded faces but Carla was still gripping that stapler.

He handed Carla an envelope with enlargements of all the photos of Gav that Petra had let him snap.

And he told them everything that he'd learned.

Carla was almost smiling. She said, "Come here, Bergeron."

She still had the stapler. "Why?"

Harry said, "Don't be a wuss, Bergeron. She isn't going to hit you with the stapler."

"Says you."

He leaned closer, and Carla Wong-Baldacci hugged him. "Thank you, Gabe."

"Of course. I was glad to do it. The thing is that Cory's worried about me."

Carla and Harry looked at one another. She said, "He thinks you're going to have to find out why he changed his name."

He nodded. "And why he was in North Carolina. And if his death was really an accident. But I'm going to be strong and put the whole matter out of my mind."

Unless Winnie asked him to delve deeper. Maybe.

"So what are you going to tell her?"

Carla said, "The minimum: that he was killed in a car accident. And show her the photos."

"Good."

Harry said, "Are you going to tell her about Aunt Petra?"

Carla said, "Only if she asks where the photos came from. Which she will."

So he went back to work and was actually not thinking about Gavin or even Thorvaldsen when Harry tapped him on the shoulder a few hours later.

Winnie and the four daughters who didn't work at GBH were filing off the elevator.

Carla was already in the conference room. He and Harry watched as they joined her around the table. He saw her pass the photos round.

She broke the news about poor Gavin's untimely demise.

After a proper moment of silence, an excited chatter arose, and Hui-wen bounced out of the room.

She was waving at him. "Dude! Get your weird ass in here."

The collective eyes of every cubicle dweller focused upon him. Paul was smiling at him.

He arose with as much dignity as he could muster. There was nothing weird about his ass...or any other part of him.

He waved at Jennifer who was standing in her doorway, face nearly ablaze with questions.

This was a sad occasion but all of Winnie's daughters were smiling at him. He did a half smile at Winnie which probably looked like a gas pain. "I'm sorry about Gavin."

But Winnie gave him a big smile and hugged him. "Thank you, Gabe."

"You're very welcome, Winnie."

"Carla told me about you but I didn't truly believe the stories."

Hui-wen said, "But you lived up to the hype! How long did it take you? A day?"

"Longer than that."

He was going to bow out, but Hui-wen said, "What was he

doing in North Carolina?"

"I don't know."

Hui-wen was staring at him. Her gaze reminded him of a cross between gazes directed at him by Carla and Aunt Flo. Hui-wen knew there was more to the story.

Carla didn't say a word.

Hui-wen said, "So where is this aunt? Did you know about her, Mom?"

Winnie shook her head. "No. But it doesn't matter."

Hui-wen wasn't ready to let it go.

But fair Francine of the flowing black hair and red lipstick spoke first. Of all the daughters, she was the least happy. "How much?"

She was clutching her purse in a death grip.

Carla said, "Francine."

"What? He didn't do this for nothing, Carla."

Hui-wen, sensing conflict and drama, said, "Yeah. Make up a bill, Dude. And don't cheat yourself. Francine is loaded."

Francine was horrified. "I am not!"

And then Hui-ting, who was invisible among her sisters, said, "He has expenses, and his time is valuable." Hui-ting was smiling at him. "I'll pay my share, Gabe."

And then the conversation went Mandarin in a big way.

He may have backed out and hidden in the Men's Room.

Until there was a knocking on his chamber door.

Hui-wen said, "Put it back in the holster and zip up because I'm coming in, Dude."

And she did.

He glared at her. "Hey! Do I come in the Ladies' Room? No, I do not."

She was inspecting the floor and the stalls and sniffing. "Not too bad. Some places are nasty."

"Why are you in here, Ms. Wong?"

"Why didn't you call me first?"

"Carla was sitting right beside me."

Hui-wen frowned. "Come on, Dude, they want you."

"I'm coming." He washed his hands even though they didn't

need it.

Winnie said, "Hui-wen's suggestion about a bill is correct."

"I'm not going to bill you. I burned some gas and made a few copies of the photos. No big deal."

Carla said, "I told you."

Hui-wen said, "We owe him for two days. At least."

Carla looked at Winnie. "Two thousand?"

Winnie nodded.

And the ladies opened their purses and started putting cash on the conference room table. Well, all except for Hui-wen who didn't have a purse. He wasn't sure where her wad of cash had been, and he didn't want to know.

Carla, being the accountant, counted. She held out a hand to Francine. "Four hundred more."

Francine extracted it with ill grace; she wasn't looking so lovely now. "I'm not as rich as you think."

Hui-wen smiled. "She's even richer than we think. Look at her shoes."

There was a lot of peering under the table. Which he didn't join.

Francine said, "I like nice things!"

Carla offered him the money.

"Thank you, but you don't have to do this."

Winnie took the cash and put it into his hands. "We are very grateful."

She smiled and headed out but not toward the elevator.

Hui-wen was smiling. "She's going to talk to Paul."

Francine said, "I'm out of here."

Yvonne, the eldest and saddest, shook his hand as she too departed. Gentle Hui-ting shook his hand and followed her sisters.

Carla walked slowly back to her cubicle.

Which left Hui-wen and Gabriel Bergeron.

"Right. Well, it's been nice getting to know you, Ms. Wong."

"Right back at you, Bergeron. You're way smarter than you look. And not the snowflake I thought you were."

"What a nice compliment."

"No. Chase told me all about Thorvaldsen and the pirates and the Chinese spies." She was looking at him with something that might be admiration but that couldn't be right? She smiled. "Dude."

He should get back to work. "Okay. Thanks. Wait. So you and Chase are dating?"

She smiled. "You might call it that. Mostly, we're banging every chance we get."

He may have blushed. "Okay."

Hui-wen said, "There's stuff about Gavin that you didn't tell Mom. Does Carla know? Yeah, I think she does."

"Nothing important to your mother's happiness, Hui-wen."

"Sure about that?"

"Sure. So why do you and Hui-ting have Chinese names and the others don't?"

Hui-wen said, "They have Chinese names: Mom is Wai-ching, Yvonne is Yu-hua, Francine is Fan-rong." She smiled a evil smile. "And Carla's is Liu."

It sounded like "Leo." Well, sort of.

She grabbed a marker that had been keeping the stapler company and locked onto his left wrist; she was surprisingly strong.

She was drawing on his palm. He didn't think he liked it. "Hui-wen, stop that!"

She smiled and put the last strokes on a Chinese character.

"Ask her what it means."

He didn't think he would. "So you don't have an...English name?" He'd almost said "American."

"Nope. I am who I am. I'm going to trust you about Gavin, Bergeron."

She hugged him cupping his ass before she loped to the elevator, probably intent on running Chase to ground.

He walked back to his cubicle smelling of sage. He put his two grand into an envelope. Why had they paid him in cash? Not that cash wasn't acceptable.

He was looking at Carla.

She had eyes in the back of her head. "What, Bergeron?"

"Nothing. So your name is Liu?"

He tried to say it as Hui-wen had but he didn't think he got it just right.

Harry spun around. "You have another name?"

"No." She maintained a laser-like focus on her computer.

"Yes."

He knew he should keep his mouth shut. "She said to ask you what it means?"

Carla froze up but then managed to say, "It doesn't mean anything. Mom just liked the sound."

This was an obvious and transparent falsehood. He looked at Harry who was frowning at Carla, but he shrugged, and they all pretended to go back to work.

He didn't think Cory would mind if he dug into this mystery, and Winnie, who was chatting with Paul, would tell him. As soon as Carla wasn't around.

And then he thought of using a translation app. He found one that allowed him to draw the character in a little box, and then select the actual character from the offerings below.

He had to hurry because his palm was sweaty, and he couldn't let Carla see.

He put the finishing touches on the drawing, and lo, the character appeared as the first choice.

He clicked.

Somewhere in a cloud server farm far away, the silicon synapses pored over his request and spat back a single word: "willow."

He smiled.

He would wait a week or so and casually work the word "willow" into a conversation with Harry; a conversation that Carla could overhear.

And watch for the reaction.

He may have been smiling at Carla.

She glared at him. "Stop that!"

"Yes, Ma'am."

He went back to work. He couldn't blame Winnie; she hadn't known how Carla was going to turn out at birth.

Maybe Carla had been sweet, graceful, and pliant as a baby?

What were the odds?

Thursday
5:00 pm

He was done for the day and for the week. He had asked Jennifer for Friday off after explaining about Gavin. And about Winnie and Paul. She seemed pleased with this bit of snooping.

He exited the elevator at the ground floor. He had expected to find Chase a desiccated husk littering the lobby floor.

Young Chase was glowing with vitality, eyes sparkling, muscles rampant and pumped full of blood.

He looked him over. He may have sniffed him in a subtle fashion; the scent of sage was cloying.

Chase said, "What, Dude?"

"Did you and Hui-wen?" He made vague motions with his hand that wouldn't actually suggest coitus to anyone.

Chase smiled, teeth gleaming. "Sure."

"Right. Okay. Good night. Have a good weekend."

Chase was smiling at him. "Why'd you ask?"

"No reason. Just nosy."

Was he the tiniest bit jealous? No. Well, maybe. But he'd seen Chase first. Not that he would ever be unfaithful to Cory.

And not that Chase was anything but rampantly heterosexual. He should be happy for Chase. And Hui-wen.

Was this cognitive dissonance? He'd have to work on that.

He shook his head and headed for his Jeep.

He was sitting in the driver's seat when Inspector Okocha tapped on his window.

He was too tired to dive for the floor.

He lowered the window. "Yes?" Okocha was giving him the full glare. "What?"

"Have you seen Thorvaldsen?"

"Nope." The general opinion was that he was a terrible liar. He tried smiling at Okocha. "Why?"

Okocha said, "Chinedum Onyewu has been expelled from the country."

"Glad to hear it."

"He may be in serious trouble at home."

"Music to my ears. So you didn't get in trouble for not preventing him getting shot?"

"No, I did not."

"Well, that's good." Okocha was going somewhere with this. "Any news about the pirates? Ms. Iwobi and Mr. Enemkpali?"

"Those were not their names."

"I sort of figured that. Do you know who they really were?"

"They are of the Ijaw people. This Nwosu was known to the police in Port Harcourt."

"So where are they now?"

"The one you called Enemkpali had a stroke and died in the ER of the Thomas Jefferson University Hospital. The woman stayed with him until he passed. She got away before I could get there."

"That's too bad about her. So where is she now?"

He shook his head. "There are Ijaw people in New York. They will help her. She will make her way home."

"Right." He'd rather she'd been arrested. "Anything else?"

"You have seen Thorvaldsen."

"Nope."

Okocha grabbed him by the throat. "You have. Where is he?"

"I don't know. Not in Philadelphia."

"He bribed you to let him go."

"What?"

Okocha said, "How much did he give you?"

"He gave me nothing, and for your information, I didn't let him go, he let me go. And I was damn glad to see the back of him."

"But you could have followed him. You do not give up. What did he give you?"

"Nothing. Really. He had a box full of diamonds, but he didn't share."

"Diamonds??" And Inspector Okocha smiled.

"Is that what you wanted to know?"

Okocha nodded. "Now it is possible that Chinedum Onyewu will be in real trouble."

And it was also possible that Inspector Okocha wanted those diamonds for himself? Or not? It wasn't like they belonged to Duke or to Onyewu.

"Excellent."

But Okocha was still holding onto his throat a bit.

"What?'

"If he didn't bribe you, why did you not follow him?"

"Because Bradley asked me not to. But mostly because I was scared of him."

But Okocha shook his head. "You are fearless."

"Am not. I'm riddled with fear."

Okocha was staring at him. "A fortune in diamonds, and you let him go for the boy? For sentimental reasons?"

Was that such a bad thing? Not that he could have gotten those diamonds away from Duke anyway.

Okocha said, "You are a very silly man."

Made in the USA
Coppell, TX
16 August 2021